BALANCE OF POWER

BALANCE OF POWER

Paul Palmer

Hodder & Stoughton

First published in Great Britain in 2000
by Hodder and Stoughton
A division of Hodder Headline

10 9 8 7 6 5 4 3 2 1

A CIP catalogue record for this title is available from the British Library

ISBN HB 0 340 70848 4
TPB 0 340 77044 9

Typeset by
Avocet Typeset, Brill, Aylesbury, Bucks
Printed in Great Britain
by Clays Ltd, St Ives plc

Hodder and Stoughton
A division of Hodder Headline
338 Euston Road
London NW1 3BH

To Newby,
For everything

ACKNOWLEDGEMENTS

A number of people provided invaluable help and support in the research of this book. In particular, I want to thank Graham and Penny Cannon, Mal MacArthur and Hayes Gorey in Washington DC; Gillian Peele in Oxford; and Sharon Churcher in New York. I'm very grateful to all of them.

I was fortunate also to be privy to the expertise of a number of public officials in the White House, Treasury and State, people who – for their own reasons – prefer to remain anonymous. Two in particular gave me privileged access; they know who they are and I'm indebted to them.

This book would not have materialised were it not for the dedication and brilliance of my agent Mark Lucas. His contribution is on every page. The same applies to my editor Carolyn Mays, whose guidance and patience were so vital; special thanks also to Jonathan Wood at Hodder & Stoughton. Sally Hughes at L.A.W. deserves a medal.

Finally, I must pay tribute to my parents Carmel and Keith and my in-laws Anthony and Yvonne. And enormous thanks to Bernadette Orbinski-Burke, Dillie Keane, Art McCulloch, Meredith Etherington-Smith and Jeremy Pilcher, John Protheroe, Adam Helliker and Venessa Corringham, Laura Patten, Camilla and Henry Mountain, Stephen Quinn, Patricia Kluge, Rod Gilchrist and Richard and Sheila at Fingal's.

And above all else . . . to my wonderful wife, Newby.

Paul Palmer
November 1999

Chapter One

On the morning of his death, President Tyler Forrester awoke early, as usual, in his bedroom in the north-east corner of the White House. He rolled over and opened his eyes. A telephone console stood on the mahogany bedside table, along with a copy of C. David Heymann's *A Woman Named Jackie* and a colour photograph of his wife, Elizabeth, taken during a sailing holiday in Provincetown ten years earlier. She was in Miami today, addressing a conference on environmental protection. Forrester always knew when he woke up whether she was or was not in the marital bed; he didn't even need to roll over and check. Something about the air, the electricity in the room, confirmed her absence.

'Morning, Liz,' he muttered to himself. Thinking of his wife made him smile; quite something, after twenty years of marriage. He yawned and ran his hand through his hair.

The President swung his legs over the side of the bed, slipped on the monogrammed blue satin slippers that he had placed on the rug the night before, and walked to the bathroom. On his way, he picked up a touchtone phone that stood, alone, on a table by the bathroom door. Before he had even placed the handset to his ear, the head of Forrester's Secret Service detail was waiting to take his request.

'Good morning, Mr President.'

'Hiyah, Bob. I'm up. I need to use the gym. Ten minutes. I'm seeing McQuogue at eight-fifteen. Oh, and if the First Lady calls, make sure she's put straight through.'

Forrester opened the door of the bathroom and switched on the soothing white lights. Ten minutes later, dressed in grey sweat pants with a bright purple stripe down the legs and across the midriff, white Nike trainers and a tangerine-coloured T-shirt that proclaimed 'My wife thinks I'M Jesus' (a present from an old drinking buddy that he would *never* wear in public), the President left the bathroom and lifted yet another telephone handset next to him.

'Bob, I'll be right out.'

Before he had crossed the beige-and-sea-blue carpet of his bedroom, the mahogany door was already open. He stepped out into the Center Hall that runs the length of the private quarters on the second floor of the White House. He immediately turned to the right, flanked by Bob Russell and two other armed agents, their oversized suit jackets hiding their weapons. The elevator was already called to the floor and open, with yet another agent inside. It was at the end of the empty cream-painted corridor, lit by soft peach wall chandeliers, that ran above the formal staterooms below. The button for 'Basement' was already flashing red.

It took them ten seconds to descend. They exited into the basement which, like all basements, was cluttered and reeked inexplicably of damp, and followed the corridor around to the right, past Elizabeth's private document room, and an entrance to the kitchens, to where two more Secret Service agents stood to attention, suits buttoned up, by a cheap teak desk, the door to the gym behind them already ajar.

'Good morning, Mr President.'

'Morning, fellas. Hey, you lot look like you should join me on the Stairmaster!' He always cracked the same joke; they always smiled. It was yet another morning ritual.

The President turned to Agent Russell. 'Bob, get me Friedman down here, will you? And leave me alone in here.

I don't think the Ayatollahs are hiding under the rowing machine.'

The President pushed the door to the gym shut. As he did so, Agent Russell took two short paces back to the command desk and picked up the telephone.

John Friedman was surprised by the early call. Instinctively, he glanced at the clock above his office door: 7.15 a.m. A call so early in the morning could mean only one of two things: very good news, or very bad. Experience had taught him that it was usually the latter. He let the phone ring four times, then picked it up.

'Friedman.'

'John, it's Bob Russell. I'm with the President.'

He listened carefully to Russell's instructions. As the First Lady's Press Secretary, Friedman would ordinarily have little contact with the President; but Tyler Forrester had taken a shine to Friedman. He often used his wife's aide as an independent sounding board in place of the battalions of vested interests who surrounded him in the West Wing.

Friedman put the phone down then checked the diary on the desk in front of him. His 8 a.m. meeting with the rest of the First Lady's staff would have to start without him. He swung round to the mirror that stood on one of the filing cabinets by his desk and checked his appearance. His suit was dark grey, single-breasted. The shine from his black brogues was as bright as the sunlight streaming through the window behind him. Examining himself in the mirror, he ran his hand through his mop of dark hair.

Friedman made his way quickly from the East Wing to the basement. In the elevator, he double-checked that his pen was working. He flicked through the President's schedule for the day, trying to anticipate any questions Tyler might throw at him. He caught his reflection in the chrome doors of the elevator: for a second, Friedman held his own stare, felt the surge of excitement and power that still swamped him every time he stepped into the

White House of a morning. He knew that at some point, when the long hours, the turf warfare, the exhausting manoeuvring had eventually taken their toll, that excitement would crumble under the weight of the cynicism that surrounded him. But for the moment he was free of such doubts: only four years out of Harvard, only two years since he was working the photocopier in the Majority Leader's office over on the Hill, Friedman was now at the very top of his profession. He was proud of himself, proud of his boss.

The elevator doors opened.

Friedman nodded towards the Secret Service agents standing by the gym entrance. He knocked on the door and waited. Almost immediately, he heard the President's muffled instructions to enter.

'Good morning, Mr President.'

'Hi, John, care to join me?'

Forrester looked at the young aide standing to his left and smiled. 'Perhaps not. We don't want your nice suit getting creased, do we, son?'

'Have you been working out long, sir?' As he waited for Forrester to reply, he walked to one of the benches set around the room and sat down.

'Long enough, goddammit,' the President replied, his breathing strained. 'I'm only doing this because you told me Elizabeth was worried about my weight.'

He paused on the machine, reached to his right and grabbed a small blue towel from the floor. 'I had to present that award to the athletes the other day, you know, the Olympic thing?' he said, wiping his forehead. 'Can you believe what one of them said to me? "Have you ever worked out, Mr President?" And then you tell me *Elizabeth* thinks I'm looking old. Jesus!' Forrester flung the towel on to the floor.

He looked back at Friedman. 'So, John, what do I have today?'

*

Elizabeth Forrester glanced at her plate. She did not like bacon. In fact, the smell of it turned her stomach. Her first date had told her she was probably secretly Jewish (she wasn't); her husband would chide her that she might have been a pig in a previous life. She would reply, sweetly, that at least she wasn't in this one.

In ten minutes she was due to give a breakfast speech for her favourite cause: protecting the threatened nature reserves of America. To her right at the table in the gold-lacquered conference room of the Miami Hyatt was Cynthia Kronfeldt, the Miami Democratic Party's chief fund-raising lady-who-lunched.

Behind her, a sea of pastel-hued wigs rustled stiffly in the breeze that came off the bay. Mrs Kronfeldt had held Elizabeth's hand since they had both sat down, as if the First Lady were a mental patient or a débutante at risk of being raped. Cynthia Kronfeldt had seen off four (exceedingly rich) husbands; the First Lady could see why. To her right was the local Senator, Dave Truelyan, a lecherous, pug-faced maverick who, when the President was fighting his primary campaign, had called Tyler 'a gutless crabfish'. Dave Truelyan was smiling a lot at Elizabeth Forrester.

She wished Friedman was with her. Instead, because the President had 'borrowed' him (something he did a lot these days), the First Lady had been assigned a young female press officer whose nervousness was reaching the point of paranoia.

Elizabeth moved the bacon around the plate with the one hand that wasn't ensnared by Cynthia Kronfeldt. 'Do you know,' Mrs Kronfeldt whispered theatrically, 'I've raised more money for your cause than Michael Milken stole!' Elizabeth smiled appropriately while secretly eyeing her watch.

When she had arrived in the White House with her husband two and a half years before, she had been an instant success as First Lady: women liked her because she was independent, without being strident; men liked her because she didn't look as if she'd break their balls. All in all, as a recent opinion poll for Prime Time had shown, Elizabeth Forrester was a huge asset to her husband. When asked for their approval rating of the First Lady, over 70 per cent of women aged between thirty and sixty-five said 'Extremely good'; the percentage of men in the same age bracket was only slightly less. And this even after she had famously told Barbara Walters that American men needed to 'think less about their baseball games and more about their women'. The White House staff had gone nuts, especially Chief of Staff Wayne McQuogue, but her honesty had, surprisingly, gone down a storm. At baseball stadiums around the country, men were holding up signs proclaiming: 'Liz, My Wife Said I Could Be Here'.

She pushed herself back from the table and stood up. Back straight and graceful, she walked to the podium. Her prepared speech was in her left hand and the audience had risen to greet her. Dressed in a light, pale blue wool suit, her auburn hair just touching her shoulders, she looked sensational. In command, but feminine. She was an immensely striking woman: more handsome than beautiful, her face long, her cheekbones high, her eyes brown.

'She's a babe, isn't she?' Senator Truelyan commented to Mrs Kronfeldt.

'She thinks you're a lecherous old drunk, so shut up and listen or I'll pull my funds,' Mrs Kronfeldt replied, turning towards the lectern, smiling and nodding as the crinkled hair-pieces of lilac and pearl turned like sunflowers towards Elizabeth.

The President sat, legs splayed, on the newly installed rowing machine, watching a little digital screen show a computerised great white shark trying to chase his rowing boat across an estuary.

'John, how's my girl doin'?' he asked Friedman.

'Fine, sir, I believe. I've just spoken with the detail in Miami and' – Friedman checked his watch: 7.50 a.m. – 'she's just about to give her speech.'

'Is she sitting next to that rednecked sonofabitch Truelyan?' the President asked, sweating and heaving himself out of the rowing machine.

'Yes, sir,' Friedman replied.

'Well, I wish that goddam electric shark would eat the cock-sucker,' the President snarled as he climbed on to the hi-tech cycling machine.

He paused to catch his breath. 'John, I've got to see McQuogue at eight-fifteen. Then I'm in Cabinet. Then I have to lunch with the Vice-President. You don't have any drugs to keep me awake in front of that dinosaur, do you?'

Struggling on the cycling machine, he ran through the rest of his daily schedule. 'Ring Elizabeth and tell her she doesn't have to come to the Mayflower dinner if she doesn't want to,' he told Friedman. The electronic clock on the bicycle machine was reaching 20, 21, 22, 23. The President watched it closely as he spoke. 'She'll be tired. I can make excuses. With the campaign coming up soon, I want her not to feel overused.'

Friedman dutifully made notes. The President's tanned legs moved rhythmically. His breath was short, his speech interrupted by the exertion of cycling up the computerised hill he saw on the screen in front of him. 'Oh, and tell her I'll be thinking of her whilst I'm dining with the wolves, and if there's . . .'

For a second, with his eyes looking at the notes he was scribbling, Friedman didn't see the President slump forward on to the screen. A fraction later, Forrester slid from the machine and crashed violently to the floor.

Everything seemed to happen in slow motion. Friedman did not have time to slam the red plastic 'CRASH' alarm button on the telephone console to his right. Instead he screamed, summoning the Secret Service men outside the room. Guns drawn, they threw themselves on to the young staffer, dragging him away from the President, who was rocking back and forth on the rubberised matting, gasping for breath.

'Shit, don't shoot! Don't shoot! I didn't touch him, he just fell over . . . Jesus,' Friedman screamed as the Secret Service agents pummelled him to the floor.

Bob Russell, shouting orders to his detail, held the President's head in his hands. 'Sir? Sir, you're gonna be OK. Hang on in there, sir.'

For a second, Forrester was able to lift his head and look down at his body. Apart from the tips of his Nike trainers, and Friedman sprawled on the floor near by, one thing caught his eye: the word JESUS spelled in capitals on his T-shirt.

Within seconds, Tyler Truman Forrester, forty-second President of the United States, had gone to meet him.

Chapter Two

Elizabeth smiled at the applause. Out of the corner of her eye, she caught a sudden movement. As she walked from the podium, her personal Secret Service agent, Lee Morrow, a handsome six-footer from the black ghettoes of Philadelphia, was the first to get beside her. 'Excuse me, ma'am, but I need a private word.'

Elizabeth stiffened. She could feel, smell, the tension off Morrow.

She was instantly surrounded by her Secret Service detail and frogmarched from the conference hall.

'Lee, what the hell is going on?' the First Lady asked as she was led, almost dragged, through the hotel's kitchen.

'Ma'am, there's a call waiting for you in the car. We'll be there shortly.'

A long concrete-floored corridor, room-service trolleys lining the right-hand side, led to a small flight of stairs. She could smell the breakfast trays. Through the exit, her limousine, door already ajar, was surrounded by more police than even Elizabeth Forrester was used to. Helmeted men were frozen in the stroboscopic lights of the squad cars. For an instant, Elizabeth felt as if she were standing to one side of all this, as if the person crouching to get into the limo, all eyes upon her, wasn't really her at all.

As the sirens started and they roared out of the service entrance, Lee Morrow handed her the telephone.

It was Friedman. 'Ma'am, it's John here . . . I'm sorry, er, to have to tell you this . . . but your husband, er . . . I'm sorry, Mrs Forrester, but the President is dead. A heart attack. In the gym. I was with him.'

With the phone still to her ear, Elizabeth looked out as the streets of Miami flashed by. People, ordinary people, standing at the traffic junctions waving. Taxis. Buses. The blaring of a ghetto-blaster. A diner and – somehow she'd always remember him – a fat man wearing a Rolling Stones T-shirt, Jagger's red tongue unfurling like a cobra.

With the telephone still held to her ear, her eyes squinted slightly, her brow furrowed. She looked as if she were thinking what she might say next. In fact, she said little.

'Thank you, John, I'll be there shortly.'

The limousine was four miles from the airport. Elizabeth turned to her right and watched the malls, K-Mart, Indigo's Jean Emporium flash by. Soon, they were on to the freeway, police outriders to either side of the car.

'Lee, stop the cavalcade, please.'

'Sorry, ma'am?' Morrow asked, his voice swamped with incredulity.

'I said stop the car,' Elizabeth snapped back. 'If you don't I'll get out myself and you'll have two dead bodies in the White House.'

As soon as she said it, she regretted it. But she was trembling with the need for air, to be alone, just to stand for a few minutes, just to have a chance, however brief, to take in what Friedman had told her. She didn't feel numb: a few days later, she would wonder why; but at that precise moment, she felt as if her senses had never been more tuned.

Morrow radioed ahead. Elizabeth could hear the voices crackling in his earpiece. She didn't care. Five minutes later, the eight police outriders, the two Cherokee Jeeps carrying the rest of her Secret Service detail, five police cars and the main limousine pulled off the freeway. The outriders had blocked the traffic both ways. Elizabeth could hear the exasperated blaring of car horns from a hundred yards away.

She stepped from the limousine. The thundering absence of trucks and cars on the turnpike shocked her; without them, it seemed as if the world had stopped.

Morrow stood silently by the car door as she took four paces and rested her hands on the rusty metallic crash barriers that lined the hard shoulder. Leaning forward, smelling the hot, cloying fumes of diesel off the tarmac, she only hoped her legs would hold her. In front of her was a scrapyard and, beyond it, three monstrous, grey, dilapidated housing projects. She could see the washing lines strewn across the tiny balconies; the multicoloured graffiti scarring the buildings' lower floors. In the far distance, a plane was taking off from Miami airport.

Tyler, is it really all over? God, I wish I'd been with you.

Grief had yet to take hold of her. She would later, much later, remember that her overwhelming emotion was anger. He had wanted it so badly; she had just wanted him. When he pushed her and stretched her almost to the limits of her endurance, when his jocularity or his arrogance, even his wildly energetic lovemaking, seemed as if it would suffocate her, consume and destroy her, she had carried on. She knew that he needed her, and she'd found solace in that.

When they'd first met at a Democratic lawyers' party in Virginia in the fall of 1971 (she wildly ambitious and frighteningly bright; he just a cultural wetback trying to muscle in on a job and a woman), she had loved him instantaneously, even painfully. But their marriage, her growing sense of losing her own identity, of being subsumed by the vastness of who Tyler was and what he wanted ultimately to be, had transformed the lust and the love they'd once had. They were unique among many political couples, the Primetime Phonies, as Tyler had called them, because they did care for each other. But in the end – *God, this was the end, wasn't it?* – in the end they were strapped into this relationship like co-pilots in a cockpit. Crash or flight, turbulence or delays, they were in it together.

As she stood on the freeway, her hands massaging her temples, Elizabeth wondered about the real price of giving so much of yourself publicly, handing over your soul, placing it on the nation's dinner plate to be examined, prodded, torn apart, eaten, and spat out.

Tyler had still been able, even after twenty years of marriage, to make her laugh, though he could rarely make her cry. But she was crying now.

As the First Lady's cavalcade continued its high-speed journey to the airport, White House Chief of Staff Wayne McQuogue was impassively dissecting his copy of the *Washington Post*. The sun's reflection from the table in his breakfast room forced him to tilt the newspaper so he could read it without squinting.

He smiled to himself. Half the leaks his staff had planted over the last few days had appeared in the newspaper. Enemies had been put in their place. Friends promoted. It was the way Washington worked, and McQuogue, a veteran of many administrations, was one of the undisputed masters. Around town, he was famed as a tough and brilliant negotiator; sometimes, when he relaxed with his drinking buddies in the library of his rambling Georgetown house, they would call him the 'real Mr President'. He didn't encourage them to do so but nor did he stop them. He would merely smile and sip his single malt.

'Wayne, the car's here.'

McQuogue's wife, Flora, turned back from the breakfast-room window. McQuogue nodded, folded the *Post* and stood. 'I'm at the Mayflower dinner tonight,' he told her, slipping into his Savile Row suit jacket. 'Don't wait up.'

McQuogue pulled the house door shut and walked slowly down the steps. For one who spent most of his waking hours under the fluorescent lights of the West Wing, he was an attractive man. He did not need to breathe in to keep his stomach flat. His large face, with its distinctive angular Scottish boning, topped by a closely cropped head of grey hair, made him look younger than his fifty-four years.

His limousine and US Army driver were waiting by the sidewalk. He had barely got comfortable in the rear of the limousine when the car phone rang. As they swerved into the Georgetown traffic, taking a left on to M Street, heading towards Washington Circle and the White House, McQuogue let the phone ring three or four times. His driver looked into the rear-view mirror.

Let 'em wait, let 'em wait.

On the seventh ring, McQuogue picked it up.

'Chief of Staff.'

It was his secretary. Through her garbled sobs he could barely make out what she was saying.

'Kathleen,' McQuogue snapped, 'put me on to Williams.'

He stared nervously at the back of the driver's head.

What now?

McQuogue's executive assistant, Johnson Williams, was on the phone within seconds. 'Sir, I have some terrible news,' he said. 'The President is dead.'

McQuogue blinked.

'Is this some kind of sick joke, Williams?'

'No, sir. He really is. It's pandemonium here. No one knows what to do, sir.'

McQuogue stayed silent for a second. His heart pounded.

'Williams, say nothing. Do nothing. Are the paramedics there?'

'Yes, sir. They've taken him to Bethesda.'

McQuogue knew the emergency procedure: the President's body would already be on its way by helicopter to the Naval Hospital in north-west Washington.

'Where is the Pres—' McQuogue began, then stopped. 'Er, where was the body?'

'In the gym, sir.'

McQuogue began to speak again, then waited. He could hear Williams's panicked breathing. Finally, McQuogue spoke. 'Williams, I want the gym sealed, and the Oval Office. No one, and I mean *no one,* is to enter either of them until I get there. Is that clear?'

'Yes, sir.'

McQuogue put the phone down. 'Sergeant, forget the traffic. Forget any fucking thing. Just get me to the White House. Now!'

Mark White didn't like to think of himself as a loser. In fact, he didn't like to think of himself at all. His ex-wife, Adele, a skyscraper of a woman, a six-foot harridan whom White had nicknamed Meyer Lanky, had thought about him an awful lot, especially when she had sat in her attorney's office five months earlier and emptied his bank account and savings of the few paltry dollars he had. She had also taken his beloved Grundig stereo, all the *Die Hard* videos and the soft-top 1967 MG he'd won at a Baltimore card game from an inebriated obstetrician.

White yawned and eased himself out of the bed. Jesus, he thought, gently massaging his scalp. He'd come to Washington thinking he'd be Bob Woodward. Now, at forty-seven, he wouldn't pass for Bob Hope.

It was Friday. In one hour, at 9 a.m. sharp, White would be required to arrive at the downtown offices of the *Washington Herald,* the scurrilous, deeply unethical and hugely profitable tabloid newspaper he worked for. White's title was Special Correspondent. But special for what? he asked himself again this morning. Somehow the title merely reminded him, cruelly, of his own failure.

Outside his studio window on Vernon Street in the Adams-Morgan district of Washington, he could hear the staff of the West Indian pitta bread café opening up.

His ruminations were interrupted by the wailing of his telephone.

'White.'

'Mark, it's me, Ron.'

As if Ronald T. Bletchman, the *Herald*'s zealous news editor, had to introduce himself to a reporter he had summarily humiliated for years. Bletchman, 'Mr Belch' to his staff, had a pockmarked face highlighted by his propensity to sweat. The news reporters had bets on what form of vegetation would take root under his armpits.

'Whitey, wake up. It's a great one. You're gonna love it! Jesus Christ, the place is going nuts . . . stay with me, I've got another call.'

White's heart sank. He listened to the computerised jangle of 'The Star Spangled Banner'. Within seconds, Bletchman was back. 'Whitey, I can't talk long. Get your ass moving and I mean pronto, ace! No messing, Whitey. He's dead. Gone. Keeled over. Jesus, the news wires said he was half fucking naked . . . Whitey, look, it will take you ten minutes. Get to the House and call me when you get there. And Whitey? Wear a goddam tie.'

Although well used to Bletchman's less than fulsome instructions, White, half naked and desperately rubbing his eyelids, missed the opportunity to halt his editor's excited string of orders and demand further explanations. The telephone merely emitted an incessant request to hang up.

'Fuck it,' White said, his bare feet tentatively making their way across the cold linoleum flooring of his flat. If the day was going to be as bad as this, there were only two remedies: a bath, and a cigarette, quickly.

The story, whatever it was, could wait. They could *always* wait.

The fifteen-minute soak slowly began to anaesthetise White's pervasive nausea. As his body and mind became attuned to the prospect of another working day, the telephone rang again. Cursing and dragging himself out of the tub, he raced back across the apartment and slumped, wet and winded, on his bed.

It was Sean James, the *Herald*'s chief photographer, calling on a mobile phone. 'Whitey, Bletchman told me you're on this one. I'm ten minutes from the White House. For fuck's sake, get your ass moving! The place is gonna be fucking bedlam.'

For the second time that morning White felt powerless and confused. He swiftly interrupted James: 'Er, Sean, can anyone tell me what's going on? I'm not quite ready to tune in to CNN yet . . . I mean, it's barely eight in the morning, and already Bletchman's been screaming at me. If it's political, why can't the political desk deal with it?'

'White, the man's dead, for Chrissakes. In the gym. Jesus, White, I'm fighting here with more traffic than a cop. Give me a break.'

White paused, sensing his colleague's tension. He asked one more question. 'Sean, give me his name, I'll run a check and be with you within the hour.'

'Name? White, are you on this fucking *planet*? OK, OK, try this . . . Tyler Forrester. Now, try this . . . the President of the fucking US of A, Whitey! Geddit? Now let me get out of this crap and meet me there.'

White let the handset fall back on to the wet sheets. He took two paces to a battered canvas chair and placed a towel over his head.

Forrester?

Christ, poor Elizabeth.

Wayne McQuogue knew the way blindfold. He entered the White House through the ground-floor entrance of the West Wing, then made his way past the suite of offices towards the main building. He reached the basement in a matter of minutes.

A lone Secret Service agent stood outside the gym.

'Is there anyone in there?' McQuogue asked brusquely, pointing at the gym door.

The agent shook his head. 'No, sir.'

McQuogue signalled for the agent to move aside.

'I want to know immediately there's any news.'

He closed the gym door behind him. To his left, a glass-doored cabinet took up half of one wall. On top of it was a pile of papers. McQuogue scanned through them: they were old press releases that had obviously been placed there some time ago. He set them back on the cabinet and turned round. He crouched down and began to fling aside a pile of red and blue cushions pulled into a makeshift bed. There was nothing beneath them. He moved on to the next pile: a pale blue towel, still damp and creased, nestled on the floor. He picked it up, wincing slightly as he did so. He could feel Tyler's perspiration, could just make out his smell. He laid the towel down again.

As he did so, he caught sight of a smudge of black under the bright metal of the Stairmaster. He stood up and tried to heave the exercise machine to one side. It was too heavy, its coasters catching on the floor matting. McQuogue crouched down, cursing his lack of agility and strength. Grimacing, he slipped the object out from where it had been kicked aside in the tumult.

McQuogue looked at the object in his hand. It was a small attaché case, more of a washbag, and the size of a man's hand. The leather was creased and battered. McQuogue immediately knew who it belonged to. Tyler had nearly always carried it with him, in his jacket pocket.

McQuogue unzipped the bag. He pulled out a small sheaf of notes, his eyes scanning them hurriedly. He checked the door behind him. It was shut tight.

He turned back to the papers in his hand: notes for a speech that Tyler was due to give at a state banquet in a few days' time.

McQuogue swore quietly to himself and rechecked the bag. There was nothing else in it. He put the speech back and stood up. He placed the bag back under the machine, and made for the door.

The Secret Service agent turned as McQuogue strode out into the corridor.

'This room is still to be sealed. Notify my office that I'm on my way up.' McQuogue hurried along the corridor. He could hear the agent behind him speaking into his radio.

McQuogue was thinking fast. He had not found what he was looking for in the gym.

John Friedman let the silence of his office consume him. Outside, in the cramped corridors of the East Wing, he knew that the rest of Elizabeth's staff were struggling to deal with the thousands of calls and faxes flooding into the White House. Friedman had retired from the fray, if only for a few seconds. He was still in a state of shock from the President's death. He closed his eyes, and exhaled. The sudden dramatic twist of events had left him stunned, depleted. He let his head rest in his hands, trying to control his breathing.

The telephone rang beside him. It was his secretary. 'John, I'm sorry but I have the First Lady on the line. She's calling from the plane. I'll put her straight through.'

He waited for the sound of Elizabeth's voice.

'John?'

Elizabeth sounded flat, almost lifeless, as if, Friedman thought, she were operating by a purely mechanical reflex. 'John,' she went on, 'we've left Miami and will arrive back in Washington in an hour or so.'

He struggled to hear the words as she spoke on the military plane's SatPhone. The line echoed and buzzed. 'John, I need you to do a favour for me.'

'Of course, ma'am,' he said, a touch too quickly. 'What is it you need?'

'John, I know the ushers will have tidied up the Residence

. . . but will you check . . .' Elizabeth's voice faded out for a second, then was back with startling clarity. 'I want to make sure,' she went on, 'that Tyler's things haven't been moved out. I want the rooms left just as he left them. I don't want any of the staff touching anything. I want . . .' Friedman heard the crack in her voice. 'I want to walk back into the room just as it was after he left it this morning.'

Friedman massaged his left temple, the phone heavy and hot in his right hand. 'Mrs Forrester,' he murmured gently, 'consider it done.' He swallowed and paused before going on: 'Ma'am, I was planning to meet you at Andrews. If I'm to do this, then I'm going to be late.'

'Stay at the White House,' she interrupted. 'I don't want any formal ceremony at the airbase. I just want to get back quickly. Wait for me there.'

Friedman heard the line go dead. He walked quickly from his office. As expected, the First Lady's suite of offices was awash with people: the secretaries, some in tears, were slamming down or picking up phones; two more staffers struggled with a fax machine in one corner. Friedman waved off their desperate pleas for guidance and hurried towards the Residence. Instinctively, he checked that his security pass was around his neck.

He turned the corner and came to the bottom of the main staircase that led to the private quarters two flights up. From habit, Friedman prepared himself for the usual Secret Service scrutiny by the stairwell before he was allowed to ascend. He looked ahead of him towards the permanent guard station. The corridor was empty. No agents. Friedman shrugged to himself and carried on up.

It took him only a matter of minutes to reach the second floor. He walked through to the Center Hall. The long, elegant corridor is the main artery of the private quarters, an impressive throughway lined with paintings by American Impressionists, an antique Chinese coromandel screen and *objets d'art* from eighteenth-century France. Friedman walked past the octagonal writing desk, a donation to the Kennedy White House, that divides the hall in two. A Wedgwood bowl full of freshly cut flowers stood resplendent on top of the dark, polished wood. He paused for a moment among the grandeur: ahead of him, at the far end of the wide corridor, the doors to the West Sitting Hall stood open. Sunlight streamed in through the fan window overlooking the Old Executive Office Building opposite the White House.

Friedman looked around him. He was surprised that there were no Secret Service agents guarding the corridor. He frowned and retraced his steps to the stairwell. To the left, a small office acted as a den for the agents assigned to the private quarters. Friedman knocked on the door.

There was no reply. He peered inside: the windowless room was empty.

He made his way back to the Center Hall and stood and listened. The quarters were unnervingly quiet. A clock ticked away to his right. The lamps were on in the hall, their yellowing glare reflecting off the mahogany Chippendale mirrors to either side of the entrance to the West Sitting Hall. Above him, the chandeliers had also been turned on, ripples of light and shadow washing across the bookcases and doors.

Friedman hurried towards the private bedroom suite in the north-east corner. He stood in front of the door and listened before knocking: it was his usual routine, and he performed it instinctively. With a jolt he realised that the President never would be here again. He opened the door and entered the room.

Darkness hit him like a shovel. The heavy gold drapes had been drawn. The room was pitch black. Friedman swayed slightly on his feet, his bearings muddled and confused by the all-consuming darkness. He fumbled to his left for the light switch he knew was there. His fingers skimmed along the thick, padded wallcovering. It was stiff and cold to the touch.

The vicious blow caught him on the right side of his head.

Wincing and stunned by the impact, he was pushed violently

back out into the corridor, pain ripping through his head. 'Jesus! Fuck!' he screamed, trying to keep his balance.

He was spun round as the heavy mahogany door to the bedroom suite was slammed into him once more, cracking against the side of his face. He could feel himself falling. The door crashed shut, its frame shaking violently from the impact. Friedman's eyes rolled back, the pain paralysing as his legs gave way and he crumpled to the floor.

Disoriented, he lay in shock for a few seconds.

What . . .

Then he heard it. Through the haze of pain and shock, he could make out a thumping of feet behind the closed door. Whoever it was was running fast.

Friedman dragged himself up. Despite the throbbing in his head, he slammed himself back against the closed door, struggling to turn the doorknob.

The door was now locked.

His chest heaving, Friedman spun around, eyes searching the shadows of the Center Hall.

What the hell was . . .

From the corner of his eye, he caught movement to his right, the briefest of shadows falling out into the corridor from an open doorway farther along the hall. Friedman threw himself forward, the pain in his head anaesthetised by his panic and confusion. He knew the geography of the private quarters well: a door led from the bedroom suite into a bathroom, which itself connected to a small anteroom. From there, a small passage led back into the Center Hall, or down to another private staircase that gave access to the state floor below and, eventually, to the White House basement.

Friedman lunged forward. He heard a door open and shut away to his right. Someone was racing through the anteroom.

He burst through the entrance to the small vestibule.

No one was there.

Friedman threw open the door that led to the private staircase: the secondary Secret Service guard post was unmanned. He could hear the pounding of footsteps from farther down the stairwell. He barrelled down the narrow staircase, taking the steps two at a time. Within seconds, he reached the state floor and threw himself round the corner.

'Jesus fucking Christ—'

Friedman saw the man's suit before his face, the two of them tumbling back against the bare wall.

'Friedman, what the fuck—'

Wayne McQuogue's face was contorted with rage and surprise.

Friedman pushed himself back, breath rasping. 'Sir, I'm sorry. I . . .' He glanced down the stairway behind McQuogue, searching for a glimpse of his attacker. 'Sir, has anyone . . . I mean, did you see anyone running, sir, down these stairs?' His voice was ragged, the words emerging breathlessly.

He caught McQuogue's incredulous expression. 'John, I've no idea, I just came in through the state door.' McQuogue nodded towards the door behind them. 'What—'

Friedman could feel those cold eyes upon him.

'John, what the hell is the matter with you?'

Friedman looked around him wildly. He dared not think what a spectacle he must present to the White House Chief of Staff. He raised his hand to his forehead. He could feel the lump there beginning to throb painfully. 'Sir, you didn't see anyone go past?'

McQuogue stayed rooted to the spot. 'Mr Friedman, what have you been doing up there?'

His voice was cold, questioning.

Friedman shook his head. 'I, well, I'm sorry, sir, I thought I heard an intruder upstairs.'

He winced inside.

Jesus, he'll think I've flipped.

'Sir, I slipped,' Friedman went on, 'and it must have, I don't know, confused me or something.'

He flinched slightly as McQuogue placed a hand on his shoulder. 'Son, none of us are exactly at our best at the moment. You get back to the East Wing and have someone look at that knock on your head. I'll speak with you later.' McQuogue stopped a few steps up and looked back at Friedman. 'Oh, and John, don't go running round corners. You're liable to get hurt.'

Friedman felt his face redden. He nodded and then pushed open the door that led through to the state rooms. A uniformed guard whom he recognised nodded in greeting.

Friedman pushed past him. He was in no mood for small talk. Then, as he was about to enter the Cross Hall, he stopped and walked back towards the guard. He remembered his name. Karowlsky . . .

'How long you been on duty?' he asked, trying to sound calm.

The guard shrugged. 'Three hours, and I've another two to go.'

Friedman nodded again and smiled weakly. He looked ahead of him. An open door led into the Cross Hall. He could see West Wing staffers hurrying towards their offices.

He turned back to the guard. 'Did Chief of Staff McQuogue just come through here?' He tried to keep the tension out of his voice.

The guard shook his head. 'No, sir. You're the only person I've seen for half an hour or so. Mr Friedman, is there something wrong?'

Friedman did not reply. His head screaming in pain, he turned away from the guard and hurried out into the Cross Hall, wondering why the Chief of Staff had lied to him.

Chapter Three

So this is what it feels like.

Elizabeth sat alone, at her own request, aboard the military plane back to Washington. She occupied the very front row, her security detail and staff four rows back. The airport in Miami had been a nightmare. Nothing had prepared her for the tumult and commotion.

She turned and looked out of the cabin window. The military plane reached its cruising altitude of 35,000 feet, a clear cloudless sky highlighting the sun-drenched coastline of Florida below her. She shivered and pulled her jacket closer around her. She couldn't begin to think of what the days ahead would hold. And she hadn't even arrived back in Washington yet.

Washington.

The thought of returning to the White House, to their bedroom, their things, chilled her blood. She hoped Friedman had managed to secure the private quarters before anything was changed in preparation for her arrival.

Selfishly, at that moment, she wished that she and Tyler had had children. At least, then she thought, she could have distracted herself, thrown her energies into assuaging someone else's grief, rather than mulling over her own loss.

She sipped sparingly at some brandy.

'Ma'am, we're about to arrive in Washington.' It was Lee

Morrow. Elizabeth could barely look him in the eyes. Even Lee, the man trained to put his life on the line for her, looked pitying. She quickly pulled herself together.

God, how much longer can I take this?

'Thank you, Lee.' As he turned back to his seat for landing, she leaned over and touched his arm. 'Will the Vice-President be at the airbase?'

'Yes, ma'am.'

'We're landing at Andrews then taking the chopper to the White House, is that right?'

'Yes, Mrs Forrester, as you requested.' She had: it was the way she wanted it to happen. Although she understood the need for protocol, for ceremony, she wanted this over quickly.

Before he left her, Morrow pulled down the window blinds. 'Mrs Forrester, I know this may not be the time to say it, an' all, given what's happened, but we all, well, we're real proud of the way you've handled it, ma'am.'

'That means a lot, Lee. And I'd like Cathy and the kids to come to the White House before I leave, if you'd like them to?' She vowed to try to keep Morrow after she had left the White House.

The military plane landed and shuddered to a halt. Elizabeth rose from her seat. Morrow and his men waited awkwardly at the door. She passed by her press assistant for the day, Margaret Cooley. 'Thank you for being here, Margaret,' she said softly, brushing her sleeve. The young woman looked distraught. Poor kid, thought Elizabeth. It was only supposed to be a quick jaunt to Florida.

She could hear the sirens and the rumbling of an expectant crowd through the aircraft door. She bit her lip and looked at Morrow. 'In your own time, Mrs Forrester,' he said, stepping back.

Time to do it. She clasped her handbag to her chest and nodded, then stepped on to the rickety stairs. Morrow was right behind her. Somewhere she found the strength to look up.

Through the sunshine, the flashbulbs still made her blink. She gripped the cold metal banister.

The Vice-President, Willard Morgan, his wife and the military chiefs stood sombrely to attention on the tarmac. Thirty yards beyond them, she could see the media battalion pressing against the crush barriers.

Now or never.

If only it could have been never.

Mark White hurried from the subway train and out of Metro Centre. Lafayette Park in front of the White House was a zoo, and you could take your pick of animals. White arrived at the same time as every TV production van, capped-tooth network frontman and foreign newshound descended on the same strip of lawn. Sean James, the photographer from the *Herald*, was nowhere to be seen amid the vast media scrum. Taking one look at the frantic battle of cameras and egos erupting in front of the White House, White went instead to find a colleague who could fill him in on what was happening. He knew where to look: McReedy's on K Street, a few blocks from the White House, would doubtless be open; its owner, a wily former Moscow cab driver known only, and inexplicably, as Mort, had moved here to escape a nasty run-in with the Russian mafia on Brighton Beach. White knew him well. The dispossessed stuck together in this town.

By the time he had criss-crossed his way across Lafayette, ducked behind the Farragut North Metro stop on 17th and squeezed his way through McReedy's glass doors, the place was busier than Friday night. Mort was pouring Bloody Marys from a three-litre pitcher and gave White a welcoming shrug. The crowd on the other side of the bar was four deep.

'Whitey! Christ, over here.' He turned to see the obese form of Michael Riordan towering above the throng. White had once shared a desk on the news floor with the famed chief news reporter for the *Washington Herald,* but Riordan's nuclear and entirely unpredictable rages – which had seen off ten computers, at least a dozen phones and, in one memorable incident, a brand new Canon photocopier – had driven even White to seek shelter elsewhere.

He joined his colleague at the back of the bar. Riordan took two cigarettes out of a packet of Marlboro Lights, bit the butts off and handed one to White. 'The Ruski's already run out of Reds,' he said, taking a slurp of his beer.

White glanced around the bar. This was his industry; his colleagues; his life. Four years at school in Wisconsin; bar jobs, waiting jobs, car cleaning jobs. He had been an honours student, a star as well. Bright, athletic, a catch. He'd dreamed of journalism. Ended writing up freeway car crashes for the *Fort Lauderdale Bugle* until, by sheer fluke, his boss recommended the young kid move to New York and make coffee for a friend on the *Village Voice.* He stayed two years; married the receptionist at the *New York Post,* covered the mayoral victories, the mayoral dollar scams, the mayoral pants-round-his-knees scandals. And, then, headhunted by the *Washington Herald,* Adele and he had come to the capital, wistfully expecting the *Washington Post* to come knocking. They hadn't. And White had stayed, and here he was. He liked to think, to convince himself, that maybe he was still a minor reporter because, in a business that relied on sleaze, he had never found that necessary percentage of amorality to go, or write, that crucial extra yard.

'Whitey, Earth requiring contact . . . are you reading?' Riordan was poking him in the side.

'It ain't been a great week,' he muttered.

'And it certainly isn't going to get any better,' Riordan said in reply, the crush behind pushing him against White's chest.

'Mick, what are we doing down here?' he asked, drawing deeply on a cigarette, his fifth of the day. 'Haven't the bozos in the office heard of CNN? Come on, let's be honest, what the hell are we going to get down here standing like pricks outside the gates?'

Riordan grunted his agreement. 'OK, Whitey, let's split. We'll file the story in the office.'

It took them fifteen minutes to make it back to the *Herald*'s office. White quickly crossed the floor of the newsroom. His colleagues were crowded round the TV set. White walked slowly towards them and watched the arrival ceremony at Andrews. Elizabeth Forrester was walking down the steps, then shaking hands with the Vice-President. As she reached the end of the welcoming line, she lifted her head and seemed to look directly into the camera.

Friedman picked up the telephone in his office. 'Lee Morrow, please,' he snapped at the White House operator.

He hoped Morrow would be in the Secret Service Command Centre buried in the White House basement. Morrow was the nearest thing Friedman had to a friend in the White House. He knew he could trust Morrow. After the attack in the private quarters, Friedman knew he had to.

The switchboard operator was back. 'Mr Friedman, Agent Morrow is with the First Lady.'

Shit.

In the panic earlier, Friedman had not checked which agents were on Elizabeth's detail.

'Mr Friedman, are you still there? Can I put you through to—'

Friedman spoke quickly. 'No, no, it's fine. Thank you.'

He replaced the receiver and sat staring at the bare wall in front of him.

The man pulled the jacket of his dark grey suit closer around him. He pushed through the crowd congregated around the south-west gate of the White House. The uniformed Secret Service guards registered the laminated White House pass around his neck. They did not stop him; they were too preoccupied with keeping the public from blocking the wrought-iron entrance.

The man strolled casually towards the Mall. A hundred yards from the White House, he removed the pass and dumped it in a trashcan. It was a fake, but a good one; he did not need to keep it. It was too risky to do so. Another could always be supplied, if required.

Seconds later, he immersed himself in the battalions of sightseers flocking through the narrow sidewalks behind the Old Executive Office Building, returning once more to welcome anonymity.

Chapter Four

Elizabeth's limousine swung through the White House gates. Within seconds she was out of the car. She paused momentarily on the white stone steps that led into the main quarters of the House. Instinctively, she looked to her right, towards the Oval Office and the driveway leading towards the West Wing.

She exhaled gently.

The Oval Office . . . but you're not there now, my darling.

The Secret Service detail and the US Navy guards formed a circle around her. 'Ma'am, I think we should go inside,' Morrow said gently, gesturing with his left hand towards the glass doors that were already open. Elizabeth nodded and looked through the entrance.

Inside, she caught sight of Friedman. The young aide looked tired, drained. Elizabeth knew how he felt. She walked steadfastly towards him.

'John, I want to go to the hospital as soon as possible. Please arrange it with Lee.'

He nodded and then began to speak. Elizabeth waved him off. 'Not now. We'll speak later. I just need to . . . to think about nothing.'

She turned away from him and took the familiar route to the private quarters one storey above her.

Elizabeth had only twenty minutes alone. The knock on the door startled her.

Oh, no . . .

'Liz?'

Elizabeth recognised the voice immediately, welcomed its familiarity. She opened the door eagerly. 'Marjorie!'

Elizabeth embraced Marjorie Wallace, her oldest and closest friend, the two of them standing in the open doorway. Eventually, Elizabeth pulled back. She was shaking slightly, her eyes red-rimmed and blinking.

She felt Marjorie lead her across the room.

'Marj, how did you . . . I mean, when did you hear? Are you—'

'Liz, don't worry about that. I came as soon as I heard. The detail let me in.'

Elizabeth watched as her friend crossed the bedroom suite and poured a glass of water. She returned to Elizabeth's side and handed the glass to her.

Elizabeth took two sips then put the glass down. She looked at Marjorie. 'Well, that's it, Marj. That's it,' she said simply, her voice little more than a whisper.

She let the silence hang between them.

'Liz, try and stay calm. Do you want to sleep?'

Elizabeth snorted in response. '*Sleep*? Jesus, Marj, I can barely think, never mind sleep.' She looked at her friend. 'Will you come with me to the hospital? To see him?'

Marjorie nodded then took her hand. 'Do you know what happened?' she asked tentatively.

Elizabeth gave the faintest of sighs. She shook her head. 'Not really. It's all been so *quick*. No one seems to know much. John said it was a heart attack. I haven't spoken to the doctors or to McQuogue yet. There's so much to do—'

She rose suddenly from the bed and paced the room, words spilling from her. 'I haven't spoken with Willard Morgan yet either. There must be some procedure for this. I mean, they must have some idea, *someone* must have some idea—'

Elizabeth felt Marjorie's arms close around her.

'Liz, not yet. Not yet.'

Her friend embraced her.

Almost immediately, Elizabeth's desperate sobbing doubled up both of them, like a punch to the stomach.

Friedman sat down on a settee by the bedroom suite. He flicked his eyes towards the door that only a few hours earlier had been slammed into his forehead. He tried to control himself, to make sense of the impossible: that an intruder, undetected by the Secret Service or a member of staff, had managed to break through the security cordon. It just didn't happen, not here, not in the White House; couldn't, *shouldn't*.

Friedman turned and beckoned to Morrow. The two men were alone in the Center Hall, the rest of the detail standing guard by the stairwell away to Friedman's right.

'Lee,' he asked, 'what would the normal detail be up here?'

Morrow frowned and sat down. 'What do you mean?'

Friedman fidgeted in his seat and glanced behind him. He kept his voice to a whisper. He could feel Morrow's professional gaze on him, assessing where this was leading. 'What I mean is,' Friedman went on, 'this morning, as you were flying back with the First Lady, neither Mrs Forrester nor the President was in residence, but there'd still be a detail up here, right?'

Morrow nodded. 'Of course. No question about it. You know that. If it wasn't one of our detail, then the uniformed guards would be on duty here, or certainly by the two entrances.'

Friedman grimaced. 'They wouldn't leave their posts? There would have to be a guard, maybe more than one, on duty on this floor at all times, right?'

Morrow nodded. 'Always. Even when the President—' He stopped and broke eye contact. 'When he or his family aren't in the Residence, this floor is continually patrolled and monitored.'

Friedman snapped his head round to face Morrow. '*Monitors*? What, CCTV?' He glanced up at the ceiling above them.

Morrow shook his head. 'No. President Forrester refused close-circuit surveillance in this corridor. But when the President or the First Lady are in their bedroom or sitting room, the infrared scanners and sensors are always working.' Morrow half smiled. 'It used to drive the President nuts,' he went on. 'We knew exactly when he was taking a leak because he'd set off the sensors every time he went into the bathroom. Same for the First Lady.'

Friedman sat forward, checking the corridor behind them. 'Can you tell from the sensors how many people are in a room?'

'Of course,' Morrow replied. He stared at Friedman.'John, why are you—'

Friedman spoke over him. 'The sensors are *always* on?' he asked hurriedly.

Morrow nodded. 'Absolutely. They're heat- and weight-sensitive. We could tell if Danny DeVito was walking round here.'

'Lee, where are those sensors monitored?'

Morrow shrugged again, his eyes wary. 'In the HQ downstairs. Have you never been down there?'

Friedman shook his head. 'No, I never got round to that particular treat. I didn't think the Service liked to advertise its expertise.'

'Yeah, well,' Morrow replied gruffly, 'we don't exactly encourage the staff to just wander in. We have a floor plan of the entire building on the computer. The perimeter sensors, round the building and the gardens, are under twenty-four-hour watch. So are the President's offices and the private quarters up here. The infrared is eveywhere. We turn off the sensors in the staterooms downstairs during the day because of the public tours; the uniformed section keep an eye on that. But all the important rooms are monitored from the Centre: in the West Wing it only applies to the Oval Office, the secretaries' offices, the Roosevelt and Cabinet Rooms and the Situation Room below. We can't keep check of every aide or staffer walking round the West Wing.

'But up here is different: if anyone enters a corridor or opens a door in the Residence, it flashes up. If someone is near the President or First Lady, we want to know who they are and what they want.'

Friedman nodded. Thinking quickly, he turned and looked at the agent. 'Is a record kept? I mean, do they keep a tally of which room was entered and when?'

'Absolutely,' Morrow replied, his tone clipped. 'Whether it's the ushers or the cleaners or anyone else moving around up here, once they've passed through the security checks at the end of the hall, we know precisely where they are on this floor and it's all recorded by the computer. We keep the logs for a month before they're sent over to Treasury to be destroyed.' Morrow's eyes bored into Friedman. 'John, you should know all this,' he said gently. 'Why're you asking?'

Friedman swallowed then told Morrow about the attack on him earlier.

'*What?*' Morrow rose quickly from the sofa, right hand fumbling for the revolver under his jacket. 'John . . . have you *reported* this?' He looked angrily at the door that led into Elizabeth's bedroom suite. 'For God's sake, John, are you telling me that Mrs Forrester is in *there* with Marjorie Wallace and there might be an intruder up *here*? Jesus—' Morrow leaped towards the small radio on the table beside him.

Friedman grabbed clumsily at his arm. 'Lee, please,' he hissed. 'Just listen to me. I don't know what the hell is going on. But I do know that there was someone here who shouldn't have been, or at least didn't want me seeing them. It was one person, I'm certain of it. Whoever it was was in the private suite. There were no agents at either of the stairwells. Is that normal?'

Morrow shook his head. 'No way. There should always be someone keeping watch.'

Friedman's voice rose just a fraction. 'Well, they *weren't* here. But someone else was. I tried to catch them on the stairwell but I lost them.'

'You said *them*?'

'I meant one person,' he replied. 'I didn't see the intruder or anyone else.' He stopped. He did not yet want to confide his suspicions about McQuogue. To do so would put Morrow in an impossible position: the Secret Service agent would have to report the entire incident to his superiors. Friedman wanted to avoid that, at least until he had spoken to Elizabeth. 'Lee, please, just do me this favour. Can you check the computer logs? Find out when this hall was penetrated and if anything was done about it.' He watched Morrow consider the request.

Neither man spoke for a few minutes. Finally, Morrow broke the silence. 'OK, John, just this once. But I'm not going to put Mrs Forrester in any danger. And if what you've said is true—'

'Lee, I'm hardly going to—'

'If it *is* true,' Morrow went on, 'then I need to discover what the hell happened and why no one was watching the Residence. After that, I'm going to have to report it.'

'Lee—'

Both men stopped talking. From the window behind them came the noise of the military helicopter landing on the South Lawn. It was to take Elizabeth directly to Bethesda. They both rose quickly from the settee. Friedman tapped gently on the door to Elizabeth's bedroom. No response. He glanced at Morrow, who raised his eyebrows and shrugged. 'Perhaps she's sleeping,' the agent said, placing his hand on the doorknob.

'No, wait a second, Lee. Let's knock again.'

Almost immediately, Elizabeth opened the door and stood before them. 'Yes, gentlemen?' she asked gently, looking from one to the other.

She no longer wore her sunglasses and her eyes were, by now, puffy, her face pale and clouded. But the most startling sight was her clothes: gone was the chic designer outfit that she had been wearing only hours before in Miami. In its place, the First Lady had on a heavy woollen black suit and patent black shoes. A black chiffon scarf was tied around her throat. In her right hand she clasped a small black purse. Marjorie Wallace stood behind her.

The two men parted to let the women through. The silence inside the private corridor was total; the only sound came from outside, the mechanical whirring of the helicopter rotor blades. The small party made its way down the stairs.

McQuogue looked up from his desk in the West Wing. The office floor was cluttered with discarded folders, squashed Styrofoam cups and scraps of paper. He sighed and pushed back the net curtains. Through the thick glass of the West Wing windows, he watched as Elizabeth Forrester walked across the South Lawn towards the helicopter. It was getting dark now and the helicopter stood bathed in light. Beyond the crowds – he spotted Friedman talking hurriedly to a Secret Service Agent – McQuogue could see the glare of television lights capturing for the millionth time today another 'historic' picture.

He left his office. In the corridor outside, all conversation stopped as he appeared. 'People, go back to your offices, wait there. You all know what you've got to do,' he said matter-of-factly, pushing through the crowd and lowering his head to avoid the inevitable panicked requests for approval and direction.

He passed quickly along the corridor that led to the Oval Office. It only took him a matter of seconds. One uniformed Secret Service guard stood rigidly to attention at the entrance, impassive as McQuogue walked towards him. The Chief of Staff did not recognise the agent. 'I'm Wayne McQuogue. Please leave this office and take guard outside.'

The young guard, pale-faced and swollen-eyed, flinched. 'I'm sorry, sir, my orders are—'

McQuogue leaned towards him. 'I don't give a damn what your orders are, son. I am White House Chief of Staff. My boss and your boss is dead. Now get out of my way.'

The guard did not hesitate. Stepping aside, his eyes remained focused on the wall twenty feet in front of him.

'Very good,' McQuogue said. 'Now, I will give you another order. I shall close this door,' he said, pointing to the entrance to the Oval Office, 'and no one, I repeat no one, is to enter. Is that clear?'

'Yessir.'

McQuogue walked confidently towards the President's desk and took a set of keys out of his suit pocket. Kneeling on the floor, he began to unlock one set of drawers.

'Are you all right, ma'am?'

Friedman stood at the door to the First Family's drawing room. Through the half-moon window behind Elizabeth, the lights were still on in the Old Executive Office Building across West Executive Avenue. Elizabeth, feet up on the sofa, was staring at the schedule of events planned for the following morning: the lying-in-state. The dignitaries and the paraphernalia of death . . .

She looked up as Friedman remained by the door. 'Oh, John, come in. Thank you, I'm fine. Marjorie has just left.'

Elizabeth didn't rise to greet him but pointed to a chair on the other side of the fireplace. 'Would you like a drink?' she asked quietly, staring ahead of her, her voice faint and muffled.

'No, thank you, ma'am.'

'Would you mind getting me one? A small brandy. I can allow myself that. It might help me sleep.'

Images from the last few hours flashed through her mind and again she felt as if she were watching herself from afar, channel-surfing through the chaos and emotions of the day. Bethesda Hospital was not the place she had expected to say her last private goodbye to Tyler. They'd done their best, laid his body in the permanent Presidential Suite. Once alone with him, she had pulled up a chair, a small metal affair that someone had placed in the corner of the room, and sat by the coffin. She hadn't said anything to Tyler; just sat there. He seemed to have his usual smile, even in death; she didn't kiss him but did something she often did when he was alive, leaned over and removed a small piece of fluff that had lodged itself on the lapel of the dark suit he had been dressed in. And – after how long, she wondered; twenty minutes? – she'd risen from the chair, laid her hand on his forehead, then turned and slowly crossed the room to the door.

Back in the White House she had disappeared into her secret hiding place, the attic structure known as the solarium which sits, glass walls on three sides, at the very top of the building. Washington, dark but lit by millions of lights, the noise of the crowds from outside the White House gates filtering up, lay before her. It was beautiful, stunning. She had enjoyed a brief moment of solace, before turning and making her way downstairs to the private quarters.

'It was good of you to come up, John,' she said to Friedman, sipping from the brandy glass. She stretched over and placed it on the table beside her. 'I wanted to ask you something. I didn't have the chance earlier. If you're not up to it now, I can understand, but I'd like to hear what happened when you were with him.'

Friedman blushed and paused.

Then he told her. All of it.

The gym, the jokes, the rowing machine, the cycling, the crash to the floor, Bob Russell pounding into the room, revolver drawn. She listened intently, legs tucked up underneath her, eyes never leaving his face.

When Friedman had finished, he leaned over and poured himself a glass of brandy. They sat in silence, the only sounds coming sporadically from the streets outside.

'There's something else, ma'am,' he said eventually.

Elizabeth nodded for him to continue.

'After you called me from the plane, I did as you asked. I came up to the private quarters to check that everything was as you requested, but something happened.'

Elizabeth frowned slightly. 'Go on.'

Friedman repeated the story he had told Morrow.

Elizabeth's reaction was surprisingly calm. 'Are you sure you were deliberately assaulted?'

He nodded. 'Certain. And whoever was in here had a key to the main door. It was locked after I'd been pushed back. They got out through the connecting doors to the back stairs. Ma'am, I've told Lee. He's checking that the sensors are working properly but—'

Elizabeth raised her hand to silence him. 'Where were the detail?'

Friedman shrugged. 'Well, they weren't up here and—'

'I suppose you can hardly blame them. The President had *died*. Their major concern would have to be Willard. So the fact that the Service had abandoned my bedroom suite for a few hours is hardly surprising. As for the intruder' – Elizabeth put the glass on the console table beside her – 'it may have been one of the ushers. I'm sure some of them are paid by the tabloids to check on us. Whoever it was was most probably trying to get some . . . some *trinket*. You can never depend on a person's loyalty, can you, John?'

She looked at him sadly, her eyes sunken and red. She appeared exhausted.

Friedman spoke again, more quietly this time. 'Ma'am, Mr McQuogue saw me as I tried to chase the intruder.'

Elizabeth's eyebrows rose in surprise.

Friedman nodded. 'Mrs Forrester, I am sorry to have to burden you with this now, ma'am. This has been a day that none of us will ever forget for the rest of our lives. But Mr McQuogue lied to me, ma'am. He had to have done so. He did not enter the stairwell from the state floor as he said. The uniformed guard told me. So, if he had come up from the basement, he would have to have seen whoever it was who had been in here, the man I was chasing.'

Elizabeth shook her head then spoke, her voice weary but controlled. 'Not true, John. I've used that stairwell myself to go down to the basement gym. McQuogue could easily have missed whoever it was coming down. There are doors off of it on the half-landings, and you can enter the stairwell from *three* different doors in the basement.'

'Ma'am—'

'John, leave it to Lee. If there was any chance that an intruder could get back in, Lee would have had me out of here by now.' She smiled weakly at her aide. 'I know you're worried about me . . . and I'm touched.'

She could feel the tears threatening again.

'But let's call it a day, John. I can't take any more dramas. Please – I'd like some time alone.'

They both rose and walked to the door. Elizabeth massaged her forehead, her thoughts elsewhere, as Friedman opened the door on to the Center Hall. Two Secret Service agents were standing guard.

'Goodnight, Mrs Forrester,' Friedman said, hesitating in the doorway.

Elizabeth looked up in surprise. 'Oh, yes, sorry,' she mumbled distractedly. 'Goodnight, John.'

When he'd gone, she collapsed on the bed, tiredness and grief swamping her. She glanced at the telephone by her side of the bed: the red CRASH button was where it should be, in the middle of the console. Elizabeth knew that if she pushed it the detail would be by her side in seconds.

Tyler, if only you were here now.

She undressed and slid beneath the covers. As she closed her eyes, she was determined not to think about what Friedman had told her. She wanted to think only of one thing.

Tyler.

She fell asleep with the smiling face of her dead husband frozen in her mind.

☆

Friedman left the private quarters and instructed the White House driver to drop him near New Hampshire. He was determined to walk home some of the way. After the terrible events of the day, the need for space and air had overridden the desire to get home as quickly as possible.

The Adams-Morgan district had changed into its night clothes. Friedman watched as a group of transvestites touted for custom outside a club on 18th. Their synthetic wigs were a kaleidoscope of reds and greens and blues, drivers slowing down and honking at the spectacle. A scattering of sodden fliers lay limp and congealed on the sidewalk. He avoided the crowds and made his way down the hill towards Dupont. He took the back route home, through the small lanes and dark streets that led off the main thoroughfares.

His house was in darkness. The only light came from the top floor, squares of white reflecting off the low roof. Friedman turned on the hall light and made his way swiftly up the stairs. Inside he tidied the clothes he had strewn across the bathroom floor, left there before the start of what he had expected to be a normal working day. He walked through the apartment. The sitting room was noisy, the windows open on to New Hampshire and the urban orchestra of late-night revellers and cars.

The telephone rang. Friedman swore loudly and reached over. 'Hello?'

It was the White House switchboard. 'Mr Friedman, I have your office on the line.'

He thought of Tyler, and a telephone call from the gym earlier in the day. He waited for his young assistant's voice. 'John?'

'Hi, Phil. What's up?'

'Nothing much, just checking out for the night. Only one thing outstanding: McQuogue wants to arrange a meeting, ideally before the funeral.'

Friedman groaned. 'What does he want?'

'Wouldn't say.'

Friedman thanked his assistant and rang off.

He was not looking forward to his meeting with the Chief of Staff. The two men came from warring factions within the White House. Once again, Friedman wondered why McQuogue had lied to him. Perhaps he'd soon find out.

Two men watched Friedman's lights go out. Their car was parked near the junction with 18th. Through the trees, the occupants of the car had an unobstructed view of Friedman's apartment.

'Well, he's turned in for the night,' one said, shuffling uncomfortably in his seat. 'Let's split.'

His colleague started the engine. The dark limousine pulled quietly away from the sidewalk, spun to the right and headed south.

As he lay back on his pillow, Friedman heard the car drive past, the headlights flickering across his walls. By the time it reached Swann Street, he was already asleep.

Chapter Five

The next morning the sun rose in an unclouded turquoise sky, the horizon still edged with a faint brush stroke of burgundy. The noise of the traffic had not yet penetrated the bullet-proof, bomb-proof, Arab-proof windows of the White House.

Elizabeth opened her eyes and was immediately swamped by an inexplicable feeling of dread. The darkness felt like a prison. She lunged for the lamp on the bedside table, fingers fumbling in the dark for the switch.

The room was bathed in a gentle pink light. Blinking and propping herself up on one arm, she looked around her. The suite was empty.

Silently, she scolded herself and tried not to think of what Friedman had told her. The attack was, she tried to reassure herself for the hundredth time, nothing more than one of the staff being caught trying to steal a memento. She pulled herself together and quickly got dressed.

She opened the bedroom door and peered out into the Center Hall. The private quarters were still illuminated by artificial light, deserted and quiet, when she left her bedroom. She turned left, walked down the stairs to the staterooms on the ground floor and immediately came across her Secret Service detail for the night.

'Can we do anything for you, ma'am?' the senior agent

asked her, eyes searching her face for any signs of worry or panic.

'No, I'm fine, thank you. But I'd like to go to the Oval Office. On my own,' Elizabeth told him, pulling her grey cashmere cardigan closer around her and blinking herself further awake.

The Secret Service agent, well schooled in the protocol of the White House, hesitated for just a second. Strictly speaking, the First Lady was a private citizen; as such she did not have a security clearance. Elizabeth sensed his reticence but, controlling her impatience, managed to smile. 'I know you shouldn't really do it,' she said, lowering her head and glancing around her at the four other agents, who stood motionless at the bottom of the stairs. 'But in the circumstances,' she went on, 'I don't think anyone will object. And if they do, then it's down to me, not you. Do you think we can proceed on that basis?'

The agent paused again for only a second. 'Of course, Mrs Forrester. I'll walk with you.'

'No, please, I really do know the way . . . and I just want to remember Tyler on my own.'

The agent nodded his acquiescence and moved aside. Elizabeth walked across the marble floors, her slippers flip-flopping on the cold surface. Sensing the agents watching her, she opened the glass doors in front of her and stepped outside. The dawn was cold and a slight wind chilled her as she immediately turned right and followed the portico that led to the West Wing. Once inside, she passed two more agents (who had been alerted to her imminent arrival) and walked up the ramp. Turning left again, she found herself in the corridor that led to her late husband's office.

Elizabeth stood for a second in the doorway to the Oval Office. Her forehead rested on the cool painted frame. She breathed in deeply, holding the air in her lungs before expelling it gently in an attempt to try to stop the trembling she could feel welling up inside her.

She thought of the last time she had seen Tyler in this office.

Eventually, pulling herself together, she crossed the threshold and walked to the desk. She stood behind it, taking in the room in front of her, silent and empty.

Suddenly, as she began to move away from the desk, something caught her eye. One of Tyler's desk drawers, normally locked tight, was slightly open. Elizabeth tugged at the brass handle and the drawer slid open.

It was empty.

Elizabeth frowned.

She looked towards the main door into the office. It was still shut tight. She crouched down and opened the next drawer down. Also empty. Not a speck of dust or a paper-clip remained in the place that had once held her husband's personal files.

The First Lady sat on the floor and thought.

Why have the drawers been left unlocked?

Feeling like a cat burglar, Elizabeth crawled behind and around Tyler's chair and tried the next set of drawers. Open. And empty.

She stood up quickly, muttering to herself. As she tried to understand why her husband's desk would be emptied only hours after his death – and by whom – she suddenly remembered something Tyler had told her after only a few weeks of being President. Joking about how he could barely do anything without being watched, and every note he made being logged somewhere, out of a sense of mischief he had decided to hide certain personal items in a special place in the Oval Office.

Elizabeth walked across the office towards the bookcase. She stretched up and pulled out a vast volume – Gore Vidal's *United States* – and, rising to her full height, peered into the back of the wooden case. She could just make out the corner of a black book and a folded piece of white paper.

The book was A4 in size, casebound, and its cover was blank. She opened it at the first page.

Tyler's handwriting.

He had his own official diary, great volumes of the thing

stored in the White House vaults. It was to be the basis of his memoirs. But this was different.

Elizabeth flicked through the pages, quickly reading small extracts. It *was* a diary, but one that he had kept secret even from her.

She closed it, and placed it on the desk. Next, she unfolded the large piece of white notepaper. It was a memo, marked 'For The President's Eyes Only'.

Urgent.
To: The President.
From: Ronald Kelly
The Pentagon
Subject: Defence Procurements.

There was nothing else attached to it. Whatever Ron Kelly had sent Tyler had been removed and placed elsewhere. The memo had been received by the President only ten days before his death.

Putting the slip of paper down, Elizabeth once again stretched up to the bookcase and removed three or four more books. Nothing behind them. She did the same for the next shelf down: nothing but dust. Tyler would never have hidden anything behind the lower shelves; anyone standing near them would have been able to see.

She returned to the desk, checked that the drawers were left as she had found them. Unbuttoning her cardigan, she placed Tyler's diary and Kelly's memo snugly under her left arm. Composing herself, she walked towards the door, adjusted the package, and with her other hand twisted the handle and pushed the door open.

'Mrs Forrester . . .'

Elizabeth looked up sharply to see Chief of Staff

McQuogue standing in front of her. 'Wayne . . . oh, I'm sorry, I was just looking through Tyler's belongings, I suppose for the last time.'

Her left arm squeezed even more tightly under her cardigan. She could feel the diary's spine cutting into her.

'You're in early, Wayne.' She managed to smile at the Chief of Staff.

'No rest for the wicked,' he replied. He shuffled the papers in his hand and looked behind her into the Oval Office.

Elizabeth said quickly: 'You know, it's so strange being here without Tyler, I just wanted to come and finally say goodbye.'

She tried to smile again. The Chief of Staff watched her intently. Silence fell between the two of them.

'Would you like me to leave you, Mrs Forrester?' McQuogue said finally. 'I can come back, it's no trouble.' His offer was accompanied by just the smallest of sighs.

'No, I'll leave you, Wayne, there's no point me getting in the way of business.' She paused. 'Is the Vice President here?'

'No, ma'am, he'll be here shortly.'

'I'd like to see him. There are a few things about the funeral ceremony I'd like to check.'

Her slight was not lost on the Chief of Staff. 'I'll tell him, Mrs Forrester . . . unless there's anything I can help you with?'

'No, Wayne, that won't be necessary. But thank you for your patience.'

She nodded at McQuogue and began to walk through the secretaries' office. Her heart pounding with every step, she made it to the door and out into the relative safety of the main corridor. As she strode towards the Secret Service agent standing guard at the top of the stairs, she glanced behind her.

McQuogue was still watching her.

Lee Morrow parked by the basement entrance to the West Wing. The morning sky had turned from light pink to an insipid watery yellow. Beyond the north-west gate the city remained silent, only the phlegmatic groan of a solitary truck briefly punc-turing the stillness of the White House grounds.

Within a few minutes he reached the Secret Service Command Centre in the basement. He slid his ID through the monitor and waited for the door to unlock. A second later, he pushed through into the office. Two agents glanced at him as he made his way across the open-plan room. Morrow waved at them, declined their offer of coffee and settled himself in front of a computer terminal in the far corner of the office suite. He could see the blurred reflection of the two agents behind him in the screen. They were not paying him any attention. Instead, one kept a keen eye on the monitors spread around the far wall.

'Oh, Lee, you should know this.'

Morrow turned round. One of the agents was walking towards him across the office. 'ADVOCATE was just on the move.' The agent used the Secret Service code-name for Elizabeth. 'She was in the Oval Office,' he went on. 'The Night Detail knew of it. She refused their request to accompany her. She shouldn't be doing that, Lee. Can you gently advise her?'

He nodded. 'Sure, but in the circumstances I think she can be excused.'

The agent shrugged and made his way back across the office.

Morrow returned to the computer monitor in front of him. Within seconds, he had called up the files he wanted.

He squinted at the screen. The sensors in the private quarters had been activated in the bedroom suite and bathrooms at 3.30 p.m. the previous afternoon. According to the guard post by the main entrance to the Residence, two authorised cleaners had entered the private quarters to prepare for Elizabeth's arrival. They had left twenty-three minutes later, their departure again reported by the guard post. At 4.17 p.m., a secretary from Elizabeth's office had also been logged in by the guards as entering the private quarters: according to the sensors, she had gone straight to the Yellow Sitting Room and had left a mere five minutes later, making her way back to the guard post.

Flicking farther down, he found what he was looking for almost immediately. The Center Hall in the Residence had been penetrated at 4.50 p.m. Five seconds later, the bedroom suite had been entered, then the bathroom. The intruder had stayed in the suite for five minutes. Whoever it was had then left the bedroom, crossed the hall and entered the Treaty Room, the office Tyler Forrester had often used instead of the West Wing. Ten minutes later, the bedroom suite sensors had flashed again: the intruder was back.

Morrow checked the guard logs on the other side of the screen. The Secret Service guard post at the entrance to the private quarters had reported no one entering the floor.

Morrow blinked in surprise.

But someone *had* been there.

He scrolled down farther. Another person had entered the private quarters at 5.04 p.m.

Friedman.

Morrow sat back and stared at the screen. From the computer records, Morrow could follow second by second the very route Friedman had taken as he pursued his attacker. The sensors clearly tracked the intruder's own frantic escape route from the private quarters. The monitors had lit up like fireworks all the way to the stairwell and the second guard post.

Morrow pushed himself back from the desk and exhaled. The computer could not be wrong. But it *had* to be. The guards had reported no one on the floor.

Controlling his anger and confusion, Morrow strolled over to his two colleagues. They nodded as he sat down next to them.

'You're in early, Lee,' one said as he sipped from a Styrofoam cup of coffee.

Morrow shrugged. 'I need to be here for when the First Lady wakes up.'

'Yeah, well, she's already done that. It's a shame you weren't here when she decided to go walkabout.'

He left the jibe unanswered. He was thinking quickly: he knew he could not alarm the two agents or they would report his suspicions immediately. Even so, he needed to check why the penetration of the private quarters had gone unreported.

He leaned back in the chair and stretched his legs, faking a yawn of his own. 'You guys been on all night?' he asked casually.

They both nodded. 'Sure have.' In unison, the two agents rolled their eyes.

Morrow affected a bored demeanour. 'How was it earlier? Before we got back from Miami?'

The agent nearest him answered. 'Pandemonium. We were both called in from home. *Everyone* was called in from home. It was chaos upstairs, apparently. The Vice-President didn't want to be rushed back here. Wayne McQuogue was ordering everyone to surround Willard Morgan, leave their posts and secure the Vice-President. You couldn't move through the West Wing, goddam staffers crowding round everywhere, people trying to rush over from the OEOB.' The agent snorted in disgust. 'Half the detail were at Bethesda or on the way. No one knew if the President was really dead or what the hell had happened.' He stopped and looked at Morrow. 'How's the First Lady?'

Morrow shrugged. 'What do you expect?'

The two agents nodded in sympathy.

Morrow decided to push a little harder. 'Who was keeping watch down here?'

The two men snorted, again in unison.

Mork and Mindy.

'A uniformed,' the other agent replied. 'If we'd been stretched any further, then we'd have to have got the goddam gardeners to stand guard. We didn't get everyone who shouldn't be here out until later. The Marines upstairs were their usual useless self. It took half an hour to secure the West Wing and empty the public tours from the state floor.'

'What about the Residence?' Morrow asked gently, not missing a beat.

The agent rolled his eyes again. 'Lee, you could have walked from Commerce to the fucking Center Hall and no one would have stopped you. According to what I heard, they didn't get people back to the guard posts until just before you arrived.'

Morrow grunted non-commitally. 'Shit happens,' he said loudly, rising from the chair.

'I think we've had enough shit for one day,' one of the agents murmured as Morrow said goodbye and left the office.

He stood in the corridor outside the Command Centre and shut his eyes.

He ran through what he had just learned: one uniformed guard had kept watch in the room behind him. Only a handful of other uniformed officers had been detailed to guard the Residence. Morrow understood all too well what had happened: in the rush to clear the main building of the public and all unneeded personnel, in the atmosphere of disbelief and paralysis that had gripped the White House after Tyler's death, the two entrances to the private quarters had been left unattended.

And someone had taken their chance.

Elizabeth checked behind her. The door to the bedroom suite was closed. From behind the windows that stretched the length of the room she could hear the early morning traffic building up along Pennsylvania.

She put Kelly's covering note to one side and opened the diary. It was inconspicuous-looking – a hard black cover, red cloth spine. Lines of dark blue ink, Tyler's handwriting. She flicked through, trying to concentrate. His handwriting was difficult to follow. By the third page, it had become even more so. Elizabeth felt as if she were translating a foreign language. Tyler had titled one section 'Funds'. The word was capitalised and underlined twice, an exclamation mark rounding it off. Beneath, he'd written:

> Kelly memo. Is this man serious?! Considering reply. M not aware of correspondence. Monitor response. Must keep check on donation. Speak to Kelly? Press reaction? Can't accept without clearance. We have no comeback. Has M committed us? Liz reaction?

Elizabeth blinked hard at the mention of herself. She wondered if 'M' referred to McQuogue.

She continued to scan the diary, hurriedly turning the pages. The next reference that caught her eye was on page six. Again it was brief. In different ink this time, he'd written:

> Reserving judgment on K. Political in-fighting? Must check with State. Vital to determine source. FBI check on K? Have spoken to M. Not concerned. Assurances that it's legal. Double-check? Must contain fall-out. Are we being cornered? M to report back.

Again Tyler had moved on, the notes now referring to his plans for a new healthcare proposal. Elizabeth reached the end of the short diary. On the final page, Tyler had written the date and time: it was the day before he'd died. Two days ago. The last entry was one line:

> K: Is this a set-up?

Elizabeth sat back. She placed the diary on the bed and glanced at Kelly's covering note. Her mind was racing. There was nothing about her husband's presidency, no worry or concern, that he had not shared with her.

But all this was new to her and she cursed Tyler silently.

What the hell was eating at you?

She stood and poured herself a glass of water. It was too late to get undressed and sleep. She could hear the staff arriving in the Mansion below, the lull before the storm of a new day. She drew back the curtains, the sunshine making her blink. She turned on the bathroom lights and began to change. Ten minutes later, she was back in the main room. The diary still lay on the bed. She picked it up and placed it and the note in her attaché case.

Chapter Six

Two hours later, White looked at the clock in the *Herald's* newsroom: 8.30 a.m. He yawned and arranged the papers on his desk into various piles. They comprised of a stack of yellowing newspaper cuttings, over fifty in all, every one about Elizabeth. This morning, Mr Belch had instructed White to read everything that had ever been written about the First Lady. White and Riordan had been assigned to cover Tyler's funeral and Mr Belch wanted White to produce a colour piece on everything Mrs Forrester did or said throughout the day.

White knew that he should check the computer databases provided to the news desk; but he preferred these ageing bits of paper, the feel of a story rather than the detached, computer-generated files he could call up on the screen in front of him. Some of the cuttings were dated five years ago, others only five weeks.

White began by reading the very first interviews with Elizabeth after her husband had announced his candidacy. They covered her life in Wisconsin, the quiet upbringing by her father, a respected but anonymous local doctor, and her housewife mother; Elizabeth's path through high school (uneventful), to college (graduating at the top of the class), and her arrival in Washington (where her peers enviously perceived her as a young woman already on the fast track to riches and power). White scribbled notes, shamelessly lifting the precious few anecdotes that had already been printed. It took him an hour and a half to make his way through the pile of cuttings. By the time he had finished, his notebook was almost half full. It was something to start with, but he knew he'd have to do better.

He raised his head and glanced across the office. It was now almost midday and his colleagues had begun to gather in little groups, rounding up partners for a lunch-hour trip to the local bar. White spotted his specific prey off to the left, heading wearily towards the coatstand. He stood up quickly and marched across the office.

'Ted?' he called out gently, manoeuvring himself around a desk.

The Assistant Managing Editor (Politics) did not bother to turn round. 'What do you want, White? I'm not drinking today, so you'll have to go and find some other victim.'

White smiled to himself. Ted Daubette was an old *Herald* hand. A gruff, implacable operator, he was known to guard his contacts and his stories like a lion his kill. But White had done him the odd favour.

'Ted, on this Forrester colour piece I'm doing,' he said quickly, 'is there anyone I should speak to? Is there anyone who *might* speak to me about how the First Lady's feeling?'

Daubette threw him a withering look. 'Mark, you're on your own. That ain't my patch. The White House ain't speaking to nobody.' Daubette struggled into his coat as he made his way towards the elevators. White followed, checking that no one was behind them.

'Ted, please, just one name. Anything. I'll give you something back, I promise.'

Daubette paused briefly by the swing-doors that led out into the lobby. 'OK,' he said wearily. 'There's one guy you might want to try. He knows her better than the rest, not that that means much. Guy named Friedman, John Friedman. Stuck-up little sonofabitch, Harvard, the usual BS, but he was seconded to fold napkins for Forrester's wife. Check him out. He'll be with the First Lady and even you might be able to track him down there.'

Elizabeth held the elderly man's hand and tried to smile. 'Clifford, thank you for coming.'

He sat down, nodding slightly as he spoke. 'You're a very brave woman, Elizabeth.' His voice was soft and patrician. 'I only wish you did not have to go through this.'

'Thank you, Clifford,' was all she said in reply. She did not need to say more.

She looked at the man opposite. Clifford Granby had the unmistakable aura of wealth. He was over six feet tall, his grey hair slicked back from his wide forehead. His eyes were a startling blue and remarkably clear for a man of nearly seventy. He had inherited his money from his father, Jack, a Scottish-born entrepreneur who had bequeathed a vast fortune. While the Granby Foundation was one of the most formidable charities in the US, the man who had inherited control of it led a reclusive and quiet life, rarely if ever seen in public.

'Is there anything I can do, Elizabeth? Did you get any sleep?'

She shook her head. 'Not really.'

'Well, you must rest.'

Elizabeth did not reply immediately. She looked at Granby and eventually spoke, this time more forcefully: 'I don't know how I'm going to get through this, Clifford. That's the trouble with thinking you're immortal, isn't it?'

Granby nodded again but kept quiet. Not for the first time Elizabeth felt a great fondness for him. She sat back in the chair and looked around the Yellow Sitting Room. 'Do you remember the first time you were here, just after we moved in? You gave us such good advice, both of us. We thought it would be easy: we'd just won the election, there were so many plans. And then you walked in, sat us both down and told us we'd probably made the biggest goddamned mistake of our lives!'

Elizabeth smiled at the memory.

'I was probably right,' Granby said quietly.

She nodded. 'You were, because you reminded us that it wasn't going to be easy, and warned us that very few people would ever say no to our faces but would damn well ensure that much of what Tyler wanted to do was killed off before he'd even signed the papers.'

'He was a great man, Elizabeth.'

She nodded vehemently. 'He was, Clifford. And so *young*, so full of ideas for what he still wanted to do. I can't . . . it just seems so horribly cruel.' She stared at Granby, her cheeks flushed, her eyes watering.

'Elizabeth, don't up—'

'No, Clifford, I have to speak. Can you *understand* that? All night I've been thinking of the great things he planned to do and now – bam! When Tyler was taking control of his presidency, really making his mark on this country, suddenly' – she clapped her hands together, hard – 'suddenly, he's *gone*.'

Granby shuffled in his chair. 'Elizabeth, you're in shock and that's understandable. But I've reached an age at which the ravages of time are something I have to accept. I can't fight them and nor can you. I would do anything, trade in all of this, to reverse what has happened. You never knew my wife, Silvie. A wonderful woman, but her own goodness could not sustain her. So you grieve, as you will, as you must, and then, slowly, you will find the courage to go on, to commit yourself to another cause. It doesn't get rid of the pain, it can't, but it helps.'

'I know . . .'

Granby coughed and rearranged his long legs. 'Elizabeth, I'm sorry to bring this up so early, but I am – how shall I say this? – I'm aware that neither you nor Tyler was independently wealthy before you came here. I cannot do anything to help you recover from your loss, but the resources I have are available to you. There is a guest house on my Virginia estate . . .'

'Clifford, that is very kind.' She smiled wearily at him. 'But given that you have never been in the public spotlight, I think my presence would be a trial for you.'

Granby shrugged. 'Then let me at least look around for you. There's a cottage for rent just two miles away. I'll check it out.'

Elizabeth blinked, trying to hold back the tears. She knew Granby was right: even now, she must consider the practicalities, however hard it was to do so. 'Thank you, Clifford. That's the kindest thing anyone has said to me since . . . since yesterday.'

'Well, I wanted to tell you directly, and I mean it. I'll wait to hear from you. Is there anything else you need?'

She shook her head. 'No. Marjorie will be here later. So will John Friedman. And thank you, Clifford, thank you for coming this morning.'

He rose from his chair and she walked him to the door. They embraced, then Granby held her hand again. 'We'll help you get through this, Elizabeth. If you need me before the funeral, you know where to find me.'

Chapter Seven

Washington seemed at its best that morning. As if the grandeur of a presidential funeral imbued the city's austere architectural sweep with a proper sense of purpose. Elizabeth looked out at the scene from her bedroom. She could see the crowd beyond South Executive Place and the Ellipse. It was the same on the other side of the White House: spectators, police, the National Guard, a huge battalion of media, all crushed into the small area around Lafayette Park.

Elizabeth let the curtains fall back into place. She was as ready as she'd ever be. There was a knock on the door. She crossed the room and let Marjorie into the suite.

'Are you ready, Liz?' Marjorie asked, taking her hand.

Elizabeth nodded hesitantly and looked around her. 'Well, I suppose it's time.'

Marjorie escorted her to the door then stood aside. In the corridor, Morrow was waiting for them. They made their way down the main stairs without speaking, following the familiar route to the Blue Room, where Tyler's coffin lay.

'Elizabeth, good morning,' Willard Morgan whispered as the former First Lady entered the room.

'Good morning, Mr President,' she answered, just a touch too loudly.

Everyone in the room stared at her, stunned by her greeting.

Willard blinked hard and raised his head, eyes trying to avoid Elizabeth's. He had only been sworn in the previous day. She looked behind him and smiled thinly at his wife, who was almost hiding.

'If you wouldn't mind waiting here, Mrs Forrester?' Morrow said.

Elizabeth stood rigidly to the left of the doorway, Marjorie beside her, as the Marine Guard lifted the President's coffin and carried it towards her. She could not bring herself to look at the vast oak casket and instead watched the faces of the men bearing her husband's body.

They're so young.

She turned and followed the coffin and then she was outside, heels clicking on the stone steps of the North Entrance.

Tyler's coffin was placed upon a gun carriage draped in the Stars and Stripes. Elizabeth, well briefed on the order of the day, turned immediately to her right and walked towards the waiting limousine.

She let herself fall back into the seat. Willard was beside her. They sat in silence as the cavalcade began to inch its way out of the White House grounds. As their car passed through the gates, Willard – still looking straight ahead – finally spoke. 'If only it hadn't had to be like this, Elizabeth.'

She could not bring herself to turn towards him.

'I didn't want this, you know. I never did. It's not really mine, I know that. I'm only here because of Tyler, Elizabeth, and I don't want you to forget that.' He coughed gently. 'You do understand that, don't you?'

Elizabeth said: 'Mr President, I am burying my husband. That is the only thing I understand.'

The limousine reached Massachusetts Avenue, heading towards the cathedral beyond the Naval Observatory. DC police outriders led the procession, followed by five horsemen and the battalions of military personnel. In front of Tyler's coffin came the 'lone horse', without its rider, stirrups reversed as a sign of mourning.

Elizabeth had never seen Washington so silent. The crowds straining for a glimpse of her seemed to do so in slow motion, in time with the rhythmic salute of the drummers.

A voice snapped at her through the intercom. 'Mr President, Mrs Forrester, we shall be arriving at the cathedral steps in thirty seconds.'

Willard played with the buttons of his black suit and stole a surreptitious glance at Elizabeth. She continued to ignore him as she placed her handbag in her lap and waited for the car to stop.

The heavy door swung open. The Marine Guards stood to attention a few feet away, Tyler's coffin on their shoulders. She stepped on to the pavement, ducking so as not to displace her black pillbox hat.

'Oh my God, Tyler,' she whispered, and felt the tears threatening.

Suddenly, she sensed that she was falling. She could see the hard pavement coming up to meet her. Her legs seemed incapable of holding her.

A strong hand took hold of her right elbow. Elizabeth allowed Morrow to take her weight.

Inside the cathedral Elizabeth moved down the aisle, past the vast stained-glass windows and stone barrel vaults. The nave rose above her, 565 feet high.

Tyler's coffin was just a few feet ahead.

We were in too much of a hurry for a church, weren't we, Tyler?

Elizabeth was seated in the front row, Willard and his wife Ethel to her right. Behind her were the Joint Chiefs of Staff, the Speaker of the House of Representatives, the Majority Leader, Supreme Court judges and senior Senators. In seemingly endless rows behind them, the world's leaders sat silently listening as the service drew to a close.

You had that terrible blue shirt on when we married. And you wore it all through the honeymoon.

'Elizabeth?'

She turned towards the voice.

'It's time for my address.' Willard passed by her and made his way quickly to the lectern. From his pocket he withdrew a handful of small white cards and placed them on the stand in front of him.

'Mrs Forrester, ladies and gentlemen, my fellow Americans. I had the great privilege of knowing Tyler Forrester for many years. He was a true leader. A committed and thoughtful President. A loving husband . . .'

You hated swimming, always did. In Provincetown I had to drag you into the boat. That time you almost fell in, I couldn't stop laughing. And then you got real mad with me, and wouldn't speak for an hour, and I still couldn't stop laughing. But we were better later . . .

'His vision of the world was of a place united in a new spirit of co-operation. He more than anyone understood the need to forgo old enmities, to build new partnerships for a new tomorrow—'

And what you ate! You would never let me change that. Nothing would do it. And you'd always chide me and tell me I was a snob, but then you'd kiss me and smile.

Your smile.

At least I've still got that to remember.

'His vision was of a new America also. A nation united by common purpose, sustained by common goals—'

That time I got drunk with you on B52s in Greece and I rang the village bell at four in the morning and all the fishermen ran out thinking a ship had gone down, and you had to hustle me home before we were caught . . .

They don't think we were still in love, do they? Funny how a President can't love his wife; and she him. But we did love each other, didn't we?

That weekend after the victory, that special two days . . . You were so antsy. And I pretended to mock you, and you stood naked in the bedroom, and told me I was committing treason by seducing the world's most important man.

Mozart's Requiem interrupted her private memorial. Having

finished his address, Willard now stood at the end of the pew and waited for Elizabeth. She rose slowly, Morrow already in place in front of her, and stepped into the aisle. As the coffin passed her, Morrow stepped forward and gently took hold of her elbow.

'Not much longer, ma'am,' he whispered, as the First Lady began the slow walk.

Oh, no, Lee, you're wrong. It's going to be very long without Tyler.

'Thank you, Prime Minister, he felt the same way about you.'

Elizabeth saw the French President standing in line to be greeted. His handsome eyes bore into her and the lights of the East Room were reflected in his bald pate.

'Mrs Forrester, my nation extends its sincere regrets.' He held her hand and leaned closer. 'Your husband will forever hold his place in history.'

'Thank you, Mr President. He tried to do so much. I only hope his work will go on.'

The Frenchman nodded and moved by.

Elizabeth signalled to the White House usher behind her. He passed her a glass of water. She sipped quickly, turned again to face the never-ending line of dignitaries. The queue – which included nine chiefs of state and twelve heads of government – stretched out of the East Room, through the Green Room and over to the west side of the building as far as the State Dining Room.

Elizabeth had returned to the White House from Arlington National Cemetery an hour ago. Tyler's grave had been prepared to the south of the immense graveyard, out of site of JFK's eternal flame. It was a deliberately simple plot, in from Hobson's Gate and in the shadow of Jackson Circle. Later, a black marble cross would be erected and the gravestone would carry Elizabeth's stark message: 'A President and a Husband'.

As she mouthed appropriate greetings to the world leaders

who passed in front of her, Elizabeth thought of that last goodbye.

In the handbag by her feet was a small plastic envelope of soil from the graveside. She could still feel remnants of the grit in her left hand.

'Thank you, your Royal Highness. I would hope to do so very soon.'

Another invitation, another offer of help.

Do they really mean it?

Elizabeth glanced to her left. Clifford Granby was making his way towards her. 'Elizabeth.' He held her hand and smiled.

'Clifford, thank you so much for coming.'

'You were magnificent, Elizabeth. And you shouldn't stay much longer in this room. The sycophants here can entertain themselves. You should go and have a rest. Are you still staying upstairs?'

'Yes, I'm here for a while yet.'

He squeezed her arm. 'I've found you a cottage. The press won't know I'm involved. Will you let me know if you want to take it up?'

'I will, Clifford, thank you.'

She looked around her. No one else was within earshot. 'There's something else I need to discuss with you privately. May I call you?'

He nodded. 'Of course.'

'We'll speak later, Clifford.'

He kissed her and turned away.

Suddenly, Elizabeth found herself alone in the vast room. Morrow walked towards her and smiled. 'That's it, Mrs Forrester. Would you like to go upstairs?'

Elizabeth looked beyond him towards the centre of the room. The statesmen and women, the princes and the kings, the power brokers and the hangers-on to power, were now focusing on Willard Morgan. He stood uncomfortably as the introductions were made.

The passing of the flame.

'Okay, Lee, let's go now.'

'God, you are so *good*.'

Riordan slapped White on the shoulder. The Irishman was standing over his colleague in the *Herald*'s newsroom. Despite his capacity for uncovering the worst of human endeavours, Riordan could barely string a sentence together in print.

'I love that bit. Jesus, that says it all!'

White ignored his colleague's excited praise and carried on writing. He had to admit that it *was* quite good. The funeral had been a truly awesome event, magisterial, brimming with the emotion and detail that made a reporter's job easy.

And yet as he wrote, White could not share Riordan's enthusiasm. He had been only a few yards away from Elizabeth when she had stumbled. He had wanted to rush forward and help her.

'Put in the bit about the heel slipping. Women will like that.' Riordan took another puff on his cigarette and flicked the ash on to the floor. 'Great, great . . . Jesus, Whitey, it's like you know this broad for real.'

He carried on typing.

> Mrs Forrester, her fine features etched with grief, managed to hold on to the door as a Secret Service agent rushed towards her.
>
> She is a woman schooled in the art of dignity and poise. She has always known the need for inner strength. Yesterday, for a second she lost it. And our nation lost it with her.

White leaned back and pushed the FILE button. The copy on the screen immediately disappeared, electronically transmitted to the subeditors who sat yards away compiling the next day's paper.

Elizabeth shut the door behind her.

'Marjorie?'

From the bathroom she heard her friend call out, 'One second.'

Elizabeth leaned back against the wooden frame, her hand still resting on the doorknob. The bedroom suite was illuminated by a cluster of small lamps. To the left and right of the door, wooden packing chests stood in four-foot-high piles. They had sunk into the deep carpet, metal grips along the bottom leaving tracks where earlier Elizabeth had heaved them to one side. The plastic wrapping was dragged back on some; others were taped and fastened. On the sides, red ink scarring the dull wood, instructions had been scribbled on to labels for the White House staff: 'Evening Wear', 'Mr Forrester's Day Suits', 'Mr Forrester's Shoes'.

Marjorie appeared in the doorway to the bathroom. 'Ignore the boxes, Liz. I wanted to get the ushers to move them but I couldn't find anyone.'

Elizabeth bit her lip as she looked at the boxes. She was not due to leave the White House for some time but already the preparations for that move had begun.

Chapter Eight

Ten days later

Friedman stood in the doorway and studied McQuogue. Their meeting, which the Chief of Staff had requested before the funeral, had been postponed several times before this evening. Friedman had accepted the excuses given to him: the White House had been chaotic since Tyler's burial. Every day the Chief of Staff's office had relayed the postponement to Friedman with a typically superior air.

Now, Friedman swayed on his feet and waited for McQuogue to finish his call.

'John, come in, come in.'

He smiled weakly and took a chair opposite McQuogue. The Chief of Staff smiled back, his demeanour surprisingly upbeat. Friedman felt that McQuogue was enjoying the drama of it all, being at the heart of an historic event. He doubted that this man had grieved for the President, before or after the funeral.

'Whisky?' McQuogue asked casually.

Friedman shook his head. 'No, thanks.'

McQuogue shrugged and poured two fingers into a tumbler. He sat down and swirled the liquid round and round. Friedman waited.

Eventually, McQuogue leaned forward. 'If you feel anything

like I do,' he said, 'then I don't doubt you're looking forward to getting home.'

Friedman nodded. 'Well, sir, it's strange to think the funeral was only ten days ago.'

McQuogue grunted. 'How is the First Lady?'

'Fine, sir. She's coping.'

'And what about . . . forgive me, John, but I need to ask you this. What about the arrangements for her departure? Have you spoken with Protocol?'

'Yes, sir. Mrs Forrester will be staying at a house arranged for her by Clifford Granby. It's near his Virginia estate.'

Friedman noted the surprise in McQuogue's eyes.

He ploughed on: 'The Service have done their security checks. Mrs Forrester is grateful that she has not been hurried. She wishes to leave fairly soon, within the next day or two. I believe that is acceptable to the President and Mrs Morgan?'

Friedman thought he detected a tiny smirk behind McQuogue's impassive expression. 'Fine, fine,' the Chief of Staff mumbled, rifling through some papers on the desk in front of him. 'Mrs Forrester must not feel that she is under any pressure. We all understand she is going through a very emotional time. We'll do anything we can to assist her.' He held Friedman's stare. 'Will you please ensure she is informed of that?'

Friedman nodded. 'Of course,' he replied. 'Is there anything else?'

McQuogue shrugged. 'I think that's enough for today, John.' He stopped and picked up a slip of notepaper from his desk. 'Oh, there is one thing . . .'

Friedman blinked and waited.

'I have not informed the former First Lady of this,' McQuogue went on, 'but you are perfectly at liberty to do so, should you decide it necessary. On the day Mr Forrester died, there *was* someone in the private quarters who should not have been there. I ordered an inquiry and I've just received the report.

Apparently, in the commotion after the President's death, the two guard posts were left unattended, which is unforgivable. Appropriate disciplinary action is being taken against the uniformed guards involved.

'However, the Service has managed to pinpoint the culprit. He is a new man in the ushers' office. He'd undergone the usual security checks and was thought to be an upstanding member of the team, but it would appear that greed got the better of him. Has Mrs Forrester found anything missing?'

Friedman shook his head. 'No, nothing at all.'

McQuogue smiled. 'Good, good. Well, this usher, Frank Danello, is from the Dominican Republic. He was caught with cutlery and kitchen apparatus as he tried to leave the premises this morning. The Service questioned him and he admitted to it all. Apparently, on the day of Mr Forrester's death, he had gone upstairs in order to steal some of the President's belongings; he hoped to sell them after the funeral.' McQuogue stopped and threw the report back on to the desk. He grimaced, his expression full of rage and disdain. 'Men like that . . .' He looked hard at Friedman. 'They disgust me.'

Friedman kept silent. He tried to picture Danello but failed: there were so many ushers. He could not remember ever having dealt with the man.

'Do you wish to press charges?' McQuogue asked.

Friedman stared back at him. 'Well, no, sir, I don't think—'

'Very well, leave it with us. He's been suspended pending a full inquiry. Is there anything else, John?'

Friedman said no.

'Fine, fine. Go home. Get some rest. We all need it.'

Friedman thanked the Chief of Staff and left the office. He headed to the ground floor and out of the main West Wing entrance. To his right, the White House was lit up, the curtains drawn in the private quarters.

As he strolled out through the north-west gate and tramped

his way round the park, looking for a cab, he was trying to retrieve Frank Danello's face from his memory.

'Lee, do we really have to deal with this now?'

Elizabeth waited for Morrow to reply. The West Sitting Hall was full of packing cases, some taped shut, others open.

She watched the agent closely as he sat perched on a chair opposite her. Elizabeth could tell Morrow was agitated; so was she. But she was grateful that the formal ceremonies had been completed. Soon, very soon, she would be out of the White House.

Tomorrow, to be precise.

Before Morrow could speak, Elizabeth asked again: 'You're certain there was absolutely no record of who had been up here before we got back from Miami?'

She waited for his answer. 'Ma'am, this is all I've been able to find out,' he said quickly. 'I've had to be careful. On the day after the President's death, I checked the computer monitors: whoever was up here took advantage of the confusion that day. I have made as many enquiries as I was able to in the last few days. The one thing I am certain of is that the guard posts to the Residence were left unmanned. As far as I can work out, they would have been so for only a few minutes. It was a mistake, a bad one. I need to report—'

Elizabeth sat forward slightly, her eyes never breaking contact with his. 'No, Lee, not yet.'

She did not want to tell him about what she had found in the Oval Office. She had barely thought about it herself amid the chaos and trauma of the last few days. 'Lee, nothing has gone missing from here,' she said, exhaustion swamping her. 'John Friedman told me about the incident. I would prefer it if this was kept between ourselves for the time being. There is' – she struggled to get the right phrase – 'there *are* things I need to think about myself. I've no doubt that it was one of the ushers up here doing or pilfering something they shouldn't have been. But I cannot take an investigation into this. Not for the time being. Is that clear?'

He nodded. Elizabeth could sense his reluctance. 'Lee, let me speak with John . . . let's see if there is some perfectly plausible explanation for all of this. I'll meet with him in the morning.'

She rose from the chair. It was the signal for Morrow to depart.

The agent left the room and Elizabeth made her way to the bedroom suite. Two Secret Servicemen were on guard at the end of the Center Hall. She bade them goodnight.

Inside the bedroom, she stopped and looked around her.

In her pocket, she carried Tyler's diary and the covering note from Kelly. Against her better instincts, she looked again at her husband's notes.

She wondered if these had been what the intruder had been looking for.

And why.

Chapter Nine

The next morning Friedman still felt weary. He thought again about his meeting with McQuogue. He was certain the Chief of Staff had been lying.

He checked the papers on his desk. There was so much to do before both he and Elizabeth left the White House the next day. Quickly, he made a list of what he would tell her at their morning meeting in an hour's time. The first thing, he knew, was McQuogue's disclosure: he had no choice, although in his heart Friedman knew that Elizabeth was thinking only of getting out of the White House.

As he compiled his list, the telephone beside him rang. He picked up the receiver.

'Friedman.'

'John, it's Elizabeth. Are you alone?'

He sat forward in his chair, pushing aside the papers on his desk. 'There's no one else here, ma'am. Do you want me to come to the private quarters now?' He stood and checked his watch: 9 a.m.

Elizabeth paused. 'No, not at the moment. But, John, do you remember that place I used to like walking? The one where we went last spring?'

Friedman thought quickly: the Tidal Basin by the Jefferson Memorial. Elizabeth had often enjoyed walking there when she had first come to Washington, especially in spring when the trees turned the park into a riot of blossom and scent.

He spoke quickly. 'Yes, ma'am, I do. Why? Is there a problem?'

Friedman heard Elizabeth sigh and caught the sound of papers rustling.

'No, there's no problem, John, I just feel like a walk. I have to get out of this place. I tell you what: meet me there at ten-thirty. And John? I'll explain later, but please don't tell anyone where you're going.'

The dark-windowed limousine left the White House through the south-east gate. The press contingent caught its departure, but without the telltale Secret Service vehicles following in its wake the assembled reporters still keeping watch on the White House dismissed the car as unimportant.

Inside, Morrow sat in the back with Elizabeth. Privately, the agent was seething. The former First Lady was on the streets of the capital, without proper back-up. But Elizabeth had insisted on it. There was only Morrow and one other agent up front with the driver. Both men were heavily armed, Morrow himself carrying two semi-automatics under his coat, his colleague the same. Still, he felt exposed.

A few minutes later the limousine parked on the edge of the Tidal Basin. Morrow was out of the car first, immediately checking around him. To his left, by the wide plaza overlooking the Basin, a group of tourists walked towards the pedimented portico.

Elizabeth followed him out of the car. The other agent, moving expertly out of the limousine, closed in behind. Morrow looked at his charge. Elizabeth nodded at him and turned to her right, following the pathway down and around the man-made lake.

Despite the warmth of the day, she had bowed to Morrow's

suggestion and was dressed in a high-collared brown coat, her face partly covered by a fake fur hat pulled down just beneath her brow. Morrow followed her as she quickly made her way around the water and took a small path that led through an orchard of cherry blossom trees, the harsh white of the Jefferson Memorial visible through the branches.

Elizabeth stepped off the path, picked her way between the trees, and walked towards a simple wooden bench placed on the edge of a small rise giving a view of the Basin below.

'Hello, John, thank you for coming.'

Elizabeth sat and undid the first few buttons of her overcoat.

'I feel like Greta Garbo,' she whispered. She took an envelope out of her pocket, opened it up and looked at Friedman. 'John, I found this just before the funeral. I've thought of little else since. It's a diary written by Tyler. But not the official diary. It's something he kept to himself, kept from me. Did you know about it?'

'No, ma'am. Where did you get it?'

'The Oval Office. I went there the night before the funeral. All of his stuff had been cleaned out.'

Elizabeth caught Friedman's surprise. 'I know. I didn't expect that either. But they missed this.' She placed the envelope between them. 'I want you to read it. It's only a few pages. Tyler must have just started it. And there's a covering note from a Pentagon official named Ronald Kelly.'

Friedman picked up the envelope and withdrew the small black book. He looked quickly around him. Morrow, standing just twenty feet away, returned his stare impassively.

Elizabeth sat back on the bench. It took Friedman only a few minutes to scan through what she had given him. He placed the papers back in the envelope and exhaled. 'What was he trying to say?' He glanced up at Elizabeth.

'You tell me.'

'Well,' Friedman replied, 'if it's about Ronald Kelly, then we need to find the memo.'

'I know, but I can hardly ask McQuogue for it.' Elizabeth leaned over and took the diary from Friedman's hand. 'If, that is, the "M" referred to in the diary really is McQuogue.'

'Mrs Forrester, the President of the United States has written in a private diary about his concern over . . . over funds and a memo from the Pentagon. That memo has now gone missing. If the President puts something like this on paper, we can't ignore it! First, I'm attacked in the private quarters; now *this*,' he said forcefully.

'John, there is absolutely nothing to suggest there's any link between the two.'

'Ma'am, whoever attacked me was looking for something.'

Elizabeth did not respond.

Friedman broke the silence. 'We're, I don't know, talking about a criminal offence if we bury this and—'

'It could destroy Tyler! Destroy his legacy!' Elizabeth was whispering fiercely. Friedman tried to speak but she carried on over him. 'Yes, they were looking for something . . . but maybe Tyler was involved, John. Maybe he'd given approval to Kelly for something. All I know is Tyler had hidden this. He couldn't even bring himself to talk about it with me, John! Do you have any idea how that makes *me* feel? For all I know, Kelly might have been blackmailing him!'

'And you think McQuogue is behind it?'

'He could be.'

'Well, he's already lied to me,' Friedman went on. 'About the attack on the day your husband died.'

Elizabeth grimaced. 'John, he's paid to lie. It's his job.'

Friedman told her then about the previous night's meeting with McQuogue.

Again, Elizabeth sat in silence for a few seconds. 'Danello?' she said finally. 'No, I don't remember any Danello. Do you?'

Friedman shook his head. 'No, ma'am. But according to McQuogue, he's the main culprit.'

Elizabeth sighed. 'Do you believe him?'

'I'm not sure. It seems rather convenient that some unknown usher is suddenly accused of stealing from the private quarters just after I've been attacked there.'

Elizabeth sat silently for a few seconds. 'John,' she said finally, 'do we know where Danello might be?'

He shook his head. 'No, but McQuogue said he'd been suspended pending a full investigation.'

'OK, John, find him, but do it discreetly.' She continued to stare ahead. 'If there is a link between the attack on you and what I found in the Oval Office, I *have* to find Kelly.'

A child's elated laugh made her turn her head to the right. Her eye fell on Morrow, still standing a few feet away.

'Perhaps there is a way, John. A way of dealing with this ourselves . . . at least until we get to Kelly.'

White hurried through the crowds outside the *Herald*'s office. It was early evening and he did not feel like Riordan's ebullient company, but he knew the Irishman was expecting him at McReedy's. He threaded his way along three blocks. He could feel sweat beginning to run down the sleeves of his shirt. He felt dirty, sticky. When he rubbed his hands, his palms clung together, puffy and damp. He eventually found himself outside McReedy's. The large plate-glass windows were steamed up; little rivulets of condensation marbled their way down.

Inside, he edged his way towards Riordan. The body heat inside the bar made him cough.

'Give us a smoke,' Riordan barked.

White threw him the packet of Marlboros. He heaved Riordan's large and dusty woollen coat off a bar stool and sat down.

The Irishman watched him through half-closed eyes. 'What have you been on today?' he asked gruffly, slinging the cigarettes back towards White.

'Belch wants me to do a further background piece on Elizabeth Forrester.'

'Do we care?'

White shrugged, puffing on his cigarette. 'Seems so. I suppose with her about to leave the Mansion tomorrow, Belch wants a write-through on what she's done, what she might do now. The usual crap. He wants to run it in two days' time.' He shuffled on his feet as Riordan ordered the drinks.

The Irishman settled back on a bar stool. 'Has anyone spoken to you about her?'

White shrugged, leaning against the bar. 'Not really. At the moment, I've got zilch.'

Riordan drew heavily on his cigarette. White could feel his friend's eyes scanning him lazily. The Jack Daniel's on the rocks felt comforting in his hands.

'What about Friedman, her press guy? Have you tried him?' Riordan asked.

'Yeah, but he didn't return my calls. Well, would *you*? Having the *Herald* on the phone is not the sort of surprise most people in this city welcome. It's like being rung up by the clap clinic. Whatever they're going to say, they shouldn't be ringing you in the first place.'

Riordan snorted his agreement and leaned closer. 'I tell you what . . . since you're on the Forrester story, why don't I try and call this friend I have at the Pentagon? Slimy sonofabitch, but I found him screwing his secretary a year ago, and held it back. He's taken my calls ever since. Gratitude or fear. He'd have come across Elizabeth, bound to have done.'

'I'd be grateful, Mick. I'll catch up with you in the morning.'

White finished his drink and thanked his friend once more. As he reached the door he turned to wave a final goodbye to Riordan. The Irishman stood alone at the bar. White watched him raise the glass to his lips, draw on it heavily and turn to face the man to his left. Riordan smiled gratefully as he recognised him. He dragged the bottle towards him and settled into conversation with his new-found companion.

It was a lonely business, drinking on your own.

'Lee, could I have a word, please?'

Elizabeth watched as Morrow closed the door to the private quarters. She poured him some coffee and told him to sit down.

'Lee, I haven't been easy in the last few days. I'm grateful I'm leaving this place tomorrow and I've got you to thank for keeping me together most of the time.'

The Secret Service agent blushed, but kept quiet.

Elizabeth allowed a moment's silence to elapse before she carried on. 'Lee, I have another favour to ask of you now. This one is what you might describe as unusual.'

Morrow looked at her, expecting a smile.

'I'm not sure how you'll do it, I'm not even sure you'll want to do it . . . and if you refuse, I want to let you know right now – and I mean this, Lee – I will not think less of you in any way. And I'm not asking you to break any laws.'

She reached over and picked up the envelope beside her. 'This is something Tyler left hidden in the Oval Office. I found it when I went there.'

Morrow still held her eye and waited. Elizabeth could see just the slightest film of sweat beginning to rise on his forehead.

'It's a covering note from a Pentagon official called Ronald Kelly. I can't remember ever having heard of him. But he'd obviously been briefing Tyler on something.'

She rose from the chair and walked towards the window before carrying on.

'I need to talk to Kelly, I really do. Ideally today or tomorrow. I know it's late, but I need it done. I was aware of this document before the funeral but, well, I don't need to explain that I had other things on my mind then.' She paused, steeled herself and went on: 'Obviously I can't go around ringing the Pentagon and trying to track him down. I'm sorry, Lee, I know this sounds bizarre, but for your own good I can't tell you why I need to get in contact with him. I just do. And I need you to do it for me.'

Two hours later Morrow arrived at his home. He picked up the telephone and made a call to a trusted friend at the Pentagon.

No, Ron Kelly was not at work today. Yes, this was his home address . . .

Thirty minutes after that, Morrow pulled out into the suburban traffic. As he did so, he did not know whether his job would be waiting for him when he got back to the White House.

Friedman pushed at the metal door, his left shoulder heaving it open. The door was heavy and rusted, the bottom scraping noisily against the scarred linoleum on the floor. He winced and stood still. Around him the flimsy apartment building throbbed: the inescapable noise of families and couples thrown together for all too brief a period, a shrill cacophony of yelps and squawks in a multitude of languages and expletives. A television blasted from the first floor, a door slammed farther up, the stairwell shaking with the impact.

Friedman checked the street behind him. The small cul-de-sac off 4th Street was quiet. It was a no-through road for cars; the tenement buildings opposite were bathed in darkness, an all-night store farther down the block the only sign of human habitation. He examined the note in his hand. According to White House records, Frank Danello lived at this address, Apartment 4E.

Friedman breathed in and composed himself. He took the stairs quickly. On the third floor, a group of Hispanic kids crowded around the open door to one apartment, dressed in what appeared to be the entire contents of a Tommy Hilfiger store. They glared at Friedman: he was white, wore a suit.

Official; an alien whose presence here could mean only trouble for them, or him. Their expressions – disdainful and animal – made him quicken his step.

He pushed past and climbed up to the fourth floor.

Apartment 4E was towards the back of the dingy, half-lit corridor. The linoleum cracked and strained under his feet as he made his way towards the door. He checked the corridor, then knocked.

No answer.

From the other apartments, he could hear shouting, cursing, a stereo on full blast. The corridor smelled of boiled vegetables and cheap disinfectant. He knocked again, then tried the door handle. The apartment was unlocked.

Gingerly, he pushed open the door.

'Hello?' His voice seemed overly loud and harsh in the dark, still apartment. His greeting bounced off the walls, echoed back at him.

There was no reply.

Friedman looked back into the corridor. He was still alone on this floor.

Holding his breath, he stepped into the darkness. He fumbled to his left for a light switch, fingers snagging on one halfway down the wall. Hurriedly, he switched it on, stepping back slightly as he did so. The apartment was small. A cramped living room, beaten-up furniture, fading prints of a Caribbean beach scene hung haphazardly on the nicotine-stained walls.

He looked around him. To his left a half-open door revealed yet more darkness. He made his way towards it, footsteps echoing within the desolate space. The door led through to a bedroom. It was equally dingy: an unmade bed; a cheap cupboard, doors closed; a flimsy patterned curtain pulled across the window. There was no sign of Danello.

Friedman retraced his steps quickly. At the far end of the living room, there was another door, this one closed.

He tapped on it gently. 'Mr Danello?'

Friedman could just make out the faint sounds of a radio coming from behind the door. He knocked again, harder, at the same time pushing the door open with his foot.

The light was on. The room was a tiny kitchenette which stank of urine and stale food.

Danello had his back to the door. He was seated in an old director's chair, head slumped forward, an open bottle of whisky on the table.

Friedman swallowed, tried to stay calm. 'Mr Danello?'

He inched his way round the table.

Danello was dressed in the black trousers and white tunic of a White House usher. The tunic had been unbuttoned, showing a grey vest underneath, a sprouting of black chest hair visible over the collar. His arms hung limply by his side; his feet were tucked under the rickety chair. Danello's forehead had turned a marbled grey, as flaccid as wet cement. His mouth was slightly open, his lips the colour of dirty bath water. A mess of rancid mucus and vomit had congealed on the bottom of his chin, staining his vest. A pool of effluent had formed round the chair legs, a puddle of urine and excreta.

Friedman spun round wildly, giving way to an animal instinct to escape from the room. He flung himself through the door and raced across the living room. The door to the outside corridor remained open. He lunged through it. The main corridor was still empty of people but he could hear them from behind the closed doors: families, TV sets, a radio.

Friedman found himself back on the stairwell. He could see the group of Hispanic youths a floor below.

'Call the police! Get the fuckin' police!' His voice sounded shrill, alien even to him. 'A man's dead!'

He threw himself down the stairs. 'Get the police!' Frantic, he pointed above him. He pushed past, feeling in his jacket pocket for his cellular phone. The youths looked at him incredulously, their expressions a mixture of contempt and amusement.

Friedman took the stairs two at a time. He had the cellular in his hand now. Catching his breath, he stopped on the first floor. His hand shook as he punched his 911.

The roar from above deafened him.

Then the rush of hot, noxious air threw him forward as the explosion took hold. Friedman cartwheeled down the last flight of stairs. His head smashed into the cold linoleum of the lobby. From above him, a swathe of violent red flame shot through the stairwell; and then, as if by magic, it was gone, the vacuum in the small space momentarily free of oxygen.

The second eruption came only a second later. Friedman dragged himself up. The heat was enough to singe his hair. He could smell a rancid odour.

He was out into the street. Glass and smouldering wood clattered down around him. Staggering forward, eyes misted and sore from the smoke and heat, he made it into the road. He looked up at the apartment building. The fourth floor was a sheet of orange-and-crimson flame. Vast billows of smoke shrouded the floors above. The brickwork around the windows to Danello's apartment was almost entirely destroyed, the blackened frames hanging down as the dark fumes swept out and upward.

Chapter Ten

Tourists would undoubtedly describe the house as 'quaint'. Architectural purists might, on the other hand, wince at the over-zealous restoration. It had certainly transformed the two-storey cottage; but the vivid lilac window frames, the pristine red brick and the riot of hanging baskets crowding its façade created the impression that the house had only recently featured in the pages of an interiors magazine.

Morrow parked his car.

The street was deserted, a few lights on as dusk began to settle. He walked to 145 Wolfe Street, carefully avoiding the obstacle course of potted plants that lined the driveway. He banged on the door as hard as he could and waited.

No response.

It did not take much of Morrow's Secret Service training to determine that Kelly was not at home. The trashcan had been emptied. He peered through the letterbox: a pile of junk mail. No smells of recent cooking.

Once back on the sidewalk, he examined the houses to either side. Alexandria was an exclusive but arty area, and Morrow reckoned on a fair degree of neighbourly camaraderie. He chose the house to the left and knocked on the door. Through it he could hear classical music.

'Who is it?'

A woman's voice, elderly.

'It's the United States Secret Service, ma'am. I have ID. Would you like me to pass it through to you?'

The woman who appeared in the doorway almost made him recoil in fright. Nearly eighty, she was swathed in psychedelic chiffon, her make-up redolent of a 1940s film siren.

Morrow could see a hint of dread in her eyes. She was not used to opening a door after dark, especially to a black man.

'What on earth do you want?'

Morrow briefly looked behind him. 'Ma'am, I'm on urgent government business. I'm trying to reach Mr Kelly.'

For a second the elderly woman looked bemused. 'Kelly? . . . Oh, you mean Ron . . . I see.' She giggled girlishly, at the same time lifting her hands towards Morrow. 'I've been painting. Can never get the damn' stuff off.'

'Ma'am, I'm sorry to interrupt, but do you happen to know where Mr Kelly might be?'

The woman raised her eyebrows and smiled.

'Yes, I do know where Ron is, or rather where he might be. He went walking. I can't remember precisely but it was, I think, just a week or so before the President died. Ron said he'd been longing for a break and just took off. He said he was going to stop off at Elkton and head on . . .'

Morrow grimaced. Seeing his confusion, the woman went on, 'My, don't they teach you any history in the Secret Service? Well, it's in Shenandoah National Park. I suppose you have at least heard of Shenandoah?'

White threw his jacket on the stool in the kitchen. His tie was off within seconds. He opened the refrigerator and pulled out some cheese. A carving knife on the worktop was clean enough to use; he cut himself two slices, grabbed his notebook and walked back into the living room.

The telephone rang beside him. He heaved himself out of

the armchair and picked up the receiver, wiping his lips with the back of his hand. 'Yeah?'

'Whitey, me.' Riordan paused for only a fraction of a second before continuing. 'Look, my guy at the Pentagon I was telling you about last night . . . the one who might know Elizabeth Forrester? I thought, "Fuck it. I'll ring him." So I did and the cocksucker was there, still at his desk! He must have a new secretary, he never used to stay till this time. Jesus, what these guys get away with. It's like—'

'Mick, are you calling with something specific, or are you just lonely this evening?'

Riordan snorted his annoyance. 'OK, idiot, why don't you get your little book and lick your pencil. My friend was not happy to hear from me but what he did say might interest you. Yes, he had met Mrs Forrester. I've got the usual "she's such a lovely, strong woman" kind of crap. I've left a memo on it in your drawer.

'But then I asked him what the feeling was about her now, anything in the wind, so to speak. And he gets all pompous, says he can't possibly divulge anything personal. So I reminded him of his after-hours sessions with Miss Bimbo and he gets nasty. Starts shouting he can't speak on this phone. Now *I'm* getting real pissed by this point so I tell him to find a Bell and call me back. And do you know what, Whitey? He does just that! Amazing what a little bit of legitimate blackmail can do in our wonderful democracy. So he starts talking about how there's wild rumours of a witch hunt about to start against all the Forrester people. Anyone associated with them will be out on their ass. Usual agency backbiting.

'But, and this is where it gets interesting, he says that there had been "problems" at Defense concerning one official, weasly guy apparently, typical nerdy bureaushite. Anyway, he's called Ronald Kelly. My friend won't tell me too much over the phone but he says Kelly stitched him up with the White House. This is, like, three weeks ago. Are you listening, Whitey?'

'Yes, Mick, I'm still here. But what's this got to do with Elizabeth Forrester?'

'Hold on, Whitey! My friend is getting real ansty at this point. He's begging me not to contact him again. I mean, crying, Whitey! He says Kelly is "bad news", that he wishes he'd never come across the guy. He's, like, tortured! I might be wrong, Whitey, I know this guy's a treacherous little asshole, but he sounded genuine to me. So then I put the pressure on some more, remind him of his wife and kids and pension . . .'

'Mick! You can't—'

'I know! I shouldn't have done it, but I did. And he took the bait nice and clean. We're meeting him tomorrow at his house. His family are away so it's his call where he wants us to go. The bad news is this: he wants it early, like six-thirty. That way, he says, it will still be dark. Are you game?'

White thought quickly. While Riordan's lead was interesting, he felt it was taking him away from the main thrust of his research. 'The thing is, Mick, it doesn't bring me back to Elizabeth. I'm not—'

'Whitey, stop! Look, Kelly's gone on permanent leave, disappeared. My friend found out through one of the secretaries he's screwing. The guy went AWOL about ten days before Forrester's funeral. So I'm like, come on, tell me something to keep me awake. He's getting real agitated at this point, asking me to go light on him. Telling me I mustn't use it, it's only background. So I agree and he starts yapping again: this morning – *today*, Whitey – my pal gets a call from the White House, one of the Secret Service. Apparently, he and this agent go back a long way. Old college buddies. My friend listens and chats and waits for the question. The agent's looking for details on Kelly, but hush-hush. Just a favour. So he tells him where he lives but also mentions that Kelly hasn't been seen for a while. This Secret Service man is not someone to mess with, apparently. My friend is *real* serious about that. And guess who the agent was, Whitey?'

'No idea, Mick. Clint Eastwood?'

'Close, Whitey, very close. But younger, apparently. And better looking. No, the agent was Lee Morrow. Have you heard of him?'

'Nah.'

'Well, you should have, dipstick. He's the head of Elizabeth Forrester's detail.'

Friedman unlocked the metal grille to his apartment building, then the door. He ran up the two flights of stairs, hands shaking uncontrollably. He slumped into the one comfortable chair and undid his tie.

He sat in silence for a few minutes before kicking his shoes off and instinctively switching on the television. The large screen leaped into life. CNN flipped up like an old friend. Friedman hurriedly downed a Bud, the chilled alcohol welcome.

He turned away to reach for the telephone beside him. The CNN newscaster's voice droned on. 'The explosion happened earlier this evening at a building in the northeast region of DC. Local police have confirmed that at least one person is dead including, CNN believes, a White House usher by the name of Frank Danello. Unconfirmed reports have it that a faulty gas connection in Mr Danello's apartment is the most likely cause of the fatal blast. Mr Danello, a native of the Dominican Republic, had been suspended from his job at the Executive Mansion following accusations of theft. No suicide note was found at the scene but neighbours said he had been depressed as a result of his suspension. Mrs Forrester has been informed.

'In other news tonight . . .'

The telephone rang beside Friedman. He snatched it up, his throat dry and sore. 'Hello?'

Jesus, who—

'John, it's Elizabeth. Have you heard?'

He swallowed hard. 'Er, yes, ma'am. I was going to call you—'

'John, did you go there?' Elizabeth's voice was tight, controlled.

'Ma'am, we need to be careful—'

'I understand that, John, but *did* you?'

He paused and swallowed again. 'Yes, Mrs Forrester.'

'Fine. You can give me a full briefing in the morning. Please be here at nine. We'll issue a statement expressing our sadness. Will the press make much of this?'

He thought quickly. 'I doubt it, ma'am,' he said eventually. 'If Danello had been depressed, and was under investigation for theft, they'll cover the story then move on.'

Friedman waited for Elizabeth to speak. Finally, the silence was broken. 'Was it him, John? The man who attacked you?'

'I don't know, ma'am. It may have been but—'

'You think it unlikely?'

Friedman paused. 'Yes, ma'am.'

'All right, John. We'll speak tomorrow.'

Elizabeth replaced the receiver and leant back into the pillows.

She closed her eyes. Ordinarily, the death of a junior member of the White House staff would have upset, rather than alarmed, her. But within a few days of being accused of an unauthorised visit to the private quarters, a good man had died.

Where the hell was Lee?

Chapter Eleven

It was an arduous drive. Morrow might have enjoyed the spectacular scenery were it not for the urgency of his visit.

The Dickey Ridge Visitors' Centre stands at the north entrance to the park. Morrow found it easily. Parking his car, he felt out of place in his jeans and windcheater as he mingled with hikers adorned with the very latest in walking gear. A young woman smiled as he approached the information desk.

'And what can I do for you today?'

'I'm looking for a friend of mine. He might have come through here, what, just under three weeks ago. I know it sounds stupid but I was supposed to meet up with him at Elkton and we kind of missed each other.'

Morrow did not have a photograph to show her. From his friend at the Pentagon he had managed to call in a very big favour and extract a brief physical description of Kelly.

Mid-forties, balding. A large black moustache and a slight scar beneath his left eye from a teenage football injury. It was little to go on, pathetically little, but it would have to do.

The young woman shook her head. 'No, I'm sorry, we simply have too many people coming through here. There's no way I'd remember him, especially if he might have been here nearly three weeks ago. But you could try Bear's Den. It's a hostel up on 601 South. If he went hiking he'd probably stop by there at some point.'

Morrow thanked her and returned to the car. Half an hour later, heading back on himself, he found Bear's Den. It was an unobtrusive stone lodge, providing the perfect starting point for the trails that led into the mountains. As he stepped from the car, a group of students poured noisily out of the hostel entrance. Pushing through them, Morrow found no one at the reception desk.

Making his way through the house, he could hear plates being stacked in the dining room. A young woman was clearing up after breakfast.

She turned to look at Morrow. 'Have you checked in yet? You've chosen the right day. Most of the bunks are free so there's plenty of room.'

He shook his head. 'No, ma'am, I'm not staying.'

Morrow then told her about his friend and waited as Kelly's description sank in. 'Yeah, I remember him. Not sure why . . . we haven't been busy these last few weeks. Sure . . . I remember he seemed to be in a hurry and he didn't have much gear with him. We offered to hire him some but he asked me to sell it to him, so I did.'

'Did he tell you where he was heading?'

'He mentioned something about Elkton and Loft Mountain. He wanted to camp. I told him the weather was going to turn and he'd be better off if he went to the official campsites at Loft Mountain, but he didn't seem keen.'

'Damn, I've missed him.'

She sat down and wiped her hands on a cloth. 'Are you a writer as well?'

'Sorry?'

'Like your friend. He said he was a writer. I remember because he had only a small rucksack and a little black case with him. I asked if he was expecting to do any work out there. He said he was a writer researching a travel book.'

Thanking her, Morrow bought a map and a pair of hiking shoes. 'It'll take a lot of luck to bump into him out there,' she told him, pointing out the route Kelly might have taken. 'If you do, let us know. It'll be a great story to tell.'

The drive led him through some of the most beautiful views within the vast expanse of the Blue Ridge Mountains.

Following signs from Elkton, he arrived by the Sapling Ridge Road. He carried on for a few more miles, until the park swept round the valley of Hawksbill Creek and reached the bottom of Swift Run, following the route of the creek. He turned left towards Sandy Bottom, the highway hugging the southern edge of the park.

He turned carefully round a sharp corner, then slowed down quickly.

The Park Rangers Jeep had swerved haphazardly across the road. Behind it was another Rangers vehicle, its doors left open. Three men in uniform stood in a group. They watched as Morrow's car came to a halt.

Trying to control his nervousness, he walked briskly towards them. At first mistaking him for a tourist, they parted to let him through. Morrow stood his ground and waited to be acknowledged.

'Can we help you, sir?'

The senior ranger looked younger than Morrow, but he was well built, his face that of a man more used to fresh air than an office desk. A brass badge gave his name as Edwards.

Morrow hesitated. To reveal that he, too, was in law enforcement might expose the clandestine nature of his visit. Someone would undoubtedly be curious as to why a Secret Service man was alone near the Appalachian Trail.

'No, I was just taking in the scenery . . . but there seems to be a problem. Is it OK to climb today?'

'Oh, yeah, don't worry.' The three men tried to suppress a laugh and one ranger turned his back to hide his smile. 'If you'd been here a few hours ago you'd have seen something else. A German couple found a body up near one of the summits. Poor bastard had been there for days.'

Morrow's stomach tightened. 'Jesus, I knew this trail was tricky but not that dangerous.'

The ranger shrugged. 'I know, hundreds do it and I've never had a stiff . . . sorry, anyone die on us. The guy must have lost his footing, banged his head and bled to death . . . but you'll be fine, sir. Just make sure you tread carefully.'

Morrow shrugged. 'Thanks for the advice but maybe I'll leave it for today.'

As he walked back to his car, he could sense the rangers watching him.

Morrow found what he was looking for back in Shenandoah. The restaurant was empty. He ordered coffee and made his way to the back. The telephone was in its own kiosk by the entrance to the kitchen. He shut the concertina door and squeezed himself on to the small bench.

The main Medical Examiner's Office was listed in Harrisonburg. The telephone was answered on the second ring.

Morrow feigned a grief-stricken voice. 'I'm sorry to trouble you but I think a friend of mine may have been in an accident. I've tried all the hospitals and the police, but they're not sure. I thought if I gave you his name you might be able to help me.'

'I'm sorry, sir, you will have to await confirmation or notification from the police. This office is not authorised to reveal that information. But the police will need someone to identify the body if your friend is dead.'

'I understand that, but I know his wife's away and I was hiking with him. We got split up and no one here seems to know whether it's him or not.'

'Where are you calling from?'

'Shenandoah. I heard there'd been an accident, someone had died, a middle-aged man, and you can understand I just panicked. Jesus, how am I going to tell Cathy? And the children, everyone—' Morrow let his voice crack.

'Well, I'm not sure I can help. Dr Loudon isn't in yet, so we won't have any information anyway.'

'Who is Dr Loudon?'

'The Chief Medical Examiner, sir. He'll be dealing with any arrivals today.'

Morrow thanked her and returned to his table. He took time to ponder his next move. Having made a decision, he let half an hour go by and redialled the number.

'Dr Loudon, please.'

The male voice was harassed and dismissive. 'Yes?'

'Is that Dr Loudon?'

'Yes.'

'Dr Loudon, it's Sergeant Grey here from Culpeper PD. I'm sorry to trouble you, sir, but we've just received an ID alert from Harrisonburg and we think we might be able to help.'

There was a pause at the other end of the line. 'Well, have you spoken with Harrisonburg PD? I don't see why I'm—'

'I've tried, sir, but Ranger Edwards is out of contact and no one's really been assigned their end.'

Loudon sighed audibly. Without a word, he put the telephone down. Morrow thought he had been disconnected, but within a second Loudon was back.

'OK, Sergeant, there ain't much. Caucasian male, just been admitted. Wounds to the head, possible multiple fractures, bruising to the abdomen. Been dead a good few days by the look of it. Physical appearance you'll know about—'

'Yes, sir, about forty-five, balding, with a black moustache. Oh, and a slight facial scar beneath the left eye.'

'Yeah, that seems to fit. But that's all I've got until I do the PM. I would guess the man has been dead for over a week.'

'And there's no clue in any of his belongings as to who he is?' Morrow interrupted quickly, immediately cursing himself.

Loudon paused before he spoke. 'Well, if there was, Sergeant, don't you think Harrisonburg would have told you in their alert?'

The Medical Examiner could not conceal the disdain he felt for the incompetent cop at the other end of the line.

Morrow continued to play stupid. 'Oh, sorry, sir. It's just that a Missing Persons report we have on a similar male mentions something about a small black attaché case his family said he was carrying. Was that found on him?'

Morrow could hear the Examiner turning a page. 'Negative, Sergeant. Until you called, this guy was down as a John Doe. Nothing on him at all, which I'll admit is strange. A Rangers' note here says that any bags he may have had on him could still be out there. They're continuing with a search, but if you give me your details I'll pass them on to the PD. It'll save them a lot of trouble. You can fax me through what you've got—'

'Hang on, sir, let me just get this dispatch . . .'

Morrow replaced the telephone. He sat back against the wooden kiosk and closed his eyes. At that moment, the only thing he knew for certain was that he had to get back to Washington.

Riordan collected White from his apartment. They drove fast along Massachusetts, heading for Bethesda. The thoroughfare was surprisingly busy: the early rush of commuter buses and vans trundling down towards the Capitol. Beyond the DC line, the road widened, with shopping malls dotted along the route, still shuttered. Shortly they were deep into the green stretch of Bethesda, the genteel homes scattered among the trees to their left and right.

They eventually found the street, Winnebago Drive. It was narrow, bracketed by looming oak trees, meandering down a steep hill towards the canal. White peered into the darkness. 'Nice place,' he said, as the homes crept past.

Riordan was sat forward in his seat, squinting to find the right number. The house was halfway up the hill. Riordan swept his sedan into the carport and switched off the lights. 'This must be it.'

White peered ahead. Just the pewter light of a small copse, and off to the right, slate steps heading up and into the darkness. 'Are you sure, Mick? I can't see anything.'

Riordan pointed above his head. High up on a ridge, buried amid the foliage, White could make out the glimmer of a few lights.

They began the climb. It was steep, the steps slippery from the night's rain. The path meandered around the bushes and trees. Finally, the steps opened on to a wide terrace. The house was deceptively large: wooden-clad, it seemed less to have been built by man than to have grown out of the forest by itself. White could see a vast plate-glass door, and through it a kitchen and sunken sitting room. Antiques and oil paintings decorated the living area.

He caught movement out of the corner of his eye. A man was crossing the hallway, coming towards them. As he reached the door, White could see him properly. He was late-thirties, gangling, his greying hair cut short and hard against his scalp. He was dressed in the trousers of a dark blue suit, his white shirt open at the neck. White placed him immediately: government employee, but senior.

'Good morning, gentlemen.' The voice was surprisingly high and tight, more of a squeak than a greeting.

Riordan made the introductions. The man's name was Jim Appleton.

'Jim, how long have we got?'

Appleton looked at his watch. 'Half an hour. I have to be at the Pentagon by eight.' High-voiced again, brittle.

They settled into the sofas in the open-plan living room. Riordan leaned forward, his large frame struggling to find its balance. 'Jim, we're grateful you invited us here.' He pretended to ignore the look of disdain his remark provoked. 'We'll be as brief as possible. I've told my colleague here about Agent Morrow enquiring after Kelly. What more do you know?'

Appleton shrugged and crossed his legs. White was presented with a view of black silk socks, polished brogues. No sign of flesh. White wondered if he wore sock garters . . .

'I can't really tell you any more, Riordan.' Appleton's eyes refused to make contact with either of the men sitting opposite. 'Kelly was anonymous. I only knew him because we'd once chatted in the gym and had arranged a game of squash, which I'd then cancelled.'

White could guess why. Kelly wasn't senior enough for this man. No point in wasting time with the likes of him.

'I've no idea why Lee Morrow should be interested in him,' Appleton muttered.

He stopped talking and flicked a piece of fluff from his trousers. Riordan filled the silence.

'Jim, don't fuck about.'

The man's face flushed deep red. White could see the fury behind his eyes, his lips clamped tight. 'Excuse me! You've tramped in here—'

Riordan shrugged non-committally. 'Jim, you said on the phone last night that Kelly was involved in some trouble with "the Mansion". Did you mean the White House?'

Appleton nodded but said nothing.

'If he was such a nobody,' Riordan said, 'why was he connected to the West Wing? I don't get it.'

Appleton had managed to subdue his anger. He sipped his coffee and placed it on a side table. From where he was sitting, White saw Appleton's hand tremble, a spill staining the polished wood. He turned back and caught White's eye.

'As I said, it's just rumour. There's no obvious reason why he should be liaising with the West Wing. People like him aren't allowed access. It doesn't happen that way, thank God.'

White spoke for the first time. 'Which department was he working in?'

Appleton considered the question for a fraction too long. White knew he had rehearsed his answer. 'Foreign Military Sales,' he said. 'Routine stuff. Export certificates, liaising with the arms industry. Nothing glamorous. No policy stuff, just filing really, as far as I can make out.'

'What sort of sales?' Riordan said, picking up White's baton. 'Tanks, planes, shit like that?'

Appleton paused again. Still trying to keep the charade up, White thought. 'Well, he'd have seen a lot of the paperwork. The system is surprisingly antiquated, you know. The Pentagon makes sure the receiving nation is not anti-American, then processes the certificates.' He stopped and uncrossed his legs, leaning forward. Forced a smile. 'Of course, the likes of Kelly wouldn't have had any say about whether the merchandise should be approved or any say in the deals. That would be dealt with at a much higher level. Even the by Secretary, if it was felt to be particularly sensitive or a close call.'

'Would the President know about it?' White asked.

Appleton shook his head. 'Hardly. I mean, this is all public-record, you know. The President wouldn't have to be informed, even as Commander-in-Chief. We're talking pure paperwork. The rules are set out. It's automatic. Kelly would have been told to stamp form A, send out the duplicates – State, Customs, CIA, just for their information – and then that would be it. I don't know what the guy was talking about.'

'Would he have dealt with anyone else outside the Pentagon?' Riordan said.

'Er, possibly over at State. The DCS is based there.'

Riordan and White waited.

'The DCS? Well, again, it's all public . . . kind of. It's the Direct Commercial Sales programme. It oversees the private sales of arms overseas. Again, routine stuff. It used to be the Office of Munitions Control, but they changed it in 1990. The DCS and the Pentagon talk to each other. Just to make sure nothing falls between the stools. They don't want another Iran-Contra.'

White interrupted quickly. 'I don't mean to be dumb, Jim, but what sort of scale are we talking about here? I mean, between Kelly and this State thing, is it big stuff?'

Appleton smiled broadly. It was genuine this time. 'You can find out for yourselves. Any deal over fourteen million dollars is registered with Congress. Not that that means a lot. There's supposed to be a monitoring body, but most of the people on it are employed by the arms manufacturers.'

'And this DCS thing, they're the guys in charge?' White asked.

Appleton shook his head. 'No, not quite. There's a programme over at State, the Centre for Defence Trade. The DCS oversees it. It's, like, favours for those countries we think deserve our help. We'll send tank engines to the Israelis, trainer aircraft to Taiwan, stuff like that. There was a big deal recently to Mexico – Hawk helicopters—'

White interrupted again. 'How many requests are we talking about in a year?'

Appleton shrugged. 'Fifty thousand at least.'

'They give the nod to that many *a year*?'

'No . . . only a small number. It depends on what the heat is like from the Hill.'

'OK, OK,' Riordan said, trying to find a way through the man's reticence. 'I'm still not getting this. You must have some idea why Morrow called.'

Appleton almost physically curled in on himself. He blushed again. His handsome face looked like strawberry ice cream, blotched white and red. White could see a film of sweat rise on his forehead. 'Look, I've already told you . . . Morrow . . . I don't know him, not really. He's just someone from college, no big deal.'

'So what did he want precisely?' Riordan's voice was soft, but his tone was steely. White glanced over at him. Riordan's eyes didn't leave Appleton's face. He repeated himself: 'Well, what did he want?'

Appleton swallowed heavily, his protruding Adam's apple bobbing in the middle of his neck like a lifebuoy. 'He . . . just wanted . . . a check on Kelly. Where he lived . . . was he at work.'

White began to speak, but Riordan lifted his right hand to

make him stop. 'Jim, Morrow is Elizabeth Forrester's Head of Detail, there's rumours Kelly's linked up to the West Wing . . . *but* you're also telling me Kelly was just small fry? It don't make sense.'

'I know, I've thought about it all night, I haven't had any sleep.' He glared at Riordan and White. 'I'm telling you the truth. That's it, all I know.' He rose from his chair and readjusted his shirt. 'I'm sorry, gentlemen' – the term was more insult than compliment – 'but I'm going to have to make a move.'

White glanced behind him as he and Riordan began the descent back to the car. Appleton had disappeared into the house, but through a small side window, White could see him hunched over the kitchen sink. He was mopping himself with a small handtowel.

Appleton left it two or three minutes. Then, grabbing his coat, he turned out the lights and secured the house. A light wind skimmed between the trees. He checked the sky. It would rain later the first wedge of cloud was moving in from the east, thick and menacing.

He made his way down to the carport. The sun was up, but not fully. His sedan was concealed among thin shadows.

'Mr Appleton.'

He stood back in shock, eyes scanning around him. 'Who—'

The man emerged from a ditch to the right of the carport. He smiled at Appleton. 'Unlock the door and get in,' he barked. In his left hand he held a small pistol.

Appleton struggled with the lock.

'Just open the fucking door.' The man walked slowly towards him. 'I'll ride with you. And you can tell me all about your visitors.'

Chapter Twelve

Morrow waved to the guards at the south-west gate. They performed a cursory check of his vehicle, then let him through. Two minutes later, he knocked on the door to the West Sitting Room.

Elizabeth opened the door herself. 'Lee . . . come in, come in.'

She directed him to the sofa in front of the window. Friedman was already sitting there. Morrow nodded at him then sat down.

'Well,' Elizabeth said, 'when can I speak with Kelly?'

Morrow swallowed. 'Mrs Forrester, you can't. I think, or rather I know, he's dead.'

Friedman lunged forward. '*What?*'

Elizabeth waved at him to be quiet. 'Go on, Lee.'

Morrow told them about Shenandoah.

'Are you sure it's him?' Elizabeth asked after he had completed his report.

'Yes, ma'am. I can't be one hundred per cent certain . . . but yes, the likelihood is that the dead man is Kelly. There's one other thing: the last witness to see him said he was carrying a briefcase. But according to the ME's office, it wasn't on him when he was found.'

Elizabeth rose from the sofa and nodded towards Friedman. 'Tell Lee about Danello.'

Friedman gave the Secret Service agent an abridged version of what had happened the previous evening. Morrow listened then grimaced. He turned towards Elizabeth. 'I heard about the explosion on the radio driving in. Mrs Forrester, Danello's death' – he glanced at Friedman then looked away – 'may have been genuine. As for Kelly, an accident like that happens all the time in the mountains. I've been out there myself, it's not the sort of place—'

'Lee, let's just look at the facts.' Elizabeth's voice was cold. 'Two weeks ago, I discover a diary that my husband had hidden from everyone, including *me. His wife!* For his own reasons, Tyler did not confide in me; he couldn't. What was worrying my husband – the President, *goddammit!* – to such an extent he couldn't bring himself to let me know about it? What was it, gentlemen? Shame? Guilt?'

She continued, face flushed, eyes blazing. 'OK, so what else do we have? The covering note from Kelly tells us nothing, but when we try and find him he just happens to have fallen off a mountain in Shenandoah. John's attacked in the private quarters and, lo and behold, before we've even told anyone, an usher none of us can remember even *meeting* is accused of theft! Then, in a depressed and humiliated state, he dies in a gas explosion. Convenient, huh?'

She glared at Morrow. 'How long have you been in the Service, Lee?'

'Seven years, ma'am.'

'And in that time, have you ever – think about this – have you *ever* been part of two concurrent investigations into White House deaths?'

Morrow shook his head. 'No, ma'am.'

'Now . . .' Elizabeth held her head in her hands and spoke quietly. 'Has Kelly's death been announced publicly?'

Friedman answered. 'No, I've checked. Nothing so far.'

She nodded. 'What else do we know about him?'

Friedman opened his briefcase. 'I pulled his personnel

records,' he said quickly. 'Don't ask how, but I buried it in a routine security check.'

'Will this get back to the West Wing?'

'Unlikely. I did it on-screen. The Secret Service will know we accessed the files, and so will security over at Defense, but the authorisation code came from the White House. They won't query it. I made sure Kelly's name was one of fifty. Just routine stuff.'

He passed over the papers. Elizabeth read them then handed the sheaf to Morrow.

Kelly's record was short. He'd studied at the University of Chicago, majoring in political science. Been turned down by State for the Diplomatic Corps fast track. Joined the Pentagon twelve years ago in Human Resources. Low security clearance. Promoted to Procurement five years ago. Parents dead. One brother, no details. FBI check confirmed his bachelorhood. Four fines for speeding. Had passed random Drug & Alcohol tests.

'Lee, can I have those papers back for a second?' Elizabeth turned to the last page. Kelly's face peered out at her. He was balding, one eye narrower than the other. Not a memorable face. A white shirt, tie pulled too tight. He could be anyone, was no one.

'Is that it?' Elizabeth held the sheet of paper away from her, as if it held an unpleasant odour.

Friedman nodded. 'He was just a clerk—'

'No, he was more than that. A clerk doesn't send a confidential memo to the President of the United States.'

Morrow sat forward, his huge bulk appearing slightly ridiculous against the dainty antique sofa. 'Ma'am, what about the paper trail?'

Friedman answered his question. 'It's difficult . . . whatever Kelly sent the President would have been processed at the Pentagon and on arrival in the West Wing. If—'

'So who would have seen it, John?' Elizabeth asked.

Friedman listed the personnel involved. 'At the Pentagon, the liaison officer dealing with the White House; over here, any number of staffers, maybe Mr McQuogue—'

'OK,' Elizabeth interrupted. 'Lee, if they were looking for Tyler's diary in the private quarters, let's just say Danello *has* been set up to take the fall. I want—'

'Ma'am,' Morrow interrupted, 'you're telling me you believe Danello was murdered to cover up a *burglary*?'

Elizabeth and he looked at each other. No one said anything for a moment. Then she spoke. 'Is there any way we can prove it was definitely Danello up here that afternoon?'

Morrow took his time answering. He exhaled heavily and rubbed his forehead. 'I've checked the sensors . . . as for CCTV, I might be able to access the general exits and entrances to the Mansion, but we're talking hours of tape. The staterooms are covered by close circuit . . . it's possible he may have been captured somewhere. I'll see what I can find.'

Elizabeth nodded then turned to Friedman. 'John, do you know anyone at the Pentagon?'

He shook his head. 'No one who'd know about Kelly.'

'I do,' said Morrow.

Elizabeth nodded for him to continue.

'An old college buddy,' Morrow said. 'He gave me Kelly's details. He might know more.'

'Can you trust him?' she asked matter-of-factly.

Morrow smiled. 'I reckon so. I've known Jim Appleton a good few years. He might be able to give me a steer.'

White sat in the office, flicking through his notes from the meeting with Appleton. As yet, he didn't quite know what it meant and whether any of it was relevant to the profile he was assembling on Elizabeth. Becoming restless, he signed on to his computer and flicked through the news wires.

Almost immediately, his eye caught a small story captioned: PENTAGON DEATH. Timed at 6.30a.m. it read

A civilian Pentagon official has died in a climbing accident near the Shenandoah National Park.

The body of Mr Ronald Kelly, a low-level adviser in the Pentagon's military sales department, was discovered by walkers at the bottom of a gully. It is believed that Mr Kelly had been dead for over a week.

Mr Kelly, 45, a bachelor from Alexandria, VA, was a keen hillwalker and is thought to have slipped to his death following heavy rain. A Pentagon spokesman said: 'This appears to be a tragic accident. There is no question of foul play or any security ramifications.'

Mr Kelly's accidental death follows the apparent suicide of junior White House usher Mr Frank Danello in the downtown gas explosion yesterday.

White sat back and looked at the screen.

Kelly dead?

He began to make calls to the usual government public relations departments. It was early in the day, but the offices were manned. Even so, he discovered little more. The answer was always the same: no further details on Kelly. Lowly figure. Should have had more sense. Sorry.

The Shenandoah Park Headquarters on Route 4 knew little more. Eventually he got through to the Rangers office near Stanley. The voice that answered dripped with boredom as White introduced himself.

'I was just calling about the government guy who fell.'

Indifference replaced boredom on the other end of the line. White pressed on. 'We're just doing a short follow-up. Can you tell me any more about the accident?'

'The rain probably got to him,' the ranger replied. 'The guy shouldn't have gone trekking in that area – the ground was far too soft. Always happens. You city types coming out here in your Reeboks, trying to turn into trappers.'

'Was he on his own?'

'Oh, yeah. He's probably got more company where he is now, but he was on his own when we found him. We didn't even know who he was.'

'What, no ID?'

'*Nada.* Well, not at first. He's been in the morgue, a John Doe. Listen, is this really important? I've got to be going.'

White's heart sank. 'OK, look, one sec. I want to go home too. Just so I know: how did you realise you had a dead Pentagon man on your hands?'

'A routine patrol farther down the hill came across his wallet a few hours after the body was discovered, just before dusk,' the ranger answered. 'It wasn't on him when he died. Must have dropped it earlier or it was blown down into the valley. Anyway, they opened it up and the ID was waiting for me here when I came on this morning. As soon as I saw it, I made the usual call to the morgue, then I let the men in uniform know that one of their pen-pushers had leaped to the other side.' The ranger laughed at his own joke.

White was by now equally keen to end the conversation. 'Well, you probably started earlier than me, so I'll let you go. Thanks for your time.'

'No problem. When you've been sitting at this desk since six-forty-five a.m., believe me, you get sick of this crap.'

White grunted a brief goodbye then scanned his notebook.

He was halfway through when confusion hit him.

At first he thought it was his mistake. According to the Park Ranger, his force was only able to identify Kelly overnight. This morning, the ranger had contacted the Pentagon as soon as he started his shift at 6.45 a.m. But the wire story had been released at 6.30 a.m. that morning.

White picked up the telephone and rang a friend at the wire agency.

'Bill, the story you guys put out this morning on the Pentagon man. What time did you get that in?'

The sigh at the other end told him that Bill, like many others, had more important news events on his mind. His friend agreed to check the logs to make sure that White had got the timing of the Pentagon announcement accurate. He was back in under a minute. 'According to this, Whitey, we got faxed the Pentagon press release at six-twenty a.m. It was put out almost immediately. To be honest, the story we ran is almost word for word this press release.'

White thanked him and rang off. He immediately called the ranger back. This time the indifference had turned to hostility. 'Goddammit, do you people never stop?'

White explained his problem. 'You see, I'm a bit confused as to how you managed to ID this guy. You say you got in at 6.45 a.m. and Kelly's wallet was given to you. You then called the Pentagon and they announced it. But the story was already being faxed to the wires twenty minutes before that.'

'Look, pal, it ain't my problem. I get in same time every morning shift. I leave same time, every afternoon. Simple.'

'Are you certain no one else had already contacted the Pentagon?'

'Oh, yeah, of course, I fucking forgot. O.J. Simpson must have told them before I arrived.'

White apologised for wasting the ranger's very important time and rang off.

'Asshole!'

He knew that what he had learned just didn't make sense. How could the Pentagon announce a man's death when only the Rangers knew Kelly was the corpse? He looked at the clock: 9.15 a.m. He emptied his briefcase and retrieved another notebook. It was the one that contained the brief résumé of his meeting with Appleton. On the final page White had written the address that Appleton had found for Kelly.

He debated with himself. He could either continue with the Kelly story, or make his way to McReedy's for an early livener. Giving a final glance across the newsroom, he left a message on Riordan's mobile. Then he booked himself a car from the pool in the *Herald*'s basement. Alexandria wasn't far. Maybe Kelly had had a room-mate.

*

White parked his car and watched Kelly's house. No sign of anyone. Locking the Toyota, he crossed the street quickly. He did not expect anyone to be home. Ronald Kelly was a bachelor. White opened his notebook. It was definitely the right address. He pushed against the gate and made his way to the front door. Through a side window, he could barely see inside. He turned and walked back on to the sidewalk.

'Can I help you, young man?'

White jumped violently. The voice came from his left. He looked towards the source. An elderly woman was hidden among hydrangeas.

'I'm press. From the *Herald*.'

'Tut-tut. Terrible paper. So right-wing, you should be ashamed. Have you got any ID?'

White unbuttoned his jacket and withdrew his wallet. He passed the elderly lady his press ID and waited. She examined it closely but had to move farther on to the road to do so. White could see her properly now. Elderly, hair thinning but still a striking woman.

'Well, that looks OK,' she conceded, handing back his ID. 'And since you're from a tabloid, I suppose you drink. Bourbon OK for you?'

She let him inside the house, leaving the door unlocked. Something furry and noisy brushed by White's ankles. He looked down. The smallest dog he had ever seen followed its mistress into the kitchen.

White examined the room. It was very small, the ceilings low. The claustrophobic effect was compounded by the huge canvases that leaned against almost every surface. The only available refuge was two small armchairs by the back window. White squeezed past and sat down in one.

The lady returned with the drinks and sat opposite him. She was evidently grateful for the company.

'I first came to Washington with the civil rights marches,' she said brightly, eyes shining at White. 'Jack, my husband, was one of their biggest supporters. Gave them everything he'd inherited . . . well, nearly everything. Then he died. And as far as I'm concerned, it all ended with McGovern. Thieves and reprobates ever since, all of them.' She stopped and watched him fidget in his chair. 'Don't worry, Mr White. I shan't bore you all morning. You're here about Ron?'

White was immediately alert. 'Yes, ma'am. I'm just making a few enquiries. Usual stuff. Can you tell me a bit about him?'

'No, not really. Not much to say. Quiet, friendly. Should never have been working for that bunch of crooks. Told him so often. He said it was all right because Forrester was a Democrat. I kept telling him—'

'Do you know that he's dead?'

She sat very still for a few seconds, then, like an engine finally restarting, regained her composure. 'My, my, how terrible. What happened?'

White told her.

'Really? The poor man. Such a reliable neighbour, though rather a sad person, I thought. Very much alone, no visitors.'

'Did you see him recently?' White was gentle with his question.

'Hmm? Oh, he came here, what, must be about three weeks ago. I know because when the President died I thought I must call Ron. But then I remembered that it was about a week since I'd seen him and then he'd told me he was going walking for a few days. I've been looking out for him since the funeral.'

He began making notes. Only half aware of what his hostess was saying, he barely noticed the fact she had stopped talking. He looked up and held her eye. She was smiling now, almost smirking. White set his notebook aside and waited.

'I have something else I can tell you but I want you to know: I do it only because they're *all* crooks, although the young man who came to see me before you was very handsome and charming. And with poor Ron falling off a mountain – such a dramatic way to go – I doubt he'll object to me confiding in you.'

She told him about her other visitor.

'I know,' the old lady continued. 'I was surprised too. When he told me he was Secret Service, I thought I'd let him talk, but I soon got bored. So I told him Ron had gone to Shenandoah and sent him on his way.'

'Do you remember the agent's name?'

'Oh, yes, I've still got my memory. Morrow, L for Lee. And there's something else.'

She rose from the chair and pushed a canvas aside. She opened the drawer of a cabinet that stood covered in dust behind White's chair. Rummaging through the papers, she cursed gently to herself. Eventually, she found what she was looking for and slammed the drawer shut. She handed White the envelope.

'This came for Ron this morning. Before he went away he asked if he could redirect his personal post to me. We always did it. Can't trust anyone these days.' She waved towards the street and sat down. 'I haven't opened it but it's the bill for his mobile phone. He had two: one for work and one for himself. He let me use it once when Bell disconnected me. Said it was OK because the taxpayers weren't paying for this one. Take it, I have no need for it. And nor, I think, does poor Ron.'

Back in the car, White opened the envelope. It was, indeed, a bill for a mobile phone registered in the name of Frank Sills. White grimaced. He checked the address at the top of the bill: it was Kelly's.

Quickly, he ran through the dates and calls: he would check them all later, but for now he was looking for any repetitions. He balanced his notebook on the passenger seat and studied the entries for the time around Kelly's death. All calls had been made a long time before his accident. Except one. White looked at the date – just under two weeks ago. Kelly had kept calling the number. White made a note of it. With his pen, he slowly marked the others above it. Kelly had tried the same number four times in a forty-eight-hour period. But the calls were all short, no more than a few seconds each.

Something about the date puzzled White.

He lit a cigarette. As he smoked, he pondered the date. Why was it special? Why—

It was the day of Forrester's death!

He threw the cigarette out of the window and grabbed the phone bill. Kelly had called this number hours after the President was dead. And had kept on calling for over twenty-four hours. They were the last calls he had made on this phone.

White started the car and turned out of the street. Two blocks down he pulled in at a Stop & Shop. There were three call-boxes, but only one working. He placed Kelly's phone bill in front of him and dialled.

'Good morning, White House operator.'

White jumped. 'Er, sorry, ma'am, I didn't know this was the White House. I was actually calling . . .'

He told the operator the number.

'Yes, sir, that's a direct line here. But the office is unmanned temporarily, sir. Would you like to leave a message?'

'Well, the thing is,' he said, laughing, 'whoever it is has paged me twice from this number but there's no name. I'll ring tomorrow. It must be the Old EOB,' he went on, referring to the office complex opposite the West Wing.

'No, sir, that number is in the East Wing.'

'Sorry?'

'The East Wing, sir. It must be someone in the First Lady's office. But all of the East Wing staff are busy. Shall I connect you to an usher?'

White had already begun to replace the receiver.

He returned to the car and began to make his way back to Washington.

He didn't see the dark green station wagon that stayed three cars behind him all the way there.

Chapter Thirteen

The Henry G. Shirley Memorial Highway stretches to the south of Washington, out past Alexandria. It cuts down and towards the turn in the Potomac River, beyond Gunston Cove and the thirty-odd sailing clubs dotted haphazardly along the shoreline like pebbles thrown by a child.

Elizabeth and Marjorie sat in the back of her limousine. Now and again, the driver would up the speed to pass the ceaseless caravan of tourist coaches on a pilgrimage to George Washington's family home at Woodlawn.

They passed through the neat landscape of Fort Belvoir. The limousine turned off Richmond Highway and headed towards Dogue Creek. A few minutes later they were there, turning left into half a mile of driveway, along an avenue of pine that had been copied from an area of Versailles, through a small copse that housed a folly. Beyond was the main mansion, hidden among birch and cedar with a view down to the Potomac.

The car drew quietly to a halt in front of Hiscock House. Elizabeth had been here before but the sight of the house always amazed her. Hiscock's pristine white façade glistened in the sunlight. The main entrance was embraced by a columned balustrade that dominated over half the house and swept fifty feet up into the roof. Seventeen marble steps led to the door.

Clifford Granby stood waiting. He was dressed casually in a pair of white slacks and a blue shirt, open at the neck. Despite the grandeur of the surroundings, Granby himself stood out: elegant and calm.

Morrow opened Elizabeth's door. The two women ran up the steps. At the top, breathless, Elizabeth stopped and looked at Granby.

'How're you doin', Elizabeth?'

They embraced, then Granby kissed Marjorie. 'Mrs Wallace, how good to see you again. Are you joining us?'

She shook her head. 'No, I'm going on to the cottage.' She turned to Elizabeth. 'I'll see you there, Liz,' she said, before making her way back to the limousine.

Granby turned and led Elizabeth into a hall cluttered with paddles, lacrosse sticks, oars, tomahawks and snowshoes. In the glass-roofed atrium the central staircase swept up in front of them. To the right, a massive gilt-edged door led into what was called the Great Antechamber, decorated with tapestries shipped from England.

Granby led her on, through room after room. Eventually, they reached their destination: the summer sitting room on the north-east side of the mansion. He guided Elizabeth towards two blue-and-gold japanned chairs that gave a panoramic view of the gardens beyond. It was where they always sat.

'Well, that's it. I'm outta there. The trucks are bringing my stuff later,' Elizabeth told him.

'I know,' Granby said. 'I saw you leave on TV. It was nice that Willard and Ethel waved you off.' He tried to keep the sarcasm out of his voice.

'You're telling me,' Elizabeth said, laughing slightly. 'I don't think she could wait to get up the stairs and settle in.'

'You've brought everything with you?'

She nodded. 'Yeah, it's all done. I wanted to pack our own things myself . . . didn't go down too well with the ushers but who cares now? That chapter of my life is closed.'

Even as she said it, she knew it wasn't true. Agitated, she looked around her.

My God this place is beautiful.

'Elizabeth.' He paused. 'I don't want to rush you. Nobody does. I'll take you to the cottage shortly. It's perfect for you. You can stay as long as you like. It's very private, but if you need me I'm only ten minutes away.'

'Thank you, Clifford. I'll go through Tyler's things, put his papers together, try and get—'

'What's worrying you, Elizabeth?'

'What?' She could feel her face reddening. 'What do you—'

'What's *worrying* you?'

She tried to look away from him. 'Clifford, how long have you been coming to Washington?' she said to cover her embarrassment.

He shrugged and unfurled his long legs. 'Far too long.' He smiled back at her. 'If the truth be told, I can't bear the place. Never could. I only visit because, given my position as head of the Granby Foundation, I sometimes have to deal with the jackals on the Hill, which rarely fills me with joy. Keep my trips to a bare minimum because of that.'

'I know. They call you the Invisible Man.'

Granby laughed gently. 'It's the way I want it, Elizabeth. In the years I've watched people blow in and blow out of the place, the only thing I am certain of is that Washington consumes those who allow it to. It devours them. Then there's nothing left; the blood has been sucked out of them – by their colleagues, their enemies, the media – until the only thing they have remaining is a last gasp before they scuttle back where they came from.' He stopped suddenly. 'Elizabeth, I'm sorry, I didn't mean—'

She held up her hand. 'Clifford, if I can't talk about my husband to you, then who else is there?' She inhaled deeply and ploughed on: 'Does the name Ronald Kelly mean anything to you?'

Granby shook his head. 'No, not at all. Why do you ask?'

'At Tyler's funeral, I said I wanted to run something past you . . .'

He nodded. 'Yes, I remember.'

'Well, it might be nothing. Jesus, Clifford, sometimes I think I'm going half crazy since Tyler died . . . seeing things that aren't there, not being able to turn to him and ask him what he thinks.' She was aware of Granby's keen stare. 'I found a diary in the Oval Office. Tyler's personal notes – I couldn't understand them. There was a covering note with the diary from a man called Kelly. He died in a climbing accident some time in the last couple of weeks or so. They only just found the body.'

Granby nodded. 'Yes, I vaguely remember reading about that. But he was junior in the Pentagon, was he not?'

'Yes, but senior enough to try to get directly to Tyler.'

'And the diary doesn't mention any names?'

Elizabeth paused. 'Well, it refers to people only by abbreviations, gives dates, minutes of meetings.'

'Do you have it on you? Can I see it?'

She shook her head. 'I've locked it away. I'm sorry, but . . . well, I'd prefer to keep it to myself at the moment. It's the last thing Tyler was writing in before he died.'

The real reason, she knew, for not handing it over to Granby was that she herself had yet to come to terms with the prospect of what her husband might have become involved with. And she could not allow anyone to know what she suspected. Not even Granby. Instead, she told him about the attack on Friedman: 'I'm not sure what that means. Maybe nothing. The White House informed John that the intruder was an usher, Frank Danello.' She looked at Granby. 'Within less than forty-eight hours Danello died in a gas explosion.'

She caught his look of surprise. 'What, the one in downtown?'

Elizabeth nodded. 'Precisely.'

'And you think Danello's death is suspicious also?' he asked quietly.

'I don't know, Clifford, I just don't know . . .' She looked at him wearily. 'Wayne McQuogue claims Danello was the intruder. McQuogue also saw me leave the Oval Office—'

'Elizabeth, you wouldn't be the first person to place blame for the world's ills on the shoulders of Wayne McQuogue. He is someone for whom power is everything. And I mean *everything.*'

'People could say the same about Tyler.'

Granby shook his head. 'No, he was different. Tyler came to Washington because he believed he could do something about this country. That was his mission, his motivation. Of course, cynics like myself could have told him there was no point: the place had become blinded by its own arrogance decades ago. But, thank God, there are still people like Tyler and yourself. You may fail' – he smiled gently at Elizabeth – 'but at least you try.'

'But you don't think McQuogue wants to even try?'

Granby grimaced. 'He is a different *species,* Elizabeth. I have come across them in every administration I've known. Men – and now some women – who really do not care what the policies are, what the mission is, as long as it is their hand on the levers of power.' He looked hard at her. 'You think there's more to it even than that?'

Elizabeth held his stare. 'Do you think Wayne would be capable of ordering a murder, Clifford? Setting someone up for a burglary they didn't commit and then silencing them before they could prove their innocence?'

'You mean Danello?'

She nodded.

Granby thought for a moment then spoke. 'If that were the case, Elizabeth – and neither of us has any proof that it is – then McQuogue would be trying to hide something monstrous.' He looked at her hard. 'Elizabeth, for your own sake, you have to *let go!* I know what you're going through but however hard this is to accept, the blunt truth is Tyler's presidency is over.'

She blinked and nodded. 'I guess you're right . . . just sometimes, I feel I should be back in the White House. Am I wrong to think that?'

Granby shook his head. 'No, it's natural. Politics was your husband's life and therefore yours. But the time has come to move on.'

She yawned. 'Talking of which, I think I'd better rest. Do you mind if I drive to the cottage now?'

To refer to her new home as a 'cottage' was to understate the manor house that rose in front of her. The façade was mock-Tudor, the dark beams harsh and flat against the white paint of the exterior walls. The top floor was decorated with brick; the windows leaded. Both sides of the house were embraced by trees; behind, a large garden narrowed to a small dip that gave a view of the Potomac through the overhanging branches.

Elizabeth and Marjorie spent a few minutes inspecting the inside together. The rooms were a riot of chintz and swags; each smelled slightly of lavender, the scented candles scattered throughout like snowdrops. They sat in a small drawing room. A fire had been lit. Elizabeth smiled to herself at the ersatz attempt to recreate an English country house. The windows in the room were open. Apart from the distant whine of a mowing machine, it was silent.

'Well,' Marjorie said finally, 'I suppose I'd better show the former First Lady how to fend for herself.'

White returned from Alexandria and parked near the Library of Congress. He made his way towards the library, entered on the ground floor and took his place in the queue by the elevator. He got off at the second floor. Following signs that directed him to the right, he wound his way past groups of volunteers and congressional aides camped in front of myriad doors. Eventually, he found the reading room he required. He filled in the necessary request forms, and made his way towards an empty desk.

He looked around him. He was virtually the only person in the immense room actually reading something on paper. The others, as uniformly dressed as they were steadfastly mute, perched in front of a bank of computer screens. White shrugged and got his bearings amid the pile of periodicals, Congressional Committee minutes and addenda spread out in front of him. It took him half an hour to weave his way through the monotonous chronicle of government business. He had no clear idea of what he might find; instead, he felt as if he were scrabbling for any detail, any concrete indication of how Kelly had spent his daylight hours.

Appleton had been right. The work of Kelly's department was all public-record, but buried so deep as to be almost invisible. The morning ticked by. He came across the first reference to the Pentagon's Foreign Military Sales department within testimony to a House Subcommittee on Human Rights. White turned to another page in his notebook. He drew a straight line down the middle of the page. On the left-hand side he wrote 'Yes', on the right 'No'.

He began listing the 'permission granted' and 'refusal' responses to export requests for arms processed by Kelly's department. After another hour he sat back and made a rough calculation. The supervisory body charged with granting export certificates had rejected less than two hundred out of more than seemingly thousands of requests for Type 5 licences. He leaned over and checked another file: Type 5 referred to the 'permanent export of unclassified articles'. He turned back, scribbling furiously. In one year, again under Tyler's presidency, the Centre for Defence Trade (CDT) had refused only forty-five out of more than a thousand submissions for export under Type 73 licences; less stringent than Type 5, this particular certificate sanctioned the 'temporary' export of unclassified articles.

White flicked back through his notes. According to

Appleton, the consultative body that counselled the Pentagon and the State Department was the Defence Trade Advisory Group. He ploughed on through the maze of cross-references. It took him another two hours. At the end the jigsaw was more complete but still unfinished. The DTAG was a committee of sixty men: nearly ninety per cent represented the arms industry. All sought, and ordinarily received, permission from Kelly's department to export their goods.

White's pad was nearly full but he remained exasperated. Half of his notes were questions rather than answers. The one puzzle he hadn't solved was Kelly. And why Lee Morrow had gone knocking on his door.

He listed the members of the DTAG in his pad, plus a passing reference to an obscure faxzine called *Guided Tour*. It was distributed every month – by fax and through its own website – to interested parties. White now considered himself part of that charmed circle.

Morrow sat in the Command Centre in the White House basement and looked at the television screen again. He was due to give Elizabeth an update at the cottage in just over an hour, and so far he had found nothing.

He rubbed his eyes and fast-forwarded his way through the mass of closed-circuit recordings of the state floor of the White House and its perimeters. He watched the public tours go through; White House staffers passing from the East Wing to the West, Friedman included; Elizabeth herself had been on one of the tapes, arriving back from Miami on the day of Tyler's death.

Morrow yawned. Around him, the Command Centre was quiet. An agent monitored the sensor panel away to Morrow's left. Otherwise, he was alone. He glanced again at the staff photograph of Danello he had discreetly got from security records, slid a tape out of the VCR and pushed another in. Morrow swore under his breath: he was only halfway through the piles of cassettes. So far, there had been no sign of Danello.

On a pad in front of him, he checked the date and time of the tape now running. The camera was positioned a few feet from the entrance to the White House briefing room, twenty yards from the official West Wing entrance. Facing east, the camera monitored all personnel entering and leaving a door which, Morrow knew, led through to the bowels of the White House and the labyrinth of corridors, kitchens, utility rooms and staffrooms hidden from public view.

He pushed the fast-forward. The video jerked into life, the human figures spinning across the screen.

Morrow checked the time on the tape : 4.41 p.m. He kept it on fast-forward.

There!

He scrambled to stop the machine.

Danello was exiting the door, pushing a metal trolley. For a second he disappeared, then was back again. On camera, Danello checked his watch, then pushed through the door, disappearing once more into the corridor ahead of him.

Morrow rewound the machine one more time. He glanced at the time counter: 5.03 p.m.

He could feel a mixture of fear and elation.

According to John Friedman, the attack in the private quarters had taken place at around 5 p.m. Morrow could do better than that: the sensors had shown two people in the private quarters between 5.01 and 5.04.

One of them was Friedman.

As to who the other person was, Morrow could not hazard a guess.

The only thing he knew for certain was it wasn't an usher named Frank Danello. The proof was freeze-framed in front of him: the dead man had been on the other side of the White House when Friedman was attacked.

*

Despite Granby's advice, Elizabeth could not settle. She forced herself to think. She was the one person in the world who had truly known Tyler: his little eccentricities, the fact that he hated heights, the way in which he never unknotted his tie when he was undressing but would just loosen it and pull it over his head like a lasso, leaving it to Elizabeth to untie it . . .

Marjorie had left her alone. Elizabeth sat back in her chair and closed her eyes. Around her the sitting room was silent and empty. She could hear the secretarial staff in the office above, the gentle thump-thump of a photocopying machine.

In her mind, she ran through Tyler's morning ritual: his bathing routine, his breakfast, the first few phone calls he would make in their bedroom suite before getting dressed, his gym bag, getting ready for his work-out . . .

The gym bag!

She sat up, trying to picture in her mind where she might last have seen it.

Tyler had always carried it with him. It was glued to his hand whenever he left the bedroom and made his way to the gym. It was small and made of leather, little bigger than a spectacle case. It contained any medication he was taking, the spectacles he sometimes wore when he was tired, and the pocket watch given to him for his tenth birthday by his grandfather. He had had the case for years; had always refused her entreaties to get a new one.

Elizabeth hadn't seen it during her move out of the White House. Could not remember packing it.

She hurried out of the sitting room and made her way up the stairs. Before her own bedroom suite, another door opened into a large guest room which had been commandeered for her personal possessions and clothes. One wall housed a large mahogany wardrobe. Tyler's clothes and belongings had been locked inside, waiting for Elizabeth to find the courage, and the time, to go through them.

She rushed into the room. The key to the wardrobe was in

the lock. She slung the doors open, the aroma of mothballs and old leather enveloping her.

She chose the biggest suit-carrier, a vast blue hold-all that sat on the floor of the cupboard. It was heavy and unwieldy. Elizabeth struggled as she heaved it across the floor.

She sat back and examined the contents. The suitcase smelled of dry cleaning, a faint trace of cologne. It smelled of Tyler.

Elizabeth squatted down on the floor and riffled through the neat pile of polo shirts, vests and jumpers. She emptied out the contents; halfway through her search, she knew the bag wasn't there.

She replaced the carrier and pulled out a small vanity case that she knew contained most of Tyler's private possessions: his pens, his wristwatch, the glasses he had sometimes worn. She carried it to the bed, the contents of the case jingling as she did so. She flicked open the catches and lifted up the lid. The case was round and two feet deep. The White House ushers had carefully wrapped smaller items in tissue paper.

She delved in, careful not to scratch or mark any of the treasured possessions.

The gym bag was there. She opened it: there was nothing inside. Furious, she returned the bag to the case and carried on searching. She shoved her hand deeper, pulling out more objects.

The pocket watch was at the very bottom. She looked at it. It still gave the right time. Slowly, she lifted it out, cupped it in her palm.

She felt as if she were holding Tyler.

The watch was round with an ornate open face and a nine-carat gold case. Tyler's grandfather had had it made for himself in 1901. The dial was of white enamel – Roman numerals for the hours, Arabic for the minutes, a standard beetle-and-poker pattern for the hands. Elizabeth turned it over, admiring the dull gold. She thought of the last time Tyler had held it.

For no real reason she picked at the opening mechanism with her fingernail. It took her a full minute to work out how the face opened, revealing the open mechanism and the space behind it, where once the watchmaker's instructions would have lain.

Eventually, the watch face clicked.

A piece of paper was folded inside. It was white, and the harshness of its colour contrasted with the faded veneer of the case itself.

Elizabeth placed the watch on the bed beside her and pulled out the piece of paper. She unfolded it.

It was a simple photocopy, the edges slightly blackened and fuzzy. The top of the original document had been removed or missed during copying. Elizabeth could see a faint smudge, an indecipherable trace of a company letterhead. Beneath it was a simple row of figures. A long printed number, then another, then a space and a date.

Elizabeth started.

The date was two weeks before Tyler's death.

Beneath the first row, in the format of a bank statement, was a short column of figures.

$150,000
$73,000
$244,000
$97,000

The numbers were in the 'Received' column of the statement. All the deposits had been made in the three months prior to Tyler's death.

Elizabeth stared at the numbers. Then she folded the paper into her pocket and put the watch in its box, packing it away again. She left the room and hurried downstairs to wait for Morrow.

Chapter Fourteen

Morrow switched off the videotapes in the Command Centre and reached for the telephone. He called Jim Appleton's office: the line was engaged. He replaced the receiver and swore to himself. Appleton had been in meetings all day. At least that was what the officious female secretary at the Pentagon had told Morrow every time he had called.

He knew it was a lie. Appleton was avoiding him.

Morrow retrieved his car and headed for Elizabeth's cottage.

'So Danello had been framed?'

Elizabeth stared at Morrow as she asked the question.

'Yes, ma'am,' he replied. 'That's what the tapes show.'

Elizabeth grimaced. 'John said Danello was dead when he entered the apartment. Within an hour, that apartment is a pile of rubble. I don't believe that was an accident.'

She reached into the pocket of her trouser suit and handed him the piece of paper she had found in Tyler's pocket watch. Morrow took it, unfolded it and scanned the column of figures. He looked back at Elizabeth enquiringly.

'It is some kind of bank statement or ledger entry,' she said, 'but it has nothing to do with our private finances. I've checked the records. So has Marjorie. None of the figures here match with our personal bank accounts, our IRS returns, nothing. There's a code on the page, but it's meaningless to me.'

Morrow nodded as Elizabeth leaned forward and took the piece of paper out of his hand. 'And you think this is linked to Kelly?' he asked quietly.

She shook her head. 'I've no way of knowing. It wasn't with his memo or Tyler's diary.' She stopped and massaged her neck, the tension threatening to develop into migraine.

'Why would your husband have hidden these figures, ma'am?'

'Because it was something else he didn't want anyone to see . . .'

Elizabeth and Morrow looked at each other. The silence lasted for a long time. Then he spoke. 'Ma'am, this is getting into a potentially criminal investigation. Mrs Forrester, I don't mean to speak out of turn, but you're going to have to—'

'Lee, I know *precisely* what I'm going to have to do.' She stood up, pulling her jacket closer around her. 'Is there anyone at Treasury you can show this to without alerting them to where it came from?'

He nodded. 'Sure. I'll say it's part of a routine security check, see if the codes are a standard banking format. If I lie enough, it should be fairly safe.'

'Fine,' Elizabeth agreed. She stood and grabbed the jacket that lay on a chair beside her. 'Please look into it tomorrow. I want to speak with Mr Granby. Will you drive me?'

Clifford Granby ushered Elizabeth into his vast office on the first floor of Hiscock House. The room was bright; Elizabeth squinted under the intense lighting. As she looked at her host it occurred to her that it was the first time she had ever thought of Granby as old; the lights were on full power because his sight was failing. He tried to hide his age, striding across the Aubusson rug, placing his glasses in the pocket of his shirt, puffing his chest out. But he could not hide the weariness evident around his eyes.

'Sit down, Elizabeth. A drink?'

She accepted a small glass of brandy, sipped it slowly as Granby settled himself opposite her by the fireplace.

'How are you feeling? Settled in? Anything you need?' he asked earnestly, the questions fired like bullets.

Elizabeth shook her head. 'You've been kind enough, Clifford. The fact that the press aren't watching me all the time is the greatest favour of all.'

'Don't worry about that. They can't get within a mile of your place.' Granby paused and eyed her. 'So,' he said gently, 'is this purely business or did you feel like keeping this fine specimen of a man company for an hour or so?'

Despite her tension, she could not help but laugh at Granby's irreverence. It was one of the things that appealed to her most about him. 'Clifford, I do need to ask you a favour. I'm sorry if—'

'Elizabeth, stop apologising and tell me what you need.' He leaned forward slightly in the chair, his blue eyes fixed upon her.

'Clifford, I found a set of figures in one of Tyler's belongings. There is a column of what appear to be bank deposits. Significant bank deposits. I don't know, Clifford . . . it *may* be meaningless, it probably *is* meaningless. It may simply be part of a ledger, some government figures he was dealing with, quite unimportant.'

Granby looked at her. 'But you don't think so?'

Elizabeth shrugged. 'Clifford, I don't know . . . what do a set of figures mean? Ordinarily, nothing, except Tyler had hidden them away, as if they were something he didn't want anyone to see. And the fact that he had hidden them surely means they represent *something*.' Elizabeth slumped back in the chair, surprised herself by the helplessness in her voice.

'Do you have it on you?'

She shook her head. 'No. I've given it to Agent Morrow.' She held Granby's stare. 'Clifford, as a federal employee Lee shouldn't even be near anything like this. It's a completely unauthorised inquiry. Please, I need this to stay just between us.'

Granby nodded. 'That goes without saying. All I *will* say is that I thought you had put all of this behind you.' He looked at her. 'You can only torture yourself with this.'

'I know, Clifford . . . but please, just bear with me for now.'

'OK. Let's see. Have you checked your personal accounts? Do these figures appear anywhere?'

'No, that's part of the problem. I've gone through everything, even back before we were in the White House. The three private accounts we held, the IRS submissions, everything. Nothing matches. If it is an account, it's not one I know about.' Elizabeth swallowed hard, trying to disguise the slight tremor in her voice. 'The thing that alarms me is that it is so unlike Tyler to have done this. First, there's his diary and the note from Kelly, then *this*. Clifford . . .' She leaned forward in her chair, knees scraping against his. 'Tyler didn't *behave* like this. I knew him! I was his wife! Why would he ferret things away unless there was something significant about them? He was the goddam President! If he wanted something investigated, something checked, he had every law enforcement agency at his disposal. He only had to pick up the phone. But he didn't! And he didn't even tell me! My husband has been dead only a short while and suddenly I'm discovering things I didn't know about him: diaries, a memo from someone who's now dead, and now *this*!'

Granby stood quickly and refilled her glass. 'Apart from Lee, have you spoken about this with anyone else? Anyone who could make enquiries on your behalf?'

Elizabeth paused for a fraction before answering. 'Only John Friedman,' she replied. 'He has left the White House payroll and is working for me as a private aide. He's free to investigate whatever I want.'

'And has he discovered anything? Something that might give you a steer on what so concerned Tyler?'

She paused again. To reveal what Friedman knew about Frank Danello would involve both of them in a police investigation. She wanted to trust Granby fully but would do so only if no one else was compromised. 'John has only just started,' she said hurriedly, hoping Granby would not sense the lie. 'It's not easy for him. He can hardly ring up the FBI and get them to do a trace on what this bank account might be. Anyway, where would they start?' Grimacing, she watched him closely. 'Was Tyler taking bribes, Clifford?'

There was silence in the room.

Granby did not answer immediately. Finally, he spoke. 'Elizabeth, I know no more than you. But we both know Tyler was a good man. Perhaps you are right to fear the worst, that's only natural. But what exactly do you have? A diary, which I have not seen but which you tell me is strange and slightly alarming; a memo that neither of us has seen or read; and a list of figures which you hope Morrow will be able to decipher. Tyler may have been secretive, perhaps careless, but you surely do not think he was corrupt?'

Elizabeth glared back at him. 'I don't think so, Clifford, but *thinking* isn't going to give me any definite answer.'

'And what if you do discover that answer but it's not to your liking?'

Elizabeth had anticipated the question. 'If my husband had done something wrong, I know he would have done so because he had been sucked into something beyond his control. Tyler was an honest man, but not everyone around him may have been so. I shall find out what happened, Clifford,' she went on, her voice rising, 'and even if it means besmirching my husband's good name, I shall do so in order to bring to justice the people who may have hijacked his presidency.'

Chapter Fifteen

Friedman knew he should go home. He had spent the day at Elizabeth's cottage, overseeing the final stage of her relocation. He was already into the city, the drive from Virginia nearly over. It was mid-week, not a time to consider a late excursion to a bar or a diner.

He decided to go out anyway. It was the first time he'd been out since Tyler had died. Five minutes after arriving at his apartment, he had changed into jeans and a white button-down. He had a hundred dollars in his back pocket; his door keys rattled in his hand. He hurried along 18th Street, falling in with the crowds making their way towards the strip of neon and glass that made up one of Dupont's main restaurant drags.

The bar was above a clothing shop, a Chinese restaurant in the basement. Potted plants lined the stairs to the bar's entrance, the flowers mounting a losing battle against the fumes from the traffic. Around the door, multicoloured posters and fliers advertised Dupont's latest attractions. He pushed against the heavy glass door, checking the road behind him.

Inside, it was dark. The ceiling lights were blue and square, set at six-foot intervals into the roofing. They threw a desultory, sombre glow. Friedman squinted into the gloom. At one end of the L-shaped room, drinkers leaned lazily against the chrome bar. He pushed through the crowd and pulled up a stool.

'Hi,' he said to the barman, ordering a Bud. He paid and retreated to a table overlooking the sidewalk. The chairs were spindly and wrought-iron. The table-top, barely bigger than a napkin, was covered with blue-and-white mosaic. Friedman settled on to his chair and began to relax.

'Hi.'

He spun round in response to the greeting. A young man, dressed in chinos and a polo shirt, stood by his table. 'Can I join you?' he asked, quickly pulling a chair towards him.

Friedman nodded his consent. The young man looked only a year or two younger than himself. He smiled at Friedman and said: 'How was your day?'

'Not bad.' Friedman laughed nervously. 'Well, not great.' He drank from the bottle of beer and placed it back on the table.

'What's your name?' the young man asked.

'Steve,' Friedman lied.

'Well, *Steve,* tell me about your fucking awful day . . . and then we'll forget all about it.' The young man leaned across the table and took Friedman's hand. 'No one knows us here,' he said gently. 'We're safe. Come on, I feel like a dance. Wanna join me? My name's Stuart.'

Back in the *Herald*'s office, White tried the number again. He wanted to speak to John Friedman directly. As he dialled, he looked up from his desk and checked the clock. It was nearly 11.30 p.m.

The line was busy.

White cursed. It had been a frustrating day: his visit to the Congressional library had yielded little; and he still could not get hold of Friedman. He rose from his desk. The *Herald*'s floor was almost empty. He opened his desk and collected Kelly's phone bill. He folded the pieces of paper and placed them in his trouser pocket. Yawning, he grabbed his jacket and made for the door.

It was raining slightly. He made his way swiftly to Farragut North Metro. The wind had picked up from the east, hurtling down Pennsylvania. White turned up his lapels and pulled the jacket closer around him. Damp and tired, he took the escalators down to the Metro platform.

The Red Line train for Shady Grove was surprisingly full when it arrived. He squeezed into the fourth carriage. It pulled quickly away, heading for Dupont. Condensation covered the windows. The air inside was lukewarm and sweet. At the next stop a man with tortoiseshell glasses pushed past him, apologising. White moved towards the back of the carriage to avoid the crush. As he did so, a gargantuan man squeezed in behind him, shoving White farther against the carriage wall.

Why do I always get them?

White placed his briefcase between his feet as he held on to the safety handles, leaning away from the open door behind him.

He felt the tug on the briefcase before he saw the hand. The bag began to slip quickly from beneath him. He bent double, swinging round. His hands scrabbled for the bag, fingers curling around the handle. Behind him, he felt a push. The train doors were closing. The fat man next to him wouldn't yield. White could see the man's hand struggling to take hold of his briefcase. He tugged viciously in response, ducking as the fat man lunged at the case one final time before darting through the closing doors.

White held the case tight against his chest.

'Are you all right?'

He turned quickly to his right. A young college student, rucksack over his shoulder, watched him in concern.

'Yeah, yeah, I'm fine,' he said, avoiding the stares of the other passengers. 'Fucking muggers come in all sizes!'

The student laughed and made his way back along the carriage.

White alighted at the next stop. He needed air. He had never been the victim of an attempted mugging. Like many DC residents, he thought crime was something best left to the mayor.

He took the escalator and left the Woodley-Park Zoo Metro. The walk home would normally take fifteen minutes. White ran and made it in under five. Hurriedly, he let himself in and rushed up the flight of stairs. The door was double-locked. Breathing heavily, and aching in his arms and legs, he opened it.

He stood for a moment and caught his breath. His breathing slowed and he dropped his briefcase to the floor. The studio was in darkness. Opposite, the Herreras were out, their flat unlit. He turned to his right, down the small corridor that led to the kitchen.

The blow hit him hard on the left side of the head.

White smashed back against the wall. His eyes were blinded by a bright light from a torch held just two feet in front of him. His feet lost their grip on the floor and he doubled up. He felt a kick in the stomach. The pain made him almost retch. He managed to drag himself along the floor, fingers scraping along the cold linoleum. Another vicious kick caught him in the left side. He spun wildly, screaming, gripped the cold edge of a worktop, trying to pull himself up.

A strong hand grabbed his hair and tugged it back. The torchlight spun erratically around the room, randomly illuminating the kitchen. White could not see his assailant's face, but in the flicker of light and dark he saw a fist swing towards him. He slumped his shoulders and tucked his chin down into his collar bone. The blow was off target, just brushing the top of White's scalp. His attacker grunted as his knuckles crashed hard against the cupboard doors.

It was White's chance.

He kicked out wildly, catching the other man full in the chest. White heard him grunt. He scrambled to his feet. The torch had fallen to the floor; its light spilled out across the kitchen. He knew what he needed: lit by the beam, his old college baseball bat stood propped against the kitchen table.

He grabbed it and turned quickly. But his assailant was quicker. In a second he was on top of White. The two men fell back, pounding against the table and chairs. White heard splinters as they tumbled once more to the floor. The man's face was pressed against his neck. White could smell his peppermint breath.

'Fuck you, you bastard!' he screamed. His hand was still on the baseball bat. He swung it hard to his right; but the man was too close for the trajectory. White felt one hand close around his throat as the man lunged towards the weapon in White's hand.

He took another swing. It connected with the right side of his attacker's neck, pushing him away. The hand around White's throat slackened as he swung again. The blow hit his opponent in the chest. He could feel the man lose strength until one sharp blow slammed hard against White's right cheekbone and nose. He howled and slumped against the worktop.

His assailant was on his feet. White lunged forward with the baseball bat, but the man avoided the swing and ducked behind him. White watched helplessly as he grabbed the briefcase from the floor and darted out through the front door.

For a fraction of a second, as light flooded in from the hallway, White caught sight of him: a side view of thick black hair and a long sallow face.

'Fuck you! Fuck you!'

White was out into the stairwell but the man was quicker. Running after him on the street, he caught sight of him flinging himself into a dark saloon car parked opposite. The vehicle was already moving, screeching forward. White began to move towards it and tripped over a trashcan. He fell violently to the ground, the sidewalk smashing into his nose and forehead.

The red lights of the saloon car were twenty yards away by now. White heard an engine's roar behind him and swivelled round to see one of his neighbour's sons returning home on his motorbike. The bike's headlight lit up the road in front. In the glare White could make out the receding car's registration number.

He dragged himself up and rubbed his forehead. The boy pointed at him and laughed uproariously. White waved back and smiled.

'Thank you, you sonofabitch,' he shouted. The boy took off his helmet and looked back at him, nervous and quizzical. 'I love you!' White screamed.

He patted his pockets. Kelly's phone bill was there, folded twice, bulky but safe. He turned back to the apartment, repeating the car's registration number to himself.

Chapter Sixteen

White rolled out of bed. His body was sore and stiff from the previous night's struggle. The telephone ringing startled him.

'Whitey!'

Riordan's wake-up call.

'Mick, listen, where are you?'

'Embassy Heights. Why?'

White told him about the attack.

'*What?*' Riordan's astonished roar forced him to lean away from the phone. His ribs ached and the graze that stretched across his nose throbbed and stung like crazy. 'You got mugged *twice*? Do you think it was a coincidence?'

'Oh, sure, Mick, what do I look like? Donald Trump returning to his Tower with a "Come Mug Me Twice" sticker on his fucking head!'

He filled Riordan in on more details of the previous night. He had lost his briefcase but he had been fortunate: Kelly's mobile phone bill remained secure, hidden behind the shelf of his bathroom cabinet.

'But Whitey, I don't get it.' Riordan swore loudly and White could hear him struggling to put more money into the call-box. 'OK, so they were obviously trailing you, but from where? And why? It's heavy shit to start breaking into someone's apartment or giving them the knuckle-kiss on the friggin' Metro, Whitey.'

'I don't know, Mick . . . maybe they picked us up at Appleton's. Or they could have been watching Kelly's house, followed me from there. The fact is they know I'm looking into Kelly, and whoever they are, they ain't happy about it.'

'Are you going to tell Belch?'

'No way.' White shifted in his seat, the pain spreading through his kidneys and down to the small of his back. 'I don't want him broadcasting it around the office. Anyway, he'll never believe it was genuine. He'll think I got laid out in a bar.'

White leaned over and retrieved his cigarettes. 'Look, Mick, last night, after the bastard ambushed me in the apartment, I got a registration number for the car he was using. Can you run a check on it?'

'Sure . . . but it'll take a while. My friend in the PD isn't back for a few days. Leave it with me.'

Riordan pleaded with White to crash out in his apartment or anywhere else he might be safe. They argued for a few minutes before White finally succumbed.

'Whitey, I'll be at your place in ten minutes,' Riordan said quickly. 'We'll take it from there.'

As he waited, White packed a few things. He retrieved Kelly's cellular phone bill from behind the bathroom cabinet. After a few minutes he heard a car horn, loud and brusque, outside his apartment window. The Irishman was incapable of ringing the bell.

Within seconds White was out on the sidewalk. He got into the car.

Riordan glanced at White. 'You sure you're OK?' he asked.

'Fine, Mick.' White flicked open a notebook in his lap. 'I want to go to—'

'Whitey, forget work! Jesus, you're checking in with me or—'

'Mick, look, just take me where I want to go, then you can

drop me off at a motel. I know one that's safe and hidden away.'

After more argument, Riordan finally relented. 'OK, where d'ya wanna go?'

White read out the address.

'Oh, by the way,' Riordan said, half laughing, 'Mr Belch was looking for you. I told him you had the flu. He said he wanted to speak with you urgently. Did you hear about the explosion?'

White shook his head.

'Well,' Riordan went on, 'some usher from the White House topped himself by blowing up his own apartment. Took three of his neighbours with him. Belch wanted you on it.'

White snorted with irritation. 'Jesus, the fat bastard always wants to engage me in a bit of mental combat.'

'Yeah, unarmed on his part.'

Riordan laughed at his own joke.

'Who was the usher?'

Riordan shrugged. 'No idea. Seems he was caught stealing from the First Lady.' He glanced at White. 'Don't worry, the city desk can cover it. It's a nothing story.'

White glanced back at Riordan. 'Kelly was trying to get hold of Elizabeth Forrester,' he said simply.

'I knew it!' Riordan shouted, slapping his hand against the steering wheel. He looked at White. 'Jesus! How d'you know?'

'On his cellular phone bill. Well, it's his but he had it registered under a different name.'

Riordan whistled. 'Hardly normal for a clerk.'

'I know. According to the bill, Kelly had been trying the East Wing up until the time he died.'

White had to hang on to the dashboard as Riordan swiftly changed lanes. 'Any other numbers of interest?' he asked.

White shook his head. 'Not that I can see so far. The question is, why would a man dealing with arms certificates be so desperate to get hold of the First Lady?'

Riordan lit a cigarette, steering the car with his left hand. 'Was he sleeping with her?'

White swore loudly. 'It doesn't make sense, Mick.'

Riordan shook his head. 'Not unless Kelly felt Elizabeth Forrester was the only person in the White House he could trust. You said the Pentagon already knew he was dead before the cops . . .' He looked at White. 'You aiming for a Pulitzer on this one, Whitey?'

'Just drive, Mick.'

It took them fifteen minutes to reach the address. White studied the building. On the ground floor workmen were constructing a coffee house. The noise of saws and hammers shattered the early morning silence. On the next two storeys grimy windows looked lifeless and blank.

'You sure this is it?' Riordan asked, peering at the façade.

'That's the address I got.' White unbuckled his seat belt and opened the door. 'Give me about half an hour, Mick. If you're moved on, I'll meet you in the diner over the road.'

He stepped between the workmen. There were three bells beside the inconspicuous door. Two carried no name beside them. But the third bore a handwritten label: *Guided Tour*. White pushed the bell and waited.

'Yeah?'

He announced himself and the buzzer sounded. He pushed through the door. The hall was tiny and dark. He nearly tripped over a bike propped against the left-hand wall. A dusty pile of unopened mail perched precariously on a splintered wooden shelf. Ahead of him stairs rose to the right. He stepped through the debris. A door opened above him, daylight flooding the dingy entrance.

White turned on to the first floor and came face to face with a man whose youth shocked him. He was dressed in an orange T-shirt and faded denims. Under them he was as skinny as spaghetti, his face lean and acne-scarred. Thinning strands of pale blond hair fell over his steel-rimmed glasses.

'You should have called ahead,' he said, stepping back into the room. 'I could have cleared the morning.'

White made his apologies and followed him into the room.

'Jeff Blain.' The youth held out his hand. White shook it and at the same time surveyed the room. It was less than twenty feet square, and every inch was covered in papers or computer equipment. He was overcome with a sense of claustrophobia: it was muggy and rank in the room, the air cloying. One wall was swamped by a battalion of bookshelves, ungainly computer reports fighting for space on them. A small window gave a view of an alley and, beyond it, the stained and sagging backs of apartment blocks.

'Coffee?'

White nodded and eased himself into a director's chair. He waited while Blain disappeared from the room. The centre of the office was dominated by an oval-shaped desk. The chaos continued there: bulging reports, their hardback covers caked in dust; computer print-outs falling like a waterfall to the floor.

Blain sauntered back into the room and handed the chipped mug to White.

'So, what can I do for you?'

He set the mug beside him on the floor. 'Your monthly magazine, *Guided Tou*r – you look at the Pentagon, right?'

Blain nodded enthusiastically. 'Sure. We're not, like, official or anything. We just monitor what they're up to. They don't care for it much, but then what do you expect?'

'I'm interested in arms sales, both in the US and abroad,' White said. 'Is that something you get involved in?'

Blain nodded again. 'We send reports over to the Hill. Sometimes a Congressional aide will get in touch with us, looking for details on a particular Pentagon programme. I run four magazines from here, two about the environment, another on the administration's drugs policy. *Guided Tour* is the oldest. We put it out on our own website. But for those who haven't got themselves into the technological age, we print it up and mail it out on the third day of every month.'

Blain pronounced 'technological' as if it were a mantra.

'I'm looking into one particular part of the Pentagon,' White said, taking a notebook out of his jacket pocket. 'It's the Foreign Military Sales office and how it links up with the Direct Commercial Sales programme over at State. Do you know about it?'

'Oh, sure, bud. Those guys are real *nice*.'

'What do you mean?'

'What I mean is they're very clever.' Blain's laughter was surprisingly girlish. 'You see, the FMS and DCS are official government. In theory, they're accountable to Congress. But these boys are employed to help US companies sell their nasty goods overseas. So they're kind of in a fix: they want to help make their friends in the private sector a nice profit, but they can't step over the line.' He laughed again.

'Are they easy to look into?'

Blain shook his head. 'No, they're the most difficult side of this job. You can try the Library of Congress, but that's like looking for a needle in a haystack . . . and you won't get the real facts there anyway. You see, they play with the books. I don't mean they make it up, but they let things disappear into the system. Make sure they don't rock too many boats.'

'What's their main line of business?'

'It depends what you mean. They're kind of nebulous. Let's say you were some little dictator running your republic and just had to have the latest Smith & Wessons for your police force. The Pentagon and State, the FMS and DCS, would let the manufacturer explain to them why the generals overseas want the revolvers. Officially, of course, the arms would be for the purposes of law and order, police patrols and the like. Acceptable things like that. So, you get the approval and everyone's happy. Only when you come to open the crates, maybe they're not the S&Ws you ordered. Maybe they're something else altogether, something much nastier. No one's any the wiser and everyone's ass is covered. And then, when the same company wants to supply arms to the military over here, guess who's first in line for the contract? Happens all the time.'

'That's illegal, right?' White asked, making short notes on his pad.

Blain hesitated. 'It is . . . and it isn't. As far as the Pentagon and State are concerned, they've given approval for one type of export. The manufacturer knows that the order is a load of baloney and so do the men in uniform opening the boxes in, say, Indonesia. But, hey, do you think they're going to say anything? I think not. So, yeah, it's illegal, but *safely* so.'

White put his notebook to one side and reached for the coffee mug. 'I suppose it's easy for someone like you to get into all this shit?'

'Easy? It's not that difficult to get below the surface, but we rarely get real deep. These people cover their tracks too well. We get tipped off by human rights groups in the country itself or sometimes by disgruntled employees here. I like to think of it as a jigsaw: we have some of the pieces but have to guess what the whole picture looks like. The thing about *Guided Tour* is that it asks more questions than we have answers to. We don't pretend to explain everything but we try to let people know that something may not be right. It's all we can do.'

'Why do you do it?'

Blain looked perplexed. 'Why? Oh, I see, you think this is some nutty, left-wing agenda, right? Nah, we're not into that. We do it because we're paid to.'

It was White's turn to look confused. 'Paid by whom?'

'The human rights lobby, donations from "concerned Congressmen", sources like that. We don't make a lot of money but it's enough. There are a lot us in this town. I keep telling people we are here to service a need . . . the need to feel *guilty*. Thank God for Iran-Contra, otherwise we'd all be out of a job.'

White tried not to dwell on the moral maze that was Washington. 'OK, OK,' he said. 'I'd like to get back to the military sales. I just need to get a grip on what scale we're talking about there. Everyone talks in code when it comes to the Pentagon.'

Blain smiled. 'I'll show you.' He leaned over and dived into the explosion of paper. After a minute he appeared again, a vast wad of reports in his hands. 'Let's see. Right, take eighteen months ago.' He stopped and looked through the pile. 'OK . . . yeah, this will give you an idea of what I'm talking about. It was just after Forrester was elected. Now, the thing was that with a Democrat in the White House, the arms manufacturers in this country were worried about Forrester's "ethical" foreign policy and the cuts he wanted to make in defence spending domestically. Forrester was hitting the arms guys at home and abroad, and they were *not* happy. The Pentagon wasn't allowed to buy their piece of shit, and the very same Pentagon was now telling them they couldn't sell the gear abroad either. Not good for morale! Before then it was basically whoever had the bucks to pay for the stuff could have it. Do you ever read *CounterPunch*?'

White shook his head.

'Well, you should. Those guys said, "Foreign policy is essentially an extension of domestic military policy . . . Follow the dollars!" They were fucking right. But under Forrester it looked as if all that would change. Only it didn't, not really. These orders are worth two billion dollars over ten years.'

'Two billion?' White stuttered.

'Oh, at least,' Blain said. 'It's all here. Take it,' he went on, handing a copy of *Guided Tour* to White. 'We wrote about it three, four months ago.'

White flicked through the flimsy pamphlet. 'OK, but I don't get one thing. If the President says no, surely the bad guys can't do business any more?'

'Mr White, in the *Herald* things may always have a happy

ending but not in this business. Oh, no. These guys aren't going to let two billion dollars disappear just because a stupid President gets worried about his image.'

White told him about his trip to the Library of Congress. 'Waste of time,' Blain said. 'You don't find anything on paper. Officially, the list of exports filed at the Library of Congress covers just small arms and police equipment, and it's *temporary* supplies. Oh, *really*? There's a lot that goes on in secret and even we only get a sniff of it, rarely any good, meaty stuff.'

White got the feeling that his companion relished the opportunity to divulge all that he knew or suspected. He flicked back through his notebook. 'There was some group I looked up . . . I've, er, lost the notes, but it was supposed to be a supervisory group, looking at the export requests, giving their approval.'

Blain snorted. 'You mean the DTAG? Ah, the Moral Police, that's what we call them. A committee of the Great and the Good who sit in judgment making sure no one knows what's really going on. You should ask yourself, Mr White, whether it's pure coincidence that the DTAG is made up of the very people who manufacture and sell these arms.'

'Is that true?'

'Totally, although they're careful. They make sure it looks completely above board.'

'Why isn't this a bigger story?' White asked. 'I mean, why haven't you done anything with this?'

Blain leaned forward, laughing. 'Well, what is there to say exactly? We believe this is what's going on but we can't *prove* it. According to the DTAG and the Pentagon, *Guided Tour* is off the planet, with the people who think the world's going to end tomorrow. We're, like, David Koresh's cousins! They spend hundreds of thousands a year publicly rubbishing us. The serious media won't touch us. Well, rarely. That's why I'm surprised you're bothering. Why are you really here, by the way?'

'Because I'm looking into the disappearance of a Pentagon

official. He died out in Shenandoah. Worked for the FMS at the Pentagon.'

Blain's look of surprise pleased White. Now he had something he could hand over. 'What's the guy's name?'

White told him. Blain made a note of it and signed on to his computer. White got out of his chair and peered over Blain's shoulder. The computer listed all the employees at the FMS. 'How the hell did you get into this?' he asked, squinting at the screen.

'We do have our friends, Mr White. And the fact is that most of the stuffed shirts at the Pentagon don't even understand computers.' He scrolled through the screen. 'We don't have anything else on Kelly. Just a list in personnel records. Let's see . . .' He flicked through the menu, fingers skimming across the keyboard. 'Come on, come on . . . damn! No, he's not in any of our files. According to this, Kelly was just small fry. He collated the export requests after they'd been approved.'

White carried on looking at the screen. 'OK, but what if he'd seen something that upset him? What if some of the licences granted to the US arms people – Type 5 or Type 73, whatever – what if they looked suspicious to him? What would happen then?'

'Well, if he was stupid he'd tell his boss. If he was really stupid, he'd take it to the DTAG, try and get them to make it public. Or tip off someone at the White House.'

Elizabeth?

'Well?' Riordan asked as he restarted the car engine.

White grimaced. 'Not much, Mick,' he replied. 'Kelly would have had to have seen any requests for arms exports. Whatever he was worried about, he kept it to himself.'

Riordan eased the car out into the uptown traffic. 'OK, where d'ya want me to drop you?'

White gave him the address of the hotel. Riordan changed lanes and headed south.

From the end of the block, a black Lincoln swung out at the same time, and slipped into the traffic, three cars behind Riordan's.

The twenty-four-hour coffee house on Dupont Circle had just finished coping with the early evening rush. From the kitchen Springsteen echoed throughout the room. The waitresses had left much of the debris on the tables and stood sullenly by the stairs, checking the clock.

Stuart sat by the window, a cappuccino in front of him. He didn't notice the two men at first. He had his back to the door, watching the people on the sidewalk. It was only when one of them joined him at the table that he took any notice.

'Good evening . . . or is it still morning by your clock?'

The man opposite him was balding, the last button of his shirt undone. He stared at Stuart, who stared back, not returning the greeting.

'Cigarette? Your name's Stuart, right?'

The young man took one, lit it himself and kept silent, waiting.

'Were you busy last night? You know, lots of people to look after?'

The question was aggressive, more of a command. It confirmed Stuart's initial verdict. Police; probably Vice.

He began to rise from the table, throwing the lit cigarette in the ashtray in front of him.

'Sit down, asshole.'

'Fuck you!'

'No thanks, you're not my type. But unless you sit down one of two things will happen: either I will arrest you or my friend over there will do the same.'

Stuart glanced behind him. The other middle-aged man sat smirking at him from two tables away. He sat down.

The man at his table leaned back. 'Now, was that difficult?

See, all we want is to have a chat. Nothing heavy.' He stopped and withdrew an envelope from inside his jacket. Opening it, he pulled out an A4 photograph and slid it across the table.

The quality was poor but Stuart could make out who it was, and where it was taken. A new john. First time. Young man, nervous. Stuart didn't care; as long as he was paying . . .

The policeman tapped his forefinger gently on the face in the photograph.

'When are you seeing him again?'

'Ask him.'

'Oh, we will, we will . . . but not quite yet.' He sighed and noisily scratched the side of his head, glancing at his colleague across the room. 'Now, I'm sorry we got off to a bad start, being that we've just met. And, hey, I understand everyone's got to make a buck, so no hard feelings, right?'

Stuart nodded but said nothing. The man motioned towards his colleague, who rose from his chair and joined them at the table. A waitress came towards them but was waved away.

'We'd like to give you this, Stuart.' The man slid a small tape recorder across the table. 'It's a great little thing, you know. You should get one of your own. What you do, see, is you push this little button here, and it records everything I'm saying. Look, I'll show you.' He rewound the tape and pushed PLAY. His grating voice repeated itself.

For the first time his colleague spoke. 'And this,' he said, skimming a white envelope across the table, 'this is for all your trouble.'

Stuart opened it and peered inside. Five hundred dollars. A lot of money to him. But still he said nothing.

'Now your new friend often likes to go to this bar on the way home. We'll page you when he's there.' The man handed Stuart a card. 'You will talk to him, suggest you go for coffee or a beer. Then, when you're somewhere in the back, nice and quiet, you have this little machine in your jacket pocket and you switch it on. You know, get him talking about you and him, about himself.

Whatever. You know the score. Then, you call us. The number is on the back of the card. No running out on us because we'll find you eventually, and then I'll have to break both your legs to stop you running the next time.'

He let the threat hang.

'Then you give us the tape and you keep the money. And, mosty important of all, you never see us again.'

Chapter Seventeen

Elizabeth watched darkness fall over the Potomac. The water looked heavy and grey, broken intermittently by a curl of surf. A mosaic of lights blinked along the opposite bank. Higher up, to the east, she could make out the wavering pulse of a car's headlights.

She turned from the window and walked back across the drawing room to the pile of papers Friedman had left for her to sign before he had returned to the city. Elizabeth ignored the correspondence and paced the sitting room. It was warm inside; the fire had been lit, the candles were burning, comforting and gentle. But she didn't feel at peace. It was the silence of the place that unnerved her most. In the White House, even among the closeted luxury of the private quarters, there were always distant sounds of people moving around. A door closing somewhere. A whisper of conversation. The bark of a telephone. The city itself rarely quietened; and even when it did, there was a tension, a brittleness, to that silence, an expectant hush before the audience burst into applause once more.

She put the fireguard in place and blew out the last remaining candles. She had asked the staff to leave her tonight; a tray of supper lay barely touched on a side table. The Secret Service had left her also, for the command centre in the stables three hundred yards from the cottage; Morrow had pleaded with her to allow an agent to stay in the house overnight, but she had insisted. The alarms were on. There was no need for extra security. Few former First Ladies bothered to request the full quota of Secret Service protection, and Elizabeth was not going to be accused of profligacy.

She picked up the attaché case containing Tyler's diary and Kelly's covering note. Then she closed the door and made her way up the stairs.

Her bedroom was on the first floor. The lights were on, the bed turned down. She tugged at one of the curtains that ran from floor to ceiling, covering the vast windows that looked out over the bay three hundred yards below the house.

Within a few minutes she had changed into her nightdress. The attaché case lay on a chair by the entrance to the bathroom. She switched off the remaining few lights, leaving only a small lamp by her bedside. She settled into the gargantuan, undulating mattress, feeling like driftwood in the Chesapeake, and flicked through the magazines on the bedside table: architectural photographs, *Vogue, Town and Country*. Faces she knew, people who had fêted her, people from whom she had not heard since Tyler had died.

Tyler.

She settled back into the sumptuous pillows. The crisp Egyptian cotton crackled under her head. She closed her eyes, grasping for sleep.

Crack.

She snapped open her eyes.

For a second, she was lost, her eyes searching for the familiar furniture of her room in the Executive Mansion. She propped herself up on her left arm and listened.

Silence.

She shook her head, scolding herself.

One night on your own in a house and you're panicking.

She listened carefully for a few seconds more. Nothing. A gentle sigh from the trees and the faint murmur of a car way off across the estuary. She laughed to herself and shrugged it off. Then she reached over and turned out the bedroom light. As she lay back her fingers brushed over the panic button by the lamp. Elizabeth knew it was connected to the Command Centre; one of the accessories of life to which she had become accustomed.

She snuggled farther into the bed and closed her eyes.

Snap.

Her head shot up. The room was pitch dark. Her eyes had yet to adapt to the blanket of blackness. She moved in the bed, the rustling of the bedcover inexplicably loud in the silence. She strained to listen. Again, nothing.

But she'd heard it, she knew that much. Certainly, she'd heard something. She struggled to replay the sound in her mind. One of the agents walking outside?

No, not that.

She flicked on the lamp again. The brightness scalded her eyes. She blinked rapidly, squinting as the room loomed up towards her.

A floorboard flexed and strained above her head.

Elizabeth crept silently across the bedroom and opened the door. Light from her room spilled into the corridor in front of her. Even so, the unfamiliarity of the surroundings disoriented her. She left the door open and tiptoed across the cold wooden floor of the first-floor lobby.

The stairs were to her left. She flicked a switch. Light from the chandelier bounced back off the cream walls. She leant over the banister, her head craning upwards to her office on the floor above.

'Hello? Lee?'

No response. Just a shuffling of feet on the floorboards directly overhead.

Fear slammed into her like a juggernaut, physical and overwhelming. Her eyes were fixed on the shadows that danced on the landing above.

'Well? Who is it?' she barked with as much arrogance as she could muster.

Someone moving. Closer now.

In a second she was through the bedroom door. She slammed it shut, struggling to find the key. The snap of the lock's cylinder broke through her panic. She rattled the handle. The door was secure. More confident now, she lunged across the bed and slammed her right palm hard against the panic button.

Where are they?

She forced herself to stay calm, to listen. Silence once again. She crept back to the bed. She could feel the tingling of shock beginning in her stomach, the slight trembling of her muscles. She breathed heavily, in, out, in, out. She ran through the anti-kidnap lectures she'd been given: stay secure. Do not move from where you are. Stay low. Respond only to your Secret Service call sign. Do not, do not *ever*, investigate an alien occurrence on your own.

Shit, there goes that one.

The door handle rattled noisily, the door itself shaking slightly. She jumped up, voice trembling and little more than a whisper. 'I'm here, I'm here!' She grabbed the handle, wrenched at the key.

'Thank God,' she stammered, pushing the door open. She half turned back into the room. 'Agent—'

The man's eyes held hers for a second.

'Wha—'

No face. Just blackness. Only the eyes.

'Who—'

'Shut the fuck up!'

A vicious whisper. Then, almost simultaneously, a hand clasped her throat and pushed her back. Fingers locked around her jaw. She was clasped tight and dragged across the room. She felt herself tumbling, a strong hand thrust into the small of her back.

Hands took hold of her and pushed her face farther down into the carpet. She could feel the weight against the small of her back.

Jesus, not like this.

Through the roar of panic in her ears, she could just make out, or rather sense, another figure moving around the room. Swift, careful steps across the carpet. Not hurried but fast, determined. She tried to breathe, to salvage some air from the dry, bristly fibres of the carpet that stifled her. She tried to scream; but all she did was breathe in more fluff. She felt she was going to choke, the wool sticking to her dry throat, and fought against the weight on top of her.

She didn't really feel the blow.

When the fist slammed into the back of her neck, she just gasped and fell into the darkness.

Friedman parked his car near Dupont then hailed a cab. He gave the taxi driver the address of J. Paul's. He didn't want to go home yet. He needed to be alone, to find some anonymity in the city, if only for a few precious hours.

Friedman took a seat at the bar and idly followed the replay of a football game broadcast on a TV set above the bar.

'You staying for the music?' the barman said while wrestling with a bottle.

Friedman shook his head. 'Nah, just downing a few before I go home.'

'I don't blame you, buddy. You government?'

'Yeah.'

'Thought so. I'm new here but I thought you looked federal.'

'I'm not FBI,' Friedman said, laughing. 'Just a boring old clerk.'

The bar was filling up now; to either side of him groups of

students and businessmen vied for service. Friedman pulled his stool farther in and downed his drink quickly.

He waved for the bill and waited.

The barman eventually came towards him. He held a glass of champagne in his hand. 'This is for you, my friend.'

Friedman smiled in response. 'I don't need a drink on the house!'

'What?' The barman looked confused. 'Nah, it's not from us. Your friend sent it over. Guy sitting by the window. Do you still want your check?'

Friedman only half heard the question. He rotated on the stool and craned his neck towards the front of the bar. To the left of the door, a young man raised his Budweiser glass and smiled. Friedman blinked once and felt his face redden. He swung back to the bar, paid his bill and picked up the champagne glass, pushing through the crowd towards the door.

'What the hell are you doing here?'

The young man laughed out loud. 'I'm having a drink, like you. What do you think? Anyway, relax. I thought you might want another before you go. If you don't, you can leave it here and get lost. Makes no difference to me.'

Friedman managed to stop himself slinging the glass on to the table and bolting for the door. He checked behind him then sat down. 'Look, I'm sorry, I just didn't . . . well, I didn't . . .'

'Think that a guy like me could be drinking in a classy joint like this?' The young man smiled. 'Listen, buddy, it's a free country. I've been in worse places than this and I've also been in better.'

The young man smiled. 'It sure is a surprise bumping into you again,' he said, holding out his hand. 'My name's Stuart, by the way. Bet you didn't remember that.'

Friedman hurried towards New Hampshire and R Street. He wanted to get home. Desperately wanted to get home.

Washington was sleeping at last. On 18th Street the last few jaded stragglers stumbled along the sidewalk. Two tramps loitered outside Safeway. At the corner of N Street, a lone police car watched them. Otherwise, it was quiet.

As he walked through the subdued streets, he frantically ran through the chance meeting with Stuart. Friedman cursed himself. Of all the things he had done, of all the pathetic, mindless, stupid acts of folly he could have committed . . .

He walked slowly up the stairs to his apartment. In the half-darkness of the hallway, he rifled through the post that his neighbour had placed on his doormat. A credit card bill and some circulars.

He unlocked the door and stepped inside. The smell of burned toast still lingered from his breakfast that morning. It was sixteen hours since he'd left the apartment.

There were no messages on the answering machine.

He leafed through the mail; the circulars went into the trash-can. At the bottom of the pile was a plain white envelope. His name was printed on the cover. It had obviously been delivered by hand because it bore no stamp. Friedman frowned and opened it up.

The type on the paper was the same as that on the envelope. Heavy, smudged, evidently from a cheap typewriter or printer.

He read it once, blinked and stood up sharply. He threw the piece of paper on the bed and stared at it.

He remained motionless for two minutes, just staring.

Then he started shaking.

And then he cried. Brutal, savage bursts, his body rocking backwards and forwards. Rocking and rocking, his cries as loud as a baby's.

The telephone rang beside him. Friedman jumped, almost collapsing sideways on to the floor. His throat ached and his face felt clammy from the tears.

Five, six rings.

He picked up the receiver. 'John?'

'Yes.'

The voice was male, the line echoed. 'I trust you received our letter?'

Friedman was too weary to pretend. 'Yes, I did.'

'And you enjoyed your little drink earlier? A strange place to meet your friend Stuart.'

'What is it you want?'

He slumped back on to his bed and waited for the reply.

'I have in my possession a tape recording, John. I shall play it to you. Listen carefully.'

Friedman could hear a faint hiss from the other end of the line. Then muffled voices. For a fraction of a second he strained to hear the conversation. But he did not need to try too hard. He recognised one voice, his own. He knew who the other person was.

'Did you get that, John?'

'Yes, I did.' He spat the words out.

'Good. Then I shall go on. We are very keen, John, that you should co-operate with us. It would be unfortunate for you if you did not.'

The man stopped talking. But not for long.

'John, how *is* Elizabeth?'

Friedman was not surprised by the question. He'd known as soon as he'd opened the envelope how this game would be played. He struggled to control himself. The apartment closed in on him. His eyes swivelled around the room, focusing on nothing.

The question was repeated. 'How is Elizabeth, John?'

'I believe she's fine, but you probably know that.'

'We do, John, but not as well as you. We would, however, very much like to know more. Do you think you can do that for us?'

'No! I won't do this! Please! Leave me alone, *please*.'

Friedman was crying again. He slammed the telephone down and shook with tearful rage. 'Oh, Jesus, you bastard.' The telephone rang again. Friedman stared at it blankly. Ten rings.

'Hello?'

'Calm down, John.'

Oh, sweet Jesus, no!

'Stay calm. It is always better to stay calm. It is important that we trust each other. We must be frank and honest at all times. We are in this together and I will not let you down. You will do the same for me. It's only proper that we stay true to each other, John.

'So, let me explain what we're going to do: if you feel you cannot help me, and I do so hope you won't, then you'll leave me no choice. I shall have to release the photographs we have and the tape. I'll have to. I don't *want* to, believe me. Oh, and in case you're thinking of trying to make contact with the young man, don't bother.

'Stuart is under our control and will remain so. I give you my word, John, my absolute word, that when all this is finished, he will not trouble you again. You and I . . . we have to keep our promises to each other.'

Friedman leaped from the bed. '*Promises?* You fucking son-ofabitch! You can't promise me anything!'

'Oh, I can, John. I promise you that if you don't help me I will ruin you. Destroy you. You will be finished. Annihilated.'

Friedman's head slumped forward and the telephone pressed into his neck. 'Oh, my God,' he whispered.

'The shame, John, the total destruction of your world. Terrible.'

He had no anger, no tears left inside him. His back was wet with sweat. He could feel it running down his spine.

'So what is it you want?' he muttered hoarsely.

'Just speak to me, John, like old friends. Just tell me about *Elizabeth*.'

'No!'

Friedman threw down the phone.

'My God, Elizabeth! Are you all right?'

Granby stood in the doorway of the bedroom suite. His face was flushed; he was dressed in a dark grey overcoat, the bottom of his pyjamas visible beneath them. Despite the shock that filled her, Elizabeth could not help but be amused by the sight of the multimillionaire dressed in his night clothes.

'I called the Command Centre to speak with you and they eventually told me what had happened!'

Elizabeth lay still under the bedcovers. Her face was grey, the veins of her neck a vivid blue. She had a sticking plaster on her forehead. Her hair was pushed back and lay untidily across the pillow.

'I'm fine, Clifford. You shouldn't have come all the way over—'

'But how did this happen? This is outrageous! Are you sure you're not hurt?' He hurried to the side of the bed. 'Elizabeth, I feel so . . . so *responsible*. I brought you here! I offered you the sanctuary of my home but you wanted to come here and' – his voice was rising, becoming cold and hard – 'these bastards attack you!'

'Clifford, please.' She winced as she tried to move. 'It's not your fault. Marjorie is on her way here and Lee is due to—'

She turned as she heard a noise by the door. Morrow stood in the entrance, surveying the room.

Granby turned. 'Thank God you're here, Agent Morrow.' He walked towards the door. 'I understand you will have to investigate this on behalf of the Service, but I also require a detailed account of what the hell happened here tonight! Is that clear? Mrs Forrester is here because of me. I shall not allow any harm to come to her!'

Before Morrow could reply, Granby marched from the room. The agent closed the door behind him. His white shirt was stained, dark patches across its crisp front and up along the cuffs and sleeves. As he walked across the carpet, his shoes squelched slightly.

'Mrs Forrester, I am so—'

Elizabeth waved him to silence and pointed to a chair. Morrow sat down, as ordered. The two of them locked eyes for a second; he dropped his gaze first, his expression embarrassed and forlorn.

'Lee, I'm fine now,' Elizabeth said, shifting slightly in the bed. The movement made her wince. Granby's doctor had been summoned to her. He had diagnosed minor bruising of the ribs, nothing broken. The concussion would make her feel nauseous for a day or two. He had wanted a head scan but Elizabeth had refused. Perhaps later, she'd said, not now.

'Have you worked out what happened?' she asked matter-of-factly, sipping from a glass of water.

Morrow retrieved a small notebook from his trouser pocket. 'Yes, ma'am. The electrical connection from the panic button console downstairs had been redirected. That's why the fail-safe alarm didn't activate at our end. We're going to have to take a more detailed look at it, but whoever played with it knew what they were doing.' He stopped and coughed. 'The agent in charge had followed your instructions and had not entered the house after your supper was served. That was at your discretion.' Morrow stopped again and looked at Elizabeth. 'Ma'am, I know mistakes were made tonight, and I'm not protecting my detail, but those instructions were—'

'Lee, I was stupid,' she said softly. 'I'm sorry. What happened was all my fault. I shouldn't have put you or the detail in that position. I'm very sorry.'

'Well, ma'am, it wasn't all your fault. The agents saw the light go on in the bedroom here, and then a few seconds later in your office upstairs.'

'My office?'

'Yes, ma'am. They were clever. They'd tripped the temporary movement alarms by the kitchen. Again, they knew what they were looking for. Those systems are state-of-the-art, you can't just hack through them with pliers. But somehow they did it. They also set up a live-wire network . . . er, well, in layman's language, they kept the circuit going. No alarms back at Control. They got in through the conservatory door. They'd removed the entire lock unit, and replaced it with a fake. Anyone checking it would not have seen or felt anything untoward. A very professional job, ma'am.

'Once they were in – and from what you've said, we can only assume there were at least two of them – they went to your office first. Putting on the light was a neat touch: the curtains were drawn, and anyone looking would have thought you'd gone up there to get something before you retired for the night. That's why you heard them above.

'The system we have here gives us an instantaneous response; the circuitry is almost impregnable. We know in a millisecond if there's a problem. But nothing was activated. All systems remained as normal.'

'So it was only when I woke and started screaming that you knew I'd been attacked?'

Morrow's face reddened. 'Yes, ma'am,' he muttered, flicking his eyes away from Elizabeth.

'They took my case,' she said, looking hard at Morrow. 'Lee, do you have the list of figures I found in Tyler's pocket watch?'

Morrow nodded. 'Yes, ma'am.'

'Well,' she went on, 'at least they didn't get that. But they did get Tyler's notes and Kelly's covering note. That's what they were looking for, wasn't it? I mean, nothing else has been stolen. It's not as if they'd dumped their Chevvy in some back lane and thought, We'll just go and hustle the former First Lady tonight, is it, Lee?'

'No, Mrs Forrester.'

'So they knew I had it. That I'd found it. But how? We kept it tight. They were very specific. They *knew*. How? How could they know?'

Morrow shrugged. 'There must have been a leak, ma'am. It might have come from Shenandoah, the people I spoke to there. I'm known as your Head of Detail. There were—'

'McQuogue.' Elizabeth whispered the name to herself, but she knew Morrow had heard it. '*But how,* Lee? That's what I can't fathom. How could they pull this off? I'm surrounded by security, there are goddam alarms and switches everywhere I turn. There's more manpower in these acres than there is at the Pentagon, and I end up with a hoodlum in a balaclava holding my head into the carpet!'

'Ma'am, when I leave here I will order a full inquiry. I will obviously have to step aside from this assignment. It's Service policy. I can't remain in place while an investigation into my conduct is under way. I have no doubt that from this we will learn—'

'You will do no such thing, Lee.' Elizabeth settled herself in the bed. For the second time she held Morrow's stare. 'You will not report this to the Treasury office. That is out of the question. You and your detail—'

'Ma'am, I have no choice but to overrule that. This is a serious infringement. It *has* to be filed! Ma'am, you've already asked me to cover up the fact that we think Frank Danello was murdered! As for Kelly—'

'Lee, I am not asking you, I am *telling* you! Listen to me.' Elizabeth lifted herself up painfully. 'If this becomes public, whoever is behind it gets away with it. What diary am I talking about? What does it prove? Where is it? Who does it name? What do I mean, Danello and Kelly may have been murdered? I'll look like a madwoman! The White House will have a field day . . . "The former First Lady is suffering from delusions, she's still in grief."

'I can hear McQuogue whispering it to the media now. Little hints about me, their worries about my sanity after Tyler's death. It would be so easy for them. They'd have a clear run. At the moment, I've got nothing but an unheaded piece of paper that may or may not be a bank statement. If you report this, your career is over anyway: Mrs Forrester attacked in her bedroom! You'll be checking bank-notes in Alaska before the day's out.

'And where will I be? I'll be the grieving, nutty widow, Friedman will be massacred as the naïve aide who helped me, and you – one of the very few people I can trust now – will be buying your kids snowboards to keep them from dying of boredom on Kodiak Island!'

Morrow began to speak, then stopped himself. The two of them sat in silence again, Elizabeth covering her eyes with her hand. The effort of the last few minutes had left her looking even paler. Eventually she spoke again. 'You haven't answered my real question, Lee.'

He raised his head to look at her.

'You said this was a professional job. That they knew what they were doing. But this was specialist equipment, secure, secret. It's not the sort of stuff you can just go and buy at the nearest K-Mart. So who would have known how to trip the circuit and get in here?'

'Someone who had dealt with it before.'

Elizabeth rested her hand back by her side. 'One of your men?'

'No way, ma'am. They're solid. I've been beside them for—'

'But someone with government or military service? Is that what you're telling me?'

Morrow sat back and exhaled. He surveyed the bedroom. 'Whoever it was must have been on the inside.'

He rose from the chair and walked slowly towards the door.

'Where are you going, Lee?'

Morrow glanced back behind him. 'To speak to the detail.'

'So you're not going to Alaska?'

'No, ma'am,' he said, turning to leave the room. 'I kind of like the heat.'

Chapter Eighteen

Friedman swallowed hard. 'I'm sorry, ma'am, they did *what?*'

He listened as Elizabeth repeated her account of the attack. Friedman gripped the telephone. He sat back on the sofa in his apartment, wearing only his boxer shorts, and shivered as he waited for her to finish her tale.

As he listened to her voice, all he could think of was another voice on the telephone. A voice which had threatened to ruin his life.

Friedman's apartment was as dark and gloomy as his mood. It was a miserable day in Washington, a reminder that any hopes of spring were premature. The sky hung low and dark, grey folds of cloud unfurling to the west. He flicked on a lamp as he listened to Elizabeth, taking slow sips of coffee from the mug in his shaking hand.

After she finished the call, he sat back on the sofa. Washington, once such a dream, was now a nightmare. Somehow, he managed to wash and dress. Afterwards he locked his apartment and ran down the stairs. He checked to the left and right as he reached the sidewalk, then stopped himself.

I'm getting paranoid.

In his jacket pocket he still had the note from his secretary detailing a call from Mark White at the *Herald*. The journalist had called a second time apparently. Friedman would ignore it. He had more vital things on his mind.

Morrow looked at the young woman sitting opposite him. She had once, before his marriage, been a part-time lover; they had both been young, and new to Washington; had sought refuge in each other.

'Lee, it's been a long time. It's nice of you to drop by for breakfast.'

Penny Graham did not look to be in her late thirties, and Morrow knew why. She had always avoided the sun, wore almost no make-up. He could still remember her puritanism, the refrigerator full of health supplements. It had worked for her: today she looked younger and more resilient than the other Treasury officials with whom she worked.

'How you been keeping, Penny?'

She smiled gently. 'Still single.'

Morrow felt a pang of embarrassment. She had once asked him to marry her.

'How's the family?' she said quickly, at the same time rearranging a sheaf of papers on the desk in front of her.

'Great,' he said, a touch too fulsomely. 'Penny—'

'Tell me, Lee.' She sat back and looked hard at him. He remembered that look: a combination of resignation and anger, like when he'd told her he had fallen for someone else. She arched her eyebrows. 'Tell me what you want. You must want *something*.'

Morrow retrieved the figures Elizabeth had given him. 'Penny, what do you make of this?'

'Not much. There's really nothing here.'

'I think it's some kind of bank statement or ledger entry.' He sat forward in his chair. 'Do the figures at the bottom mean anything to you?'

She squinted at the slip of paper. 'It's hard to say. The one on the right might be an account number. As for this one' – her finger ran along the line of figures on the left-hand side of the statement – 'there's a possibility it's a routing number. You have no idea which bank we're talking about or where it might be?'

'No, that's all I have,' he said. 'The letterhead was torn off or not photocopied.'

'There's a lot of money going into this account.' She checked the dates of the deposits. 'Lee, you're talking about over half a million dollars deposited in the space of *three weeks*! Who was the payee?'

It felt strange to be under this barrage of questions; it was he who normally played the role of interrogator. 'I'm not sure,' he replied. 'That really is all I have.'

'OK, let's see what we can find out.' Penny swivelled round on her chair and leaned across to a bookshelf behind her. Morrow watched as she pulled out two large volumes from the bottom shelf. He helped her lay them on the desk in front of them.

'These,' Penny explained, 'are the treasured *Thomson's Financial*.' She looked at Morrow. 'Have you seen them before?'

He shook his head. 'No, never.'

She opened Volume One as she spoke. 'They're compiled in Skokie, Illinois, roughly once a month. They list every bank and financial corporation in the US according to a set formula of digital codes.'

'Every one?'

'If they're registered with the American Bankers Association, then yes.' She caught Morrow's eye. 'Do you think this bank is legit?'

He shrugged in response. 'No idea. Is there any way of telling?'

She shook her head. 'Not really. If they're in here, then they're a financial corporation recognised by the Federal Reserve. OK,' she continued, 'let's see.' She peered closely at the statement. 'As I said, the figures on the left could well be a routing transit number.' She looked again at Morrow. 'Every bank in the US has an identifiable code, a "flagging" mechanism so that banks can talk to each other by computer: the Minc. line tells you which bank the cheque or statement is from and, in what region within the US the cheque or statement was issued.'

'A Minc. line?'

'Jesus, Lee, didn't they teach you anything in Treasury goon school?'

Morrow tensed at the jibe, but didn't reply.

Flicking through the compendium, Penny explained what she was looking for. 'Magnetic Incorporated Character Recognition lines contains all the information you need about any bank. They are marked at the bottom of every cheque in the US. When the cheques are fed through high-speed reader sorters, they're processed according to the information provided by the Minc. line. Not all banks include the routing transit number on statements, but some do.' She heaved the *Thomson's* nearer to her and glanced at Morrow. 'These volumes have been put on to CD-ROM but we public officials do not yet have that luxury.'

Morrow looked at the directory over her shoulder: page after page listed lines of nine-digit numbers, and beside them the relevant bank and region within the US. 'Right,' she sighed, 'according to this the routing number is 900456577. If it *is* a routing number. If it *is* a statement.'

Her finger ran down a column of figures. 'No, it's not here.'

She closed the first volume and pulled the second towards her. 'If I was at First Boston, I'd be charging you by the minute.' She expertly thumbed through the hefty catalogue, flicking back and forth between pages. Finally, she stopped at one particular page. 'Got ya! Yeah, you were right. This *is* a bank statement.'

Morrow could feel his heart quicken. 'Does it tell you which bank?' he said, leaning closer.

'Sure.' She looked again at the directory. 'The routing number is from the NordFund Group.' She scanned the page. 'NordFund has only two branches: both in Richmond, Virginia.'

'Have you heard of them?'

Penny shook her head. 'No. Of the thirty thousand or so financial institutions within the United States, NordFund is not one I normally talk to. I deal with the Social Security departments: if someone is drawing welfare and wants it put directly into their bank account, we can verify through *Thomson's* which is the right bank. But, from looking at this, I doubt NordFund has any clients on welfare. I can't be certain but at a guess I'd say it was a private bank, and if that's the case, then whatever this is about, you're going to have one hell of a problem tracing whoever holds this account.'

Morrow knew she was right. The Bank Privacy Act prevented the disclosure of an account holder's name or details unless backed up by a warrant.

'Where in Richmond?' he asked.

She looked again at the directory. 'The two branches are at what appears to be the same address.' Penny glanced back at him. 'Is this enquiry official, Lee?'

'Kind of,' he replied quickly, walking back to his seat.

'Kind of?'

'It's just something I'm looking into before I report it.' At least, he thought, he was only half lying. 'Penny, would you write down those details for me?'

She did as he asked. He took the paper from her. 'Thanks, Penny. Thanks a lot.'

She looked at him and smiled. 'It was good to see you again.'

Please don't say 'Call me'.

She turned away from him, back to her computer screen. 'Hang loose, Morrow. I'll see you around.'

White flicked through the notebook again. He was crouched by a small table in a back room of the Windsor Court Hotel near Dupont. The place was quiet, to the north-east, a perfect refuge. He leaned over to his left and switched on a small lamp. He was still sore from the beating he'd received the day before. His right arm ached like hell, and every time he tried to write the pain was excruciating.

Riordan sat quietly in a chair opposite him, puffing on a Marlboro Red.

'Have you run a check on that car reg. I gave you?' White asked him.

'It's being done, Whitey. The PD move at their own pace. If I hassle them, they'll only start charging me more.' Riordan crushed his cigarette on to a saucer, exhaling deeply. 'OK,' he said, rearranging his bulk in the tiny chair, 'what more do you know about Lee Morrow?'

White shrugged. 'Very little. He's been with Elizabeth Forrester since the beginning.'

'And suddenly he's interested in a dead Pentagon official. Or rather, we know he was trying to track Kelly down . . . and suddenly Kelly falls off the mountain?'

White grimaced, shaking his head. 'Mick, are you seriously suggesting Lee Morrow *killed* Kelly?'

They looked at each other.

'OK, OK,' Riordan said quickly, 'let's just say Morrow was genuinely trying to find Kelly for whatever reason . . . but almost certainly at Mrs Forrester's request. Do you think that investigation is authorised or freelance?'

'Could be either,' White replied. 'But what we haven't got is *why*. What the link is between Kelly and the Forresters. There has to be one. What was he working on when he died? Who was his contact at the Mansion? I mean, who *was* he? For a start, why is someone who's supposed to be a number-cruncher at the Pentagon living in such a swish place in Alexandria?'

Riordan lit another cigarette. White allowed him to do so even though the room was fuggy and hot. 'Kelly had a nice pad?' he asked.

White nodded. 'Very.'

'But he can't have been earning more than, what, forty, forty-five thousand a year, right?'

'Maybe . . . I'm not sure.'

Riordan leaned forward in his chair. 'Well, he was seeing a lot of paperwork. We're talking big figures, millions, maybe billions. You think he was taking paybacks?'

'Mick, I haven't got his bank account. Nor have I looked under his bed.'

Riordan smirked. 'No, but what about the house, Whitey? If it's rented then we're going to have problems. But if he owns it, we can check how much he paid for it and when. *If* he paid for it.'

'Where do we start?' White asked.

'I'll show you.'

The Old Town Courthouse in Alexandria was a reminder of the town's colonial past: a redbrick edifice with a white cupola, the structure as pristine and elegant as the day it was completed. White followed Riordan into the building. They stopped and examined a laminated directory by the entrance. 'First floor,' Riordan said.

They hurried up the stairs.

The Records Office reeked of old paper and stale coffee, the ubiquitous smell of officialdom. A middle-aged woman sat behind the counter. She smiled as the two men approached her. Riordan did the talking. 'Ma'am, we're interested in a property in town. We're not sure if it's rented or privately owned. Can you do a check?'

'Of course, gentlemen,' the lady replied. She seemed delighted to have callers. 'But if it's rental then the records won't be here. Do you have the address?'

White hurriedly pulled out his notebook. He wrote down Kelly's address and passed it to her.

'I won't be a minute. Please take a seat.'

They sat down. Riordan glared at the No Smoking sign and fidgeted in his seat. They did not have to wait long. Within a few minutes, the clerk was back. 'Right,' she said briskly, 'I've checked that address and made a copy of the land records. If the owners rent it out, then you'll have to approach them, I'm afraid. We don't keep any records here.' She held out a piece of yellow paper. 'Who wants this?'

White took it and thanked her. The two men hurried out of the office and stood in the empty corridor. White scanned through the details as Riordan slumped against the wall opposite. The land record was cursory: it gave the full address of the property and brief details on the size of the site, its tax classification and history.

The name of the owner was at the bottom: according to the files, Kelly's house was registered to a company called Vale Investments Inc. White looked up at Riordan. 'You were right, Mick.' He handed the record over. 'Kelly didn't own the property. Or if he did, he had it registered under a company name.'

Riordan whistled as he glanced at the document. 'And why, my friend, would he do that? . . . Vale Investments Inc., franchise tax reports registered in Virginia.' He stared at White. 'Where's there a phone?'

White pulled out his cellular and handed it to Riordan.

'Come on, Whitey, we'll get better reception in the lobby.'

Downstairs, Riordan balanced his notebook on a desk by the door. He called Assistance, got the number he was looking for, then dialled. White listened as Riordan pressurised the person on the other end of the line. The Irishman scribbled notes frantically as he spoke. After ten minutes he was done. Riordan handed the cellular back to White and smiled at his colleague. 'Let's walk and talk.'

Outside, the morning had given way to a warm and muggy afternoon.

'OK,' Riordan went on, his voice wheezy, 'according to the Secretary of Commonwealth's office in Richmond, Vale Investments was set up nine months ago. There are no details as to its line of business, not that that means much. *But,* and here's the interesting bit, the registered agent is based in DC.' Riordan smiled at White. 'And it isn't Mr Kelly. The company might own Kelly's house, but Kelly doesn't own the company. Nor is he a company officer. The house was bought for him.'

'But who the hell are Vale Investments?'

Riordan paused by his car. 'It doesn't matter who they are, Whitey, it's who they *represent* that matters. The question is, who *owns* Vale Investments . . . who's giving out the money?'

'You've got the address, right?'

Riordan smiled, reaching for his cigarettes. 'Sure do. And I've got even more than that. According to the Franchise Tax Report, the company is represented in Richmond by a private bank: NordFund Corp.'

The two men sat forward in the car, alert. 'Do we check what they were after in there?' one asked his companion.

'No, there's no point. We're to get them at the hotel.'

'Fine.'

They slipped into the Richmond traffic, Riordan's blue Honda clearly visible ahead of them.

Chapter Nineteen

Elizabeth replaced the telephone receiver. She was sitting in the study of the cottage, a pile of press cuttings spread out on the table in front of her. Friedman sat beside her, a legal pad on his lap.

'Morrow knows for certain that it's a bank statement,' she muttered, as much to herself as to him. 'A Richmond bank account. But without a warrant, there's no way we can discover whose account it is.'

She tried to keep her voice level, controlled. But inside, an inescapable feeling of dread had begun to envelop her. The very thought that Tyler might have been ferreting money away in a secret bank account left only one inference: the husband she had loved, had known as a decent and honest man, had been corrupted. Had crossed the line.

The thought chilled her. 'I just can't believe it, John.' She looked at him in anguish. 'Why? *Why*? Tyler . . . taking kickbacks! And for *what!*' She held her head in her hands. The repercussions of what she had found in her husband's pocket watch were too enormous for her to contemplate. But contemplate them she must, that much she knew.

'John, I just feel so *powerless!*' She could feel her face blazing. 'I go public and Tyler's name is mud. What am I supposed to do? Ring up the FBI, the Speaker . . . let them loose on my husband

and everything he did . . . even though I don't know *what* he did? That's what would happen. You know it and I know it! And all the time, I sit here and I know, I *know*, that Tyler wasn't dishonest, goddammit! I know that, John!'

Elizabeth frantically tried to control herself. She exhaled deeply, her throat raw and tight. Somehow she managed to control the tremor in her voice. 'Let's look at this calmly . . . what if Kelly included that bank statement in the package he sent to Tyler? For whatever reason, the name of the bank and the account holder had been removed: maybe Kelly did it, maybe he wanted to hold something back just in case Tyler' – she stopped and averted her eyes – 'just in case he was also party to the fraud.'

Elizabeth winced.

Somehow, she managed to keep speaking. 'Perhaps it was Kelly's insurance. If Tyler had refused to act on the information Kelly had given him – whatever that information *was* – then Kelly could have gone public. He would have sent Tyler enough to show him what was going on, but not everything. If Tyler was determined to uncover what had gone on, then he'd have responded to Kelly's bait and met with him . . . or had someone do it for him.'

Friedman placed the pad on the desk. 'But, ma'am, the President *didn't* act! There's no record anywhere that your husband ever met with Kelly. I know: I've looked. None of the White House records detail any such meeting.'

Elizabeth felt the feeling of dread take even tighter hold on her. 'I know, John,' she said eventually. 'I know. But if Kelly had compiled a report on fraud at the Pentagon, and Tyler had been in on it, there's no way my husband would have written what he did. I know, John! I could sense it as I read the diary; that's what so infuriates me! Tyler was terrified of something, John. Absolutely petrified. If he was receiving illegal funds, he wouldn't have written what he did. No way. He just *wouldn't!*' She sat back in the chair and closed her eyes.

Christ, I hope I'm right.

Friedman interrupted her thoughts. 'Then why did he hide the statement, Mrs Forrester?'

The question hung between them.

'For the same reason he hid the diary,' she replied, again hoping against hope that it was true. 'For the same goddam reason he didn't tell me what was eating him inside! Because he couldn't trust the people around him! Tyler was the world's worst procrastinator. He'd have sat on this, mulled it over, waited, and then he'd have acted. But if he felt that he was being fed wrong, or biased, information, he'd have waited a little longer. He would have told—'

'McQuogue?'

Elizabeth nodded. 'Precisely. He said as much in the diary. McQuogue would have been empowered to investigate. But if Tyler had even the faintest inkling that McQuogue was holding something back from him, then he'd have waited. If he hid the bank statement, it would have been for only one reason: he suspected McQuogue wasn't being truthful. Only Tyler didn't have the chance to find out for sure, did he, John?'

Friedman remained silent.

'And with Tyler dead, McQuogue had to make sure there was no other evidence. He had to have everything of Tyler's; couldn't take the risk of anyone else having access to Kelly's information.'

'Which is why they went to the private quarters?'

Elizabeth nodded. 'And why they came here. Kelly was killed for what he knew; Danello because there had to be a suspect after the attack on you.'

She sat back and silence fell between them. Gradually calm returned. Elizabeth glanced at him. 'John, I want you to find out what you can about NordFund. I can't ask Lee to continue: he has risked too much already. I can tell that the rest of the detail are curious about where he has been. The only way we can move forward is by discovering who the hell was receiving this money.

Talk to Clifford Granby – he has connections everywhere. Ask him about NordFund.'

At nightfall, Riordan dropped White outside his hotel. White crossed the lawn in front and entered the main reception area. He wanted coffee and the hotel laid on free mugs day and night. He climbed the stairs. There was no one behind reception. He took a Styrofoam cup from the pile, poured himself regular from the percolator.

'Ah, Mr White, you're back.'

He stood sipping the scalding coffee as the reception manager came round to join him.

'Some friends were here for you earlier. They said they'd knock on your door. I told them—'

White threw the coffee into a trashcan. 'How many of them were there?'

He looked urgently behind him.

The receptionist blushed. 'Well, two men. They said they'd wait outside after they'd tried your door and—'

White was already pushing the man back towards the corridor that led to the rear of the hotel. 'Is there another way out here?' he whispered, his hand grasping the receptionist's shoulder as he checked behind them.

'Sorry? I mean, is there a prob—'

White propelled the startled clerk along. 'Is there a goddam service entrance? Just tell me!'

'Yes, there is. But normally guests don't—'

'Where the fuck is it?'

'In the basement, sir. It leads through to the street. We use it for laundry and so on. But it's locked now. The cleaning staff have gone home for the day.'

'Have you got the key?'

'Yes.'

'Then take me.'

White pushed the other man forward. He followed him past the lifts and to the left. He glanced behind him again. No one. As they reached the end of the public corridor, he heard the main door to the hotel crash open. He manhandled the clerk along, constantly checking behind. They hurried through the service area of the hotel and reached some stairs.

'Mr White, this is most unusual. If there's—'

'Just get the fucking keys!' he screeched. He could hear heavy footsteps on the floor above. The clerk had the keys out, but his hands were too unsteady. He dropped them to the floor, scrambling to stop himself. White shoved him aside and retrieved the heavy set. There were ten keys on the ring.

'Which one? *Which one, goddammit?*'

The clerk trembled. 'The one with the red marking!'

Above them a door was flung open. White could hear urgent shouts.

Feet pounded on the steps.

He grasped the door handle, unlocked it and crashed hard against it. Street light flooded into the narrow corridor. He lunged forward. To his left an iron staircase rose to street level. He bounded up, flinging the keys aside. As he reached the sidewalk, he could hear a scream from the clerk. 'Please, he went that way! *Please!*'

White was out on to 16th. The main hotel building was to his right. Parked in front was a dark sedan. He raced to his left. The traffic was heavy again. He reached the kerb and, without looking, propelled himself into the road, missing a cab by inches. The squealing of horns attracted the attention of his pursuers. They were only a minute behind him.

He was on the east side now. Blood pounded through his temples. His chest tightened and his legs felt unwieldy.

Please, don't give up on me now.

He raced on to Corcoran Street. As he swept left, in the darkness he glimpsed the men chasing after him. They were a block away. Two of them. Fast.

He willed himself to make it to the junction of 15th. With each step his chest was seared by pain. He struggled to keep going, left hand clasped to his ribs.

He glanced behind him. They were half a block away.

He tore across Church Street. He had no time to think about where he was heading. He just had to run.

'Whitey? Over here, *quick!*'

He turned at the sound of his name. Riordan's blue Honda, its headlights streaming across the sidewalk, ground to a halt on the south-east side of the junction. Riordan's bulky torso was hanging out of the window. White sprinted into the road, waving at a truck which came thundering towards him. The driver roared his disapproval, at the same time swinging the vehicle hard to the left. White reached the passenger side of the car. The door was open. He heaved himself in, half falling on to Riordan in the driver's seat.

'*Fucking* go!'

The Honda lurched to the right, crashed through a pile of beer crates and jumped the sidewalk. White looked behind. The men were twenty feet away. One was struggling to retrieve something from inside his jacket.

Riordan put his foot to the floor. The sound of horns deafened them as he swung hard and fast on P Street, heading towards Logan Circle. At 14th, as Riordan jumped a light and nearly collided with a school bus, White stopped looking over his shoulder.

'Fuck, Mick! How did you get here?'

Riordan glanced at him briefly, keeping his foot on the accelerator. 'I was heading back to Embassy Heights when I saw you trying to kill your fucking self on 15th! Jesus, I had to take two bad turns and go down the one-way by Corcoran. Are you OK?'

White exhaled heavily and massaged his chest. 'Sure, apart from feeling like I'm about to die.'

From Logan Circle, Riordan headed east towards Shaw-Howard U.

'How did they find you?' he said, closing the window.

'I don't know, Mick. I didn't telephone anyone. Only you knew where I was.'

Riordan picked up the note of suspicion in his voice and turned slightly to face his friend. 'Mark, don't fuck with me! I never told a goddam soul! I swear—'

White slammed his hands on the dashboard. 'Fuck, I've got it now!'

He rested his head in his arms and began moaning gently. 'Christ, how could I be so stupid? Jesus, the credit card! The fucking credit card! The hotel ran it through the machine this morning. It's the only way they could have known I was there.'

'Not possible, Whitey. To get into those records, it takes time. Unless you're Federal, it's almost impossible to monitor an account by the second.' Riordan spoke quickly, watching the road ahead. 'You need to be linked up real good. There's not a chance in hell these thugs could have—'

Riordan stopped. White watched his face closely. They sat in silence as the car carried on along 14th. Then White spoke.

'They managed it, Mick! They *were* keyed in! They were waiting for me to surface. And I made it so fucking easy for them!'

Riordan glanced at him sideways. 'Whitey,' he said, 'this is serious business, my friend.' He scratched his forehead and fumbled for a cigarette. 'Jesus! What have you got yourself into?'

'I don't know, Mick. I don't fucking *know* what they want!' He slammed his hand against the dashboard.

'Where d'ya want to go now?'

'To the *Herald*. Go through the carport and drop me at the back escalators. I don't think they'd dare try and grab me in the middle of the office.'

Riordan turned the car around and headed east.

Chapter Twenty

'Mr Friedman, come in, come in.'

He accepted Granby's invitation. Inside, he glanced around the drawing room of Hiscock House: it seemed to go on for ever, a succession of oversized sofas scattered throughout. He waited as Granby finished a call. Friedman studied him closely. In the time he had worked for Elizabeth, Friedman had had very little to do with the elderly man sitting opposite him. He knew of Granby's reputation, of course: he was famed within the White House as one of the Invisible Men, the Grand Old Men of Washington who discreetly counselled Tyler; Friedman knew also that Granby had reinvented the very meaning of anonymity. Whatever it was that the old man did, and Friedman had heard of the vast fortune at Granby's disposal, he had only a hazy understanding of how the multimillionaire operated.

'John, apologies. That was Japan.' Granby smiled. 'You ever been there? Ever dealt with them?'

Friedman nodded. 'Now and again. But only at the odd function in the White House.' As he spoke, he could sense that Granby's mind had moved on, his thoughts were elsewhere.

'How is Elizabeth?'

'Fine, sir,'

Granby grimaced. 'I wish she would move in here.' He looked at Friedman. 'She thinks she's protecting *me!*'

Friedman laughed. 'Maybe she is . . . I don't think you'd appreciate the media outside your door.'

Granby nodded. 'Well, they haven't worked out that I found her that house so I suppose we've got away with it so far. Elizabeth has spoken to me about a bank account. I believe you have some more details?'

Speaking quickly, Friedman filled Granby in on what Morrow had discovered about NordFund. 'The problem, sir, is that we cannot determine exactly what the purpose of this account was unless we go public. At the moment, Mrs Forrester does not wish to do so. Her reasoning is that she has little concrete evidence: we do not even know if the late President was directly benefiting from this account. Even—'

'What you're saying, John, is that Elizabeth cannot bring herself to be the one who destroys her husband's reputation?'

Friedman nodded but kept silent.

'Well,' Granby continued, 'that's hardly surprising. For a woman like Elizabeth, someone who supported her husband through everything, the very fact that Tyler had allowed himself to become embroiled in . . . in this affair is devastating.' He held Friedman's stare. 'So, son, you want me to make a few calls and see what I can find out?'

The two men smiled at each other. 'Yes, Mr Granby.'

'Just give me the details, John.'

'Sir, this is the account number and the name of the bank.'

He handed over the details of NordFund.

Granby glanced at them, then put the piece of paper in his pocket. Friedman stood and made his way towards the door. 'Mr Granby, I know that Mrs Forrester will be eternally grateful for this.'

Riordan checked the *Herald*'s carport. It was half empty, the day-workers having long gone. He turned and gestured to White. The two men hurried towards Riordan's car. Within seconds they were out on to 19th, heading west. Riordan checked the rear-view mirror then glanced at White. 'No one's on us.'

White grimaced. 'Not yet, Mick. Let's just get this over with.'

'You sure you want to stay watching this place all night?'

'Maybe.'

It took them half an hour to find the address. Under the streetlights, the entrance to the office building was well lit. White and Riordan watched from their car parked across the street. The building itself was six storeys high, sandwiched between residential apartments in Embassy Heights. The entrance had a plate-glass door; beyond it, a small lobby and reception desk led through to a long corridor. At the end was an elevator.

White shuffled in the car seat. His legs had gone numb and Riordan's cigarette smoke was irritating him. 'There's no night guard,' he said, staring at the entrance.

Riordan opened the window and threw his butt on to the sidewalk. 'No guard, but the super locked the doors.'

'Mick, we're wasting our time,' White groaned, knees aching from the cramped space. 'The building's locked and there's no question that Vale Investments' office will be as well. What are we going to do, break in?'

Riordan stared ahead. 'Trust me, Whitey. I'm going to show you an old trick. It just might work. Give me your phone.'

'Mick—'

'Give me the friggin' phone, Whitey.'

Reluctantly, White handed him the cellular. The Irishman pushed five numbers, waited, then spoke. 'Fire service, please.'

White lunged for the phone. 'Mick, they'll trace my number! Jesus, give—'

Riordan pushed himself as far away from White as he could, his bulk scrunched up against the driver's door. He put his hand over the mouthpiece and snarled at his colleague: 'Shut it, Whitey, OK? I've punched in a block on your number. The only fuckin' thing they'll have is my voice.' He spoke into the phone again. 'Hello? Yeah, thanks. Is that the fire service? OK, look, there's smoke coming out of a building in Embassy Heights. What? Yeah, yeah, smoke, shitloads. It's an office building . . . what? I don't know, ma'am, I think everyone's left but I'm not sure. They have their own key to get out . . . what? Yes, ma'am, it's by the Holiday Inn.'

He winked at White.

'No, ma'am, I'm not the super. You can? Oh, fine . . . yes, yes, no problem. What? No, no, I can't stay on the line, ma'am. My kid's sick, I've got to go. But you better get someone here real fast, ma'am.'

He flicked the phone shut and handed it back to White. 'Now just watch,' he said smugly, settling into the seat.

It took ten minutes. First one fire truck roared up to the building, the crews jumping out as the vehicle lurched to a halt, its siren wailing. A minute later, another truck arrived, screeching round the corner, nearly thundering into the first. Almost immediately the building's super appeared at the entrance. Incredulous, White watched as the firemen and the super rushed into the road, looking up at the dark building. Then the super hurried back to the entrance. He unlocked the door, stepping aside to let three firemen into the building.

'Mick, for fuck sake—'

'Just wait!'

The super was being pulled aside by what appeared to be the fire officer in charge of the crews. White could see the two men conferring, the super pointing towards an alley by the side of the building. The fire officer ran towards it, the super struggling to keep up, a set of keys in his hand.

Riordan moved quickly. 'OK, let's go,' he muttered, heaving himself out of the car. White followed, the two of them bathed in the pulsating lights of the fire trucks across the street.

Riordan began running away from the trucks. White hurried to keep up with him. He had no idea where his friend was heading but had little choice but to follow. They turned right down a small street, ran along the side of an apartment building, then turned right again. Twenty yards down, White could make out the darkened opening of an alleyway.

Riordan turned to him. 'Come on, but slowly.'

Thirty yards into the alleyway, they could see the super struggling to unlock the back entrance. White and Riordan stayed hidden in the blackness as they carefully inched their way forward. Finally, the man managed to get the better of the lock and the unwieldy back door swung open. White watched as the super and the fire officer stepped inside then reappeared almost immediately. Two seconds later they ran back along the alleyway towards the street, away from White and Riordan, disappearing round the corner.

The back entrance was left unguarded.

'OK, Whitey, now!'

The two men rushed down the alleyway. Riordan leaped through the open doorway. White followed and found himself in a small, brightly lit lobby. Riordan propped himself against the wall, his breath coming in short, agonised gasps. 'OK, Whitey, we haven't got long. They'll be back in a few seconds with reinforcements. Which floor did you say the Vale office was on?'

White struggled to catch his own breath. He could not believe what Riordan had done. 'Er . . . the fourth, I think. Yeah, yeah, the fourth.' His lungs were screaming for mercy.

The emergency stairs were in front of them. They hurried up the steps. Halfway up the first flight, Riordan turned and pulled White towards him. 'Now,' he whispered, 'we have to be careful. The crew that went through the front door would have gone straight to the top of the building. That's the procedure. So we only have a few minutes to get to the office. If we're caught, we tell them we just left the building and returned to see what was happening.'

White could have picked holes in Riordan's impromptu plan but thought twice before saying so. In silence, they climbed the stairs, stopping at each floor. Below they could hear the second fire crew entering the building, shouts and commands filtering up the stairwell. Within a minute they'd reached the fourth floor. Riordan pushed through the lobby door in front of them. As White followed he could hear the voices of the fire crew more clearly now. They were only a floor away. 'Mick,' he hissed. 'They're right behind us!'

Riordan waved him off and lunged down the darkened corridor. In the half-light, they could just make out the names of the companies on the ten or so doors leading off the corridor.

They followed the corridor round to the right. The Vale office was at the end. The name-plate said simply: 'Vale Investments'. The two men leaned against it, trying to catch their breath.

'OK, Mick, fuckin' brilliant! So what's the plan now?' White whispered in between gasping for breath. He looked at the lock on the door. 'There's no way—'

Riordan motioned him to be quiet. The Irishman tried the door, then, with surprising dexterity, sank to his knees. White watched as he pulled out a small black case. He unzipped it and withdrew a set of thin metal prongs.

'Mick, what the fuck you doin'? Jesus, you're breaking in! How the—'

'Whitey, shut it! They'll hear you!' The sound of metal scraping against metal seemed inordinately loud in the hushed corridor. 'I learned this a few years ago,' Riordan hissed, 'from a piece I was doing on DC burglars. One of the fraternity showed me this particular trick. I used to train with him on weekends at my apartment building.' He looked back at White. 'When I knew my neighbours were out, we'd play with their locks. We wouldn't go in or anything. We never stole nothing. Well, I didn't anyway.'

'Jesus, Mick, you're fuckin' crazy! This is criminal! I mean, what did Nixon ask you to do? Become a plumber?' White stopped whispering. He could hear the heavy tread of the fire crews from around the corner behind him. Their shouts echoed in the deserted space. 'Mick, they're—'

Riordan gave one final twist to the lock. He stood quickly and tried the door handle. 'Yes!' The door swung open. He turned and pulled White through the open doorway. The office was in total darkness, windows covered in Venetian blinds. White could pick up the faintest trace of cigar smoke.

'Down, Whitey, behind here!'

The two men crouched behind a filing cabinet to the left of the door. Beyond it they could hear the fire crews drawing closer. Almost immediately the door into the office swung open. Torchlight quickly swept the room. 'Clear!' a fireman shouted, before slamming the door shut.

'What if they lock it?' White muttered. He was surprised by how calm his voice sounded.

'They won't,' Riordan replied confidently. 'They don't care if the door isn't locked. They're just looking for smoke traces.'

They waited for ten minutes. Eventually, the voices receded from the corridor. Riordan tugged White to his feet.

'Mick, what if they close the back entrance? We'll be stuck in here!'

'They won't. The super will have to check every floor before he leaves, starting at the top. The Chief Fire Officer has to be with him. Through *every* floor. They always do one final check before they're done. It'll be in the insurance. We have' – Riordan squinted to read his wristwatch – 'about twenty minutes. Maybe half an hour, but we shouldn't push it. So, where do we start?'

The office was small: two cheap desks, three phones, a two-drawer filing cabinet by a wall. On the far side, an old-fashioned typewriter and next to it a fax machine. The flooring was carpet, torn in places. Riordan fumbled in his pocket and found what he was looking for: a thin beam of light lit up the wall opposite White.

'Jesus, Mick, what else do you have in there? A fuckin' SWAT team?'

'Could be arranged.'

'Christ.'

With only one torch, they could not divide the tasks. First, they tried the drawers to the desks: all were open. They crouched down on the floor, checking through the paperwork. White's eyes ached as he tried to read the documents by the paltry light. Most were rent forms, a catalogue of income from properties in DC and Maryland. There was no mention of Kelly or his house.

After five minutes they put the papers back and closed the drawers. The filing cabinet stood opposite them. 'OK, Mr Watergate,' White sneered, 'how're we going to get past those locks?'

Riordan ignored the question. He marched back across the office. By the window, a metal chair was propped against the wall. Riordan picked it up, then waited. The only sounds were the voices of the fire crews outside in the street, and the slamming of truck doors. Riordan counted to three then brought the chair down hard against the side of a desk.

'Mick!'

The noise was deafening, metal torn from metal as the Irishman pulled a shattered leg from the chair.

White watched silently as Riordan pulled at the first drawer in the filing cabinet. Breathing loudly, cursing as he did so, he managed to tug the metal drawer open a quarter of an inch. Then, pushing down with all his weight, he prised the metal leg into the small gap. 'Whitey, come and help me.'

They pushed down hard. Just as White thought the leg would snap, he heard the sound of yet more metal creaking and splitting inside the cabinet. With one final push the ancient lock mechanism gave in, the drawers shaking and buckling as the metal rod inside snapped free.

Riordan flung the chair leg to one side. 'Well,' he said, 'they'll certainly know someone's been here. But they won't know it's us.'

Quickly, they pulled the top drawer out. The files were alphabetical. White flicked through to the K's. He pulled the documents out and examined them by the light of Riordan's torch. There was no reference to Ronald Kelly. White returned the files to the drawer. He looked at Riordan; the Irishman's face was bathed in shadow. 'There's nothing here.'

'OK, try these,' Riordan hissed as he pulled out a folder marked GENERAL, then hurried to the door and listened. There was no sound from outside.

White pulled out the files. He laid them on the floor and began flicking through, the torchlight guiding him. 'Mick! I've got it.'

Riordan crouched down beside him on the floor.

The first document was a registration form with the Secretary of the Commonwealth in Virginia. It confirmed the establishment of Vale Investments as a trading company. White tossed it aside. Beneath it was notification from NordFund Corp. of Richmond establishing banking facilities at a branch on Wilbur Street. There was nothing else in the file.

White jotted down the bank details: there was no account number, only the name of the banking officer who had dealt with the application. 'That's all there is.'

'Shit! Did Kelly use any kind of pseudonym or a cover name?' Riordan whispered, glancing at the door.

'Yes! He had a cellular phone registered to "Frank Sills"! I couldn't get anything out of the phone company but Kelly had tried to get Elizabeth Forrester on that phone. "Sills" was his cover.'

White retrieved the S files.

The first document was a copy of a NordFund bank statement. The account was in the name of Frank Sills. White swore under his breath – $370,000 had been deposited in the account over the last three months.

He made a note of the account number and flicked to the next page. He read it, then looked at Riordan.

'Jesus, Mick!'

The document confirmed the purchase by Vale Investments of a house in Alexandria at a cost of $560,000. It was Kelly's address.

'The guy was up to his neck in kickbacks!'

'OK, Whitey, calm down.' Riordan glanced at the closed door again. 'Take the bank stuff and the purchase note. Put the file back in the drawer.'

'*Mick.*'

White was staring in the half-light at the second page of the document. He handed it to Riordan. This page showed another account, one made out in the name of James Appleton: $125,000 had been banked in it.

Riordan swore under his breath. 'The lying little bastard!'

White grabbed the page back. 'Mick, this payment was made four days ago . . . *after* we'd been to Appleton. They're paying people off left, right and centre!'

Hurriedly, he replaced the documents in the filing cabinet.

They waited at the office door for a second, the only sound that of their own breathing

Silence from outside.

Riordan opened the door. 'Let's get out of here.'

Chapter Twenty-one

Elizabeth worked her way through the pile of correspondence. It had been nearly a month since she had left the White House, and her staff had become smaller, the postbags bigger. It seemed as if the entire country remained fascinated by her, eager to hear her pronouncement on any topic, however large or small.

She pushed the papers aside. They could wait; by the end of the day she would have noted her replies and handed those notes to the two secretaries who beavered away on her behalf.

When she heard the knock on the door, she sat forward. She knew who it was.

Friedman joined her in the drawing room. Elizabeth could see the tiredness under his eyes. She had begun to worry about her young aide, had begun to notice a tension, a brittleness in him that she had never seen before.

'John, are you OK?'

He smarted at her concern. 'Well, yes, Mrs Forrester. Why do you ask?'

Elizabeth shrugged off the question. 'OK, let's run through the outstanding things.'

For half an hour, the two of them discussed the interview requests from the media, invitations to appear in support of Democratic candidates across the country. Elizabeth edited out some of the names. She laughed angrily at one request: 'Christ,

John, this guy never stopped criticising me behind my back. Now he wants me to endorse his Senate campaign!' She scrunched the letter in her hand and hurled it swiftly into the burning fire.

Friedman ignored the gesture and carried on. After a short while he was done. He gathered the papers together and put them back in his briefcase.

'John, have you had a chance to speak with Clifford?'

Friedman nodded. 'Yes, ma'am. Mr Granby had been away for a few days but, yes, we have spoken.'

'Good,' she said. 'What did he say?'

Before he could reply, the telephone rang. Elizabeth picked it up. 'Hello?'

'Elizabeth, it's Clifford here.'

'We were just talking about you! Are you at home?'

'Yes, I am . . . my apologies, but that matter we discussed – I have a few details but not much, I'm afraid. Can I come over?'

'Please do. We'll wait for you.'

Elizabeth ordered coffee from the kitchen. Friedman reorganised his papers. She found his presence strangely disquieting tonight; the young aide seemed nervous and offhand.

Elizabeth groaned inwardly. The last thing she needed was Friedman to wilt on her.

When Clifford Granby arrived, he waved away Elizabeth's offer of coffee.

'I've made some tentative enquiries about your problem,' he said quickly. He glanced at Friedman. 'I'm afraid I'm going to disappoint you . . . My friends in the banking sector have heard of NordFund. It's a small, private concern, not big enough to make a mark on the national, or even local, scene.'

'And there's no way we can discover who owned that account?'

'No, Elizabeth. That is impossible unless—'

'I go public and convince a judge to issue a warrant?'

He nodded solemnly. 'And if you do that—'

'It might turn out that my husband was the account holder?' No one answered her.

Tyler, what have you done?

Elizabeth could feel her face reddening. 'OK, gentlemen. Your advice is – what? Do *nothing*?'

Granby kept silent for a few moments. Then he spoke. 'In the circumstances, Elizabeth, unless you become aware of anything else, I have to conclude that that would be your best course, yes. I do not see that you have any other choice.'

She looked at Friedman. 'John?'

He seemed startled. 'Er, yes, ma'am . . . yes. I can only agree with Mr Granby.'

Elizabeth did not agree but she kept her own counsel. An idea was taking final shape in her mind, one that had been there for many days but which, until now, she had dismissed as preposterous.

'OK, is there anything else?' she said to them both.

'Oh, there is one final thing,' Friedman told her.

She nodded at him to go on.

'There's a poll about to be released by NBC. They've been compiling it over the last few days. They want a reaction from you before they air it.'

Elizabeth motioned for him to continue.

'Well, they've asked the recipients who they would rate most highly as President.' He stopped and pulled a folded sheet of A4 paper from his jacket pocket. 'I don't know whether the White House have been faxed the results as well, but the network is keen for a response from you. I told them that—'

Elizabeth interrupted him quickly. 'John, no way. I am not going to make any public comment about Willard's White House. I've told you that. I don't care what the poll shows about him or Tyler, I will not get involved.'

Friedman sat forward, avoiding Elizabeth's stare. 'The poll isn't about Willard *precisely*,' he said quietly. 'It features him, of course. And not that well, it must be said.' He examined the line of figures on the paper in his hand. 'The poll is actually about *you*.'

Elizabeth glanced towards Granby. Her friend shrugged and nodded to Friedman.

'What does it say, John?'

He handed the piece of paper to Elizabeth.

'Jesus, this is all I need!'

She shoved the fax towards Granby, who read it hurriedly.

'Elizabeth—'

'Mrs Forrester—'

Granby and Friedman both stopped and waited for the other to continue. Elizabeth seized her chance and spoke quickly. 'No! No way! I don't care. I am not going to comment on this. It's a freak. People just feel sorry for me. I can't—'

'Mrs Forrester, you are way ahead of Willard in that poll. That's a fact. You can't just ignore it.'

Elizabeth was growing increasingly agitated. Her forehead glistened and a swathe of red ran from her throat down to the top of her breasts. 'No! You two know me better than anyone else in the world. How can you both expect me to look at this rationally? You saw what I went through with Tyler. You saw how much I bled for him! How it nearly destroyed me *and* him! And now you're both talking as if this is an amusing diversion! For God's sake, the presidency fucking *killed* him!'

She was shaking now, eyes blurred by tears. Her chest heaved and she felt nauseous. She needed air. She wanted to rage some more, to keep shouting in the hope that this would all just go away.

But she knew she couldn't. Elizabeth might scream and shout at the two of them for as long as she liked. But her anger was not because of them; it was because the poll had brought into focus a challenge she knew she must meet.

In the hours since he had arrived home from his meeting with Elizabeth and Granby, Friedman had tried to control his panic.

He pulled at his tie, letting it fall to the floor. He felt filthy, polluted. He had not as yet betrayed Elizabeth, but he carried the prospect of it with fear and loathing.

He rested his head against the kitchen cupboards.

He was too intelligent to believe his self-pity was in any way justified; too terrified to think about anything other than himself.

They had come to him because they knew his secret. And they had guessed rightly that he would know more about Elizabeth than anyone else.

I can control this.

His head began thumping again, the nausea returning.

He breathed in slowly. His apartment was icy cold, the AC on full. It gurgled and thumped noisily in the corner. Friedman ignored it. He craved the brittle, freezing air, as if it might whip away his own anguish.

He reached over and turned out the lights. The wispy yellow glow of the streetlights bathed the room. He would try to sleep, if he could, just sitting in the chair. He didn't have the energy to make it across the hall to his bedroom. Eventually he rose from the sofa and checked in the refrigerator. It was almost empty. He grunted with irritation. He had ignored the hunger pains but now they grew pressing. He hurried to the window and peered outside. The street was deserted. He turned back and found his suit jacket. He pulled it on and made for the front door.

The night was warm, the heat dense and airless under a thick layer of cloud. Friedman made his way up New Hampshire. He checked behind him once or twice, cursing his own paranoia. There was no one about. He tensed as two couples came towards him; but their laughter was reassuring. At 18th he swung right. The lights of the all-night store shone one block ahead. He waited at the kerb to let a taxi edge past.

Friedman stepped into the road. He was halfway across when he heard the car. He glanced behind him nervously, at the same time hurrying towards the opposite sidewalk. The car's lights bore down on him. He quickened his step, keeping the headlights in view.

The car was coming towards him fast.

He began to run.

In a second, he had made it to the sidewalk, sweating and trembling. He whipped round as the car swept past. He was safe.

Friedman sighed with relief.

He paused, catching his breath. He thought he heard the car stop, but an elderly woman emerged from an apartment building behind him, distracting his attention for a second. She eyed him suspiciously. He turned his back on her and spun round.

The car had stopped thirty feet ahead of him. It was a black Lincoln, parked illegally.

Friedman moved quickly to the right of the sidewalk, his arm brushing against the metal grilles that protected the storefronts. His eyes were riveted on the Lincoln.

It was only ten feet away now.

He quickened his pace. The all-night store was within running distance. He didn't want to run. He tried to convince himself he was being ridiculous.

But he kept his eyes on the Lincoln.

Five feet away.

The passenger window rolled down electronically. Friedman felt his stomach somersault but he kept moving, his right shoulder pressed hard and awkwardly against the glass of a storefront.

The window was two-thirds open.

Friedman lunged away from the car, his lungs screaming for air. The all-night store was within reach.

The Lincoln's engine roared into life. Out of the corner of his eye, Friedman thought he caught movement from the window. But the car was lurching forward. He pushed himself back into the shadows. The Lincoln accelerated aggressively into the road, picking up speed before disappearing round the corner.

Friedman watched it go, then sank heavily against a metal grille. His head slumped forward. He could feel the reservoirs of sweat under his arms. His lungs sucked in oxygen as he struggled to maintain his composure. He lifted his head and checked the sidewalk. It was empty. The spot where the Lincoln had been parked was clear.

He straightened up, his fear giving way to laughter.

It was the streetlight reflecting off the envelope that caught his attention. The package lay in the middle of the sidewalk. A4 size, in a commercial brown envelope.

Friedman carefully edged his way towards the package. He could see a white sticker on the front. He leaned forward and looked down. His name was on the sticker.

He picked the package up, then turned it over and peeled open the envelope. He tugged at the bulky, slippery contents. The photographs almost spilled out on to the sidewalk.

They showed a woman. There were ten shots of her, clear and precise. She was walking down a street. Her face was distinctive, striking. Her hair was light auburn, cut into a fashionable bob. She was wearing a cream trouser suit and black pumps.

Friedman felt the blood rush from his face.

His mother, Patricia, looked as beautiful as ever.

Trembling, he flicked once more through the ten prints. Attached to the last was a short scrawled note.

'Do you really want Patricia to know?'

Chapter Twenty-two

'So, do I go in alone or do you want to come with me?'

White turned to Riordan. He watched as the Irishman puffed on a cigarette, and grimaced. 'However you want to play it, Whitey.' Riordan shuffled in his seat. 'Personally, I don't think we should have fucking come here in the first place. If they picked you up from here before—'

'Mick, we've gone through this! I have to put pressure on Appleton. He's our one link.' White turned away from his friend and watched the house from the silent street. 'There's no point waiting any more. We're just wasting time. Everywhere we've turned over the past few days has led us nowhere. We know Appleton's in there, OK?'

Riordan nodded.

'Wait here, Mick.'

He got out of the car and walked up the lane. He passed by the carport and began to climb the steps to Appleton's house. Halfway up, he could see that the sliding doors which led to the outside deck were open and the lights on inside. Appleton was nowhere to be seen. White carried on, the house coming into view properly as he turned the last corner.

White stood on the deck and waited. It was silent up here, the trees muffling any noise from neighbouring properties. He tapped lightly on the door. 'Hello?'

There was the sound of a toilet flushing, then a door slamming shut. Appleton appeared from around a corner, a towel in his hands. He looked at White, stopping dead in his tracks. 'What the—'

White raised a hand in apology. 'Jim, I just wanted to talk with you privately.'

Appleton was walking swiftly towards him, a look of outrage on his face. 'You people! You have no respect for anyone's privacy or—'

White knew he had to be brutal. 'Appleton, either you speak to me or I inform your bosses of the payment you received from a company called Vale Investments.'

Appleton jerked back as if he had been scalded with boiling water. 'I . . . I . . . what . . . get out!' He lunged at White, his face contorted in rage and disbelief. 'Fuckin'—'

White pushed him back and closed the door behind him. 'Jim, sit down and shut it. OK? Either you speak to me or you can read about why a Pentagon official is being secretly paid by a shelf company that also just happened to have Ronald Kelly on its books!'

Appleton stood rooted to the spot, his face blotchy, eyes scanning the doorway behind White. 'What do you *want* from me?' he hissed quietly, checking the deck once more.

'Jim, there's no one else about. Please, can we just talk?'

Appleton nodded finally and stood back. White followed him into the spacious house. They crossed the open-plan living room. Appleton slumped into a chair by the fireplace. White sat perched on a dining chair a few feet away.

'Jim . . . I know this is difficult for you, and I'm not here to try and cause you any further problems.' He could see Appleton's face blanch. 'But I know also that you weren't telling us the whole truth when we were last here. You've been taking money, Jim. A lot of it. I think you should tell me why.'

Appleton remained still. His lips trembled slightly as he

struggled to find the right words. 'Mr White, I did not lie to you, or to Riordan. I hardly knew Ronald Kelly. We spoke now and again but we weren't friends.' Appleton spat the word out as if it was an alien concept. White wondered how many true friends the man had.

'So why were you and Kelly being paid by the same people?' he asked, his eyes never leaving Appleton's face.

'Look, I think you're on the wrong track here. Kelly was losing his grip. You could see it, the man wasn't thinking straight. He—'

'Jim, you were on the same payroll. Only it isn't the Pentagon sending the cheques!'

Appleton swallowed hard and sat in silence for a few seconds. White could see he was having a private debate with himself. Finally, he spoke, his voice weary and hoarse. 'Will this be published? I mean, will you—'

'Jim, if you don't tell me what you know about Kelly and Vale Investments, then yes. Before I even talk about protecting you, I need to know precisely what happened.'

Appleton nodded, his hands shaking as he massaged his forehead.

'Let's start with something simple. The Pentagon issued a press release before the Park Rangers in Shenandoah even knew Kelly was dead. Why was that?'

Appleton leaned back in his chair and closed his eyes. His voice was thin and little more than a whisper. 'No one knows. The media relations people were handed the release by the Procurement Office where Kelly worked.'

'And no one queried it?'

For the first time, Appleton smiled. 'Mr White, sometimes it is better to remain ignorant.' The smile disappeared. 'I wish I was . . . either Kelly was being watched by his own people—'

'And they knew he just happened to fall off a mountain?'

'—or they got lucky.'

The two men stared at each other. White spoke first. 'OK,

Jim, let's go back to the beginning. What do you really know about Kelly?'

Appleton answered in a faint whisper. 'About ten days before President Forrester died, Kelly came to see me in my office. I was, to be honest, a bit pissed with him! I hardly knew the guy, but one afternoon he breezes in, casual as anything. I mean, I am much senior than him.'

'What did he want?'

'He didn't say at first. He asked me how things were going. We talked about what we were doing over the weekend. Then he asks me about the White House.'

White waited. He nodded at Appleton to go on.

'Every day, certainly most days, a package is sent over to the West Wing. It's for the President's Eyes Only. He is literally handed what's in the box and goes through it himself. If the Defense Secretary isn't *in situ* then his staff compile the relevant reports. Every department head sends things up the line, papers or decisions they want the Oval Office to know about. It's a lottery . . . you hope your report will get on to the President's desk, then maybe you'll get a call from the West Wing or a note from the man himself. It's all vanity.'

White could picture the competition to get things in front of the President. He'd wager that Appleton would be a master of that particular game.

'So,' Appleton continued, 'Kelly starts asking me about the box. It was a strange conversation. I mean, he wouldn't even get *near* it. It's not as if they put the thing in the fucking Pentagon lobby and anyone can send a love note over to the White House!'

'So why did he want to know about it?'

Appleton shrugged. 'He didn't say. I'm trying to get rid of him but he won't move. He keeps saying the same thing: "Wouldn't it be funny if someone could get a stupid note into that box, wouldn't it be hilarious?" He was rambling, not making any sense. As I said, he wasn't normal, he was panicking over something. He asked me if I'd ever been able to get my reports in there. I said that I had . . . that, in fact, later that day I was due to go down to the Security Office and forward a report on NATO to the White House. I'd been working on it for weeks; the West Wing wanted a full breakdown of what our allies were doing militarily about the tensions in Turkey and Macedonia.' Appleton glanced at White. 'I was stupid . . . I shouldn't have . . . well, you know what it's like when the President wants something from you.'

'And Kelly?'

'When I told him I'd been directed to put my report in the box, he gets all agitated, starts running through how I'd do it. I mean, it's no big deal. If you've got clearance you go down to the Security Office on the E-Ring, by the river entrance. The list of what's to be included in the box is there and you hand over the report or file, whatever, to one of the Marines. Half an hour later, it's in the White House, on the Commander-in-Chief's desk. There's no big secret. They just make sure that only papers that have been authorised or that the President has personally requested get in there.'

Appleton stopped again.

White allowed him the pause, fearful that any prompting might shatter the man's fragile composure.

'I . . . well, Kelly then leaves my office, laughing about my report and congratulating me. I'm, like, this guy needs watching! He's a loose cannon. A bit later, I go down to the Security Office with my report. I'm running about five, maybe ten minutes late. I'm shitting my pants: the printer in my office was on the blink, so I'm trying to print up the final draft for the fucking President and thinking I'm going to miss the deadline! I rush down there with only a few seconds to go. The Marines are getting ready to leave and I burst in, just praying that I'm on time. I tell them this report has been requested by the White House, that they've got to include it in the box. They're looking all confused.

'One of them goes back through the log and says that all the files have already been delivered to them from the relevant departments. There's nothing more to be included. Everything's been ticked off the list. I'm real unhappy by this stage. So I grab the fucking list out of his hand and there it is! My name, department and the report that's been requested. But there's a tick by my name! Seems *my* report was handed over to them an hour before I'd even got to their office! I can't believe this is happening. I manage to ask him who delivered it. The Marine looks at the signature next to my name: it says "Jim Appleton" but it ain't my writing. Christ! I scream at him to tell me what the sonofabitch looked like . . . so he describes him.'

Appleton looked at White. 'It was Ronald Kelly . . . well, the description matched him. I'm fucking furious, livid. Kelly! I storm out of the office, check the personnel records, find where Kelly's shitty little office is. It's in another part of the complex. I'm by the river entrance. So, I'm marching along the corridor, about to murder this guy, get him fired, prosecuted, torn apart. I want Kelly *dead.* The bastard has screwed me! *Me!* But when I get to his office, he's not there. I'm asking around: Where is he? *Where is he?* No one knows! I leave him a note, threatening to crucify him. I get his numbers from Human Relations and I ring him at his home and on his cellular. No answer anywhere. That night I come home and I'm just waiting for the call: Why did you put an unauthorised report in the President's box? Jesus! I don't even *know* what Kelly had sent over there. It could have been *anything,* signed in under my name!

'But nothing happens. I go into the office the next day, shitting myself, not knowing whether I should own up to what happened or just let it go . . . see if anyone notices. All day I sit there, waiting. I can't work, can't think. Just wondering when the roof is going to fall in on me! But nothing happens. I try and find Kelly: he's gone AWOL. That scares me even more. What the fuck had he put in the box? I can't ask too many questions otherwise people would start wondering. So, I keep quiet . . . the day passes, then the next. Still no sign of Kelly. He's disappeared. Three days later, the call comes: "Where's the NATO report!

The Secretary wants it! So does the President!" I'm about to explain what happened, but they don't want to hear excuses. Before I even start telling them, the—'

'Who was this?' White asked.

'Oh, the Office of the Chairman of the Joint Chiefs of Staff. Room 2E878. When you get a call from that extension, you know you've got to get moving, fast! So I say I've got it and they're, like, "Well, bring it up! Now!" So I go over there, hand it to them, and I'm just so goddam happy that no one's asking why the report wasn't sent over three days before.'

He looked at White. 'Within a matter of days Forrester was dead. After the President's death, I mean, no one is doing any work, it's paralysis. I forget about Kelly amid the bedlam. Then, around ten days after the President's funeral, out of the blue I get a call from Lee Morrow. We were at college together. Morrow rings up, wants to know about Kelly! Morrow is the Service! Jesus, I'm dying inside. Kelly has used me to get to the White House, I haven't reported it and suddenly Morrow's on the phone! So I tell him that Kelly's gone AWOL; all he wants in return is Kelly's address. I'm trying to stay calm.

'I put the phone down on Morrow and try to do some work. A few hours later Riordan rings me. I'm, like, thinking the world is about to fall in! Riordan wants to know about Mrs Forrester and before I can stop myself I blurt out about the call from Morrow.' He stopped, his head slumping forward. 'Jesus, if only I'd kept my mouth shut.'

White sat back and examined the man opposite. Appleton looked as if he had just heaved an enormous weight from on top of him. 'And you still don't know what Kelly put in the box?'

Appleton shook his head. 'No idea.'

White knew he wasn't lying.

'You can't use *any* of this! Please! My job is—'

'Jim, Kelly was on the payroll of Vale Investments . . . the company owned his house. How come they also owned *you*?'

Appleton let his head slump forward. He gave a small groan

then breathed deeply. 'After you first came here, I was approached.' He looked up at White. His eyes were blazing, fear and desperation etched in his face. 'Jesus, White, the guy was armed! He starts talking about my family. I can't believe this is happening. He wants to know about you and Riordan . . .'

White could feel his heart quicken. 'What did you tell him?'

'That you were journalists . . . that you were asking abut Kelly.'

So that's how they found me!

'Then, a few days after, I'm leaving the house and my cellular rings. A man tells me that they are grateful for my co-operation. He says that in return for my discretion, his partners have authorised him to make a payment to me. I'm thinking, This is a set-up! I turn the cellular off, can't get my head round what's going on!'

Appleton exhaled and rubbed his eyes. 'The very next morning, a package arrives here: it's a bank statement, made out in my name! A hundred and twenty-five thousand dollors! The bank is—

'NordFund.'

Appleton looked up sharply. 'How do you—'

'It doesn't matter. Go on.'

'White, they *knew*! I'm up to my neck in debt. This house is mortgaged three times. I'm haemorrhaging money. But I know I can't accept this, it's bribery, a federal offence . . . so I put the statement in the safe here. That afternoon, *yesterday*, the phone rings at my office. It's the same guy as before. He tells me that the money is mine but I am not to speak about Kelly or anyone else. The phone could be bugged or anything! I'm about to tell him to shove it when he interrupts me: "If you try and go public on this, Appleton, remember your family and remember that the account is in your name." He says that, White! I know what he's getting at: if I cause a stink about this, my family are in trouble and my own career is over. You only have to look at the bank statement: the account is in my name. They've got me both ways!

How can I say I never received a dime when the fuckin' account is in *my name*? And I don't even fuckin' know who they are or what they want!'

'How are you supposed to withdraw the money?'

'I can have it wired to my own bank in DC or, I suppose, withdraw it from Richmond.'

'And you've never met anyone other than the guy who first threatened you?'

Appleton shook his head. 'No. All dealings have to go through the bank.'

White stayed silent and studied him. There was no question that the man was in fear of his life. But White had an idea; he only hoped Appleton would play ball. 'Jim,' he said gently, 'where are the family?'

'There's no way you're going to involve my—'

White held up his hand. 'Jim, where are they?'

'They're in Baltimore. They went there two days ago. The kids aren't back at school for ten days.'

'Jim, I need you to trust me.' White told Appleton about the attack at his apartment. 'They must have followed me from here—'

Appleton was on his feet immediately. 'And you came back?' His voice was shrill. 'Jesus, White, you're—'

White remained seated. 'Jim, you haven't got any choice but to help me. I was very careful. We weren't followed here and there's no one watching the hou—'

'You don't know that!'

White finally stood up. 'Well, there's only one way of finding out. Pack a bag, Jim, and don't fuckin' argue! You're taking me to NordFund.'

'No way! I'll—'

White threw him a withering glance. 'You'll *what,* Jim? Spend the rest of your life waiting for them to tap you on the shoulder again? Wondering who it is they're trying to protect? And when they might get to the point of doing to you and your family what they may have done to Kelly? For whatever reason, Jim, they've decided to pay you off rather than bump you off, and you should be fuckin' grateful! But there's no way you're going to take the risk they might suddenly change their minds about you.' White could see Appleton debating with himself. 'Jim, you might hate my guts but at the moment you've got no choice but to trust me.'

As he waited for Appleton to decide, White hoped he was right.

Friedman tried to steer the car and reach for the cellular phone, which rang incessantly. He swore to himself and checked in the rear-view mirror; there was no traffic behind him on the road back into DC. He steadied the car and picked up his phone. 'John Friedman.'

'How was your meeting with Elizabeth, John?'

Oh no!

He tried to concentrate on the road ahead. He felt his throat constrict, a knot of fear hard and rigid in his stomach. 'Who is this?' he managed to mumble, his mouth suddenly dry.

'John, don't fuck about. You got our package?'

He dropped his speed, cradling the cellular behind his left ear. 'Listen, you *fuck*! You dare touch my mother, you piece of—'

'John, John! Relax!' Friedman felt his anger threaten to explode at the patronising tone of the caller. 'We were only giving you an example. We can get anywhere, John. Anywhere we want.' The voice was even more mocking now, cold and arrogant. 'Your mother's a pretty woman. You take after her! That's nice.' The man emitted a steely laugh.

'You *bastard*!' Friedman hissed back, his mind spinning furiously. He struggled to keep his car steady as the signs for DC drew nearer. 'How dare you call me on this phone?'

'John, you have a choice. I will give you some directions now. We need to meet with you. Tonight.'

'Go and—'

'John, I'd like to explain to you in person what will happen if you don't co-operate.' The man dictated an address in the north-east of DC. 'Be there.'

The line was cut.

McQuogue surveyed the men in front of him. There were twelve of them in all, seated around the conference table in the Roosevelt Room. He had positioned himself nearest the fire-place, just to the right of the President's chair. There were no windows in the room, which was womb-like and oppressive. The ceiling lights were bright and reflected off the long, polished table. The heating was on full and McQuogue balked at the airless, cloying atmosphere. He smelled coffee and the sweetness of male sweat.

He had called the meeting to thrash out the build-up to the meeting of the Democratic National Committee, which was scheduled for two weeks' time. The host city was Houston, a place McQuogue neither liked nor loathed. The meeting was designed to bolster Willard's run for re-election in a year's time. McQuogue was determined that Houston would be the launch of that campaign. 'OK,' he barked, calling the meeting to order, 'let's start.'

He allowed his deputy to run through the planned schedule. As he waited, he watched the reaction of the other men around the table. Some of them he liked; others he despised, but charmed. He was more prone to the former, but good at the latter. To his right, the chairman of the DNC was sweating and sighing loudly. McQuogue found Ron Fuller irritating; during Tyler's presidency, McQuogue had sidelined him. He had even, at one point, begun a campaign of leaking examples of Fuller's incompetence to the media. But the old codger had hung on, adroitly riding the storm, secure in the support of the party bigwigs over on the Hill.

McQuogue doodled on the pad in front of him, only half listening to the monologue that came from the other end of the table.

'OK, OK,' he cut in finally, eager to move the meeting to a quick conclusion. 'I'll present this plan to the President for his . . . er . . . approval.' He allowed the room to digest the reminder that it was he, rather than Willard, who essentially called the shots. 'I want a complete breakdown on campaign finance,' he went on, 'and predictions for how much more we need and where we'll get it from. Any questions?'

The men around him remained silent. McQuogue nodded and began to rise from his chair.

'Just one, Wayne.'

Half out of his chair, he stopped and glared at Fuller. 'Yes, Ron. What is it?' McQuogue sat down noisily.

The DNC chairman pulled himself up and smiled. The old man's suit was faded, the cuff of one sleeve frayed a little at the edges. The shirt did not match the tie,which did not match the suit. But for all his lack of style, Fuller was a wily and unpredictable foe. The others were watching him closely. 'Well, Wayne,' he purred, scratching the nape of his neck, 'I was just wondering about Elizabeth.'

McQuogue sat down, trying hard to contain his irritation. The room fell deathly silent. Fuller waited for just a few seconds more, then spoke again. 'I mean, we're all sorry about Tyler's death and wouldn't wish anyone to forget him. I know that Mrs Forrester would want us to carry on as normal. I haven't spoken to her today' – Fuller smiled gently at the hint of his (spurious) closeness to the former First Lady – 'but after the press stories about her supporting Willard, wouldn't it be right to include her in Houston? I mean, she's the most popular woman in America. I think we'd be insane not to utilise that.'

McQuogue shuffled his papers and thought quickly.

Elizabeth's public endorsement of Willard would be priceless. But McQuogue didn't trust her to play by the rules. 'Well, Ron,' he intervened, eager to regain the initiative, 'that is obviously a factor. Mrs Forrester's support is, I know, unconditional. But I'm not sure what you're getting at. We have to control this convention very carefully. Would it be wise to introduce a wild card?'

Fuller affected an astonished look. 'Wild card?' he barked, just a touch too loudly. 'I don't think anyone would consider Mrs Forrester to be that. After all, she is—'

McQuogue interrupted hurriedly. 'No, no, I didn't mean to denigrate her contribution, but Elizabeth will only say what she wants to say. She won't play ball for anyone other than her husband . . . well, his memory anyway.'

Fuller raised an eyebrow and glanced towards the end of the table.

'I don't agree, Wayne.'

The voice came from the far left. McQuogue leaned forward to catch sight of the speaker. Raymond Swains, one of the party's main fund-raisers. McQuogue willed himself to remain calm. He knew he had been ambushed. He had no choice but to allow Swains his moment.

'Carry on, Ray. I'd appreciate your thoughts.'

Swains waved away the compliment. 'Wayne, I agree with Ron. Mrs Forrester's endorsement would be a great boost. We need her in Houston. As far as I can see, if we don't persuade her to come on board, her refusal will haunt us throughout the campaign. And that ain't something that fills me with joy. Simple as that.'

'So?' McQuogue said perfunctorily. 'What do you have in mind?'

Fuller picked up the baton. 'Ask her to give the welcome speech. Get her on board, *quickly*. If Elizabeth Forrester welcomes the President to the meeting – I can just see it now – we're talking ten, fifteen points in the polls. The Republicans will crap themselves! There ain't nothing they can throw at us to beat that.

I tell you, that picture, Willard and Elizabeth embracing on the stage, it's dynamite. We've got to get her.'

McQuogue was thinking hard now. The plan had some merit.

'I'll run it past the President and see—'

'I already have.'

Fuller again.

McQuogue failed to conceal his astonishment. 'I'm not aware that the President is—'

Fuller was beaming from ear to ear. 'Oh, he is fully aware, Wayne. I spoke to him only this morning, before I came here. There were a few things he wanted to run past me.' He paused. 'Anyway,' he rushed on, his voice excited and rising in pitch, 'I just mentioned that Elizabeth would be a great bonus to his re-election campaign and he was mighty pleased by that suggestion. Shall I drop you a note on it, Wayne?'

'Fine,' McQuogue replied tersely, rising from his chair again. 'That's something we'll look at closely.'

The meeting was over, the swords resheathed.

McQuogue turned on his heel and was out of the door. He headed to the left, past the Oval Office (Willard was at a hospital opening in Boston), and marched back to his own office.

He entered the anteroom where his secretary, Kathleen, sat. He ignored her and strolled past into his office. Before sitting down, he turned back to close the door behind him. He was surprised to see Kathleen standing in the doorway.

'Mr McQuogue, there's an urgent message for you.'

He took the note from her hand and dismissed her gruffly before glancing at the message slip. McQuogue pulled his cellular out of his jacket. He did not need to recheck the message slip. He knew the number by heart.

Elizabeth yawned. Her head ached terribly. She sat back in the chair and massaged her neck, trying to release the tension. After a few seconds, she got up and crossed the drawing room. She opened the heavy oak door and walked into the hall. The Secret Service detail were two doors down; in the lobby of the cottage, the chandeliers reflected off the marble walls. At the sound of her heels on the floor, a young agent appeared in front of her.

'Good evening, Mrs Forrester. Is there anything you need?'

'No, I'm fine. Has Lee gone?'

'Yes, ma'am.'

'Fine . . . fine. Goodnight.'

Her legs felt heavy as she walked slowly towards the staircase. She clasped the handrail and willed herself to keep going. She didn't want an agent to see her so defeated.

On the mezzanine landing her staff had thoughtfully placed private pictures of her, ones they had brought from the White House. She stopped and looked at them.

Tyler was in every one.

She sat down on a bergère sofa and breathed out. She heard the agent quietly close the door downstairs. She was alone again. One more flight of stairs and she would be in her bedroom. But she felt far too exhausted to manage those last few steps. So she sat for a while, looking through the photographs: Camp David, Houston, a visit to Hawaii. She picked up a large silver frame and admired the image: it was a formal shot of herself and Tyler, taken for their Christmas card. She was wearing a purple Donna Karan evening dress, a diamond choker round her neck. Tyler was in black tie.

Elizabeth looked into his eyes: they shone in the photograph but to her, the woman who had known him best, they seemed lifeless, bland. She could feel her own eyes smarting. She did not want to blink, did not – *I'm going crazy* – did not want to miss anything.

'Were you, Tyler? Were you someone I didn't know?'

She flinched at the sound of her own voice echoing back at her in the empty hallway. She looked around. She was still alone.

She tried to recall her happiness when this picture was taken.

But she couldn't. She thought only of what Tyler had hidden from her, what noose had tightened around his neck. And what she had, finally, resolved to do about it.

Chapter Twenty-three

Thirty minutes later Friedman parked his car on 18th Street and hailed a cab. He tried not to think about Elizabeth. He sat back in the cab and gave the driver the address. Friedman allowed the driver to thread his way north. He watched as the neighbourhood gradually swallowed them up. In the dark, his destination looked almost exciting. Nightfall had softened its edges, smothered the blemishes and the scars, like a vigorous coat of black paint. In daylight it was different, of course. The shambles of its shuttered storefronts, the tornado of graffiti, the desolate weariness of the dead-eyed men who shuffled along its decrepit sidewalks like a chain gang deprived only of its restraints, all typified the decay of this neighbourhood, which was within sight, but not sound, of Capitol Hill.

The driver double-checked the address with him. Friedman ignored the curious stare in the rear-view mirror. Few people ventured here after dark. Even fewer in a suit and tie, and then only if they were in search of something illegal and lost enough to accept that they'd be lucky to venture back out unharmed.

Friedman played nervously with his watch. He tried again not to think about Elizabeth. Instead, he thought about himself, and his mother.

He checked the time. A full thirty seconds since he'd last done so: 12.30 a.m.

Friedman tipped the driver well and looked around him. He stepped off the sidewalk and hurried across to the call-box as instructed. The small bulb above it had been smashed; the metal canopy was battered and bent. He picked the receiver up; amazingly, a dialling tone purred back at him. He had the vague sense of being watched. There were certainly enough shadows around him.

When the signal came it was not from the telephone. He heard the engine before he saw the car, a low mechanical growl from around the corner. He tensed, more concerned that it might be a police vehicle than a criminal. As the sound grew louder, he tried to think up a cover story. In the end, he didn't need one. The car was an ordinary sedan, dark-coloured and in need of a wash.

The window was wound down, by hand. In the gloom, Friedman could not see inside.

'Get in the back.' The voice was nasal, East Coast, almost certainly New York. It was different from the polished, elegant vowels of the man on the phone.

Friedman hesitated, unable to think or to move. He wasn't allowed to hesitate long. 'I said get in the fucking car, otherwise you're gonna wet your pants.' The back door swung open. Friedman left the inadequate shield of the phone booth and moved towards the car. He bent down, stepping head first into the enclosed darkness.

'Good evening, John.'

He ignored the greeting and heaved the car door shut. 'I'm here for the first and only time. I mean that! How dare you—'

'John, shut the fuck up for a minute!'

The inside lights were switched off, the windows blackened. As his eyes adjusted to the darkness, he could make out the silhouette of a man sitting in front of him. His head was wreathed in the pale shadows.

It was the same voice. 'You do know that you have done the right thing, don't you?'

Friedman nodded, then realised his companion couldn't see him.

'Yes,' he murmured.

'Good. Excellent. I wanted to speak to you about a man called Mark White. He's a journalist. Do you know him?'

Friedman instinctively shook his head. 'Er, no . . . that name doesn't mean anything to me.'

'Are you sure?'

'Of course I'm fucking sure! Give me a break!'

'John, I find it hard to believe you do not know Mark White. It just doesn't make sense. We know Elizabeth sent an agent to Shenandoah. He was careless. A report was filed by the rangers there. We were able to trace a vehicle back to the Secret Service. What you have already told us confirms it was him. That wasn't very clever, blundering around Blue Ridge. Mr White also appears interested in Kelly. And you say you know nothing about White or anything else relating to Kelly?'

Friedman leaned back. The hard cover of the seat pressed uncomfortably against the small of his back. 'I've told you before, Mrs Forrester was, well, she was worried about Kelly. The agent went—'

'This was Mr Morrow?'

'Yes, it was. He went to Shenandoah but he didn't find anything.'

'Why is Mrs Forrester so keen to find out about Kelly?'

'I'm not sure.'

'Don't waste my time, John.'

'I'm *not!*'

'Has she seen the memo Kelly sent over to the White House?'

'No . . . or if she has, which I doubt, she hasn't told me.' He lied.

'John, there's a problem we'd like you to solve for us. You see, we want to make sure that Mrs Forrester stops looking into Kelly. Can you do that for us?'

Friedman's mind was reeling. 'No. What do you mean? I can't

tell her . . . look, how do you expect me to keep on at this? They're going to know it was me! They'll have to. I can't keep feeding you stuff without getting caught! I'll be ruined. You might as well publish those fucking pictures, it won't *matter!*'

'John, that's not going to happen. You know how this town works. Everyone has their spies. Listen to me – all you're doing is protecting yourself. Mrs Forrester will soon disappear into the background, and then all of this will be over. You'll get yourself another job, and you'll be in the clear. We have our own contacts, John. We can help you. We make sure that we look after the people who have helped us. Believe me, you're not the only one we deal with.'

'Oh, yeah,' Friedman snarled. 'What are you, all of a sudden? My mentor? Jesus!'

'I'm sorry you hate me, John. And I'm sorry if I hurt your head that day in the White House.'

Friedman struggled for breath. Panic overwhelmed him. 'My God, it was *you!*'

The man remained silent.

'Jesus! Oh, my God . . . you and Danello too? You . . . you *killed* him! Fuck, what am I doing—'

The man let the implied threat hang in the air for a while longer.

'You see,' he went on eventually, 'it's very important you tell us precisely what Elizabeth is up to. We don't go around mindlessly threatening people with violence. Have we ever threatened to harm you, John? Or your mother?'

'Oh, *right!* You—'

'John, let's keep it simple.' The man stopped talking and sighed noisily. 'If you come across Mark White, you must call us. And you must ensure that Mrs Forrester does not persist in her somewhat inconvenient obsession with Kelly. Is that clear?'

Friedman mumbled a reply. 'I have to go now . . . I've got to go! Mrs Forrester needs me early tomorrow—'

'Good, John. It's good you're being so professional about this.'

Friedman flinched as the door beside him swung open. He looked back into the darkness of the automobile.

'We'll be in touch, John,' came the familiar threatening voice from inside.

Chapter Twenty-four

'Good morning, John.' Elizabeth pushed her breakfast tray away. 'My God, you look *terrible*! Are you all right?'

He glanced up. His face was pale and skeletal. The skin around his cheekbones was pinched, his eyes deadened. 'I'm just tired, Mrs Forrester.'

Elizabeth sensed a nervousness about him. She put it down to fatigue and poured him coffee.

'Anyway, how are you feeling, ma'am?' he asked quickly.

She shrugged. 'Physically, I'm fine. What's new?' she asked casually.

Friedman grimaced. 'What I'm hearing,' Friedman replied, 'from the White House, is that they're still worried about how you'll stand regarding Willard and the election.'

He had Elizabeth's full attention now. 'Go on,' she muttered quietly, leaning back into the sofa, her eyes fixed on his face.

'One of the Communications people told me that McQuogue is going to approach you about giving the welcoming speech at the DNC meeting in Houston.'

Elizabeth laughed incredulously. 'He can't seriously expect me to do *that*? He's forcing Willard to overturn or dump nearly everything Tyler held dear, and now he wants me to throw my weight behind them! He's worried, isn't he, John?'

Friedman nodded. 'I would imagine so.'

Elizabeth snorted in disbelief. 'What does he really want? To make sure he can silence me? Get me on board in the hope I'll just forget the small matter that my husband may have been involved in a fraud with Ronald Kelly?'

'McQuogue doesn't necessarily know that.'

Elizabeth raised her hand. 'No . . . but he never does anything unless there's an endgame. He thinks that by flattering me he can prevent me from continuing with our investigation.' She stopped and held Friedman's stare. 'So when are they going to ask me?'

He took a manila folder from his briefcase and flicked through the pages. 'According to my source, later this week. Willard doesn't want to call you himself—'

'I bet he doesn't!'

'—so McQuogue will do it.'

'Incredible.'

She ran through the pros and cons of the White House offer in her head.

'OK, OK . . . where's this coming from? Who's put them up to it?'

Friedman shrugged. 'I can only guess it's the DNC. I hear Swains and Fuller are bending over backwards to get you on board.'

Elizabeth smiled. 'I know, they've both called me.'

He glanced up in surprise. 'They *what*?'

'They called me yesterday. One on the phone in the morning, the other following up with a "How are things going?" call later on. It wasn't exactly subtle but those two never were. Mind you, they supported Tyler, fought for him tooth and nail, so the least I could do was play along with them.'

'What did you tell them?'

'That I would think about it . . . I'd consider any suggestions but I would want to speak to Willard himself.' She was grinning now, unable to control herself. 'They said something else too . . . both of them.'

He responded to the hint. 'What?'

'They wanted me to think about the campaign . . . about how I might get involved a bit more. What my thoughts were on Willard. I was careful, very careful, but they'd expect that. It didn't stop them pushing, though. Certainly not Fuller. He could barely hold back from getting to the point of his phone call.'

She wanted to drag a response from Friedman, use his reaction to open up her own emotions.

'Mrs Forrester, you're torturing me here!' He smiled for the first time.

'John, they both asked me if I'd consider standing alongside Willard . . . if I'd be prepared to have my name put forward. They wanted to know if I'd accept a nomination for Vice-President.'

She savoured his incredulous stare. 'Get us some more coffee, John.'

Elizabeth paused, allowing the silence to linger. She examined him out of the corner of her eye. 'I need your advice,' she went on. 'I'm sorry, but you're just going to have to sit there and listen to me.' She smiled. 'I've been thinking hard, John, about what I should be doing, what people want me to do. And the more I think about what *I* should do, the more I keep coming back to Tyler. Why he did what he did, and why I stood by him even when I knew that our lives would be turned upside down. I kept at it, kept my mouth shut, because I loved him and respected him, and because I thought he could make a difference. God, I don't know . . . I thought I *knew* what I was going to say to you, what I needed to say, but . . .'

She rubbed one eye with the palm of her hand, reached over and took a sip of water.

'John, I don't know where this is going to lead us. I want you to tell me honestly whether I'm going half crazy or if I'm just angry because Tyler is dead and I've been left to pick up the pieces, to half kill myself worrying about what went on under his administration!'

'Mrs Forrester, are you saying you simply want to become Vice-President so you can launch an investigation into all of this?'

Elizabeth was startled by the astonishment in Friedman's voice. 'Well,' she said hesitantly, 'let's look at that as an option. What's the downside?'

He shrugged non-commitally. 'It's hard to say . . . first off, the party and the media would love the fact you were standing. Willard is hardly glamorous or exciting. With you on the ticket, he'd be almost guaranteed re-election. You know that. You were the most popular First Lady of modern times. After the President's death—'

'I'm the most popular widow?'

'In a sense, yes. The downside? The Republicans will start taking you apart. They'll try and crucify you on policy. What do you stand for? Are you just a clothes-horse? That would be the first line of attack.'

Elizabeth nodded her head wearily. 'Christ, is that all they can throw at me?'

'Well, it would only be the start. As VP, you'd be heir to the throne. Would the country accept a woman that close to the Oval Office? It's almost impossible to quantify, Mrs Forrester. You'd bolster Willard enormously, but you might harm yourself in the process.'

'Are you saying I shouldn't even consider it?'

Friedman fidgeted with his tie, coughed sharply, his face reddening. 'No, ma'am, I'm not. I just think you need to understand that you might be doing more for Willard than you would do for yourself. If you began to bring his ticket down, then McQuogue would heap the blame on you. In public they'd stick by you, but if Willard won then the White House would sideline you. At the moment you're of use to them. That's obvious. The polls are saying it nearly every day. You're right in one respect: people don't expect you to disappear. But they might not swallow you taking the nomination. Plus, you've been through a national campaign. Do you really want to put up with that again?'

'I know the risks, John. I was there with Tyler. What if I say no?'

'Then no one will ever know you were approached. But the party will still expect you to be onside. You're cornered: whichever way you turn, you're going to have to swing behind Willard. Your husband appointed him—'

'And anything I do to the contrary will look as if I'm putting Tyler down?'

'Yes, ma'am.'

'So as far as they're concerned, I've been caught. If I do support Willard, they'll take my endorsement and give me nothing in return and it means I won't be best placed to find out what was going on in Tyler's White House. They'll be able to watch my every move, and cover their tracks. If I *don't* back him, they'll say I'm just being spiteful?'

Friedman nodded.

'But what if I don't accept the nomination for Vice-President . . . what if I do something else?'

She saw the confusion in his face. 'What, John, if I refused just to play second fiddle? If I'm that important to the party, if I really want to uncover those bastards, maybe I should consider the things that drove Tyler to make *his* stand. Would that be the most ridiculous thing you'd ever heard?'

Elizabeth had expected Friedman to be shocked. She had had almost the exact same conversation with Tyler five years ago. It seemed such a long time now. Another universe, one in which they had felt elation and terror in equal measure.

But Friedman's reaction was more than just surprise. Elizabeth struggled to define it; this was a man who looked to be in fear of his life.

'Are you serious?' he said eventually.

Elizabeth clasped her hands together and peered off into

the middle distance. 'As serious as I've ever been . . . and as petrified.'

He said nothing in response.

Outside the sun had relinquished its presence at the window and the room was becoming dark. Elizabeth rose from the chair and switched on a lamp. She turned back to Friedman. 'You think this is just because of Kelly and Danello? Because I want to find out what the hell terrified my husband so much?'

'No, ma'am . . . I mean, the Kelly issue is separate—'

'Not entirely, John.'

'What do you mean?'

Elizabeth stood by the fireplace, her back to him. 'I'm not considering doing this just because I want to expose the bastards who sent these men to their deaths. As far as I know, they might have killed Tyler too.'

'Mrs Forrester—'

She waved aside the interruption. 'Oh, I don't mean actually killed him . . . but Tyler had been a fit man. Jesus, he'd had more medical check-ups than a certified hypochondriac. I don't know, maybe the stress, the fear . . . whatever it was that had been eating at him, whatever it is about that bank account, contributed to his death. In the days before he died, he was more . . . I don't know . . . withdrawn, *tense*. Maybe I'm rewriting history, seeing things with hindsight that weren't really there in the first place . . . but Tyler had read that memo from Kelly, whatever was in it, *wherever* it now is, and he kept that knowledge even from me.'

'And you think by doing this you can make it right?'

Friedman's voice almost cracked. Elizabeth glanced at him curiously. His eyes had sunk further into his gaunt face. He picked at his nails. He would have to get used to the pressure again; they all would.

'No, I don't think I can right it. I can hardly bring Tyler back . . . but I can at least pick up where he – where we – left off. I owe him that much surely. Perhaps I also owe it to myself.'

*

The Greyhound pitched a little as it took a curve, the sudden change throwing White against his companion. 'Sorry, Jim,' he muttered, pulling back the curtain.

Appleton ignored him.

White settled back into his seat in the economy section and looked around him. The commuters were engrossed in the morning's papers or sleeping. He yawned again; he did not envy people whose careers demanded such an early start. He looked out of the window, could make out the thin claret-coloured line on the horizon that heralded dawn. For the hundredth time that morning he pondered where he was, literally, heading. Appleton had reluctantly agreed to accompany him to Richmond; the Pentagon official had called in sick and, in darkness, Riordan had driven them to the bus station before returning to the *Herald*. White and Appleton had waited for the first early morning shuttle south.

Throughout the hours Appleton had been in White's company, he had hardly spoken. White worried that his companion was not up to the plan they had agreed, though he knew he had little choice but to go ahead with it.

From Richmond bus station, they took a cab into the city. The morning traffic was heavy and slow. Richmond was shrouded in a thick, grey mist, the streets sodden after intermittent downpours. When they reached downtown, the cab inched its way north.

Suddenly they shuddered to a halt. White looked at Appleton as he paid the driver. 'Jim, are you ready?'

For the first time he spoke. 'Mr White, don't you ever curse yourself for the lives you ruin?' White could see the tears forming in his eyes.

'Jim, I know—'

Appleton flung open the door. White hurried out after him and looked across the street. The office building was off to the left, a small, slightly dilapidated ten-storey structure that was dwarfed by its gleaming, cocksure neighbours. He looked at Appleton. 'Let's go.'

The two men entered the lobby of the building. In front of them, a black-and-white notice-board listed the resident companies. NordFund was on the fifth floor. They took the elevator and exited to find themselves in a circular lobby. In front of them two women sat behind a reception desk. They smiled as the men approached.

White felt slightly nauseous. It was up to Appleton now.

'Can we help you, gentlemen?'

Appleton hesitated only a second before replying. 'Yes, ma'am, we need to speak with Mr Cannon. He's with NordFund. Please tell him Jim Appleton and his attorney are here to see him.'

One of the women smiled back then spoke into a phone. 'Please take a seat over there,' she said eventually, pointing to a small office across the lobby. 'Mr Cannon will be with you shortly.'

They did not have long to wait. A well-groomed but featureless man in his late forties entered the room after a few minutes. He shook both men's hands. White watched him closely for any signs of tension or suspicion; outwardly, at least, there were none.

'So, Mr Appleton . . . Mr White . . . what can I do for you?'

Appleton spoke quickly. 'You hold one of my accounts here, Mr Cannon, although this is the first time I've visited you. My attorney and I are in Virginia on business. I wish to make other deposits to the account but I also have some queries. Can you check the present balance?'

Cannon smiled. 'Of course. May I see some ID?'

Appleton handed over his driver's license. Cannon glanced at it briefly, then handed it back. 'What is the account number?'

Appleton passed over the document he had retrieved from his safe.

Cannon looked at it, smiled again, then spoke. 'Come with me, gentlemen.'

They followed him along a corridor that led towards the

back of the building. Finally he opened the door to a small but expensively furnished office. He waved them towards two leather armchairs, then sat opposite them behind the vast antique desk that dominated the room.

'So, first of all, Mr Appleton, may I say it's a pleasure to meet you at last. NordFund is always delighted to welcome new customers.' The smile was glued on to his face. 'You mentioned you had a query on your account. What specifically?'

White prayed that Appleton would remember the pitch they'd rehearsed in DC.

He need not have worried. 'Mr Cannon, the deposit of one hundred and twenty-five thousand dollars of five days ago was made by Vale Investments. We are currently in business with them and I understand you are also their bankers. However, that payment should not have been made.' Appleton smiled weakly. 'I'm afraid we are in the unique position of having to query a deposit. Are you in a position to return the moneys to Vale Investments?'

Cannon nodded. 'Certainly. The papers can be drawn up immediately. Let me just check.' He signed on to the computer in front of him. After a few seconds he grimaced then typed in more codes. White watched him; he wished he could see what Cannon was reading.

'Mr Appleton, you are correct . . . Vale Investments is registered with us so reimbursing them would be no problem. I do not handle their accounts, however. That is done by Mr Calthorp, our Chief Executive Officer.'

White intervened for the first time. 'Forgive me, Mr Cannon, but my client wishes to contact Vale Investments. He—'

'Sir, you must surely have some idea where Vale Investments operates from?'

'Yes, we do,' White went on, 'but, you see, we have been unable to get any reply from them, despite extensive correspondence. My client wishes to reimburse them the money but we have to be certain, in the circumstances, that Vale Investments is still trading. Mr Cannon, I am here to ensure my client doesn't repay a company that, as far as we can tell, no longer exists.'

Cannon did not reply at first. He checked the computer screen in front of him, then looked back at White and Appleton. 'I'm sorry, gentlemen, but there is absolutely no way I can divulge any details of Vale Investments. And I have to say this is a most peculiar request. NordFund is a private bank, Mr White, and as such we are not obliged to divulge any details about our clients.' He smiled at the two men. 'For example, you would hardly wish me to hand over your own private details.'

White glanced at Appleton then back at the banker opposite him. 'Mr Cannon, we have not been entirely truthful with you.'

He watched as Cannon shifted in his chair.

'You see,' White went on, 'the money from Vale Investments is only part of what they owe us. We do not wish to return *any* moneys to them – we wish to get more out of them. Can you assist us in that matter?'

Cannon shook his head. 'Absolutely not. I'm afraid, gentlemen, this is a matter for the civil courts, not for us.'

'And Mr Calthorp will be of no assistance?'

Cannon appeared uncomfortable with the question. 'I doubt it. Do you wish me to ask him?'

White thought quickly. 'Yes,' he replied. 'If you could . . .'

Cannon picked up the telephone. White heard him speak briefly to Calthorp and explain the situation. He looked at the two men sitting opposite him then replaced the receiver. 'Mr Calthorp wonders if you would mind waiting for a few moments in reception.'

White and Appleton returned to the lobby. White watched the clock: after fifteen minutes of sitting in silence he nudged Appleton. 'Jim, I need to have a smoke . . . I'll tell them we'll be back in fifteen minutes.'

White informed the receptionists then joined Appleton in the elevator. They exited the building into the mid-morning crowd. Across the street a diner was open, its plate-glass windows advertising the daily specials, limp lace curtains looped back unevenly. White took hold of Appleton's elbow and led him across the street.

The sound of a car screeching to a halt made him spin round.

White watched as three men got out of the car, which had come to a halt directly in front of the NordFund building. He could hear Appleton's voice from inside the diner. 'White, are you—'

He stepped into the hot, busy diner. Through the windows, he watched as the men rushed into NordFund. Within a minute, they were back on the sidewalk. They had been joined by a middle-aged man in his fifties and one other: Cannon. The bank official seemed bewildered.

The small group hurriedly checked the sidewalk to either side of them, desperately searching the crowds.

White had a good idea who their quarry was.

Then, Cannon suddenly pointed across the street. The men turned and stared at the diner.

White felt his stomach lurch.

Cursing to himself, he dashed to the back of the room. Appleton sat in a chair, his head slumped forward. White hurried up to him and whispered, 'Jim, get moving! Do *not* fight me! *Just go!*' He took hold of Appleton's arms and dragged the man after him. Swing-doors led into a small corridor. To the left were the bathrooms, a small hatch opening on to the kitchen. White pulled Appleton along with him. At the end of the corridor was a fire door. White yanked at the handle, then kicked the door open on to a courtyard.

'They're on to us, Jim! Just keep *moving!*'

An alleyway ran off the courtyard. The two men threw themselves down it. Within a minute they were on to the sidewalk. Opposite was a department store, its windows festooned with sales signs. White grabbed hold of Appleton again and lurched into the oncoming traffic. The sound of car horns and drivers suddenly braking shattered the calm of the street. White knew it would advertise their presence but he didn't care.

Within seconds they were in the store. They pushed through the crowds of shoppers, hurrying towards the back. White checked behind them. There was no one on them. Not yet.

They sped through the sports department, White pushing aside the rails of clothes. A sign marked 'Personnel Only' was visible to their left. He grabbed Appleton and pushed him through the door. They were into a large cavernous storeroom. At the far end, yet another door opened on to daylight. They reached it within seconds and hurried through. The delivery area was busy, trucks and forklifts parked to their left. A burly man turned towards them, a look of astonishment on his face. 'Hey! You can't—'

White picked up speed, propelling Appleton forward. They crossed the lot and hurtled through the gateway. White could feel his lungs closing in on him. Appleton did not seem breathless, but when White glanced at him his face was devoid of blood, his eyes fixed in a terrified stare. Passers-by muttered expletives as the two men pushed past.

The crowds opened up. White could see a cab rank opposite. He almost cried with relief. They lunged into a cab and White screamed instructions. 'To the bus station! Now! Quick! Go!'

The startled driver threw the vehicle into gear and gingerly pulled out into the traffic. White leaned towards the man and screamed again, 'I said move it, bud! Like *real* quick!'

The driver shot him an outraged look but followed his orders. The cab shot through the traffic and hurtled round a corner.

White swivelled in his seat and looked behind him. Two men had just exited the delivery yard. They stood motionless, glaring at the crowds around them.

He caught his breath and looked at Appleton. 'You OK?' he said gingerly, wiping the sweat from his forehead.

Appleton had begun crying. Tears saturated his cheeks; his

eyes were red and swollen. He looked accusingly at White. 'What have you done to me? What—'

'Jim, listen to me!' He grabbed Appleton's shoulder. 'Have you somewhere you can go? Where are your family? Jim?'

Appleton had begun sobbing. White ignored a contemptuous stare from the cab driver. 'Jim, answer me, for fuck's sake! Have you got somewhere to go? I'll—'

'My best man's place.' Appleton's voice was garbled, choked. 'It's in Baltimore. My family are staying with him for a few days' vacation.'

'Can anyone trace you there?'

He shook his head. 'No . . . no.' His voice broke again and he slumped forward in the seat.

'Jim, go there. Ring your office. Tell them you're sick. Do not tell anyone where you are!'

Appleton suddenly lunged at him. His hands took hold of White's jacket and his face was thrust forward, eyes blazing. 'And what *then*, White? What *then*?' Spittle soaked White's face, making him blink. 'Can you answer me that, Mr Journalist! What *then*?'

White gently took hold of Appleton's fingers and peeled them off his jacket. Appleton put his head in his hands. White stared ahead as the cab hurtled towards the bus station.

'I don't know, Jim,' he muttered. 'I'm sorry, I just don't know.'

White watched the *Herald* building. He was at the back of the complex, in a small sidestreet used only by the security staff. He had remained in the shadows for nearly half an hour: he'd checked that the cars to his left and right were empty and there were no passers-by. He held his breath and ran across the street.

The small entrance opened up to a Plexiglas-screened reception area. White smiled at the guard behind the window. He pulled his ID from his jacket and pushed it up to the screen. 'Can you ring up to Mick Riordan? Tell him to meet down here?'

The guard shrugged and made the call.

Riordan emerged from the elevator within two minutes. 'Whitey! What—' He stopped and looked at White. 'Are you OK?'

White put his finger to his lips and nodded at the door behind him. The two men left the building. 'Mick, I'll tell you what happened but you've got to get me someplace safe.'

Riordan didn't answer. He checked the street ahead. It was empty apart from a Federal Express truck parked by the far corner. He turned round and waved at White. An alleyway led round to the left. The two men walked down it quickly. Ahead was a small blue door. Riordan yanked it open. It led through to the carport of the office building behind the newspaper. They scurried across the echoing chamber.

'Mick, where are we going?' White hurried to keep up with his colleague.

'Whitey, just stick with me.'

They exited on to 17th Street. The parked cars were thicker on the ground but there was no one on the sidewalk. Riordan turned right and picked up speed. He was almost running.

'Where's your car, Mick?' White whispered, his breath short.

Riordan shook his head. 'Nah, we don't need that. You're staying at Mort's. There's a bedroom above the bar. He'll clear it for you. No one knows it's there.'

'Mick!' White stopped and threw his hands up in frustration. 'If they've managed to follow me home, and trace me to the hotel, then they're damn well going to check I'm not propping up the fucking bar at McReedy's! I haven't even told you what happened with Apple—'

Riordan walked back and tugged at White's jacket. 'Later, Whitey! Mort's is the best place. It's all alarmed and there's a panic button connected to the PD. It's the best I can do within three minutes.'

It took them five minutes to make it to the block that backed on to McReedy's. Riordan knew the way blindfold. The entrance was dark, the only light from a security lamp by the street corner.

'How the hell do you know every back alley in DC, Mick?'

Riordan grunted. 'I've spent my life in the gutter, Whitey. It helps.'

Twenty yards down, the alleyway veered off to the right. Cardboard boxes were stacked along one wall, the narrow space slimy and covered in litter. Riordan checked around them once more. He then knocked on an unmarked wooden door. One knock. Then two. Then two more. The recognised signal to be let in.

Mort appeared in the shadow of the doorway. He didn't speak but waved the two men in. Once the door was locked shut, he peered at his visitors. 'Whitey, what happened to your face?'

'I'll tell you in a sec.'

Riordan pushed Mort back into the bar then reappeared within a minute. He held up a key. 'This is for you.' He handed it to White. 'Come with me.'

White followed him up the stairs. At the top, Riordan unlocked a small door. Inside, the room was tiny but clean: a day-bed and desk, a curtained window. Riordan opened another door ahead of them and glanced back at White. 'You've even got an *en suite*.'

White slumped on to the bed. 'What the hell is this? A brothel?'

'Nah. Mort sometimes spends the night in town. He used to let the staff use this room; his own is next door.' Riordan looked closely at White. 'So, tell me.'

White related what had happened in Richmond.

'Then NordFund is in on the scam?' Riordan said finally.

White nodded. 'It has to be.'

'Are you sure Appleton will be OK?'

White nodded. 'I put him on the bus to Baltimore. I've told him to stay quiet for two weeks . . . then to call you, leave a number and we'll get back to him.'

'What *with*, Whitey?'

'You're not the first one to ask me that.' He yawned and looked around him. 'Mick, I need to sleep.'

Riordan made his goodbyes and left him alone. White tried to settle in the strange room. A few seconds later, he heard footsteps on the stairs.

'It's only me, Whitey!'

'Mort, don't worry about me. Just lock up tight and set the alarms. I'm fine. I've got Riordan's cellular, it's—'

'If you think I'm leaving you in my bar alone, then you're stupid. I don't care who wants to break your legs. You're not getting near my vodka.'

Chapter Twenty-five

The next morning, White slipped back into the *Herald*'s office. Riordan met him at the security entrance. 'You sleep?' he asked, holding the elevator open.

White nodded. 'Yeah. I just thought it would be better to meet you here.'

He had banked on the fact that security was tight in the *Herald* building. CCTV cameras covered every entrance. Two guards sat at reception only yards from his desk.

White couldn't help but appreciate the irony. Only a short time ago he had loathed coming into the office. Now it was his refuge.

Almost immediately, he rose from his desk and quickly made his way towards the reference library at the back of the news floor. He swung through the doors and walked towards the counter, breathing a sigh of relief. One of his favourite librarians stood facing him.

'Jesus, Whitey, you look like shit. Are you—'

'I'm fine, Brett. Can I just use the terminals at the back? If anyone comes asking for me, I'm not here and you haven't seen me.'

White hid himself at the back of the room, behind a stack of reference books. He picked up the phone in front of him and dialled Riordan's mobile.

'Yeah?'

The Irishman's customary bark made him flinch.

'It's Mark. Where are you?'

'Jesus, I've only just left you! I'm on my way to a drugs bust-up over in Shaw-Howard. Whaddya want?'

'I forgot to ask you, have you got that vehicle registration check yet? Can you do it now?'

'Fuck, Whitey, your timing is perfect. My friend hasn't come back to me. OK, listen, I know what I'll do. I'll be with some PD guys in, like, ten minutes. I know one of them real well. I'll see if he'll slip over to the black-and-white and run it through for me. I'll call you back, Whitey.'

'The library number. I need to do a check on NordFund.'

Riordan grunted his approval and signed off. White replaced the receiver and pulled his notes from his jacket pocket. He checked the details he remembered from the meeting at NordFund. After ten minutes, he was finished. He rose and strode towards Brett.

'Can I smoke in here?'

'Whitey, it's a fucking *library*, man. What do you think?' the young man replied, rolling his eyes.

Before White could argue with him, the telephone behind them rang. White dashed back around the bookshelf and picked it up.

'Whitey?' It was Riordan. 'Are you sitting down?' Despite the jocularity, White could sense the tension in his friend's voice.

'What is it, Mick?'

'Okay, I don't know what this means but this is what I've got. According to my guy, the car outside your apartment was registered to a company . . . Vale Investments.'

'*Jesus*! We were right!'

'I know.'

'Is there any more?'

'No, just the fact that it's registered to that company and the address for the office building. Well, that's what he said. Do you want me to check it again?'

'No, leave this with me.'

White finished the conversation and returned to the computer screen. Having signed on, he chose the databank he wanted and waited. The instructions appeared in front of him. He typed in Vale Investments and waited for the search to continue. After a few seconds, the screen purred into life.

The list was long. The business search had uncovered over two hundred companies of that name. White began flicking through them. It took him fifteen minutes to find the right one.

The address in DC matched that given to Riordan by the local cops. But there was no other information on the company. No mention of a registered agent or any other directors. White turned away from the screen and signalled to the librarian.

'Brett—'

'No, you *still* cannot smoke.'

'It's not that,' he said, turning back to the screen. 'Do you know how to work this thing?'

The young man joined him at the terminal.

'What are you looking for?'

'Well, this company . . . Vale Investments. It's not giving me any more info. What the outfit does, who owns it, the directors . . . that sort of shit.'

Brett shooed White out of the chair and took his place in front of the screen. He began searching through different directories. Each time he came up with nothing, he scratched his head and clicked his tongue in frustration.

'You think these guys are still trading?' he asked White.

'Not sure. Why?'

'Well, there's nothing coming in on them. Tax accounts, employee directory, trading associations. Nothing. How old is the company?'

'Nine months.'

'Mmm. But they could have been shut down, right?'

'Maybe.'

Brett returned to the screen. 'Ah, here you have it,' he said finally as his fingers skimmed across the keyboard. 'Thought so. It's defunct, Whitey. No records. They must have gone under.'

White swore loudly and banged his fist against the desktop. 'That's not possible! I've been to their office.'

'Well, there's nothing on them . . . you could try the business guys, see if they have anything. But I don't think they'll be in the office yet.'

'OK,' White said, double-checking the name of NordFund's Chief Banking Officer. 'Try Calthorp and a bank, NordFund, based in Richmond.'

This time the computer responded positively. Five articles appeared. The first four were purely financial, reporting the bank's role in one or two deals. Brett scrolled down. The last feature was more informative: it covered a controversy three years ago when NordFund and Calthorp had been named, among others, as major players in a bad property deal in New Jersey. White noted that it had been in the first month of Tyler's presidency.

'Is there anything else on NordFund?'

Brett scrolled down farther. 'No, all the quotes come from an anonymous PR company. No names.'

White swept his eyes across the room. Then he stopped and looked at Brett. 'This whole place is computerised, right?'

'Most of it.'

'What about the old cuttings files, the paper ones? Are they all gone?'

'No. You see, the thing about the *Herald* is that it's virtually the only paper in the entire country that hasn't fully switched over yet. The bosses are too tight-assed to make the investment.'

White nodded. He had heard about it. Although their newspaper now operated on computers, the *Herald*'s holding company, a conglomerate based in Chicago, refused to give the tabloid the very latest equipment. It had been a long-standing sore point with the newspaper's management: the overlords viewed the *Herald* as a profitable but disreputable sideline. They seemed almost embarrassed about owning it.

Brett leaned back and smiled. 'And then, of course, there's Mr Belch.'

'What about him?'

'Well, when the management told him they weren't going to make the investment he wanted, he refused to throw out all the old files. It was a stand-off: they wanted to sell off parts of the building, but Bletchman said he wouldn't have the old files cleared out until the new computers were brought in. Seems he held his corner. We only started moving them last week.'

White smiled and slapped the young man on the back. 'Brett, can you take me down there, like, now?'

'Whitey, I'm the only one on. If there's a prob—'

'Five minutes, Brett. Please?'

They descended by the back stairs. It had been years since White had ventured into this part of the building. The corridors were decrepit and dark; the carpeting ancient. Most of the floor was deserted, waiting for the Chicago bosses to lease it out. Brett led White to the far end of a narrow corridor. A steel door blocked their entrance. The young man unlocked it, swung it open and turned on the lights.

The smell was overwhelming. A dank, musty odour of old paper. It wasn't unpleasant, just strangely unsettling. The fluorescent lights were dull and sporadic. Much of the room was in semi-darkness. In front of White, metal cabinets ran the length of the wall. Each cabinet contained stories published by the *Herald* before 1970. They were categorised by subject and name.

'Where do we start?' he asked.

Brett shook his head sadly. 'Well, remember, before the paper was bought in 1970, it was called the *Washington Star*. So a lot of these files will be from the *Star* days. They're all alphabetical and cross-referenced. But it won't be easy. They're in one hell of a mess.'

White nodded towards the line of filing cabinets in front of them. 'OK, let's go play Alphabet City.'

For twenty minutes, they carefully read through the ancient bits of newspaper. The N package contained no mention of NordFund or Calthorp.

White picked up the Vs. Some of the cuttings were so old that the print had faded, the paper torn and yellowed.

From time to time, Brett would dart to the back of the room, cross-checking another file. White lit a cigarette and ignored Brett's objections.

He had completed two packages when Brett spoke. 'Er, this might just be something . . .'

White looked at him. Brett was unfolding a double-page feature.

'Well, it might be nothing. But this was under Building Works. One of the Vale companies was cross-reffed to this package.' He stopped and began reading the feature. 'It's dated 1967. According to this, a building won a design award and this Vale company was part of the consortium. The original cutting had the company down for Oakview. But you said DC, right?' He handed the cutting to White.

> One of the contractors, Vale Wishman of Oakview, was so pleased with the results of the Arlington project that it has raised the possibility of moving its Headquarters there. Senior vice-president Leonard Calthorp said: 'Business is always on the move!'

Calthorp worked for Vale?

White laid the cutting at his feet. 'Would there be anything on Calthorp in these cuttings? Can we check?'

'Sure.'

He waited as Brett retreated back into the filing stacks. He could hear drawers being opened and closed.

'Only a little, Whitey,' Brett shouted as he made his way back to the front of the room with a small envelope. He handed it to White. 'I've got to get back to the office, otherwise—'

'OK, OK.'

Back in the library, Brett rushed to answer a phone. White retreated to his desk and opened the Calthorp package. The first few articles were from the late seventies. Nothing had been written since then. He began to read. The stories covered the period of urban growth around the Beltway during the Nixon and Carter administrations. The Calthorp mentioned in the story was by now the sole director of a major property firm. According to one short profile, he had come to Washington from the south a decade or so before.

White read on.

The rest of the stories were inconsequential, fleeting references to Calthorp's involvement in condos and marinas in Maryland and the Washington suburbs. There were no quotes from him and, according to the directories, no cross-referencing on photographs. There was no mention that he had joined NordFund.

White continued reading. His eyes were aching. The last story covered a meeting that had taken place in the late seventies of an organisation called the Christian Organisation for America. According to the small report, the COA had opened an office in DC a year or so before Reagan's victory. It was a lobby group dedicated to spreading Christian values in business. The meeting had only attracted attention because one of the organisation's directors, Ralph Pierce, was a former associate of Robert Welch. In the late fifties, Welch had steam-rollered the John Birch Society, the right-wing group that had immortalised Birch, a Second World War casualty who had become a figurehead for anti-communist radicals in the US. The John Birch Society grew rapidly in the early sixties and came closest to legitimacy when right-wing Republican Barry Goldwater launched his presidential campaign, before scandal and dissent weakened the Society's core.

At the very end of the story, a list of Washington businessmen involved in the COA included the name Leonard Calthorp.

White returned to the main search directory and typed in COA. He waited for the computer to respond. A handful of leads flickered up on to the screen. According to the files, the organisation had only flirted with Washington under Reagan. It seemed to have petered out in the mid eighties.

White restlessly read through. Neither Calthorp nor NordFund warranted a mention in any of the stories. He scrolled forward to the last few and called them up.

He almost missed it.

At the bottom of the final story, lost amid the mundane quotes above it, Calthorp's name was mentioned. The first computer search had not found him. He and Brett had been looking in the wrong directory.

White leant forward and studied the screen.

> The COA was surprised to hear yesterday of the defection of one of its associate directors. Mr Leonard Calthorp, a former director of Vale Holdings and CEO of NordFund, was said to have retired from the board because of a 'crisis of conscience'. No details were forthcoming from Mr Calthorp.

White reread the story and made notes. He turned off the screen and retreated to the front of the library.

'Brett, will there be anyone on in Pictures?'

The young man raised his eyes from the magazine he was reading. 'No, I doubt it. Why?'

'Well, I just want to cross-check on the picture files. See if they have anything on this Calthorp guy.'

White quickly found the relevant cabinet. The drawer he was looking for was halfway down. He opened the 'Cal' files and began flicking through.

He found it almost immediately.

He retrieved the photograph from the envelope and looked at it. It showed a group of men, all in suits, obviously standing on some sort of podium. The photograph was dated 1979. He quickly read the line of names along the bottom. Leonard Calthorp was the last. White looked at the man in the photograph.

Calthorp was dressed sombrely, in a black suit. The men with him were laughing and smiling, but he was impassive. White could not be certain but it seemed that Calthorp was moving in the picture. His face was slightly blurred and his right hand had risen to his forehead, as if to shield himself from the camera lens. White walked back to the reception desk and opened his attaché case. He began to put the photograph in it. Then he stopped. He had missed it the first time. His entire attention had been focused on finding Calthorp. He examined the photograph again.

That familiar smile and strong jaw, two men down from Calthorp.

Wayne McQuogue, later White House Chief of Staff to Tyler Forrester and Willard Morgan.

The house was the size of a suburban garage. A small window was to the left of the front door. Above it two more windows. The flower boxes were full of red-and-white daisies. The quaint colonial style was accentuated by the slope of the street, the entire house leaning to the right as if resting.

Friedman stood opposite it for a few minutes. Down the hill he could see the yachts of Annapolis harbour. Tourists in garish outfits wandered aimlessly, gawking at the quaint marina. A couple of midshipmen, dressed in pristine white, sauntered along the sidewalk eating ice cream.

He waited for a tourist group to pass by before crossing the road. He lifted the brass knocker, let it fall loudly against the blue door, and waited. After a few moments it was opened.

'John, my God, what a surprise! What time is it?'

He kissed his mother.

Patricia Friedman was shockingly beautiful. Her auburn hair had just been washed: he could smell the shampoo. Her face was long, the bones fine, tilting upward to eyes that were green and round. She wore a simple lilac trouser suit, no jewellery.

'Why didn't you ring, John, and let me know? Are you alone?' Patricia Friedman scanned the street behind her son.

'Yes, Mom. Just me.'

Friedman pushed past his mother. He heard her lock the door behind them. He carried on down a small hall and into a huge room, much bigger than the outside dimensions of the house would suggest. It ran all the way through to a large garden at the back; a study and dining area were through to his left. He could smell coffee.

'There's nothing for dinner,' his mother said. 'I ate earlier, but if you want I can—'

'Mom, I'm fine. I was just near by, thought I'd say hi.'

'Were you working out here?' Patricia stood looking at her son. 'Well, what's the news? Tell me all.'

She strolled through to the kitchen, Friedman following her. She fussed with a bottle of wine, taking two glasses out of a sideboard. 'Open this,' she said, handing him the bottle. 'You know where the opener is. I've left the radio on upstairs.'

She hurried from the room. He could sense her excitement, the jerky movements of her steps revealing her joy at the arrival home of her only child. He closed his eyes, steadied himself.

He was grateful for the time alone. He had wanted to come here, saw little enough of his mother as it was, but he had driven to Annapolis because his family home had beckoned to him like a lighthouse. Now that he was here, he had to try to avoid the emotional rocks.

The futility of his own actions made him tremble again.

Friedman knew that if his tormentors wanted to get to his mother, they could. Maybe would. There was little, if anything, he could do about it.

'I spoke to Aunt Judy. She sends you her love.' Patricia handed him a glass. 'She wonders why she hasn't heard from you, but by now we all understand that someone as *important* as you can't give much time to your own family.'

The criticism was tender, unaccusatory.

'Anyway, she's invited me . . .'

He half listened as his mother recounted the family news.

He felt like crying out to her and struggled for control, panic battling with the desire not to alarm the person who loved him more than anything else, whose instincts were selfless.

'Mom, there's something—'

'And then I hear a knock on the door and it's a young man you once knew at Harvard.'

He snapped to attention. '*What?*'

'Yes, he was in your class. Oh, what was his name? Er, Jack . . . yes, Jack something.'

I don't know a Jack.

His mother looked at him expectantly. Friedman hoped his panic didn't show. Silently he scanned his memory, willing his college days to reveal a familiar face, a recollection that would assuage his galloping terror.

I wasn't at school with any Jacks.

'He came here?'

His mother nodded. 'Yes, a few hours ago. Oh, what a shame you missed him! He said he was in Annapolis on business, had your old address and was just dropping by. I told him you were up in DC. He stayed for half an hour, talking about your college days. You never told me about Courtney! Why didn't you—'

Friedman managed to place the wineglass on the table beside him without spilling its contents. 'Mom, this is *real* important! How does he look this . . . er, Jack?'

'Oh, a bit older than you. He said he'd joined the class two years late. Nice man. Told me he was spending a few days in Maryland, might drop by again if you were around. I said I thought that was unlikely. You didn't manage to get out here much.' She looked at her son. He recoiled before the loneliness etched on her face. He longed to tell her that his own isolation was more paralysing. But, of course, he couldn't. No son could tell a widowed mother that.

'Damn it, I nearly forgot!' she went on, oblivious to his inner torment. 'God, I'm getting old. He left you a number. Said you should call him.'

She rose from the chair and opened the drawer of a lowboy. The polished antique wood glistened in the light from the fire. She turned back, handing him the piece of paper. Friedman looked at the telephone number. It was a 202 area code. Washington.

He blinked, forced another smile and pocketed the note.

'Honey, why don't you rest here for a few days? Take some time off,' she went on. 'We'll take the boat out. The yard are still taking care of it for me, it will be fun. Can you do that?'

Friedman longed to say yes, to collapse in front of her and let *her* protect *him*.

Instead, he shook his head. 'No, Mom.' He glanced at his watch. 'And I'd better go. I just wanted to say hi.' He put the glass down and stood up. He hoped she couldn't see he was trembling.

'But you've been here less than five minutes, John! I've opened a bottle specially. Honestly, I don't—'

He leaned forward and kissed his mother on the forehead. She sank against his chest, her bony arms holding him tight. He could smell her perfume. She felt small – *so small* – in his grasp, as if he could snap her in half, as if he were comforting her, not the other way round. He would call her tomorrow. When things were different, if not better. Tell her to go to Aunt Judy's, invent a reason. He didn't want to alarm her now. Didn't have the strength to explain or to lie.

Her head rested against his breastbone, their breathing in

unison. Friedman peered over her shoulder at the warm, welcoming fire.

He wondered at what point other children saw that their parents were merely mortal. When they finally realised that the child had become the protector. That they had to lie to them. Often.

Chapter Twenty-six

It was the kind of evening Elizabeth would have marvelled at once. The sky was turquoise, the first grey of early evening diluting the brightness. On the Potomac, a neat flotilla of pristine white boats slid downriver. The lawns lay thick and faultless in front of her.

Elizabeth turned to her right, making her way to the back of the house. The shadows gathered here, limp and cool. She nodded to the young agent who stood guard.

The impotence of her own position infuriated her.

She carried on walking, loafers sinking into the carpet of grass. Morrow followed behind. A small copse opened up just a little to the west of the house. A narrow path led down and through the curtain of moss and branches. She followed it, watching her step. It was cold under the canopy that rose and swayed above her. She stopped and looked around. It was so quiet, the only sound her own breathing and the snap of a branch as Morrow came to a halt ten feet behind her.

Tyler.

It all seemed to close in on her.

She pushed the thoughts away.

There was something else she had to concentrate on.

She emerged from the woods. She was surprised by how far

from the house she'd walked, and she waited for Morrow to catch up with her. 'How long have I been out, Lee?'

'Nearly an hour, ma'am.'

She smiled. 'Is John here yet?'

He nodded. 'Yes, he's just arrived. The detail radioed but I didn't think you wanted to be disturbed.'

Elizabeth thanked him and strode towards the house.

Friedman rose from his chair as Elizabeth entered the room. She began talking immediately, barely giving him time to sit back down.

'If I do this, John, and I'm not saying that I will, there's something you should know . . .'

He did not interrupt her. He perched on the edge of his seat, his knees tight together. His hands were clasped and rested in his lap. Elizabeth thought she noticed them tremble slightly.

'I have to trust you, John. I do anyway, but what I'm about to tell you will shock you. I have to face up to things that happened a long time ago, and which I now regret. You're the only person who will hear this. I never told Tyler. I don't think our marriage would have survived it, and I've lived with that thought ever since.'

Then she told him.

'I didn't like him at first.' Elizabeth smiled and closed her eyes. 'So after we'd been introduced I played the usual games, pretending I didn't know who he was, ignoring him at lectures. He probably thought I was a snob. I ran with a set that spent its time photocopying anti-war leaflets, picketing the dean's office, marching along Main Street.

'I was lying to myself, of course. There was something about him . . . I couldn't stop thinking about him – whether I'd been so rude he would just get bored and find someone else. Anyway, after we'd stopped fencing with each other, he invited me for a drink and I went. It was the first time he made a pass at me. I hit him. Hard. Then I stormed out of the bar and vowed never to speak to him again.

'I didn't see him for ages until at a lecture he suddenly plonked himself down right next to me. I was mortified . . . but flattered, so damn flattered. He sat back, stretching his long legs out in front of him, hands behind his head, just smiling to himself. God, he was infuriating! Afterwards he chased me down the hall, begging forgiveness. I went with him for coffee, but only, I told him, in order to make him stop his pathetic whining. Coffee went on into dinner and then he walked me home, not even asking to be invited in.'

She watched Friedman blush. She had never been this intimate with him before. But now she had to be. If they were both in this together, he had to know. However hard it was to tell him.

'We fell in love very quickly. Neither of us actually sat back and analysed it. I was too embarrassed to admit I was falling for one of the campus Lotharios. I kept it from my friends; refused to get up in the morning until his room-mate had left. Amazingly, no one ever found out. At lectures I insisted on ignoring him, and to meet me he would have to drive ten miles to a bar where I knew there would be no students. It went on like that for three months. He was my first. I knew I wasn't his.'

'Mrs Forrester, you don't have to tell me—'

'John, I do! If it comes out, then you and I will have to deal with it. You're going to be the one handling the damage limitation.'

Elizabeth shrugged her shoulders and sat back in her chair.

'I told him I was pregnant five weeks later. He looked at me like I was playing a joke. But then he could see I was trying not to cry and he told me it was OK, that we'd sort it out. "If you want the baby, then we'll have it. We'll settle down after college. It will be fine." I fought hard not to believe him. I didn't want to settle down, I wanted to move up – in the world, in the legal profession, in my life. But I also wanted him, desperately wanted to stay with him. So I started shouting and crying. "I don't want to have the baby. I mean, I'm not twenty! I want to get rid of it." I kept talking and crying for most of the night, holding on to him so tight he could barely breathe at times.

'The next day, we sat down and planned it. I would go to my parents and tell them. He would come with me. We'd arrange for an abortion. Then we would marry, set up home in college and get on with our lives.

'I kissed him goodbye the next morning. I would drive to his apartment at four that afternoon and we'd head off to my parents'. I arrived ten minutes late. There was no answer at his apartment. So I went and sat in the car. I waited for an hour then drove to his favourite bar. His friends said he'd gone to make the train. Had to spend a few days with his brother in Cleveland. He'd be back in a while. Some family emergency.

'It took me three hours to drive to my parents'. It was gruelling. Trucks thundering past me. The road endless.

'I cried all the way.'

'How old were you exactly?'

By now Friedman stood looking out of the window. Elizabeth remained seated.

'It was three days before my nineteenth birthday. So, I eventually arrived at my parents' house. I just walked in, put my bag down in the hall. Usual stuff: class warrior comes home carrying the real knowledge of the world back to the closed-minded victims who just happen to be her parents. So, we're sitting round, organising my things, and I just drop it in. Real casual. "Hey, Mom, Dad, I'm pregnant! Yup, it's happened!" Like I'd just spilt the milk or lost my purse. I started laughing, still sorting my things, watching them out of the corner of my eye.

'My mother did what she always did when something went wrong: she pretended everything was all right. Started cooking, making little jokes. My father just sat in the lounge. I remember he sat there for two, three hours, staring at the wall. Saying nothing. So, I had my mother behind me talking about coffee mornings, and my father in front of me refusing to speak.

'Boy, it didn't take me long to lose my sense of humour, I can tell you. I mean, what planet were these people on? Oh, I knew it was all my fault. I was the one who'd done something stupid. But I couldn't let them think that I was sorry. *No way*. I was too damn arrogant to allow that. What I wanted was a *reaction*. So I just started shouting, running back and forth between the kitchen and the lounge. Screaming at my mother: "Will you listen to me?" She just kept busy in the kitchen. "Calm down, dear." *Calm down!* So then I'd march straight back into the lounge and stand in front of my father and scream at him! What was wrong with these people?

'So I'm standing like this, shrieking and shouting. "Jesus, so I had sex!" Very loud this time. I was going to make them *pay* for their inhibitions! So Dad looks over at the door. Mom comes in, walking very slowly. And she comes up to me, and I'm thinking: "OK, now I can really tell her. Really show her what a superb new young woman I am." And she hits me straight across the face. Two hard slaps. Left, right. She's perfectly calm. Just whacks me across the mouth. Then she says: "You think *we're* pathetic?" That blew it. I just collapsed on the floor, crying, crying non-stop.

'So Dad gets up and puts his arms round me and holds me, and I'm crying and saying I'm so sorry, I'm *so sorry*. And Mom stands there, stroking my hair. Just the three of us. You know, I've never felt so loved. Then I knew. Oh, I really knew. There were only two people who'd ever really love me and they were both holding me, just letting me cry.'

Friedman reached into his briefcase. 'I think we may need one of these,' he said, taking out a battered packet of Marlboro Lights.

'I didn't know you smoked.'

'I keep them for those occasions when you fear the world might end.'

Elizabeth smiled slightly. 'I guess we're in one of those.'

He came across the room towards her and leaned against the table. His arm brushed against the side of Elizabeth's chair. They shared the ashtray.

'I'm sorry, Mrs Forrester, but I'm going to have to know all of it. We don't have to say anything publicly. The story may not even surface, and if it does we'll just tell them it's crap. But—'

'It will come out, John. I always knew it would at some point. I didn't tell Tyler when he ran because it would have distracted him. Jesus, I spent the whole campaign wondering when it would happen. I'd wake up every morning and think: "OK, maybe it's today I'll have to tell him." When *nothing* happened, I couldn't believe it. The sheer relief of not having to admit to my husband I'd had an abortion.'

She'd said the word.

'Who performed the surgery?' Friedman asked, still staring at the floor.

'The local doctor. He was a friend of my father's. We drove to see him the next day – Dad must have spoken to him on the phone the night before. I woke up about three hours later. Dad was beside me and I was back home by the end of the evening. Spent the next three days in bed; the pain was terrible at times. Slowly, we began to put it behind us. Tried to pretend things were normal. But they never were, of course. Dad died two years later, Mom six months after that.' Her voice caught. She could feel the tears threatening.

No, I can't cry again.

'I don't think they ever really forgave me,' Elizabeth went on. 'With one stupid act I'd destroyed their world. Their brilliant little girl had betrayed them. I'm sure that's what they thought, although they never said anything to me. But the next time I came back from college, I got up in the night to fix a drink or have a cigarette. I crept out to the porch, but as I reached the screen door, I could hear a noise from outside. I looked through the window and my mother was sitting there. In her nightdress, one of those horrible nylon things. She always wore it. She was just sitting there, trembling a little, crying into her hands. Little shaky sobs.'

'Does anyone else know?'

'What? Oh, no. The doctor and the nurse died a few years later. There were no records – I'd asked dad that shortly before his illness. He said the doctor pretended it had never happened.'

Elizabeth crushed the cigarette into the ashtray. Her fingers trembled slightly as she did so. She rested her head in her hands.

Friedman stared at her. 'That's not all, is it?'

She pulled her hands through her hair. 'No, it's not. I lied to Tyler. I told him the reason we couldn't have children was because I was infertile due to a birth defect. He'd so wanted kids; he was wonderful about it, said it didn't matter. But we stopped . . . well, you get my drift. It wasn't the same after that. I felt I'd driven him away. It was all my fault. I could never escape from it. The responsibility . . . knowing that my whole life was ruined because I was so stupid. My parents, my marriage, never being a mother . . . *Christ!*'

She rose from the chair and strode across the room. Her shoulders slumped against the window. Her neck pressed into the glass and she could feel it, cold and hard. She fiddled with her wedding ring, tugged at her jacket buttons. Friedman did not turn to face her. Elizabeth watched him puff urgently on his cigarette.

'Who's the father?'

She knew the question had to be asked. Would be.

'If you mean will he say anything, well, he hasn't so far. Didn't during Tyler's campaign. I was terrified the office would call me one day and say he was on the phone. Then I'd know it was all over. But he never did call. I think it's because he felt so bad he wasn't there when I had the operation. Afterwards, he took me on holiday, to the Cape. It was his way of saying sorry for being scared. He knew he'd been a coward. But the trip was a disaster and we never really saw each other again. Sometimes we'd bump into each other on campus. I'd be embarrassed or still furious with him. He'd look so guilty he could hardly talk. So we'd just sort of nod at each other and walk on. I suppose the only reason he never profited from it was because he still felt so responsible. We did love each other. We loved each other terribly. It was the real thing for both of us. On the last day at college, I got a note from him. He said he still loved me and wanted me to go out west with him, try and start afresh. I never got back to him. Two months later, I met Tyler.'

'And he's still, you know, *alive*, this guy?'

'Oh, yes, very much alive.'

'Who is he?'

'That's the strange thing. He works in DC. He's a journalist called Mark White.'

White replaced the telephone. He crossed another name off the list in his notebook; yet another contact had never heard of Leonard Calthorp or NordFund. He yawned and pushed himself back from the desk. He crashed into the wall behind him, cursing. The office at the back of the *Herald* was tiny. Not for the first time, he felt as if he were caged.

Suddenly the door in front of him swung open, smashing against the side of the desk. White's styrofoam cup of coffee careered on to the floor.

'Shit, Whitey, sorry!'

Riordan closed the door behind them. 'We can't stay here long. Bletchman keeps asking me how your flu is going. I think he reckons you're going for another job.' Riordan smiled down at him. 'Are you?'

'Not now, Mick. I'm a fucking fugitive not an applicant.'

The Irishman smirked at him. 'Your friend Elizabeth Forrester has been busy.'

White looked up sharply. 'What do you mean?'

'Well, according to the imbeciles on the political desk, they've picked up a rumour that the lefties might want her to stand as VP. They're taking a chance with it in tomorrow's paper.'

'You're kidding me? Elizabeth?'

Jesus!

Riordan nodded. 'That's what they say. Some crap about them wanting her to glam up Willard's ticket. Do you think she'd do it?'

White shook his head. 'Unlikely. She's too—'

'Deep in the shit with Ronald Kelly?' Riordan lit a Marlboro and inhaled deeply.

'Mick—'

'Talking of which, what have you got?' Riordan said, nodding towards the telephone.

White told him about Calthorp. Riordan grimaced. 'A new one on me. Does anyone know him?'

'I've tried my contacts. Zilch. No one's ever come across him. But he has to have been around the White House, because he goes back a long way with McQuogue.'

'Not necessarily,' Riordan replied. 'McQuogue's the sort of ruthless bastard who dumps people along the way.'

White shook his head. 'It's too neat, Mick. Kelly is trying to dish the dirt on the White House and the people trying to stop me finding out why just happen to know McQuogue.' White picked up his notebook and put his jacket on. 'And,' he went on, 'I can't exactly ring the White House switchboard and ask to be put through to the Chief of Staff's office.'

'In the circumstances, no, that wouldn't be the best of moves.'

'Mick, I've got jack-shit I can write . . . if I blow Appleton's cover, we may never find out who was behind it. They'll throw him to the wolves and the bastards behind this will have covered their tracks.'

The two men left the office. White locked it and handed the

key to Riordan. The corridor ahead of them was empty. They began to make their way towards the back exit.

'Where do you want to go now, Whitey?'

'Can you suggest anywhere other than Mort's?'

Riordan shook his head and put his arm around White's shoulder. 'Well, by tomorrow morning there might be someone you can approach.'

'Who?'

'Elizabeth Forrester. If she stands alongside Willard, then Appleton and Kelly become a very, *very* hot property, my friend.'

White didn't answer him.

Chapter Twenty-seven

It was the first time she had been back to the White House since Tyler's death, and in the time since she had confessed her past to Friedman Elizabeth had pondered what it would feel like. She looked around the room, pacing all the while. She fiddled with her jacket, a bright blue two-piece. Marjorie and Friedman watched her. 'I look like a mistress in this thing.' She examined herself in the mirror. 'It was very kind of Willard and Ethel to let me use their home,' she said sarcastically.

The Treaty Room was in the private quarters of the White House. It was dominated by a dark mahogany desk and Healy's portrait of Lincoln. Tyler had used it as his own office, a refuge from the intrusions of the Oval Office itself. Elizabeth examined the room more closely. It was almost as she remembered it. The photographs of herself and Tyler had been removed. One of Willard and his grandchildren adorned the mantelpiece in front of her. She looked away quickly.

Below, in the Blue Room, the entire White House press corps, complete with film crews, crowded into the elegant space. Summoned only a few hours before by Friedman, they had been told little, other than that the former First Lady was to unveil a portrait of her late husband that had been completed only two days before his death. It was Elizabeth's first public speech since the funeral. The network bosses had allocated a slot in the news broadcasts later in the day. None had decided to carry it live. Mrs Forrester was news, but she was not the President.

Friedman checked through the speech she was about to make. Marjorie sat by the fireplace, silent.

'It's all ready, Mrs Forrester.'

Elizabeth turned and took the cards from Friedman's outstretched hand. She glanced at them briefly, placed them in a small leather attaché case and began to walk towards the open door.

With Friedman following, and Morrow shadowing them both, she walked the length of the Central Hall of the private quarters and began making her way down the Grand Staircase. As she turned into the Cross Hall by the North Entrance, she could hear the commotion in the Blue Room.

'Prepare for a busy day, John,' she said as Morrow ushered her in. She waited for him to smile. He looked at her blankly, then nodded.

'Yes, of course. I'm sorry, I think I've got a bug.'

'Get some paracetamol,' Elizabeth said, turning away from him. 'You're going to need it. And I need *you*.'

She made her way past the expectant press. She was surprised to see Wayne McQuogue at the edge of the crowd. She smiled and nodded to him.

Poor Wayne, here goes your day.

A small podium, borrowed from the basement briefing room, had been placed in front of the windows. Elizabeth turned to face the crowd.

'Ladies and gentlemen, thank you for coming at such short notice.' She looked into the familiar faces. 'I'd like to begin by saying that during my time in the White House you all showed me the greatest courtesy, even when I could see your eyes sometimes glazing over when I spoke to you.'

The room erupted in laughter and she raised her hand to silence it. 'You all know that I loved my husband very dearly. At times we were not always as happy as we had once been. I was aware of Tyler's weaknesses and he, too, was aware of mine. No marriage would be complete without the occasional hiccup and Tyler and I were no different, except our hiccups made the evening news.'

It was at this moment, the media agreed later, that they knew something was up. Imperceptibly, the atmosphere in the Blue Room changed. A sense of urgency swept over the audience, an attentiveness that had not been there earlier. Elizabeth sensed it too, and smiled inwardly.

'We came to the White House by virtue of the support of the American people. Tyler's mission was to change much of what was wrong about our nation, and to celebrate all that was good. I believe he went a long way to achieving that noble aim. His presidency was, and will always remain, one of the most challenging and important administrations in recent times. And it is for this reason that I passionately believe that his work must continue.

'I have mourned his death more than anyone. But from that mourning I have also learned that from grief comes strength. I hold dear my husband's memory. Equally important, I know that the future is what should now concern us. We as a nation can gain from our loss.

'Outside of this room, poverty still plagues our cities. Our children still fall victim to drugs. Our young women still carry the burden of teenage pregnancy. Our environment still remains darkened by the evils of pollution. So much is right about our great nation, and yet so much is wrong.'

Elizabeth paused and arranged the white cards in front of her. 'Willard Morgan and the entire team in the White House and beyond are all aware of what my husband set out to do. That impetus cannot stop, must not stop for one second. I left the White House in sadness and in grief. I return today to unveil this portrait of Tyler. Now that I am back, I cannot help but remember what the Forrester presidency meant to this country. Ladies and gentlemen, the White House may no longer be my home. My husband may no longer sit in the Oval Office. He will never do so again.' She stopped and swallowed hard. 'But one day very soon, I myself hope to be back for good.'

Out of the corner of her eye, Elizabeth could see McQuogue flinch. He glanced across the room at Friedman, who adroitly avoided his stare.

'I have been First Lady, I have been a supportive wife.' Elizabeth paused. She had the full attention of the room. 'Now, ladies and gentlemen, I intend to go one step farther. The press reports in the last few days have not been accurate. It is, however, my intention to begin assembling a team around me to begin what I believe will be a crucial fight to keep the Forrester legacy alive in this building and in this country.

'It is for that reason I am taking this opportunity to announce my intention to stand as a candidate for President of the United States.'

At the very same moment, President Willard Morgan was attending a ceremony at the Jefferson Hotel, a few blocks from the White House.

The first inkling that something was amiss came, ironically, from one of the waiters. Bored with the presence of a mere President, he had retired to an anteroom for a cigarette. He listened to the radio through an earpiece. As McQuogue observed later: 'Typical of Willard to hear it from a busboy.'

The waiter told his boss about Elizabeth's announcement; he told a Secret Service agent who told a member of the White House team. When the news was passed on to Willard himself, twenty pagers went off simultaneously, a chorus of bleeps breaking out in the assembled crowd.

Willard was ushered to a side room. He was handed a secure telephone with a direct line to the White House. Back in his office, McQuogue was waiting for the call.

'Jesus Christ, Wayne! Why didn't we know? I mean, what am

I paying you people for? Is it too much to ask that I should have known, had some idea, this was going to happen? And in the White House!'

Willard was short of breath but he carried on talking. 'I mean, fuck, Wayne, this is Elizabeth Forrester we're talking about. Jesus, she's standing against *me*! I'm in a room of people you say will finance my fucking campaign and now they're looking at me like I'm nothing. The big bad wolf spoiling Little Red Riding Hood's finest hour!'

Willard took another long drag on his cigar. 'I'm not going to be Dan Quayle, Wayne.'

'Mr President, you carry on as normal. Nothing changes. You are in charge, you are running the country. You *are* the President. Sir, say nothing as you leave the hotel. You are due to return here anyway for your twelve o'clock. Business as usual, sir.'

There was no response from the other end of the line. Willard had put the phone down on him.

Friedman sat opposite Elizabeth in the limousine. Her face was flushed, her eyes bright. She radiated energy. He could almost feel the heat coming off her, could imagine the rush of adrenaline in her veins. They turned out of the White House, heading north.

He heard Elizabeth say something but kept his eyes fixed on the floor.

'John?'

He looked up. 'Sorry, Mrs Forrester, I'm just thinking about who I need to speak to at the networks.'

'Well, forget that for a minute. How do you feel it went?'

He smiled. 'Very well, ma'am. The surprise was perfect. I watched the reporters the whole time you were speaking. I don't think they could quite believe what they were hearing.'

'Well, they'd better believe it.' Elizabeth fussed with the handbag on her knee. She retrieved a sheaf of papers and began making marks with a pen. 'I'm in this race, for what it's worth, and I'm going to do my best to win it.' She looked out of the window. 'And I'll win it for Tyler as much as for myself.' She turned back to Friedman. 'Has there been any reaction yet from the White House?'

He shook his head. 'Not yet. They'll gather their troops, wait and see how the networks play it this evening.' Friedman tried to keep the enthusiasm in his voice. 'I expect Willard will shrug it off, compliment you on your time as First Lady, damn you with faint praise.'

Elizabeth's smile widened. 'Poor man, he can't have expected this.'

Friedman nodded his assent. 'No, Mrs Forrester. I don't think anyone expected this.'

'That's the trick Tyler taught me, John. I watched him do it. He would tell me to keep people's expectations low, make them feel a false sense of security, then hit them with it. I've never forgotten that. We did well, John. I'm grateful. And now our secret is out.'

He concentrated on her words but did not really hear them.

As Elizabeth's limousine sped north, two blocks away White eased himself out of the bed in Mort's staff room. He retrieved his watch from the small cabinet at the end of the bed: 10.12 a.m. He grunted and got dressed.

White stopped at the door that led into the main bar. He peered through the crack: Mort was watching television, shouting his approval in between the newscaster's pronouncement. There was no one else around.

'Morning, Mort.'

'Ah, Whitey! You're awake. Coffee's over there, ashtray beneath the counter. Help yourself.'

White sauntered to the end of the bar. 'Do you want a refill?'

The Russian shook his head. He glanced at White. 'You'll

have a busy day today, my friend.' He pointed at the television screen.

The local network was live outside the White House. White's journalistic training picked up the urgency in the reporter's voice. But he wasn't looking at the man. Beneath him, across the bottom of the screen, a subtitle flashed on and off: 'Mrs Forrester runs for President'.

Chapter Twenty-eight

It was an uninspiring storefront, made more so by the dull metallic glow of early evening. Dirty windows. The glue from old bills stuck to the windows like old beer on a bar. Venetian blinds, twisted in places, blocked the view of inside. The door shook when opened and the hall carpet, putrid red, was stained and torn at the edges. Twenty desks, old, chipped. Boxes of Canon computer equipment piled in one corner. Beside them, two new black office chairs, the plastic packaging dusty.

Elizabeth stood in the middle of the room. 'I never did thank you for spoiling me, John,' she said brightly, turning to Friedman.

This unprepossessing office suite would now act as the war room for Elizabeth's embryonic campaign. She looked around her. The grime, the bare, dilapidated reality of political graft, had not changed much, she thought, since Tyler's first local campaign. Elizabeth walked to a suite of offices that lined the back of the war room. The largest had been commandeered as a conference room. She slumped wearily in a chair. Friedman perched on the edge of the table.

Almost immediately, the door to the conference room crashed open.

'Mrs Candidate, welcome to the land of the living dead.'

Benmont Greenhalgh's voice could cut through glass. Bullet-proof glass. He was a short man, barely reaching Elizabeth's shoulder. His most obvious feature was his nose, bulbous and arched at the same time. His one affectation was a cravat, usually a knotted blue one.

Greenhalgh removed his jacket. Simultaneously he threw a dirty black satchel on the table in front of Elizabeth. He looked at his candidate across the table.

'When we win, I want Jerry Garcia to play me in the movie.'

'He's dead, Benmont.'

'Even better.'

Elizabeth waited for Greenhalgh to become serious. 'OK,' he said, 'at present we've had ten approaches from people who worked for you at the White House. Ten *proper* approaches.' He slid a slip of paper across to Elizabeth.

She flicked through the list quickly. 'They're all good people . . . can we afford to pay them?'

Greenhalgh shook his head. 'Not yet . . . but that isn't an issue. They'll come over regardless. Anyway, how're you really doin', Mrs Candidate?'

Elizabeth smiled back at him. 'Wondering if I've just made the biggest mistake of my life.' She glanced at Friedman and held his eye.

'Well,' Greenhalgh replied, 'you were there with your husband. You know more about this bedlam than either of us.' He grinned up at her.

Elizabeth shook her head. 'There's a great difference between watching someone else doing it and putting yourself in the firing line, Benmont.' She looked again at Friedman, who glanced away quickly.

'OK,' Greenhalgh went on, 'I've spoken to Doug Fraser in New Hampshire. The local network is there, could be better, but we're working on it. How're funds?'

Friedman winced. 'Slow.'

'I've gotta have my slots on the TV, John,' Greenhalgh barked. The table shook as his elbows rocked on top of it. 'No good the candidate just sitting with Jay Leno by the end of the month. We're making four ads. We must break them soon. Fast. We're gonna lose the impact otherwise.'

Elizabeth watched silently as her two most senior advisers catalogued the twists and turns of the campaign. It took an hour. Eventually Greenhalgh thundered off to prod yet another state party official into saying nice things about his candidate, Friedman to brief the media.

Elizabeth took the phone call. She felt embarrassed, almost as if she had betrayed the man she was about to speak to. 'Clifford, good of you to call.'

She glanced back across the office suite. She couldn't see Friedman, but Greenhalgh stood in the middle of the office, arms waving like an orchestral conductor's. She smiled and turned away. 'Clifford? Are you still there?'

'Yes, Elizabeth.'

She was surprised by Granby's tone. The old man seemed subdued, bereft of his usual energy. 'Is everything all right?' she asked, dreading the answer.

Granby took his time before speaking. 'I wish you had told me, Elizabeth.'

She felt her face redden. She was glad Granby was not here because she knew he was right. She had trusted him with most things, but had pulled back from confiding her announcement to him because she knew he would have tried talking her out of it. She told him as much. 'Clifford, I had to do it this way. If I'd sat down with you and told you what I was planning, you would probably have had me incarcerated!'

'Elizabeth, you're quite right,' he replied, his voice slow and measured. 'Are you *sure* you've done the right thing? This is one hell of a step. You can't disappear now. You have no choice but to go on with this.' Granby paused; she could hear him sip on a drink. She could imagine him, sitting alone in his vast house, fretting over her decision. 'Elizabeth, I want you to know that I accept that you are now in the running but I am concerned by your motives.'

She flinched slightly, but said nothing.

'You see, Elizabeth, it appears to me that it is not you that is running. It is Tyler's ghost.'

She was about to snap back at him, again because she was worried that he was right. Instead, she said: 'Clifford, I am not doing this because I am obsessed with what I have discovered about Tyler's White House.' She wondered too late if the telephone was secure. She carried on quickly, 'I *will* find out what happened with Tyler. I will because I must. And the only way I am going to do that is by putting myself in the firing line. If I am successful, then I am free to pursue that investigation. If I am not, then I will have shown that I am not someone who will just disappear from view. I want them to know that about me, Clifford.'

'Well, they do now. I wish you luck, Elizabeth. Genuinely. I admired your husband and I admire you. And it is for that reason that I worry about you, that you have taken a step that will expose you to all manner of unforeseen circumstances.'

She let her head drop forward. Granby's concern for her was, she knew, genuine and honest. Apart from Marjorie and Friedman, he was the one person she had relied upon, and she would continue to do so. 'Clifford, I'll take care. I saw it with Tyler,' she said gently. 'And Clifford? Thank you. I remember my friends and I count you as a very special one.'

'Good luck, Elizabeth.'

She replaced the receiver and stared straight ahead.

White settled back on to his chair. Through the floorboards he could hear the raucous laughter from the bar downstairs. He was both pleased and irritated by it: he welcomed the comfort of having people near by, but felt the frustration of not being able to join them.

Leaning forward, he thought of Elizabeth.

In one grand, extraordinary move, she had transformed the landscape – as, he knew, only she could. From a distance he had followed her career in the public eye. He no longer felt envy towards her or Tyler. As far as White was concerned, a better man than he had won her. In the years during which they had gone in differing directions, she skyward and he so much lower, White had tried to close his mind to her; not because he no longer cared for her, he still did, but more because every time he pondered her accomplishments, it served only to remind him of how little he had achieved in his own life. So it had been better to ignore her. His motivation had been self-survival and self-respect.

He could recall her, though. Every nuance of her voice, the way she held herself. The images of her that had become part of the folklore of Tyler's presidency had been far removed from White's own recollections. In his private reminiscences she had always been, and would always remain, a woman who had shown him what it meant to love someone unconditionally, and how that love could terrify even those who considered themselves to be strong. How it diluted one's own courage until all that was left was the instinct to run away.

He had done that. He had hurt her. Wounded her terribly. And in so doing, he had hardened her. He could see that. She wasn't entirely the person he had once known; what she had done in her remarkable life, the things she had seen, the vicious political battles that had polished and honed the rod of steel that he knew held her together like an emotional backbone, those experiences, the negative and the positive, had transformed her from the eager, naïve student he had wooed and seduced such a long time ago.

White wondered what she was like now. How tough she really was. And as he sat like a prisoner in McReedy's, he was also frightened.

He had never divulged what he knew about Elizabeth, the

pain they had once shared. Guilt had been the primary reason. He had abandoned her when she needed him most. His cowardice had been instinctive and fulsome, and because of that it had taken a long time to accept his own culpability. At times he congratulated himself on his discretion. It had watered down his shame. He could have made his name by revealing what he knew. Were others to know, they would urge him to abandon his loyalty. After all, what had Elizabeth done for him? But he had never created the opportunity in which to receive that advice. He had trusted his own instincts almost for the first time. By keeping quiet he had thought that Elizabeth might be grateful to him, might consider him out of her debt. His refusal to capitalise on their secret was the only thing he was truly proud of in his life. Through the years it had given him a particular satisfaction to know that he had not let her down again. And then, once she had become famous, once she shared the most renowned address in the world, the shame that he had felt developed gradually into unconscious denial. Elizabeth had become a chapter in his life that he had, with varying degrees of success, closed for good.

Until now.

Friedman returned to his cupboard of an office in the war room. The list of tasks he had in his hand ran the length of a page. The people who could help him were few. It was going to be a long evening. In his pocket, he had the telephone number his mother had given him. It was time, he knew, to make the call.

He closed the door and sat down. He checked that the blinds in his office were closed. No one could see inside.

He dialled the number. A male voice answered. 'Yes?'

'It's me,' Friedman said, tripping over the words. 'I—'

'John, thank you for calling.' There was no surprise in the man's tone.

Friedman knew that he sounded hollow, inadequate. 'If you

even think about harming my mother, I promise you, there won't be anything you can do to me that will hurt me. Do you fucking *understand* that, you evil *bastard*?'

'John, I'm sorry.'

Friedman felt his chest tighten. He gripped the telephone receiver as if it were a loaded weapon. 'How dare you go to her house?' he said. 'Her *home*! I've met with you once—'

'John, you didn't tell us what your boss was about to do. That annoyed us.'

'I didn't know until three *days* ago! Look, I've told you before, I don't know what the fuck you want. I've told you Mrs Forrester was looking into Kelly—'

'John, please don't repeat yourself. Mrs Forrester's decision to stand has changed everything, you must know that. And as a result your information becomes even more valuable. We went to your mother's house – nice lady by the way – because we had to show you that we were serious. Now, we want you to do something for us.' The man coughed lightly. 'We believe Mrs Forrester has a certain bank statement.'

Friedman spat out his reply. 'Yes.'

'We want a copy.'

'I *can't*!' he half screamed. 'I've got the fucking campaign team around me, I'm in the middle of—'

'Just get it, John. And meet us at the same place. Eleven p.m. Tonight.'

The line was cut.

Friedman slammed the receiver down. He stared at it for what seemed like a lifetime. Then he rose slowly from his chair and looked out into the war room. Elizabeth was at the far end with Greenhalgh, Morrow by the main door beyond the reception area.

Friedman left his office and turned away from them. The lights in the conference room were off. He unlocked the door and closed it behind him. Through the half-closed blinds, the light from the office suite outside was diffused and grey.

Elizabeth's attaché case was in the corner, propped against the conference table. Friedman hurried towards it. He knew the combination for the lock; he swivelled the dials, squinting in the paltry light. Elizabeth's case clicked open. He could smell the leather and a faint trace of her perfume. The NordFund bank statement was tucked into the back pocket, where he had last seen her place it.

His hands trembling, he put the statement in his pocket and relocked the case. Holding his breath, he dashed back across the room and peered through the blinds: the campaign team were away to his right, half hidden behind a concrete pillar. Friedman slipped out of the room. To his immediate left, a Canon photocopier had been pushed against the bare wall. He yanked the lid open and put the statement face down.

'John.'

He spun round, his face burning. Morrow was strolling towards him. Friedman could hear the whirr of the machine beneath his hands, the plastic warm. He managed to smile. 'What's up, Lee?' he asked, positioning his body so that Morrow could not see the slip of paper rolling out into the copier's tray.

'A few queries on the schedule.'

Friedman saw Morrow glance towards the out tray. He moved again to block the agent's view. 'Sure, Lee,' he muttered, retrieving the two pieces of paper and folding them in half. 'Let me get this away and I'll come and find you.'

Friedman could feel the sweat on his forehead. He blinked it out of his eyes and hurried back to the conference room, placing the original copy back in Elizabeth's case. Thirty seconds later, he was back on the main floor of the war room, looking for Morrow.

Chapter Twenty-nine

Two hours after the meeting in the war room, Elizabeth and Friedman returned to the cottage. In the early evening darkness, the gates were surrounded by media cameras. The limousines swept through and, in a few short minutes, Elizabeth found herself back in the relative sanctuary of the house. Friedman followed her into the sitting room, Morrow closing the door behind them. Elizabeth settled into an armchair, removing her jacket. She watched Friedman closely.

The young aide opened his attaché case and pulled out a sheaf of papers. He looked up and smiled at her. 'It's late, I know,' he said, 'but you should cast your eye over this.'

Elizabeth took the papers and read the media schedule. Eventually, she handed it back to Friedman, nodding her acceptance of it.

'John, I need you to answer me a question,' she said finally. 'It's about Mark White. We have to consider the possibility he will capitalise on what I've done.' She fiddled with her gold bracelet and watched the darkness deepen through the leaded windows. 'He hasn't up until now, but there's a great difference between me being First Lady and actually standing for President. I want you to make contact with him.

'We have to know if he is going to spill the beans,' she went on. 'I might be deluding myself but Mark has never harmed me, not once. I can only imagine it's because he feels guilty, even after such a long time, although heaven knows it's not often in this line of work that you find yourself on the receiving end of other people's discretion. Or loyalty. I know you understand what I mean.'

Friedman coughed lightly and smiled back. 'Mrs Forrester,' he said quietly, 'I think you're making a bad decision. Mark White is a problem only if we make him into one. Surely it would be—'

She raised her hand. 'John, I know what you're going to say. But I can't continue along this road with his shadow behind me. If we speak to him, and he gives me a personal guarantee that he will do nothing, then perhaps I can meet with him and thank him. If, however, it is obvious that he is about to reveal what he knows, I have no choice but to pre-empt him.'

'Mrs Forrester, that's an appallingly risky course of action to take.' Friedman was talking quickly. Elizabeth was surprised by the vehemence of his objection. But she kept quiet and listened. 'It might provoke him,' Friedman said forcefully. 'It might be the case that any approach we make to him simply legitimises what he will do. If Mark White were to come out and say this, our response would be simple: where's the proof? The fact is there isn't any. We can just portray him as an embittered former boyfriend who's trying to profit from your fame. We'll—'

'No, John, I am not getting into that kind of McQuogue territory. I am not going to start this campaign with a lie. I learned that from Tyler. There's no point secretly tying one hand behind your back – he always said that. You will have to trust me on this. Call Mark and arrange a meeting. Tell him you have my full trust and authority. Let's see what he has to say. At least we'll be forearmed.'

Elizabeth changed the subject. She was confident Friedman could control Mark White. He'd have to. She couldn't bring herself to face the possibility of what might happen if he didn't.

*

Friedman drove himself away from the cottage. At the main gates, the press were still camped on either side of the road, like little packs of beagles ready for the chase. The media captured his departure on camera. Friedman put his foot down and checked in the rear-view mirror. He was alone on the road. There were no headlights behind him. He pulled over ten minutes later, before the turnpike, and took his cellular phone out of his jacket. As he did so, the photocopy of the NordFund statement crackled in his pocket. He checked the time: 10.12 p.m. He dialled the *Herald*'s number and asked the operator to be put through to Mark White.

An aggressive male voice barked a greeting.

'Er, could I speak to Mr White, please?' Friedman asked.

'No, he's not here.'

'Tell him it's John Friedman. I—'

'Hang on, hang on. I can transfer your call.'

Before Friedman could speak, he heard two clicks, then a strange voice.

'Hello, is that Mr White?'

'Yes.'

'Mr White, my name is John Friedman. I'm Elizabeth Forrester's Director of Communications and—'

'I know who you are. How can I help you?'

'Mr White, there's something I need to discuss with you. I have been talking with my candidate and I am authorised to approach you and ask you some questions. I wonder if that would be convenient?'

White paused for a second before replying. 'Mr Friedman,' he said hesitantly, 'I don't mean to insult you but I do need to check that you are who you say you are. I need—'

'Mark, it's about your time with my candidate. And what happened before that. Elizabeth has spoken with me. Now, can we meet?'

*

Friedman watched the street ahead of him. If anything, it was quieter than the previous time he had been here. The vague roar of traffic, way off to the north, was the only sign that there was anyone alive near by. Despite the warmth of the evening, he stood shivering on the sidewalk. He tugged his jacket closer round him.

He didn't have long to wait.

The vehicle was different from the last time: a black Cadillac, darkened windows. Friedman watched as it rolled towards him from the other side of the street. When it was almost parallel with him, the headlights were flashed. Once, then again.

He hurried towards it, checking left and right. The passenger door swung open. He crouched down and got inside. A dark plastic screen divided the passengers from the driver's compartment. Friedman could just make out the silhouette of two men in the front. The AC was on and he felt almost naked under the chilling blast of air. He settled back in the seat, trying to control his breathing.

'Good evening, John.' The man's voice was crackly: he was using the intercom. 'Have you got it?'

Friedman nodded. He pulled the NordFund statement from his pocket and leaned forward. The plastic partition slid open, and an outstretched hand took the paper from him. 'Thank you, John.'

Friedman readjusted himself in the seat and glanced out of the window.

'Is Mrs Forrester still pursuing her investigation?' the man asked.

'No . . . at least, not yet. Her focus is on the campaign.'

'And have you managed to find Mark White for us?'

'No,' Friedman said. He would not tell them that he had tracked down White; not yet, not until he discovered precisely what the journalist knew. 'I've told you, he's not someone I've ever dealt with,' he lied.

The man did not reply immediately. Then he said: 'You

should have told us Elizabeth was thinking of standing, John. You—'

'I didn't *know*! I fucking told you! She came out with it only, what, three days ago? It was as much a surprise to me as anyone else! Jesus, I couldn't *believe* she was thinking of standing. You don't know her! Mrs Forrester will wait and wait and then she'll act. It's the way she's always been. She's not the sort of person who sits you down and tells you everything she thinks.'

'So we've noticed.'

Friedman remained silent.

'And she will continue with her investigation into Kelly, will she, John? If she is successful in her campaign. Is that the idea?'

'I don't know,' he mumbled.

'The problem, John,' the man went on, his voice echoing in the car, 'is that we don't entirely believe you. You see, there had to have been some warning, some hint that your boss was about to declare. You're a professional, John. And so am I.' The slot was pulled open again: an envelope was pushed through the gap, tumbling into Friedman's lap. In the half-darkness, he opened it: there was only one photograph.

His mother was standing in her drawing room, a young man's arm around her shoulders. Friedman thought he was going to be sick.

'That picture was taken an hour ago, John. The man beside your mother is your old college buddy, Jack. The cameraman is a friend of his. At this precise moment' – the man paused, then spoke again – 'Jack and his friend are convincing your mother to join them for dinner.'

Friedman felt the bile rise in his throat. The car seemed to close in on him. For a full minute, he was unable to speak. He stared at the photograph. 'I've been telling you the truth!' he moaned eventually, his hands trembling.

'Good, John. That's very good. But, you see, the landscape has changed dramatically. And it's important you advise us of a way that we can stop your boss.'

'I *can't!* There's nothing—'
'John, you have no choice.'
So Friedman told them.

Chapter Thirty

The next morning, Friedman parked his car on F Street and walked two blocks. The library building was dilapidated and deserted. He stood in the doorway and peered inside. Towards the back a row of desks ran along one side of the room. Friedman walked towards the man sitting in the farthest corner. The shadows were longer here.

The man stood. 'John?'

He nodded and shook White's hand. 'Are you sure we're OK to talk here?'

White looked around them. 'Yeah, we're fine.'

They settled on to two small chairs. Friedman checked the room again. At the opposite end of the line of desks, he suddenly saw a large, burly man reading a newspaper. 'Who's that?' he asked White nervously.

'A friend. Don't worry. He doesn't know why we're meeting.'

Friedman did not enquire as to why the journalist had felt the need to bring a bodyguard. 'Mr White—'

'Call me Mark. I think your knowledge of me is intimate enough.'

Friedman forced a smile. 'Well, *Mark,* this isn't an easy conversation to have. You obviously understand that my boss is in the process of launching a very serious, and we hope successful, campaign against Willard Morgan. There's a lot of ground to cover, and we both know the White House is one extremely dangerous enemy to make.'

Friedman stopped. White stayed silent, watching him.

'Mark, I know about the, er, *relationship* that you had with Mrs Forrester. And what happened afterwards. She is understandably nervous that any campaign might become embroiled in scandal were the facts ever to become public.'

White sat back in the chair as if he had been whipped. 'Are you suggesting that I'd *betray* her?'

Friedman blushed and tried to avoid his stare. 'Well, yes, you are a tabloid journalist!'

'Friedman, I've never fucking told—'

'Mark, she merely wants to know if . . . I don't know . . . if she can *continue* to rely on your discretion.'

'She was a *kid*, for fuck's sake.' White struggled to keep his voice low. He leaned forward, whispering harshly, 'We both were! We made a mistake, that's all. And if anyone did something bad, it was me, not her! I left her to it, I abandoned *her*, not the other way round. I'm—'

'You won't reveal this, then?' Friedman said, watching him. The journalist's face was flushed, his fury obvious. 'Mr White, only the three of us know you were the father of the child.'

And when it's revealed, you'll be blamed, White.

White nodded. 'Oh, for fuck's sake, you people . . . of course I'm not going to say anything.' He shook his head slowly. 'Her secret's safe with me. Oh, and thank her, John. Thank her for expressing such trust in me!'

Friedman blinked quickly, then gathered his things. He rose from the chair.

'One last thing, John.'

Friedman looked back. White's smile was unconvincing. 'I'll do a deal with you. I'll keep quiet if you tell me why Elizabeth is so interested in a man named Ronald Kelly.'

*

White relished the moment. The young aide opposite him stood wide-eyed. White could almost smell the fear coming off him. He knew he had landed a home run.

'Mark, I don't know what—'

He waved Friedman back towards him, keeping his voice to a whisper. 'John, Kelly worked for the Pentagon signing off export requests. I know these licences are easy to get, if you have the right connections. I also know that Kelly's disappearance was somewhat convenient, and in the days before he died he was trying to get in touch with Elizabeth. That is one hell of a coincidence.' White calculated quickly how far he could go with Friedman. 'So what does she know?' he asked carefully.

He watched and waited. Friedman was obviously thinking on his feet. After a few seconds, he spoke. 'My candidate is concerned that something in the White House alarmed her late husband. But she is not involved in anything that pertains to Mr Kelly's activities.'

White nodded. The answer was meaningless and both of them knew it. He decided to take a risk. 'John, speak with Elizabeth and tell her that unless I am given help on this one, then, who knows? I may have to use the story.' He let the threat hang for a moment. 'I don't *want* to threaten her but I need to swap notes. I believe she can do that.'

Friedman stood up quickly. 'Is that all?' he asked perfunctorily.

White nodded. 'But I think we should talk again.'

'Mr White, that's impossible. I'm with the candidate solidly so—'

'So when, then?'

White watched as Friedman once again waited before answering. 'I should be able to make it in a day's time. But it will have to be the evening.'

'I'll see you there at six,' White said, handing over a card.

Friedman put it in his pocket and walked away. White watched him go. Then, he motioned to Riordan. They gave it five minutes and left by the side entrance, checking the street behind them.

An hour later Friedman strode into the war room. The latest campaign posters had arrived. An enthusiastic volunteer had plastered Elizabeth's face around the small space. Friedman felt her unblinking eyes watching him as he strolled towards his office.

'John?'

He looked back. Elizabeth was coming towards him across the floor. Behind her Greenhalgh hovered, his ear glued to a cellular phone. Friedman tensed and smiled. 'Mrs Forrester, how are things?'

'Better than I'd expected. No one yet sees me as menopausal maniac, I hope.' She looked back at Greenhalgh and then took Friedman by the arm. 'Let's talk in your office.'

He shut the door behind them. Elizabeth pulled the rickety office chair towards her and slumped down. 'Well?' she asked simply.

'I spoke to White . . . and he's onside. He won't reveal anything.'

Elizabeth exhaled. '*Thank God.*' She held her head in her hands and breathed deeply. 'How did he look?'

Friedman blushed. 'Fine . . . younger than I'd thought.'

'Why will he keep it quiet?'

'He said he had never planned to embarrass you, and that he wouldn't do so now.'

'Thank you,' Elizabeth muttered to herself, not looking at Friedman. 'Thank you, thank you, *thank* you, Mark.'

'But he wanted something from us.'

She looked up sharply. 'What?'

Friedman sat down. 'He knows about Kelly.' He saw her surprise. 'He's been looking into it. He's surprisingly well informed. He also said that Kelly was trying to get hold of you before he died.'

'*What?*'

'That's all he'd say. But he wants our co-operation. Thinks we should swap notes. He claims to have looked into the export requests—'

Elizabeth sat forward on her chair. 'Does he know about Tyler's diary?'

Friedman shook his head. 'He didn't say so, and I doubt it. But what do you want me to tell him?'

Elizabeth fell silent. Through the windows she could see Greenhalgh pacing the room impatiently. Finally she spoke. 'John, we have no choice but to work with Mark. Neither you nor I can exactly chase around Washington. At the moment we're no closer to finding out anything. Tell Mark what we know.' She stood up and went to open the door. 'I think we can trust him. Mark isn't an evil person. He's just, well, *weak*. So you'll see him again?'

Friedman nodded. 'Yes, ma'am.'

'If he sticks by what he said, Mark will be the man we can thank for saving my candidacy.' She looked back at Friedman. 'It's ironic, isn't it?'

He nodded again. Forced a smile. 'It certainly is, Mrs Forrester.' He watched Elizabeth join Greenhalgh and disappear into the conference room. Then he picked up the phone.

Riordan appeared at the doorway of Mort's spare room with a bottle of Jack Daniel's. He handed it to White, who produced two plastic tumblers from the small bedside table. They drank quickly and in silence. Riordan took another large slug, then settled back on the only chair in the room. 'Do you trust him? Friedman?'

White shrugged. 'It doesn't look like I have any choice. Appleton can't help us any more. There's no way we can crack NordFund, it's watertight.'

'And they won't be exactly pleased to see you again.'

'Precisely.' White accepted a top-up. 'If my instincts are right, Elizabeth must be able to supply the link between NordFund and the White House. She's got to have known something. If Wayne McQuogue is an associate of Calthorp, then whatever Kelly uncovered goes right to the White House.'

Riordan nodded but his face was impassive. 'Unless the Forresters were in on the scam?' He glanced at White. 'They may have buried Kelly's memo, kept it nice and tight.'

White shook his head. 'No way, Mick.'

The Irishman snorted his irritation. 'How do you know?'

'I just know, Mick.'

I just know.

Elizabeth had been arguing with Greenhalgh for an hour. As an old Washington hand, he had been badgering his candidate to make the necessary courtesy calls on the Democratic bigwigs in the Capitol. Elizabeth knew that he was nervous about their support: as First Lady, she had had only passing dealings with the men who day to day tested the temperature within the halls of the Legislature. She was wily enough to appreciate that this was how Washington worked. She didn't like it but she knew she couldn't change it. Even so, she wasn't going to pay homage until she had to.

She turned away and checked the sheet of paper that lay on the desk in front of her. 'OK, OK,' she said, 'I'll do it. But not tomorrow. Maybe next week. They'll have to wait.'

Greenhalgh grimaced. 'Liz, you have got to hit the ground running and get the support on the Hill that you need.'

'Benmont, I've got to take this campaign out into the country. It's no good me sitting in Washington talking to the Fat Men if, in the end, they're not going to back me anyway. I understand they want to feel involved. And I'll meet with them face to face when the time is right.' She slid the schedule across the table. 'Have a look at my marks then come back to me.'

Greenhalgh slipped the paper into his document case and stood.

'Benmont.' She looked up at him and waved him back to his chair. 'Sit down for a minute. There's something I've got to ask you.'

Greenhalgh obliged. He reached into his jacket and removed a packet of cigars. Elizabeth rolled her eyes but allowed him to continue.

'Benmont, I don't know if this is the right time to raise this issue, but I'm going to anyway.' She peered over his head to make sure the door was still shut tight. 'It's about John Friedman. Does he seem OK to you?'

Greenhalgh shrugged. 'Sure. Why do you ask?'

Elizabeth shook her head. 'I don't know . . . I can't quite say. It's just that I have a feeling, call it whatever you want, that he's not performing properly. Firstly, he looks exhausted half the time. That I can understand. None of us is exactly having a vacation at the moment, but there's more to it with John: he's lacking somehow. It's like he's sitting at the back of the room, watching all of this going on around him, and when I try to get an idea of what he's thinking, he clams up! I'm sorry if I sound harsh, but I can't have somebody on board who isn't committed. I'm incredibly fond of John, you know that. He was there when . . . well, when Tyler died. But every time he's around, there's just this feeling that maybe he doesn't really believe in what we're doing. What do you think?'

Greenhalgh looked nonplussed. 'Liz, I've known you for, what, over a decade?' He drew heavily on his cigar. 'You always do this. You spend more time worrying about the people around you than about what you should be doing out on the street. John's *fine*. Sure, he's a bit antsy now and again, but who isn't? We've all put our butts on the line over this one, and there's no going back.'

'Has he said anything to you?' Elizabeth's voice was pleading. 'I need to know, Benmont, because if there is something wrong, then I can try and sort it out for him. You know what John is like: he keeps things so tight' – she slapped her chest in frustration – 'it's like he's constantly refusing to open up.'

'*Tight?*' Greenhalgh mimicked her hand gestures. 'Liz, he's probably terrified! I know I am. And so should you be. You're standing for President! You're the best candidate this country has had since, since . . . OK, maybe since your husband. But only maybe. Even he had his faults.'

'Benmont, why are you—'

'Liz, I'm making you see facts!' Greenhalgh waved his cigar like a baton. 'Sure, John isn't his usual urbane self. What do you expect? You were a great First Lady, the best yet. But you've committed yourself, and us, to the most savage, disgusting, goddam *unbelievable* torture in the modern world!'

His hands fell gently on to the table between them. 'Liz, I'm sorry if I'm being harsh. But you've got to understand that this is the easy part. At the moment, you're up in the polls, there are people knocking on your door, you've got half of Congress wanting to put their arms round you. You're the hot ticket! But it ain't going to last. You saw that with Tyler, and so did John. D'you know why he's a bit out of sorts? Because he knows that around the corner is the biggest fucking gigantic mountain we have to climb. He's a trooper, Liz, we know that. He's young. Maybe too young, I don't know. But what I am sure of is that he's sitting there terrified that he might do something to harm you, and he doesn't want to let you down. Has he ever let you down?'

Elizabeth shook her head.

'Well, there you are. Don't worry about John, Liz. He's with us all the way.'

Chapter Thirty-one

'Ladies and gentlemen, please welcome the next President of the United States!'

Friedman watched Elizabeth rise from her chair and walk towards the podium. The applause in the hall was deafening.

'Congressman, thank you very much. It's great to be among friends again!'

The applause erupted once more.

As the audience finally went quiet, Elizabeth settled into her speech. In front of her, the TelePrompTers scrolled down slowly. Friedman tried to concentrate on her speech.

'My message to you today is a simple one. America deserves the best: in our schools, in the workplace, at home. More care for the elderly and sick of this nation. More opportunities for business, for those of us who have had to struggle day and night to make our enterprises work. I want America to be a nation of ambition *and* compassion. It is to help us achieve this that I propose—'

Friedman looked at his notes. She was due to finish in ten minutes. Then, there would be a quick walk-through in the conference room of the Baltimore hotel before moving on to the next engagement.

Elizabeth was into her closing remarks. 'So I thank you

for listening and for coming here tonight. If I have convinced only one of you in this room, then it will have been worth it.'

'We're convinced! How about dinner?' a man at the front of the audience shouted. The rest roared their approval.

'You know where to get hold of me, sir. Very soon my address will be 1600 Pennsylvania Avenue. Thank you!'

The crowd was on its feet. Elizabeth and her entourage swept through the room, Friedman struggling to direct her towards the important party officials. It was no use. Sheer momentum carried her along. The chanting was deafening.

'E-LIZ-A-BETH! E-LIZ-A-BETH!'

Out into the hotel lobby and on to the sidewalk. The limousine was waiting and Elizabeth and Friedman were bundled in. Within seconds, the entourage was moving, heading for her first major television interview.

'Mr President?'

Willard Morgan looked across the Oval Office. He remained seated on the sofa and waved McQuogue in, throwing a copy of the *Times* back on to the table. 'I just don't *get* it, Wayne. I mean, what does this woman stand for? Where has she *been*? She's never held elected office in her life but they're talking about her as if she's the Great White Hope.'

Willard sat back and rubbed his eyes. McQuogue placed his briefcase on the carpet and sat down.

Oh dear. This was going to be a long one.

'Mr President, your support in the party will hold up. I'm sure of it. I've been speaking to—'

'Yeah, yeah. I know, Wayne. I also know it's *bullshit*. Those guys would lick a buffalo's ass if it helped them.'

McQuogue tried to calm him. 'Sir, her speeches and interviews will be forgotten by the end of the week. You have the G8 in a month. There're more important things to get on with. The media will tire of her.'

'No, they won't.'

'Mr President, these are literally very early days. Elizabeth hasn't got a proper organisation yet. She hasn't staked out her position on a whole range of issues. You will cement your supremacy at the conference in Houston. Elizabeth Forrester is a novelty that will wear off, I promise you.'

Willard stood up. 'Walk with me, Wayne.'

They made their way through the secretaries' office and past the Cabinet Room. McQuogue followed Willard down the ramp and to the right as they began the short walk back towards the Residence. The Service opened the French doors that led on to the West Terrace. They were outside now, the evening warm. The Rose Garden was to their right, illuminated by the lights of the West Wing. Willard stopped halfway along the colonnade and, stepping down, walked into the middle of the garden, his feet dragging slightly on the earth. In front of him, the White House lawns spread out beyond the trimmed hedges. He lit a cigar. The flame of his lighter briefly illuminated his face. McQuogue recognised that look: despair, confusion. He had seen it in other people; men who questioned the purpose of going on, their strength bleeding away.

'First time I came here was for Tricia Nixon's wedding,' Willard said, walking round the garden. 'Goddam Nixon put me on the worst table, right over there. I had the ushers crashing into me every five minutes. When I thanked him, the bastard said: "Thought I'd need a map to find you!" But I kicked his ass on the committee. I should have sent him his own map so he could find his way back to San Clemente.'

Willard chuckled softly. McQuogue's feet sank into the grass. It had rained earlier. Looking down, he saw that his shoes were covered with little specks of green.

'Aw, we'll see in the morning,' Willard said finally, placing his arm around McQuogue's back and guiding him towards the colonnade. The Chief of Staff could smell the President's breath: stale tobacco, a hint of alcohol. 'Things always look brighter then, eh? Send my best to Flora. Ethel's playing bridge with her tomorrow, right? Good. Tomorrow. Right, well, we'll see. Tomorrow.'

McQuogue watched the President make his way along the dimly lit corridor. Then he retraced his route back into the West Wing. He passed the framed photographs of Willard, walked down the stairs and out again on to West Executive Drive. His car was waiting. It made its way through the guardpost at the south-east gate and turned towards 17th Street, heading north.

McQuogue let his head fall back against the seat. He opened the window, enjoying the warm night air.

Willard's falling apart.

Flora was asleep when he arrived home. McQuogue let himself into his first-floor study and switched on the lights. He sat down at his oak desk, then picked up the telephone. He checked the time: 11.30 p.m. He dialled the familiar number. It was late, but he knew the man wouldn't mind being woken.

Chapter Thirty-two

White opened his eyes and sat up, dazed. He squinted and tried to get his bearings. Rolling out of bed, he got dressed and strolled down to Mort's office. A copy of that morning's *Herald* was on the table. Elizabeth's picture dominated the front page. White groaned and was about to pick up the paper when the door swung open.

Riordan looked at him and smiled. 'You OK?'

'Been better.'

The telephone interrupted them. Riordan leaned over and snatched it up. 'Yeah?'

White listened as he grunted into the phone, making short notes on a pad between them. 'OK . . . fine, many thanks,' Riordan said, looking at him. 'I've no idea how he is . . . what? Well, he's had the answering machine on for a while—' He looked at White. 'Yeah, well, thanks for letting me know. I'll pass on the message if I speak to him.'

'Who was that?'

'The office.'

'How do—'

'I told them I was dropping by to see Mort.' He looked at White. 'They still think you're ill.'

'I fucking must be,' he grunted, 'crashing out in this dive.'

Riordan threw his Styrofoam cup into the trashcan. 'Well, you've got a message . . . some old lady called you. She wouldn't leave a name. Lives in Alexandria. You know her?'

White nodded. 'Yeah, she's Kelly's neighbour.'

'She left a number,' Riordan said, pushing the note across the desk.

White leaned over and pulled the telephone towards him. He dialled the number. It rang and rang. He was about to put the receiver down when the call was answered.

'Yes, who is this?'

'My name's Mark White. From the *Herald*. You called me earlier?'

'Oh, yes, thank you, dear! Yes, that's right, I did call you. I couldn't for the life of me remember where I'd left your card, so I searched the whole house. I knew it was here somewhere, but with all my paints and canvases sometimes things just—'

'Ma'am, is there something you wanted to tell me?'

'Yes, there is. Mr White, there was a letter for Ron this morning. I only found it when I got back. It wasn't addressed to him, of course. It was under the name he used for his phone, the cellular one.'

'Yes, ma'am. His private one.'

'That's right. Anyway, I thought, given that poor Ron won't be coming back, I should open it. So I did. It's the same thing I gave you before, a bill. This one has a call on it. Only one. I thought it might be of help to you. Stay there and I'll find it.'

White motioned to Riordan for a pen. He hurriedly took the pad and made a note. According to the neighbour, the call had been made the day after Forrester's death.

'Are you sure that's the date?' White asked.

'Well, that's what it says here. The last bill had lots of numbers on it but—'

'Ma'am, they send the bills out at specific times. This call has obviously been passed on to the next month's billing. Is there anything else on the bill?'

'Yes, there is . . . there's the time it was made eleven-seventeen p.m. And a number. Shall I read it to you?'

White took down the number. He didn't recognise the area code.

'Ma'am, I'm very grateful,' he said.

White replaced the phone and showed Riordan the number. 'Do you know this area code?'

Riordan leaned over and squinted. 'Yeah, how could I not know it? It's Irishtown. Boston.'

'Are you sure?'

'Of course I'm sure. Why? Whose is it?'

White shrugged. 'I don't know. But Ronald Kelly called it just before he fell off the mountain.'

Riordan sat back in surprise. 'Well, there's only one way you're gonna find out who he was calling.' He nodded at the phone. 'Try it.'

'It's a bit early, Mick, and I don't—'

Riordan snorted his irritation. 'Fuck the time, Whitey. If anyone's going to be at home, it's now.'

White dialled the number. A man's voice answered after three rings. 'Hello. Who is this?'

White quickly ran through his introduction. 'I'm sorry to trouble you so early,' he said, 'but I'm calling about Ronald Kelly. My name's Mark White. I'm a journalist from the *Herald* in Washington, DC. Who am I speaking to?'

'For heaven's sake, it's before breakfast!' White could hear a door slam. 'I really don't think this is the kind of hour to be calling someone about their dead brother. Can you people never leave others alone?'

Kelly's brother?

'And anyway,' the man went on, 'I don't talk to the media, let alone a sleazy tabloid.'

White's patience evaporated. Resisting the instinct to scream down the telephone, he spat the words out. 'Listen, I don't fucking care if you think I'm slime! But since I've been looking into your brother's death, I've been physically threatened, chased—"

'I said *good day*, Mr White.' The voice was harsh, final.

He panicked that he had gone too far. 'Sir, your brother happens to have been murdered.'

There was silence from the other end of the line. 'On what evidence do you base this?' the man said finally.

'On very little, to be frank. But if you care to listen, I can try and explain.'

'Be quick.'

White ran through what he knew. 'He was reported dead in Shenandoah. Did you know that?'

There was silence.

'Shenandoah?' The voice was hesitant.

'Does that surprise you, sir?' White looked up at Riordan and gave the thumbs-up.

'Yes, yes . . . it does.'

'You didn't see it in the press?'

'No, I don't read newspapers. I didn't even know Ronald was dead until a friend told me he had read about it. How predictable . . . Shenandoah . . . of all the places to have gone . . .'

'Why do you say that?' White asked hurriedly, flipping over to a new page of his notebook.

'Why? Oh, because that's where our father went. Hawksbill Creek. He had a cabin there. I've never been but Ronald did, many years ago.'

'Where is this cabin?'

'No real idea . . . along the trail, near Elkton, if I remember rightly. My father cheerfully named it Empty Creek, although my recollection is that the area was officially known as Baldor . . . Bentore Hollow, something like that.'

'Sir—'

'Did you say your name was White?'

'Yes, sir.'

'Fine. I hope I've been of assistance. But please, Mr White, don't call again.'

'You've no interest in how your brother died, Mr Kelly?'

There was a short silence. 'Not really. At my age you are only truly interested in your own death.'

The line went dead.

White looked at Riordan. 'Kelly's family had a cabin in Shenandoah,' he said, closing the notebook. 'That must have been where he was heading.' He checked back through his notes as Riordan lit a cigarette and passed it to him. 'Have you ever been out there?' he asked the Irishman.

'Never.'

'Mick, I'm seeing Friedman this evening. There'll be maps at the Barnes and Noble down the block. We can check there.'

Riordan followed him out of the door.

Friedman left the war room and walked two blocks. He hailed a cab, giving the driver the address. The evening was warm and cloying. Friedman was sweating into his clothes; the interior of the cab was airless. He slumped back in the hard leather seat, closing his eyes. His eyelids felt heavy, dank. Each time he shut himself off from the world around him, Elizabeth's name ran through his mind like a jammed CD.

Fifteen minutes later, the cab swerved to a stop at the corner of 4th and K Street. 'You sure you wanna get out here, bud?' The driver turned and looked at Friedman.

He nodded in response and paid. The sidewalk was quiet. Across from him, a small deli was closing up for the night. Beside it a carport rose seven storeys. Friedman looked around him. The hotel was in the middle of the next block. Its sign was blood-red and half broken: the Beau Regarde. The entrance consisted of a brown metal door beyond which a seedy lobby housed a small desk, metal grilles protecting an obese man sitting behind it. Friedman pushed through the door. A TV set blasted out a baseball game, the noise deafening. The reception clerk did not bother to raise his head in greeting.

'Excuse me,' Friedman had to shout to make himself heard.

Lifeless eyes fixed on him then turned back to a supermarket tabloid. The man was dressed in a filthy green turtleneck, the front dusted in cigarette ash. 'Twenty dollars for an hour,' he roared, 'thirty-five for the night. Bathroom's shared—'

Friedman felt a surge of shame. 'I'm not here to take a room,' he snapped abruptly, checking behind him. 'I'm here to meet someone. A friend. There should be a reservation in the name of White.'

The clerk rolled himself to the left. He opened a large black register and ran his podgy finger down a short line of names, his head still bowed. 'Room twenty-four, end of the second floor.' He slung a thick copper key across the desk.

Friedman looked at it warily. 'Is he not here yet?'

'Nah. But let yourself in. Elevator's through that door.'

The elevator opened on to a dark and dingy corridor. The ceiling lights were caked in grime, the milky brown linoleum torn and spotted with dirt. Friedman's eyes slowly adjusted to the gloom. He peered at the door numbers, and made his way to the left. Room 24 was the last one, at the end of the corridor by the fire escape entrance. Friedman stopped outside and listened. There was no noise from within. He tapped quietly on the door just to make sure.

No response.

He looked behind him and knocked again. He could feel himself trembling. He snatched his hand back and waited some more. Then he unlocked the door and stepped inside. The room was surprisingly large. A double bed to the left, two windows overlooking the street. A small desk and an old-fashioned TV. The curtains were thin and pulled back, the one on the right partly falling off the rail. Friedman closed the door and sat down on the bed.

He would speak with White. Afterwards, he would wait for his blackmailers to call, and then he would finish this game for good.

It wasn't the best of angles, but it would have to do. The carport was nearly full, the top floor open to the elements. There had originally been five security cameras on this level, linked to a control panel at the main entrance in the basement. But vandalism and indifference meant only one was working now.

His sight was hindered also by the sun, which was tilting to the west and head-on. Apart from these irritants, the man was calm. He had done this kind of job before. Would do so again.

He crouched by the side of the scarred concrete balcony. To his left and right were two cars, and behind them a small pick-up truck. He unfurled the FR-F2 sniper rifle from its packaging and leaned back against the wall. The weapon was perfect for the job. Made in France, it was designed to deliver its bullets in a first-round hit, at a range of six hundred metres. A good sniper could place ten shots on a human-sized target within a circle of only twenty centimetres. Any closer, and an expert could group the shots within five centimetres.

The man liked to think of himself as an expert.

White hurried through reception. He marched towards the desk and banged his hand hard against the top. The fat clerk sat back in surprise. 'Wha—'

'Room twenty-four. Have you got the key? I paid you earlier, remember?'

The clerk turned back to his newspaper. 'Your *friend*'s already up there.'

White swore loudly. 'When did he get here?'

'Five minutes ago.'

White turned and strode towards the elevator. As he waited for it to descend, he heard the clerk muttering behind him, 'Goddam faggots.'

He controlled his anger, looking at the line of numbers above the elevator door. Someone was holding it on the top floor. He cursed again and pushed through to the stairs, running up the two flights. The fire escape door was heavy and rusty. He heaved it open and found himself opposite Room 24. He knocked quickly. 'John?'

The door swung open immediately.

'White, where the fu—'

He pushed past Friedman. 'I'm sorry, I had to go a different way to get here.' He saw the surprise in Friedman's eyes. 'Well, we don't want the media following us, do we?' he lied, then took in the room. 'Do you like this place? Not quite what a White House staffer is used to, eh?'

Friedman pulled a small chair towards him and sat down. 'Look, Mark, let's get this over with, if you don't mind. I've spoken with Elizabeth and she's given me her authorisation to discuss Kelly with you.'

White sat on the bed opposite. The late sun shone through the grimy windows. Friedman's face was in shadow, his narrow head framed by the square of light behind him. 'OK,' White said, 'let's not waste any more of your time.' He took out a small tape recorder and placed it on the bed. 'Do you mind this?'

Friedman shook his head.

White smiled. 'A strange place to have an interview, isn't it?'

Friedman did not respond to the humour. 'OK. This is what I can tell you. Shortly after the President died, Mrs Forrester became aware of Ronald Kelly. I can't tell you how—'

'John—'

'Mark, just listen! It doesn't matter how she found out, the fact is that Kelly seemed to be warning the White House that things were not as they should be over at the Pentagon. You know he worked for the Foreign Military Sales office?'

'Yeah, and I also know he tried – and maybe did – get a memo to Tyler Forrester.'

Friedman looked up in surprise. 'How—'

'It doesn't matter,' White said. 'Have you seen what Kelly sent to the Oval Office? Has Elizabeth?'

Friedman breathed deeply again. 'No. Mrs Forrester suspected that Kelly had alerted the President to the fact that some of the contributors to his campaign may have been getting favours from elsewhere in the administration. There's no proof, just suspicion.'

'Is that why she sent Morrow to Shenandoah?'

Friedman nodded. 'Yes. We were eager to talk to Kelly. But, well, you know the rest.'

White leaned forward, trying to keep his balance on the soft bed. 'No, I don't, actually. Are you saying Kelly was murdered?'

'We don't know. But he's not here to tell us anything more, is he? Mrs Forrester believes that he had seen something at the Pentagon that wasn't right. For whatever reason, he thought he could trust the President. But we don't know what Kelly told him.'

'Why not?'

Friedman paused and shook his head. 'Because Kelly had given the President a memorandum . . . but we can't find it.'

White jerked back. What Friedman had just said tallied with Appleton's interview. 'You're telling me Tyler Forrester knew about this and nothing was done? Jesus—'

Friedman raised his hand. 'I'm not saying that. It's all conjecture. Mrs Forrester has decided she herself can't make this public because she has no solid proof of what she suspects. That's why she's agreed for me to meet with you.'

'John, you're talking in code here.'

Friedman hissed back at him, 'I'm doing my goddam best!

You wanted to swap what we had, so here we are. Tell me what *you* know.'

'OK.' White held his stare. 'Kelly and the FMS office are the last place the export requests for arms go to. Since I've been looking into this, I've been followed, beaten up, fuckers have been to my home. I don't—'

'*What?*'

White ignored the interruption. 'Look, none of that matters now. Tell me one thing: Leonard Calthorp. He runs NordFund. Does Elizabeth know him?'

Friedman sat back and turned his palms towards White. 'No.'

'John, Calthorp knows McQuogue.'

White could see the fear in the other man's eyes. 'The Chief of Staff is the link to NordFund?' Friedman asked.

White nodded. 'They're old friends. It was McQuogue—'

The first bullet thundered into the crooked picture above White's head. At a speed of 850 metres per second, it had taken a quarter of a second to cross the street from the carport opposite. Even less to shear through the window in front of White, ploughing into the wall behind him. The second bullet was nearer, slicing off the top of the tape recorder in his hand, plastic and wiring embedding themselves in his face.

'Fucking hell!'

Friedman screamed and lunged forward. White threw himself to the floor and grabbed Friedman's arm, dragging him back into the room. Three more 7.62 mm bullets carved through the bed like a knife through butter. White rolled on to his left side, wincing as the splintered glass from the window cut into his shoulder and back. Friedman crawled after him. 'Jesus, White! What—'

'Stay down! Stay the fuck down!'

The bullets were coming faster now. The television exploded in a violent snowstorm of sparks and shattered tubing. The vanity desk crumpled under the assault, the cheap Formica splitting as it lurched and fell forward. White scanned the room. A small door was ahead of them. He kicked it open with his feet. It led into a bathroom. White crawled through. 'Follow me. Come on, move! Keep *down!*'

The bathroom was shared with the room next door. White hurled himself through the door, spinning on his knees as he did so. Friedman crouched behind him. To White's right was another door. He calculated quickly: it must lead back on to the hotel corridor.

He tried to stand. Another round of bullets obliterated the light switch and thundered through the thin plaster walls, crushing the line of tiles above the bath by his head.

'Jesus!' White sank back down. Friedman was prostrate on the floor, whimpering and trembling violently. 'John, come on! We've got to move! Come *on!*'

Friedman lay rigid with fear. He moaned, his face wet with tears. 'It's them! They—'

'John, not now! *Come on!*' He tried to pull Friedman towards him. But the young man refused to budge. The mirror exploded behind White, shards of glass hurtling through the tiny room. He felt a sting on his cheek. He ducked again, kicking Friedman's ribs. 'John—'

'They were blackmailing me! ' Friedman was screeching with fear, his face contorted. 'They got to me! Oh, Jesus! Oh, no. My God, it's *them!*'

'John, not now! We've got to get the fuck out of here!'

Friedman scrambled to his feet. His face was cut, blood matting his hair. 'Mark, I told them about Elizabeth! About the abortion! They said they'd ruin me. They'd got to my *mother!* They asked me about Kelly . . . wanted me to stop Elizabeth looking into him. They know about you and—'

White tried to grab his legs, to get him down. But Friedman stood up again, his jacket half off him, swaying on his legs. 'It's got to be them, the bastards!' He lunged towards the door that led back into the bedroom. 'My God, my case! Where's my case—'

'John, no!'

The bullet caught Friedman in the thorax. The severed artery found its new opening within a second, Friedman's blood erupting on to the walls and floor. Another bullet took off the right side of his face. He hovered in the air, arms outstretched, his handsome features crumpled like tissue paper as he twisted in terrible agony then fell to the floor.

White flung the corridor door open and rolled out, his face scraping along the torn and filthy linoleum. The door to the room opposite swung open. 'Jesus, buddy, what're you doin'?' The man was half naked and sweating. White could hear a radio blaring from within.

White pushed him back into the room then made it to the fire escape, his clothes sticking to him. He slammed against the door at the bottom and found himself in a small parking lot. He started running, keeping away from the main sidewalks, dashing through the alleys that criss-crossed this part of town. He saw no one but did not dare check behind him. One long alleyway ended at the outskirts to an industrial park. White stopped and leaned against a chain-link fence. His hands were covered in blood and dust. He dared not think about his face.

White stood shivering on the corner of 17th. The lights from McReedy's fell across the sidewalk. Through the glass he could see drinkers in a solid row. He watched as two women came out, the noise from inside shattering the tranquillity of the street for a few seconds. He checked around him. There were no cars and no pedestrians. He retraced his steps around the block, walking east and away from the bar. He hurried along the sidewalk, hugging the shopfronts. He doubled back again, now on 18th, and entered the alleyway that led down to McReedy's trade entrance. Crates of empty bottles lined one wall. White pushed the connecting door open. Immediately, the noise and fumes of the bar enveloped him.

Mort saw him immediately, nodded, and then leaned forward, whispering into Riordan's ear. White let the door slide shut and waited. Two minutes later, his friend joined him in the small lobby.

The Irishman recoiled in fright. 'Jesus, Whitey, what the hell happened?'

White tugged at his sleeve and pointed upstairs. The two men took the stairs quickly, then crowded into the tiny bedroom. White slumped on the bed. His face was chalky, eyes red-rimmed, a streak of dried blood swathed across his forehead. Riordan disappeared back into the hall to return with a handful of wet napkins. He handed them to White.

'Friedman's dead.'

'*What?*'

White told him. He spoke in short bursts, his voice hoarse and tremulous. Riordan leaned back against the door jamb, his huge frame engulfing the narrow space. 'Did anyone see you leave?'

White shrugged. 'One guy but I hadn't booked the room in my own name.'

'The cops still won't be able to trace you.'

'Fuck, Mick, I know that! And what would I tell them anyway? "Oh, yes, I did arrange the meeting, but I didn't know he was going to have his head blown off!" Jesus, he exploded in front of me.' White began to tremble. Riordan pulled a small silver flask from his jacket pocket. He unscrewed the top and handed it over.

White drank greedily, the warm liquid scorching his throat. It tasted bitter and dry. He swallowed hard, the heat from the whiskey filling his chest. He looked at Riordan. 'The cops are going to think I had a hand in this! Jesus, Mick, this is murder we're talking about. First Kelly, now Friedman! Elizabeth knew he was meeting with me. She'll think I had—'

'Whitey, take it nice and slow.' Riordan sat down on the bed, his thick thigh pushing into White's back. He took the flask from out of his friend's hand and sipped at it. 'What did Friedman say?'

White told him. 'Then the stupid asshole tried to get back into the room! He was trying to find his goddam briefcase!' He struggled to control his breathing. 'He kept screaming about "them", about how they'd blackmailed him, that he'd told them about—' He sank his head in his hands. 'Jesus, Mick, the guy just had no idea what he was dealing with.'

'He was being watched.' Riordan's loud breathing ricocheted around the room.

White moaned softly, his head slumped against his chest. 'And so they killed him because he was talking to me?'

Riordan nodded. 'Did he give you a name?'

White moaned again. 'I'm not sure. When I mentioned Wayne McQuogue, he nearly collapsed. The guy was almost shaking from fear.'

The two men looked at each other. Then Riordan threw White's jacket at him. 'Come on, we're getting you out of here.'

White waited as his friend disappeared down the stairs. In seconds he was back, Mort hurrying behind him. White followed the two men into the basement of the bar. The cavernous space was badly lit, bags of rubbish and empty crates vying for space. In the middle was a large blue van. Riordan pushed White into the back of the vehicle as Mort got in the front. Seconds later, the garage door rose noisily. White and Riordan crouched in the back. The van turned left and stopped. Mort got out again. 'What's he doin'?' White asked, pushing his head against the window.

'Locking up,' Riordan snapped, legs splayed out in front of him. The floor of the van was smeared with grime and dust. 'This goddam suit cost me a hundred bucks,' he moaned, adjusting his weight as he struggled to get comfortable.

Mort pulled out into the evening traffic. Riordan barked directions. 'We'll hole you up at Roxie's,' he told White. 'Time you met her anyway.' The Irishman examined his clothes and cursed again.

'I've got to try Shenandoah, Mick.'

'Yeah, yeah . . . but Mort doesn't know the way there.' He looked at White. 'And you need to lie low tonight. I'll stay with you.' Riordan turned away and muttered, 'Christ, why am I going out on a limb for a sonofabitch like you?'

White didn't have the energy to thank him.

Chapter Thirty-three

'Mrs Forrester?'

Elizabeth waved for Morrow to enter. He remained standing and waited until she ended her conversation. 'Yes, Senator, I am willing to extend the grants in that regard,' she said, her voice smooth and polished.

Elizabeth put the receiver down and looked at the desk in front of her. She picked up the briefcase next to her and withdrew some papers.

'Mrs Forrester?'

She looked up again. 'Lee, oh, I'm sorry, I was miles away. Forgive me. Good morning.' She smiled at the agent. Then the smile vanished.

'Mrs Forrester, I'm afraid I have some bad news.'

She held his stare. *Oh, no, not again!*

'It's John, ma'am.'

She looked at him, horrified. 'What?'

'He was found in a Washington hotel, ma'am. He'd been shot. I'm sorry, Mrs Forrester, but John is dead.'

'Oh, no! How? Wh-wh- what . . .'

Elizabeth's anguished cry echoed through the room. Her head slumped against the desktop. She could smell the polish. She pressed her forehead harder against the glistening wood.

She stayed like that for a very long time.

*

McQuogue let the curtains fall back. The West Wing was beginning another day. He yawned and stretched himself, glancing at the television set in the corner of the room. The sound had been turned down and he waited as the commercials finished.

He blinked and looked at the screen. Friedman's face stared back at him.

McQuogue scrabbled for the remote control. As he did so, the images changed. Police cruisers on a downtown street. TV cameras. A small crowd. He upped the volume.

'We are going live to a crime scene in downtown DC this morning on the infamous "Brothel's Alley" neighbourhood north of Union Station.' The anchorman's voice was dark and smooth as liquorice. 'The body of a young man discovered last night at approximately eight p.m. has been officially identified this morning as that of Mr John Friedman, Director of Communications for Elizabeth Forrester's primary campaign. A 911 had been made by the hotel's reception after gunshots were heard from a room on the second floor of the building last night.'

McQuogue stood transfixed, his suit jacket limp in his hand. He saw a body-bag being brought out of the hotel entrance. The reporter's excited tones boomed loudly from the TV set. 'Mr Friedman apparently died in a hail of bullets. Police sources have confirmed that another man was seen leaving the building shortly after the incident. As yet, the authorities have not revealed whether they know the mysterious man's identity although we are told that Mr Friedman had arrived at the hotel for a meeting. The Beau Regarde is a hotel associated with the sex trade and notorious as a hangout for male and female prostitutes. Witnesses have confirmed that a man was seen—'

'Jesus fucking Christ!'

McQuogue spun round and lunged for the telephone. He barked at the signals operator, 'Get me the President!' then issued a further list of staff to be brought to his office. McQuogue threw the receiver back down and perched on the edge of his desk, trying to decipher the clues from the TV report. His calculations were swift and unhindered by emotion. It wasn't John Friedman McQuogue was thinking about. It was Elizabeth.

Friedman was a nail in her coffin.

'MRS FORRESTER! DID you speak to him BEFORE he DIED? FRIEDMAN!! FRIEEDMAN! Mrs Forrester?? FRIEEEDMAAANN!'

Elizabeth could hear the reporters' shouts through the car window as the limousine swept away from the cottage. She could see the local police herding journalists away from the entrance, waving the car forward. It suddenly lurched to the right, picking up speed. Ahead of it a police car, siren wailing, stormed forward, another to the rear of the limousine.

Two quick, violent turns and they were heading towards DC.

Elizabeth stared wildly around.

It wasn't meant to be like this.

Half an hour later, they drew up alongside the war room.

'Lee, they're here as well!'

The door to the office suite was blocked by the media. Morrow peered through the windscreen, shouting at the driver. 'I don't fucking care!' he screamed. 'Mount the sidewalk. We're going to mount the sidewalk!'

He urged the driver forward.

'Lee, someone's going to get killed here!'

Morrow shouted again. 'Get us to the door! Now!'

The limousine half-mounted the sidewalk, forcing the reporters to make a hasty retreat. Morrow quickly kicked open the door, taking Elizabeth's hand. 'NOW!'

They were out of the car, the pack closing in on its prey. 'IN! IN!' Morrow shouted, still holding her hand. Elizabeth tried desperately to find her step. 'IN! The door!'

Finally, they were through. Morrow slammed the door closed behind him, the DC police speedily forming a guard against the media.

Elizabeth was looking at her shoes as she entered the war room. One of her heels had nearly broken in the scrum. She examined it, muttering under her breath. She thought she was alone: the only noise came from outside – violent banging on the window, shouts and screams, a chorus of protests. But when she looked up she realised that she wasn't. There were over a hundred people staring at her. Every one of them was silent. Her campaign workers shuffled aside and eventually made a space for her to walk through. Still no one said anything. The shock of Friedman's death – *his murder*! – had left them mute.

Elizabeth hurried to the back of the room. Greenhalgh held the conference room door open for her. She fell through it, slamming her handbag against the wall. He let the door fall shut and closed the Venetian blinds, blocking the view from outside.

'Sit down, Elizabeth.'

She glared at him, eyes on fire, cheeks flushed crimson.

He spoke softly this time. 'Please, just sit down.'

'Jesus, Benmont, have they no shame? Those people . . . John's just died, and look at them!'

'Liz, your chief campaign manager has just been gunned down in a seedy hotel! What on earth do you expect?'

She glared at him again.

'I'm as devastated as you are, Liz. John was my friend, too. But we have to think of a way to deal with this.'

She leaned back violently in the chair, nearly tipping herself over. '*Deal* with it? John's not an exit poll, Benmont! Can't anyone just show some respect for the man? For us? For his mother? Christ, his mother . . . I haven't called her.' She stood up, lunging for the phone. Benmont leaned forward and placed his hand over hers.

'I've spoken to her already. I told her you would call as soon as things quietened down. She understood, Elizabeth. She knows what's happening up here.'

Elizabeth slumped back in her chair and cursed again.

'Liz, I'm sorry, but we have to take stock of what's happened. I've been speaking to Simons at NBC—'

'*Benmont!* John is dead and you're talking *business!*'

Greenhalgh began walking round the room. 'Elizabeth, when Tyler died, how did you feel?'

'What?' She had begun crying.

'How did you feel? Your husband was dead. And . . .?'

Elizabeth stared at him. She swallowed and managed to speak. 'I felt – I *feel* – devastated. He was my husband!'

'So why do you want to be President?'

'Benmont, do we have to do this now? Christ, John is in some morgue and you're interrogating me. You bastard, Benmont! You unfeeling, mother—'

Greenhalgh put his arm round her.

She cried again, terrible, raking sobs, anger and grief fuelling her rage, her fist slamming on the table-top. Eventually, she managed to compose herself. 'Oh my God, Benmont, what have I got us into?'

'Did you know who he was meeting?' Greenhalgh asked gently.

Elizabeth hid the lie behind her anger. 'No. He was due to get back to the cottage late last night but he never arrived. I suppose the police will want to speak with me?'

Greenhalgh nodded. 'They've already been on to us. They'll come over whenever you're ready. You saw the reports?'

Elizabeth had. A photocopy of the scene-of-crime notice was in her attaché case. The police would inevitably ask her why her young aide was meeting someone in a sleazy hotel. She couldn't tell them. Not yet. Not until someone had spoken to Mark White.

Where are you, Mark?

She pushed the thought from her mind. 'What do we do now?'

'Well, we have a statement prepared. We'll release it. Then, as arranged, you will give your speech this evening—'

'No!'

'Yes, you will. You will speak about John. You will speak about Tyler. You will speak about yourself.'

Elizabeth tipped forward in her chair. 'I'm not sure I can go through with it, Benmont. Not any more,' she whispered, staring at the table-top.

There was a heavy bang on the door. They both turned and looked at it. Greenhalgh raced around the table and threw it open.

'I told you. No interruptions!'

Claire Perry, a slight young woman with auburn hair who worked as Elizabeth's advance team manager, stood in front of him. 'I'm sorry, Benmont, but I think you should take this call.'

'For God's sake, can't you deal with it?'

Elizabeth watched the young woman closely. She was tense, all of them were tense, but Perry was trembling, her face red. 'Benmont, I really, really think you should take this call!'

Greenhalgh glanced back at Elizabeth and rolled his eyes. 'OK, OK. Who is it?'

'Martins from the network.'

'Jesus, the locals! Give me a break. I'm not talking to some scum who thinks—'

Perry thrust the message slip into his hand. 'Take it, Benmont!'

Elizabeth watched as he took the call.

'Hi, so what can I do for you today?'

Greenhalgh's tone was light. He sat back in his chair, shoulders open, one foot on the edge of the conference table. 'Yes,' he went on, 'Mrs Forrester will be making a statement about Mr Friedman's death.' He paused and caught Elizabeth's eye. 'No, I can't give you an exact time yet. The candidate is obviously distressed by events and is also insistent that we protect Mr Friedman's family from any further upset.'

Elizabeth nodded vigorously, rising from her chair. She walked to the front of the conference room and peered through the blinds into the main office. The campaign workers were mostly on the phones, doubtless fielding yet more enquiries about the tragedy that had struck her campaign.

'I'm *sorry*?'

Elizabeth turned sharply at Greenhalgh's tone.

'Er, I don't know about that,' he said into the phone. 'No, I can't make any statement. I mean, are we talking rumour here or fact? Because if this is just a smear, then believe me—'

Greenhalgh stopped. He listened for a few seconds more. Elizabeth returned to her chair opposite him, desperate to catch his eye. 'You're kidding me! What? This is outrageous! OK, OK, here's the deal. I will speak to the candidate about this, although I don't see why she should even bother with this kind of crap. And I'll tell you now: if this is a pile of horseshit, which I have absolutely no doubt it is, then you'd better bury it, pal!'

Greenhalgh replaced the receiver. He untied his cravat and dabbed at his forehead, letting out a deep sigh. Then he looked at his boss. 'Liz, that was one weird phone call.'

'Well, tell me. What was it about?'

He looked down at his notes. 'Jesus! Where do they get this crap from? I mean, we knew the White House would play dirty tricks, but this is disgusting! Contemptible! I'm gonna nail these fuckers *to the wall!*' He threw the notebook to one side. 'They claim you had an abortion when you were . . .'

Elizabeth listened in silence. She did not, could not, move.

Eventually, she spoke. 'I'm sorry, Benmont. It's true.'

Chapter Thirty-four

Elizabeth felt it had been a lifetime since she had heard of Friedman's death. In fact, she realised, as she tried to compose herself, it had been only a matter of hours. She looked in the mirror. No message, no relief, came back to her from the eyes that met her own. She stepped out of the bathroom and back into a private office at the war room.

'How're you feeling?' Marjorie asked, gathering Elizabeth's case from the table.

'Like they're loading the rifles for me,' she replied, straightening her skirt and examining herself in the mirror. 'Did you read my speech?'

Marjorie leaned across the desk and retrieved the cards. 'Yes, I did. I think you're very brave, Liz.'

'Brave or stupid. But we'll find out soon enough. What's the time?'

'Five-thirty. We should go now.'

The two women left the room. One of the campaign advance team stood by the door, waiting for Elizabeth's instructions. Greenhalgh was on the phone in an adjoining room. His voice echoed as he ran through the schedule with a network executive. Elizabeth waited in silence for him to finish. After a few seconds he strode towards his candidate. 'Well?' he asked gently.

'I'm ready.'

'You sure you want to do this tonight?'

She nodded and made her way towards the war room's entrance. Through the plate glass, the media stood twelve deep; they had been informed by Greenhalgh that Elizabeth would be making a live statement this evening.

Her limousine made its way down Massachusetts. Its destination was an office complex near 7th and F Street. It was where Tyler had based his own war room during the campaign three and a half years earlier.

In the car, Benmont ran through the plans. 'We've shipped in your husband's desk, Liz. The one he wrote his victory speech on. The backdrop is a picture of yourself and Tyler and the flag. That's it. Nothing else. The focus will be just on you.'

Elizabeth nodded. She was only half listening to Greenhalgh. She knew the details; had planned much of it herself. Out of the car window she watched as they made their way east on K. She caught a brief glimpse of the White House as they neared Lafayette Square, heading towards the National Portrait Gallery. As they reached F Street, she turned towards Greenhalgh.

'Did we contact Mrs Friedman, Benmont? I said I'd keep her informed of everything that was happening.'

'Yes, we did, Liz.'

'Good. I'll speak to her myself later this evening.'

They spent the rest of the journey in silence.

Elizabeth was hurried across the sidewalk and took the lift to the seventh floor. During Tyler's campaign, she had spent many hours in this office suite. As the lift doors opened, she stepped out and surveyed the room. Images of Tyler and his campaign team flashed through her mind. The late-night meetings. The laughter and the tension.

I wonder if you're watching me now, Tyler.

'We're ready, Liz,' Greenhalgh said, stepping aside.

She walked across the office suite. As she passed Marjorie, she squeezed her hand and smiled. There was no need for words.

Elizabeth took her place at the desk. The camera crews and

the lights were focused on her. She allowed make-up to be applied, cautioning the nervous assistant that she required very little. That over with, she checked that the TelePrompTer was positioned correctly. She placed the small cards in front of her and joined her hands together. The senior floor manager counted her down.

'Four, three, two . . .'

The red lights flicked on. She was live.

Elizabeth rose slightly in the chair, leaned forward and smiled.

'Good evening, my fellow Americans . . .'

'This morning, I was informed of the tragic death of my aide, John Friedman. His death, at such a young age, has come as a terrible personal shock, not just to myself but to all of those who worked with John. We knew him as a friend, and we must find the strength from each other to deal with his murder. I have spoken with the authorities in Washington and we will assist their investigation in any way we can. All of us are adamant that the full facts about what happened yesterday should be established quickly. The circumstances of his death are something the local police and government agencies must determine for themselves. It would be premature of me to venture any opinion as to why John was in that hotel, and why he died in such a brutal and savage way. Our prayers are with him and his family and friends. I know that you will join with me in praying for his soul.'

Elizabeth paused but kept her eyes on the camera lens in front of her. 'You will also be aware of a news report broadcast at lunchtime concerning my early years. I knew that when I entered public life with my husband, our marriage and our lives would be changed for ever. I have endured through my time in the White House the unrelenting pressure of media exposure. I make no complaint about it. In a democracy like ours, it is incumbent upon those holding or seeking office to open their lives to scrutiny and investigation. As First Lady, I frequently found the constant invasion of every aspect of my day-to-day life inconvenient and often painful. I fought off the temptation to respond or to resist. My role was to support my husband, a man I loved more than anything and whose memory I have sought to serve.

'I have decided to make this broadcast this evening because it is only right that you hear from me the precise facts. It is deeply painful for me to speak about this aspect of my life. I have never spoken of it before, not because I believe I have something to hide or to be ashamed of, but because to have done so while Tyler was alive would have been to embroil him in an issue over which he had no control, and a situation to which he did not contribute.

'I was nineteen years old when, as a student in Wisconsin, my world collapsed around me. Up until then, I had concentrated on my studies and, as you all know, on my deepfelt belief that the war in Vietnam was a cancer that was destroying our society. I look back on those times with a fondness and a pride that grow more profound with every passing day. My one private regret is that, in a moment of naïveté and adolescent foolishness, I became pregnant. When I realised what had happened to me, I felt the same desperation and horror that many women, even today, experience. I was disgusted with myself for being so stupid and for being in a position where I could not give my child the care and the life that I would wish to. I had my own life ahead of me and yet I had another life inside of me. I was terrified, alone and without either the courage or the humility to seek advice and counsel from my family and friends.

'The decision I took was a selfish one, in the sense that I alone decided that it was in my interests that I delay becoming a mother. I am not proud of that decision, but nor am I disgusted by it. Many women, many couples, in this country have been faced by precisely the same dilemma. In my ignorance, and perhaps my arrogance, I believed that it was the best, and only, course of action. I come from a proud and private family. My parents were role models to me. Their marriage had been the happiest and the most content I had ever witnessed. As their only daughter, their only child, I felt the pressure to do well, to repay them with my own success and my own independence. Their love for me, and their desire that I live as full and rewarding a life as I could, was something that held me together then, and still does to this day . . .'

McQuogue watched Willard. Only the two of them were present in the Oval Office. The television was on. A tray of coffee lay between them, untouched.

McQuogue felt elated. He turned back to the television screen. Elizabeth looked tired. Her eyes were puffy, her cheeks overly flushed. He thought he saw her hand tremble slightly. She had begun her broadcast tentatively, her vowels swallowed, the rhythm of her speech erratic.

'She's struggling,' he muttered.

Willard waved at him. 'Hush. I want to get all of this.'

McQuogue allowed the President to concentrate on the broadcast. Willard sat crouched forward in the chair, his whole body rigid with tension. McQuogue did not need to listen to Elizabeth's words. As far as he was concerned, she was finished. The suddenness of her appearance on television only confirmed his belief. He knew Elizabeth. She would not carry on, could not. He relaxed farther into his chair. He resisted a smile and waited for the words he knew would come. He wondered how she'd phrase it. How sorry she'd be. How she'd tell America she was pulling out of the race.

'My mother and father were traditional people. They were from a different generation – one that had lived through a war that was worth fighting. People who knew the value of family and morality. Two people who wanted their child to be happy and fulfilled. I let them down terribly and, to this day, I feel the shame and the guilt of that.

'I spent many years afterwards thinking about what I had done. I met my husband: a wonderful, loving man. I saw in him the stability and the strength I had experienced in my own home. Tyler gave me the rock on which I could stand. His ambition, his sense of purpose, his incredible lust for life, all of it diluted the pain that I carried with me every day. I did not lie to my husband, but nor did I confess to him. A marriage is a contract between two people that does not, and should not, require hidden subclauses. There were no secrets between Tyler and myself apart from this one. I did not tell him because I discovered, very early on in our marriage, that I could not have children. The operation had been successful but it had also removed my ability to become a mother. A tragic but irreversible accident.'

White grimaced. He felt as if he were watching his own betrayal, his own cowardice exposed to an uncomprehending world. Riordan stood behind him, his girlfriend Roxie cross-legged on the floor by his feet. White struggled to control his emotions. He felt sick and ashamed.

'Interesting.' Riordan's mumbling had accompanied the beginning of Elizabeth's broadcast. Roxie snapped at him to be quiet.

White knew that Riordan was judging Elizabeth's performance as a journalist. He wished he could do the same. Instead, his mind fought to deal with the images, the emotions, that threatened to swamp him. Terror. Shame. Incredulity. That it should come to *this*. That their fumbling, passionate union so many years ago, the lust of two young people fuelled by arrogance and excitement, should end up *here*, silenced and appalled him. He wished he could do anything, something, to help her. He had never been there for her. Never. He'd kept quiet, but it was Elizabeth who was now exposed. He'd told her it would be all right, but it was Elizabeth who had suffered the pain. He'd tried to make amends, but it was Elizabeth who had severed the contact between them, and found the strength to go on. His own weakness compounded in the face of her resolve.

He could hear her words, but it was her eyes that enthralled and captured him. Filled with pain and courage, they stared back at him. He willed her on, felt a tremor of hope.

Jesus, she's mesmerising.

'That knowledge almost destroyed me. Tyler had recently been elected a State Senator. Our life was perfect. We were blissfully, unconditionally happy. The news that we could never produce our own children was something I had to tell him. It was the hardest moment of my life. Tyler would have made a fantastic father. His own childhood had often been marked by tragedy and discord, but he carried with him a desperate, consuming need to prove that he could be a better father than his own. I deprived him of that opportunity.

'I know there will be those among you who will be repelled by what I did. I ask not for forgiveness but for your understanding. I ask you to respect the decision I made even if you yourselves would never have done what I did.

'One week ago I announced my candidacy for the presidency of this nation. I did so, as I have said in the days that have passed, because I know and feel that I can make a difference. I have been stunned and amazed by the groundswell of support that I have received. In talking to the people I have met, I am yet more convinced of the need to right what is so wrong with our nation. I have been wounded. I make no pretence about that. I know that there are those of you who will no longer listen to me in the way you may once have done. But I will continue with this campaign because I believe it is right to do so.'

☆

'Jesus fucking Christ, she's crazy!' Willard spun round. 'Wayne—'

McQuogue upped the sound on the TV. Both men stared at the screen in incredulity.

'I have spoken to you this evening with honesty and with hope. Honesty because finally I have laid bare the motives and the fears that drove me so many years ago. In the last few hours I have been counselled by many people as to what I should say this evening. I have listened to that advice. I have weighed the options ahead of me. But what I have said tonight is from my heart. There is no spin, no deceit. I have not set out to rewrite my history, nor to excuse it. I know I shall make a President of which this nation can be proud. I am not giving up.

'I ask you to look not at what I have done, but at what I can do.

'Thank you. Goodnight, and God bless you.'

They were down the stairs and out into the limousine within seconds. Elizabeth peered out of the window and waved to the small crowd. Marjorie and Greenhalgh sat facing her. She shut her eyes for a second, willing herself to stop shaking. She felt depleted, raw. She had done it. Had spoken about something she had thought long gone, long buried. She lowered her shoulders and opened her eyes. Marjorie and Greenhalgh were smiling.

'Well?'

Greenhalgh placed his briefcase on his knees. 'Mrs Candidate, that was one of the most extraordinary speeches I've—'

'It was the truth, Benmont.'

'I know, that's why it was so incredible!'

'Well, now it's an even playing field. There's nothing else the bastards can throw at me.'

Elizabeth turned away to look at the streets. She realised that she had spent most of her formative years watching the world watching her. She felt both relieved and full of trepidation. She'd vowed to carry on. It wouldn't be easy. All she could do now was fight to survive.

Chapter Thirty-five

At the war room the next morning, Elizabeth groaned at the spectacle visible out of the window. Despite the early hour, demonstrators competed for attention on the sidewalk outside. Across the street, Pro-Lifers howled their contempt for her. Their banners were brutal: 'Murderess!', 'Rot in Hell!', 'Baby Killer!' The crowd was three thick, police cordons pushing them back. The grey light of early morning gave the spectacle a theatrical quality: the rhythmic throb of the police lights, cars whizzing past, their headlights spotlighting the crowds, the candles and torches of the demonstrators. It was both beautiful and menacing, as if some giant beast lay immovable at her door.

Elizabeth winced and felt anger rising. Nearer to the war room entrance, on the opposite side of the street, another, larger crowd tried to shout down opponents. This mainly female contingent was as vociferous in its protests. Banners summarised its position, 'Liz Made a Choice!', 'A Human Being, Not a Politico!', 'Mothers Back You!' The placards were handwritten, moving like sunflowers every time a network TV crew scanned the crowd, the camera's torpedo of light searching for a target. The media pack swarmed across the street, charging back and forth to the opposing sides, like tennis balls over a net.

She turned and looked at Greenhalgh. 'Jesus, it's a carnival out there.'

He shrugged. 'What do you expect? You've got—'

'I know, Benmont.' She walked away from the window. 'Instead of sitting at home watching reruns of my speech last night, every zealot in the entire DC area is now camped outside my doorstep. It's hardly the way to win Middle America, is it?'

She marched back towards the conference room. Greenhalgh followed.

Morrow closed the door behind them.

It was he who spoke first. 'Mrs Forrester, I really need to run through the Houston visit with you.'

Elizabeth nodded. 'OK, Lee. I suppose it's time to get back to business as usual.' As she said it, she only half believed it.

Morrow took a collection of papers out of his attaché case. He passed a set to Elizabeth, another to Greenhalgh. The three of them fell silent. Elizabeth looked through the schedule. The first two pages were a formula she knew well, a breakdown of the personnel travelling with her.

Elizabeth glanced at Morrow and Greenhalgh. She knew what they were thinking. John Friedman's name should have been on the list. Someone had hurriedly retyped it to exclude him.

She grimaced and carried on reading.

'How many students at the College of Law?' she asked.

Greenhalgh shrugged. 'Four hundred so far. The Q&A session isn't scripted. That's been made clear to the media. The talking points are being finished outside.'

Elizabeth looked at Morrow. 'Lee, any remarks?'

'None, ma'am.' He looked at his watch. 'I'd better push on, Mrs Forrester,' he said briskly, and gathered the schedules together. 'I've got a meeting at the White House.'

Elizabeth raised her eyebrows in surprise. 'What's that about, Lee?'

'Routine, ma'am. I'll be back shortly.'

After Morrow had left, Elizabeth leaned over and picked up a set of poll figures. She read them quickly. 'It's not *too* bad, Benmont, is it?'

'No, Liz. In fact, you could say it's rather good. Even if every nut in DC is standing outside.'

'So, what's the plan?' she asked, sipping from a glass of water.

He sat back and shrugged. 'We carry on as we always intended. Since your broadcast last night, the focus groups have put you eight, nearly nine points ahead of Willard. The media coverage helps, of course.' Greenhalgh waved distractedly at the pile of newsprint spread out on the table.

Elizabeth knew he was right: since her television announcement, debate had raged about her abortion. Greenhalgh passed her a preliminary review of the network coverage last night. It was almost universally favourable. Inevitably, as she had known would happen, those on the far right had lampooned her as a 'murderer'. There had been death threats telephoned through to the war room only minutes after her TV address.

'The focus groups like your honesty and your guts,' Greenhalgh said simply. 'The line about "it's not what I've done but what I can do" registered double positive.' He looked at the figures again. In the small focus groups he had set up in the crucial primary states, voters had watched Elizabeth's announcement live. They had been given a set of buttons to push throughout her broadcast which registered 'negative', 'favourable' or 'positive'. Amazingly, she had emerged with stronger support from the voters after her broadcast than before, especially from the women. The results had been faxed through to the war room before Elizabeth had even left the TV studio. This morning, the same groups were being questioned again. Greenhalgh was set to leak the results to the media in a few hours' time.

'We still don't know who leaked the story?'

Greenhalgh shook his head. 'No, ma'am. And at present, John's death is being put down as mistaken identity.' He looked at his candidate. 'There's nothing else you need to tell me, is there, Liz?'

'No, Benmont. I don't know what John was up to. You know that.'

Her lie was a means to an end. White would get in touch, if he was still alive . . .

McQuogue rocked gently back and forth on his feet. The door to the Yellow Oval Room opened. A Secret Service agent stood in the doorway. 'Mr McQuogue, the President will see you now, sir.'

Willard looked up as McQuogue entered.

'Wayne, get comfortable. Whisky?'

The Chief of Staff nodded and watched as the President strolled to a side table and poured the drink. Willard joined him by the fireplace, handed him the glass and relaxed into a soft, large armchair. McQuogue took the small one opposite.

'Well?' the President asked. 'It doesn't look as if the abortion revelations have exactly taken the wind out of Elizabeth's sails, does it, Wayne?'

'It all depends on Houston, sir. Forget the polls for the moment. Once we get the party behind us after this weekend, Elizabeth won't have the means to keep this going. She's going to run out of money, fast.'

Willard grunted in reply. The President was jacketless, his shirtsleeves rolled up. McQuogue could see the bottom of his thick biceps. For his age, Willard Morgan remained a fit man.

'I don't want to go to Houston with Elizabeth still breathing on me, Wayne. I don't trust those fuckers. I want it tied up way before then.'

'It will be, sir.'

Willard shifted in his chair and placed the crystal glass on the carpet by his side. 'If only she hadn't given that goddam broadcast last night! She was dead in the water. Jesus, in one day she had Friedman dead, then the abortion story hits the networks. But all she has to do is flash her smile, tell everyone she's nothing less than a fucking victim, and up and down the East

Coast they're falling at her feet. According to the networks' polls, she's even up in North Carolina—'

'Mr President, if I may interrupt?'

Willard nodded for him to continue.

'Mrs Forrester is strong in certain areas. Yes, sir, it's true that she has maintained her lead in the polls. But she's running out of money, and she's weak on the ground. In most states the local party is behind us. We have more troops on the ground, and we can kill her on commercials. She simply can't sustain her campaign through the odd national broadcast.'

'You say that, Wayne,' Willard replied, undoing his dark blue tie and throwing it over the back of his chair. 'But that fucking scumbag Richards has pulled out of the race and declared for her! Bastard thinks he'll get the VP slot. Christ, the things I've done for that man on the Hill . . . Cocksucker always hated me. Thinks he's the intellectual of the party. Goddam it, he can barely write his own name without moving his lips!' He pointed his finger at McQuogue and carried on talking. 'Richards' people will go over to her in droves. It might see her through.'

'Mr President, after Houston you will be ahead. I have no doubts about that. We cannot exhaust ourselves on this campaign. The big push comes after Houston.'

'You'd better be right, goddam it,' Willard replied, rising quickly from his chair. 'What are we doing tomorrow?'

'Des Moines, sir. Then Houston. And I need you to look through some papers before that.'

Willard smiled. 'Great. The glamour of politics.'

Morrow eased his car through the south-west gate. The White House was quiet, the Secret Service Command Centre was empty. He entered the Centre and sat at one of the desks. He flicked through some files on the table, trying to find a schedule of Willard's movements.

The door opened.

'Lee, thanks for coming.'

Bob Russell, the most senior agent assigned to the White House, stood in the doorway. Russell had been Morrow's mentor. He had been the one who had recommended Morrow be assigned to Elizabeth's detail. He was also the agent who had cradled Tyler's head as his life slipped away.

Morrow stood. 'Good morning, sir.'

Russell pulled a chair towards him and sat down. Morrow sat also.

'Lee, about Houston—'

'I've just run through the schedule with Mrs Forrester. I was planning to copy it to Sixteenth Street in the morning.' All security arrangements for individuals under the Service's care were filed there. Analysts did their own deskbound checks and ran the names of people meeting the candidates or targets through the Service's own computer. The results were instantaneously passed to the on-site details concerned.

'Lee, Sixteenth can look at the Forrester schedule. I want you to look at something else.'

Russell passed over a manila folder. Morrow examined it. It was an almost identical schedule to the one he had checked for Elizabeth. But there was one important difference. This schedule was for President Morgan.

Morrow looked up at Russell. 'Sir, is there something I need to be checking for in this?'

Russell shook his head. 'Just read it, Lee.'

Morrow flicked through. He quickly came to the motorcade Assignments for Willard's own arrival in Houston. The United States Secret Service detail contained a long list of names, over thirty in all. After Bob Russell, the lead agent, the rest were in alphabetical order.

Morrow's name was on the list.

He looked again at Russell. 'Sir, why am I part of the President's deta—'

'Lee, you're being reassigned. I'm sorry it had to be done this way but—'

'Sir, you can't! I'm Head of Detail for Mrs Forrester. I'm the one who knows exactly what she'll—'

'Agent Morrow.' Russell's voice was hard and brisk. 'I am not authorised to explain the reasons.' He held up his hand to stop Morrow interrupting. He spoke quickly, his tone more sympathetic this time. 'Son, I know this has come out of the blue but there's nothing you or I can do about it. The instructions did not come from Sixteenth Street. They've just been informed of this as well. It is no reflection on you, Lee, but the orders came from the West Wing.'

'But, Bob, she needs me.'

'I'm sorry, Lee, it's already decided. You're off the Forrester detail.'

Morrow sat in silence as Russell stood and collected his papers. 'The new man is Ben Shaw. I'll make sure the Forrester people are told. You should call Shaw on this number.' Russell slid a piece of paper across the desk. 'Link up with him. The rest of the Forrester detail will cover until Shaw's in place.'

Russell left the room.

Morrow sat quietly, seething. He had expected to be with Elizabeth throughout the campaign . . . perhaps even returning with her to the White House. Although he could never say so publicly, had had to smother his affection for Elizabeth, Morrow privately wanted her to win. After Tyler's death and Friedman's murder, he had seen the private grief; but he had also seen her strength. More than anyone, he had got to know the extraordinary courage that lay beneath her groomed exterior.

And now he had been promoted! He didn't enjoy the moment.

He picked up the telephone and managed to speak to Shaw. They arranged to meet at Sixteenth Street HQ in one hour. Morrow opened a notepad and began writing. He wanted to be prepared for his meeting with the new Head of Detail. For half an hour he composed his report: everything that Shaw needed to know about every aspect of Elizabeth's life was in it: her staff; her friends; her homes; the rest of the detail. Morrow opened his briefcase and extracted the detailed plans of the war room and the Virginia cottage. He prepared a comprehensive breakdown of Elizabeth's Approved List, the venues she visited frequently, the people who had instant access to her.

He strolled across the office, photocopying the schedules for Houston, and the next month of campaign stops. The pile was three inches thick by the time he had finished. It was all there, the minutiae of Elizabeth's life. A neat, lucid breakdown of everything, and anything, the new Head of Detail needed to know about her. But Morrow knew it wasn't really complete. It didn't capture the *woman,* the person he had come to respect and admire.

No, he thought, Elizabeth couldn't be summarised by a Secret Service agent's report.

'Ma'am, I have some news.'

Morrow's voice was crackly and distant. He was on his cellular. She stiffened slightly at his tone. 'What is it, Lee?'

'Ma'am, you will be informed of this officially from Sixteenth Street . . . but, well, I wanted to tell you myself. I'm off your detail, Mrs Forrester.'

'*What?*'

'Mrs Forrester, the West Wing has requested that I rejoin the presidential protection team. There's nothing—'

Elizabeth could not control her fury. 'Who the goddam . . . let me speak to McQuogue . . . no, I want to speak to Willard. *Now!*'

Despite her rage at the insult the White House had delivered to her, Elizabeth listened to Morrow's reply. 'Ma'am, I'm sorry, but I don't think there's anything you can do. In this instance the West Wing have the final say. I'm sorry, Mrs Forrester, but I think it's best that we allow them to do this. For the time being.'

Elizabeth thought quickly. She knew he was probably right: were she to make waves, to complain to the White House, it could embarrass Morrow. Might blight his career. She did not wish to do that.

She breathed in heavily, her outrage at not being informed of his transfer scalding her like hot coffee. 'OK, Lee,' she said finally, 'they can have it their way. They're trying to play games . . . as usual. The day before I'm in Houston, lo and behold, the White House insist on rearranging my detail! Well, I suppose we'll just have to keep on smiling and not let them think we've been got at.'

Morrow did not reply. Elizabeth knew he could not, should not, agree with her. The Secret Service, not Elizabeth, was his employer.

Finally, Morrow spoke again. 'Ma'am, I will be in Houston . . . with the President's party. I've spoken to the new Head of Detail – Ben Shaw. I don't know him personally, ma'am, he's new to the Service, but he will have my full report. If there's anything more he needs, then he can call me.'

Elizabeth thanked him.

'And, Mrs Forrester . . . well, I know I shouldn't say this, ma'am, but . . . well, good luck. I'll be thinking of you.'

'Thank you, Lee. Thank you very much.'

Another friend was being taken from her.

'Send my love to Cathy and the kids, Lee . . . we'll speak very soon, I hope.'

'God bless you, Mrs Forrester. And take care.'

Elizabeth replaced the receiver. Greenhalgh held her stare. 'Morrow's off the detail,' she said quietly.

'Jesus Christ! Was this the West Wing?'

Elizabeth nodded. 'There's nothing we can do.'

Greenhalgh snorted. 'No, that's where you're wrong, Mrs

Candidate! There's a lot you can do! You can, for starters, make sure you're back in the White House.'

Elizabeth smiled. She was grateful for Greenhalgh's attempt to raise her spirits. She was aware also that he was sending her another message: we have to concentrate on the campaign. Personnel problems, however hard and dispiriting, cannot be allowed to interfere.

She knew Greenhalgh was right. But she felt more alone than she had ever done before. Tyler, John, Lee . . . the men she had trusted, the people who had always been there for her, all gone.

She rose from the table and started out across the deserted office suite.

Houston was tomorrow.

Yes, she'd be alone. But not totally. The last time she had visited Houston was with Tyler.

Somehow, she knew he'd be watching her this time.

Chapter Thirty-six

White drove as Riordan dozed beside him. Twenty minutes out of DC, they were past Fairfax, heading west on the I-66. The traffic was light. White kept a careful eye out for any cops and watched his speed.

Two hours later they reached the outskirts of Elkton, Virginia. According to Kelly's brother, the family cabin was on private land near Hawksbill Creek. White examined the maps they had bought in DC. He quickly found the area, seven or so miles to the south-east of Elkton. The highway out of the town followed the route of West Swift Run, a creek that cut through the valley between Hanse Mountain and Dolly's Knob. The National Park skirted around Hawksbill Creek itself, a small finger of privately owned land, ten miles long and four miles wide, falling away from the heights of Beldor Ridge and, beyond it, the Norfolk and Western Railway and the valley of the Shenandoah River. According to the map, there were a few cabins along Hawksbill Creek, but none were named.

He swore and threw the map aside. 'We'll try in the town,' he said to Riordan. The Irishman nodded.

White followed the route into Elkton, and parked opposite a diner. The windows were steamy and obscured. 'I'll be one second, Mick,' he said, crossing the street. He stepped inside the diner and got his bearings. An elderly waitress, her hair thin and white, stood towards the back of the room. She watched him come towards her.

'Excuse me, ma'am, but I wonder if you know this area?'

The woman smiled. 'Should do. Been nowhere else, hon'. What you looking for?'

'A place called Baldor or Bentore Hollow. It's supposed to be near Hawksbill Creek. I wond—'

'You mean Beldor Hollow?' She pronounced the last word 'Hollar'. 'Honey, I hope you've got strong legs and enough provisions! You're looking for someplace people don't go much. You can only drive so far, then you're going to have to walk.' She wiped her hands on a cloth and beckoned White. 'You got a map?'

Ten minutes later, he was back in the car.

'You find it?' Riordan asked.

'Kind of,' White replied. 'According to a waitress, the private cabins are along the edge of the National Park. She hasn't heard of the Kelly family or any land belonging to them. But she showed me where to look.'

They carried on along the I-33. Five miles outside Elkton the road twisted and turned, small lanes branching off to either side. White and Riordan kept their eyes on the road signs. Ten minutes after Swift Run, White slowed the car down as Riordan checked the map. They just managed to spot the turning: the road to Hawksbill Creek was easy to miss.

White turned the car off the highway. The lane was shielded by thick woods, sunlight disappearing as the road dipped and turned into the valley. The small car groaned and spun on the gravel. White struggled to keep the vehicle moving, his hands tight on the steering wheel.

An hour later, the lane passed by Beldor. White parked the car under the cover of some trees. 'We'll have to walk from here, Mick.'

Riordan grunted and got out. The air was thick with the smell of pine. Ahead of them, where once the lane had carried on, was a narrow path. The gravel under White's feet was solid and dusty, nature's own cement. There were no tyre marks, nor any other evidence of recent human intrusion.

'You sure Kelly would have made it this far?' Riordan asked.

White shrugged. 'Well, we have.'

He retrieved the map and locked the car. Riordan stood back and surveyed the forest in front of them. 'How do you want to do it?'

White looked at the map. According to the Rangers office, Kelly's body had been discovered at the bottom of a ridge roughly four miles from where they stood. 'Mick, I'm going to head west.' He didn't insult Riordan by pointing out that this route looked the hardest. 'You try the south.' White checked his watch. 'We'll meet back here in two hours. If either of us find the cabin, we can go back to it together.' He handed Riordan his own map.

'Jesus, what a fucking day out,' the Irishman snorted.

They headed off in opposite directions.

Under the canopy of foliage, the air was crisper. White was grateful for the cover. The midday sun was strong, but the greenery shielded him. He followed the path, checking the map every ten minutes. It took him two hours to reach the finger of private land that matched the outline given on the map. The slog had seemed twice as long. His face was itchy and sticky from the dust and pollen that engulfed him. Finally, he emerged into a wide, oblong clearing.

To the west, the ground dipped and fell towards a small creek. White could hear the gentle lapping of water thirty metres below. Around him, the forest seemed to lift and fall with an energy and life of its own. It whispered and muttered to him, the sporadic rustle of leaves unnerving.

He wiped his forehead and checked around him.

There was no sign of a cabin. All White could see were trees, endless blocks of them, the ridges steep and thick.

Jesus, this is impossible!

He sat down on a spiky granite promontory and tried to get his bearings. From the time of day and position of the sun, he knew he was facing towards the west. He tried to match his position against the terrain shown on the map. It was a difficult, infuriating task: the land seemed to fall and rise of its own accord, the spindly creeks and sharp ridges bearing little relation to the contours of the map. He stood up, wondering where the nearest inhabited place was. He had not seen a home site back on the highway, and had come across no other people.

White decided to follow the path to the right. The alternative looked uninviting: a sharp incline that appeared to fall away towards the creek below. He lunged forward. The path leaped and dipped through a seemingly impenetrable blanket of pine and oak. He pushed through, the branches snapping back at him like angry dogs.

He carried on wearily for another hour, before collapsing gratefully on the ground. He opened his bottle of water. The liquid was warm and cloying. The forest shimmied and leaped around him.

White stood up and looked once more at the map. He was, he calculated, on the eastern side of Hawksbill Creek. The most likely position for any cabin was to the south, where the land was more approachable, the terrain less inaccessible. He pocketed the map and pushed on.

The path rollercoasted through the forest. In the middle of a particularly abundant stand of trees, White tried to negotiate a difficult incline.

'Shit!'

He found himself falling, slipping helplessly. He slid down ten feet, reaching out for a handhold. His fall was broken within seconds as he plunged into a nest of nettles, their sting vicious and instant. He cried out again, hurriedly tugging his hand back. His elbow scraped savagely against something hard. He swore again and stood up. The graze was deep, the blood oozing slowly through the broken film of skin.

He found his footing and looked down. The nettle bush had been trampled, and at first he thought it was a small stake buried in the middle. He kneeled down and looked more closely. Reaching out, his fingers carefully pushed back the branches. Hidden deep in the bushes was a concrete block, about two feet high, a matchstick-thin metal spike – brown and rusted – rising out of the top for a foot and a half. The outer edges of the block were chipped and scarred, its battle against the encroaching army of greenery lost.

He looked around him. The post was definitely man-made. It was also very old, the moss along its side thick and dark. A hole the size of a dime ran through it; the rim was scuffed and worn. It appeared to be all that remained of an amateurish trap.

A trapper's cabin might be near by.

White crawled back up the hill, plunging deeper into the forest. The light was almost non-existent here, the gloom heavy and inviolable. Beneath his feet, the ground was cracked and crumbling. He blundered on, slipping on the dry, withered earth.

He pushed back another curtain of branches.

It was there, but only just.

The cabin looked as if it were part of the trees that enveloped it, a lone child among a roomful of adults. The structure was wooden, the walls turned black and greasy. It appeared as solid as a canvas tent. The sloping roof was made of corrugated iron, the rust claret-red, a small round chimney in the far corner. A two-foot wall of brick secured the cabin to the ground, the undergrowth eating its way upwards, obscuring much of the foundations. The surrounding forest pushed hard and solid against the outer walls.

White stopped and caught his breath.

This might be it. It was worth a try.

He pushed his way to the left, crunching through the woods. A small clearing, two feet wide and only a foot deep, marked the cabin's entrance. White stepped forward. The trees shoved and elbowed him as he tried to reach the door.

There were no windows at the front of the cabin. The door itself was made of steel, the once shiny metal now smudged and darkened by rainwater and slime. The handle was wooden and chipped. White grabbed hold of it, the wood cold and wet to his touch. The door stuck a little. He kicked hard against the steel with his foot.

It creaked noisily as it swung open.

'Good afternoon! You must be Mr White.'

'Benmont, this schedule isn't right.'

Elizabeth looked at her watch: 4.30 p.m. She was due to get a night flight to Houston in three hours. She slid the dossier across the conference room table. Greenhalgh took it and flicked through the stiff, typed pages. 'What's the matter with it?' he asked, sitting back and holding Elizabeth's eye.

She took it back from him and pointed to the second page. It was the afternoon and evening schedule for her arrival at the Hyatt in Houston the following evening. 'I don't know, Benmont . . . I do the Bates speech and then I'm at the Hyatt . . . I don't think they've given me enough time on the evening speech, and I can't do a proper meet-and-greet if I'm holed up in my hotel suite. According to this, I'll be spending more time talking to men in suits than to the people I need to get out and vote for me.'

Elizabeth sighed and examined the schedule once more. She had her pen ready, scribbling notes in the margin as she read it. 'There isn't enough time, Benmont.' She made some final changes to the schedule, then handed it back to him. 'Pass it to the new Head of Detail. I want a copy agreed within the hour.'

He nodded.

Elizabeth looked out of the office window across the war room. 'Where *is* the new head, anyway?' she asked, gathering her papers.

Greenhalgh shrugged. 'No idea. As far as I know, he's supposed to link up with us at the airport later.'

Elizabeth smiled. It was what she expected. The White House were playing games.

They could have their games.

She had her game plan.

White knew he couldn't run.

He stood in the doorway, terror paralysing him. The gloom inside the cabin was total. White could just make out the shape of the man in front of him: he was standing, legs slightly apart. In the faint light that came through the open doorway, White could see the reflection off the gun pointing at him.

He stood his ground, trying to control his breathing. The door jamb pressed into his arms. He felt as if he were in a makeshift prison, knew that in a way he was.

'Step back two paces. Do not even attempt to run.'

The voice was American, the accent unidentifiable. White inched back.

'Put your hands out towards me. No! Not that much. Lower them a little. Good, that's better.'

White watched as the man stepped forward. Despite the gloom inside the cabin, White could see him properly now. He was powerfully built, dressed in black track pants, grey sneakers and a dark green T-shirt. Around his waist was a navy blue bum-bag, zipped and pulled tight into his stomach. The man was about forty, his face lined and tanned.

White tried to speak, his mouth dry. 'Look, I think—'

'Shut up!'

The order was clipped. 'If I want you to talk, I'll fucking tell you. Until then, keep your mouth shut.' The man smirked. 'Mind you, who's going to hear you anyway, Mr White? You *are* Mark White, aren't you?'

He nodded.

'Well, that makes things slightly easier. It would be unfortunate to dispose of a total stranger.'

White understood the threat.

The man readjusted his position. He kept the gun pointed straight at White, at the same time rummaging with his left hand in a pocket of his pants. He pulled out a small radio. His eyes were cold and victorious. He barked into the hand-held device. 'Control.'

White heard the crackle of the radio in response. The man spoke into it again. 'Yeah, we have an unexpected result here. Mr White has joined me for an afternoon in the country.' He grinned and winked at White. 'Sure, I'll be over shortly.' He repocketed the radio. 'You really have made our job a lot easier, you know? This way, I can leave you here. We've been looking for you. It's not good for morale when a piece of shit like you is able to get away.'

White desperately willed himself to work out a plan. Opposite him, the man slid a long, dark object out of the bum-bag around his waist. White heard a crisp crackle from within the small bag, caught a glimpse of paper. He glanced back at the object in the man's hand. It was cylindrical, roughly a foot long. White watched as he attached the silencer to the muzzle of the gun. He screwed it on quickly, his eyes never leaving his prey.

White wondered why the gunman needed it. He knew that all he could do was play for time. 'Why did *you* come here?' he asked tentatively.

'I thought I told you to—'

'Hey, you're going to kill me anyway, right? So at least answer the question.'

The gunman steadied himself, flexing his hand around the pistol. 'I came here for the very same reason as you, Mr White. Kelly thought he could hide out here. We didn't know that he'd actually reached it. We caught him trying to make his way back to Hanse Mountain but . . . well, I suppose I can tell you now that he wasn't carrying something we'd hoped he'd have. So we did our own search. Took us quite some time to find out where he might have stopped off.' The man checked that the silencer was secure. 'How did *you* find out about this place? You impress me.'

It was White's turn to smile. 'Contacts,' he said, shrugging, trying to keep the dread out of his voice. 'You're one of McQuogue's people, aren't you?'

The man waved the gun at White and tut-tutted. 'Mr White, I don't think this is the right time to do an interview, do you? Perhaps if you spoke to my agent, then we could arrange something.' He sneered back at White.

'Who's your *agent*? McQuogue? Calthorp?'

'I have been known to work with them, yes.'

Bastard.

White's knees trembled a little, and his thighs felt lifeless and thick. His feet had gone numb. He fixed his eyes on the gun pointing at him. 'I'd like to meet your boss some time. I could tell him something that might be useful to him—'

'You know shit!'

'Why don't you radio your friends and pass on the message? Tell them I know about Vale Investments, NordFund . . . and I'm not the only one. I've got—'

'White, we don't care what you know or fucking don't know, asshole. A dead man can't write news stories, right?' The man chuckled at his own joke.

'I've sent what I know to my bosses.' He tried to give the lie as much resonance as he could muster.

It provoked the first sign of interest from the gunman. 'Well, aren't you a clever boy! What have you told them? That you've uncovered a *conspiracy*? You're amateur night out, White, so cut the bullshit.' The man glanced round the darkened cabin. 'And I'm getting bored. It's time to go. Come on, move out, slowly.'

White stood his ground. If he was going to die, he'd try to postpone it. 'You're the one full of shit!'

The man's eyes narrowed, his expression as venomous as that of a cobra. 'White—'

'Oh, you can kill me! Go on, fuckface, do it! But when you've reported it to your boss, you might like to tell him that, no, you didn't think of bringing me to him!' He held the man's stare. 'You're the one that killed Friedman, aren't you?'

The smile still taunted White. 'Let's just say I was a little surprised that you chose such a salubrious venue for meeting your pretty bum-boy.' The smile vanished.

'Yes,' White sneered in return, 'but I bet you didn't like telling your boss you'd missed me, did you?' He could feel the adrenaline coursing through him. 'That can't have been pleasant, macho man. What did they call you? Asshole? Imbecile? Or—'

'Out, White! Cut the—'

White stayed where he was. 'And you don't *know*, do you? You don't know what Friedman told me and you fucking well don't know what I did with it. So think about that, *asshole*! Tell your people you fucked up again!' White could see just the slightest doubt in those cold killer eyes. He pressed on: 'Tell your bosses Jim Appleton told me everything and he is in a place where you can't find him! Radio your friends and tell them I've handed everything Appleton told me over to a third person, Rambo. See what they have to say about *that*.'

The man blinked once. White knew he was pushing it very far. Death, the very real threat of it, hung in his nostrils like petrol fumes. The gunman kept the pistol aimed at him. Deftly, he pulled the radio back out of his pocket and switched it on. 'Control.'

The radio crackled.

'Yeah, our friend thinks he's being smart. He wants to pass a message on.'

More crackle.

'I said he wants to talk to the man himself.'

The gunman scowled. The radio was noisy but interference made it impossible for White to hear what was being said on the other end. The gunman had the handpiece held to his ear. 'Jesus!' he snarled. 'OK, OK. I'll wait. But make it fucking fast.'

He kept the radio in his hand. The cabin was silent again. White could hear the breeze blow through the branches outside. The wind was picking up, the forest coming alive behind him. The cabin shook a little, walls groaning and bowing under the pressure.

White spoke first. 'How much are they paying you for this?'

'Fuck off.'

'Must be a lot. I mean, it's hardly the sort of thing you do for peanuts, is it?'

The gunman shook his head. 'And next you'll ask me how I got into it!'

White laughed. He was surprised by how genuine it sounded. Maybe that was what fear did. Sharpened your emotions, even your sense of humour. 'You killed Kelly as well, right?'

The man exhaled wearily. 'Jesus, you think I'm going to tell you that?'

'Did you push him down the ridge or kill him first and then dump the body?'

'I said, shut the fu—'

'I bet it was easy. He was hardly a big guy, was he? Must have been a piece of cake. There he was, trying to make his way back to a cabin he hadn't seen in forty years, heaving himself over the ridges, you guys strolling along behind, just waiting for your moment and—'

The man rolled his eyes. 'I said—'

'Mind you, you can't kill all of us, can you? It's not like you can get rid of me, the people at the paper, Elizabeth Forrester's people, all those who know—'

'Forrester? Jesus, you know shit.' The gun was rigid in his hand.

'I mean, she knows.' White swallowed, the trickle of saliva hot and gritty. 'She's got enough on Kelly to take you people to the nearest penitentiary and throw away the key. She's—'

'History.' The man smirked. 'Now—'

The radio crackled into life. The gunman reached for it, the gun's muzzle dropping slightly as he did so. He listened, his eyes always on White. 'Fuck! OK, OK, I'll do it. Where are you?' He listened again, then put the radio back in his pouch. He nodded at White. 'Step outside. *Slowly*.'

White inched his way back through the door. The gunman followed. He motioned at White to turn round. As he did so, White felt the steel of the silencer push into his back.

'Now, we're going to take you to see someone, asshole. Keep three paces ahead of me at all times. I'll tell you where to walk.'

They headed away from the path White had taken, following a small ridge at the back of the cabin. White struggled down an incline, his feet scrabbling for a hold. He could hear the gunman behind him.

'Straight ahead, past that copse to the right.'

White did as he was told. As he scrambled along, he tried desperately to think what he could do next. He had to think. Fast. The path meandered at a gentle gradient through the trees. Ahead of him, White could see a small clearing, beyond it a thick curtain of trees.

'There are bear traps along here, you know,' he shouted, trying to glance over his shoulder.

'*Just fucking move!*'

As White turned back, he caught the briefest glimpse of movement away to his left. He held his breath. He didn't want to meet the gunman's colleagues yet. He had no idea what he was going to tell them.

Very carefully, as he limped forward, he watched the trees. Another quick movement, a smudge of blue.

The gunman gave no sign he had seen it also. White gingerly stumbled ahead, his heart pounding. Beyond the clearing there was a small dip, the entrance to yet another path enveloped by thick bushes.

'OK, White, slide through the opening, but slowly. I'm behind you.'

He had to crouch down to get through the small gap. His hands scraped against solid earth. He could hear the gunman's boots crunching on the briars behind. White slid forward then began crawling down the steep hill.

The deafening scream made him gasp and lose his grip. He tumbled forward, his head smashing against a branch, blinded for a second as he felt himself falling. Almost immediately he heard the crash of something heavy rolling down through the bushes above him. He opened his eyes, his own fall now swift and brutal. Finally, he slumped hard against a thicket, legs splayed in front of him. In a flash, he saw the gunman plunging towards him, arms flailing, one hand still holding the pistol. The gunman's face was contorted in rage and surprise as his eyes met White's.

The man tried to stop his fall, his body lunging helplessly at the bushes by White's feet. As his hands scrabbled for a grip, White kicked out viciously, his foot slamming into the gunman's face. The man screamed in desperation as he tried to bring the pistol round. But his body could not stop itself: the gunman shot past White, spinning and twisting through the maze of branches, hands still failing to find any grip as he descended loud and hard through the dense forest. White clamped his arms around the branches, trying to hold himself tight against the hill. He looked beneath him.

With one final flip, the gunman was whipped through a patch of nettles, thin, spindly branches splaying out under his weight. His neck was flung back and, with a hopeless roar, he was spun around again, the metal spike of an animal trap piercing his Adam's apple, the rusty pole of steel exiting out of the left side of his head.

White looked around him. Suddenly the forest had gone silent. He had no idea what had caused the gunman's fall. All he could think of was escape, survival.

'Whitey! Whitey! Jesus!'

Riordan.

He almost laughed out loud with relief. 'Mick!' he screamed, and heard Riordan stop running high above him. 'Mick, I'm down here.'

White looked above him. Riordan's red, flushed face peered down. In his hand he held a thick black branch.

White waved at him to stay where he was. Then he began to scramble back up the hill, hands gripping the roots. It took him nearly fifteen minutes. He lunged over the lip of the incline and fell breathlessly to the ground.

'Jesus, Whitey! Are you fuckin'—'

'Mick, what the fuck happened?' White managed to stand, his hands sore and cut. He looked at Riordan. Despite the sweat and dirt that marked his face, the Irishman was laughing. He held up the branch in his hand. 'I heard your voices through the trees,' he said. 'I'd got fucking lost. I was about to jump out when I saw the bastard had a gun. It was the only thing I could think of: as he tried to crawl through the gap, I just fucking gave it to him with all I had.'

The two men looked at each other, then exploded into laughter. The raucous sounds swept through the forest. Finally, White managed to quieten Riordan. 'Mick, come on, come on! There's others with him.'

Riordan nodded. 'Which way do you want to go?'

White looked around him. 'I'm not sure . . . but we've got to get down there.' He pointed down the hill towards the gunman's body.

'Whitey, are you fucking mad! I'm—'

'Mick!' White hissed. 'If there was anything in Kelly's cabin, that bastard has it on him.'

They eased their way to the left, hugging the hillside, watching their step carefully. They reached the bottom within twenty minutes. Pushing through the trees, they came to the gunman's lifeless body. White tried to catch his breath, his lungs trembling, his limbs stretched like wire.

The forest was silent again.

He scrabbled towards the body. He tried to avoid looking at the obscene spike, its tip red and peppered with brain tissue. They heaved the man up.

Pulling at the belt of the bum-bag, White twisted the nylon holder round the limp body. He unzipped it, checking around them.

Only the sounds of the forest.

He peered into the hold-all. It contained a round of bullets and some sheets of paper, folded and squashed. White pulled them out.

In the darkness cast by the canopy above him, he had to squint to read what was on the paper. The type was small, the paper thick and expensive. There was no covering note. But the first page – entitled PROCUREMENT – was dense with print.

'Whitey—'

A radio crackled.

'Fuck!' Riordan screamed, slipping on the dirt.

White leaped back, Kelly's memo falling to the ground. The radio barked again. The noise was smothered by the body on top of it. Even so, they could hear the unrelenting fuzz of shouted commands.

The gunman's accomplices would be expecting a reply.

White spun round and got his bearings. The path that he had taken from Hawksbill Creek was to his left. He tried to think. They had no choice but to return the way he had come. To do otherwise would be to venture even farther into the unknown and darkening forest. He directed Riordan through the trees. As he did so, he retrieved the package of documents and placed them in his hip pocket.

They reached the edge of Hawksbill Creek within an hour. The sun was lower, the breeze slashing at them as they hurried along, the route of the creek guiding them until a large clearing opened up before them.

The hire car was still there.

White motioned at Riordan to stay quiet. They watched the

car for a full five minutes as they hid among trees to the north. There was no one about. White scanned the other side of the clearing. Nothing. No reflection from anything metallic, no sign that anyone had been here since they had arrived four hours earlier.

'Now, Mick!'

They made it to the car. White threw Riordan the keys. 'Mick, you drive. I want to read this,' he said, pulling the papers out of his pocket.

Riordan reversed the small saloon out of the clearing. He slowed as they negotiated a hairpin bend, the bushes reaching out from the crowded hedgerows.

The sudden explosion of light blinded them both. A car was heading towards them: it was silver and roaring round a sharp bend ahead, the sun reflecting savagely off the bonnet. Riordan flung the steering wheel to the left as White held on to the dashboard.

'Jesus!'

The other car lurched away from them. White could see two men in the front, their eyes wide with shock. The passenger held a radio to his ear. He was in his twenties, sandy-haired with a round, fleshy face. His eyes bored into White. In his other hand he had a gun. He was gesticulating wildly.

'Mick, keep going! Keep going!'

The two cars swept by within inches of each other. White's eyes locked on to the driver, and the two of them looked at each other; in that moment it dawned on both of them. They both *knew*. They had met once before: White had been winded and panting on the floor of his kitchen, the driver of the car lunging through the doorway of White's apartment before disappearing into a waiting saloon as White had lain helpless on the sidewalk.

'Jesus, Mick, fucking go!'

Riordan floored the accelerator. White looked behind them: the other car had stopped. The passenger had turned round in his seat and was trying to get out of the door. The driver was frantically attempting to turn the car round in the narrow lane. But it was too tight. They were marooned.

Riordan roared out on to the highway and spun right. He glanced at White. 'Give me a fucking cigarette!'

As he reached for the packet, White froze the image of the driver's face in his mind. He struggled to remember the passenger. All he could recall was sandy hair, a surprisingly young face. He tried to stop shaking.

Neither man spoke until they reached the outskirts of Elkton.

Chapter Thirty-seven

Riordan parked round the corner from Roxie's apartment. He and White watched the building. After five minutes they sped across the street. Within seconds they had reached Roxie's door.

Inside, White pulled the papers from his pocket and began reading again. The first page had been stamped with the seal of the President's private secretary. The memo was also marked 'Level Five'. White did not understand the categorisation. He made a note to check it later.

> 'Mr President, for the past four years I have been employed in the Foreign Military Sales Department at the Pentagon. I have for the last eighteen months been seconded to the Procurement Approval Office, liaising with the Centre for Defence Trade at State. I have full security clearance, to Level Five.
>
> Sir, I have taken the liberty of writing to you directly because of what I have seen, and because I do not feel that I can trust anyone else. I have not copied this memo to any one. Only you and I will see it. I understand that this memo will go through the clearance procedures within the West Wing and the Oval Office, which is why I have channelled it through Level Five priority in your

> Pentagon box. I know this will reach you, sir, because I have also labelled this package with the current password. I apologise in advance for my subterfuge, but I felt I had no choice. I am willing to co-operate with any inquiry resulting from the attached.

White marvelled at Kelly's ingenuity. It tallied with what Appleton had told him.

He carried on reading.

> In my role within the Military Sales, I am authorised to collate and store the arms export licences forwarded to us by State or generated from within the Pentagon. Since you took office, the number of licences approved from within this office have increased by *thirty per cent.* In my role, I have collated in the last five weeks a hundred and fifty-five export requests. I was under specific orders to process these requests immediately. There was to be no delay. The attached list is a summary.

White flicked to the last page of the memo. The list was long: Type 73 licences for temporary export of unclassified articles; Type 85 licences for temporary or permanent export of classified articles or technical data. In brackets alongside half the licences approved, the same company was registered: Vale Investments.

White returned to the memo.

> The majority of requests are legitimate and have been filed with Congress which is also my job. However, in the bimonthly tally that I conduct within my office, I have noticed a number of alarming discrepancies. The export licences filed with Congress do not match with the number that have passed my desk. I have tried to conduct my own investigation, but have been thwarted at every turn. The numbers do not match. The disclosure rules to

the Senate committees are not being adhered to. At first I thought it was my own mistake. But I have carefully checked the numbers again and again. I was prepared to accept that the discrepancy was due to inter-agency confusion. That is, until last week.

Without your knowledge, sir, 'blind' export licences – Types 5 and 73 – have also been privately agreed. This contradicts Presidential Orders, and your stated public policy and published Code of Conduct. The export requests are for law enforcement material, a subclause of Presidential Order 1197, which allows 'non-combat' export of law enforcement materials.

In the past seven days, I have been required to collate a series of export requests for Vale Investments. These illegal licences total $230 million.

The illegal profits are channelled through a Virginia bank called NordFund. Through my own investigations, I have discovered that NordFund is a privately owned bank overseen by a former director of Vale Investments, Leonard Calthorp. Mr Calthorp is a former business associate of your Chief of Staff, Mr Wayne McQuogue. I enclose copies of a series of NordFund bank statements that prove the illegal payment to members of your administration.

White flicked to the next page: it was a bank statement, the account holder Flora McQuogue. He could feel the knot of panic tighten in his stomach: $900,000 had been paid into the account in the last eight months. There had not been one withdrawal.

He flicked on to the next page. The piece of paper had been torn in half: what was left was the letterhead of NordFund and one line of type, giving the name of the account holder. The account was made out to Wayne McQuogue.

White examined the rest of the package; there was no sign of the other half of the McQuogue statement. He turned back to Kelly's memo.

> I also enclose a series of bank accounts from which the payments were made to your Chief of Staff. Vale Investments is the conduit for payments from all sides, but it is merely the front for an organisation that I believe is the ultimate beneficiary of the deals. It is my understanding that the level of profit attainable from the granting of these requests runs into billions of dollars. I have copied all of the NordFund accounts I had access to.

White rifled through the package: there were ten pages in all, a list of figures from a plethora of NordFund accounts. He hurriedly examined the account holders; the names meant nothing to him. The figures were immense: millions of dollars shifting between five accounts. There was no clue as to whom the payments had been made to. Again, White checked the name of the account holders: McQuogue's name was not on any of the other accounts. He finished reading Kelly's memo.

> I have tried to alert my superiors to the discrepancies, but I have been told that a Level Six order has been placed on the files. At present my superiors have ordered me to desist from my enquiries. I am available for FBI or Senate investigation.
>
> I am scared, Mr President. I have been a supporter of yours since the beginning. I know of your commitment to humanitarian causes. I understand that by removing the relevant documentation I am in contravention of my Employee Code and my Level 5 clearance. But I felt that I had no choice but to proceed in the manner that I have.
>
> A loyal citizen,
>
> RONALD KELLY

The man watched the Houston Hyatt from the sidewalk. It was just as they had described it. The main entrance under the canopy. The bus terminal and cab-stand to the left and right. He crossed the street and strolled nonchalantly towards the main doors and into the lobby. A banner stretched above him: 'Welcome to Houston, Mrs Forrester'. The man turned left, avoiding reception. Above him, the lobby rose thirty floors to a domed roof, glass 'bubble' elevators clutching the sides of an immense concrete column. He waited for an elevator to descend, placing the large suitcase by his feet.

He pushed the button for the twenty-fourth floor, exited the elevator and found the room easily enough. Suite 2423, in the far eastern corner. He withdrew the plastic entry card from his pocket and pushed it into the slot. The red light turned green. He pushed the door open and stepped inside.

The suite was empty. They had made sure of that. He stood by the closed door, taking in his surroundings. Two sofas were arranged around a mahogany coffee table; in front of them, a line of windows gave 180-degree views of downtown Houston and the freeways beyond. He hurried across the sitting area and opened a door. An anteroom, cupboards to the left and right, led into the bathroom. It matched the plan he had been given.

He turned on the lights in the bathroom, placed the suitcase by his feet, careful not to mark the newly cleaned marble floor, and opened it. The specially adapted Vaime SSR Mk 2 rifle lay among the sponge padding. He pulled out a small leather case from one compartment, unzipped it and squatted down on his knees. He placed the tools on the floor in front of him and crawled towards the sink unit.

The space was tight. He took off his jacket, laying it over the bathtub. Breathing slowly, he picked up a pair of pliers and carefully worked his hand around the pedestal. The ceramic column was secured tight to the bathroom wall. But just underneath the bottom of the basin, a small hole was hidden from view. He grunted as he squeezed his hand into the space and began to unscrew the back nuts. He worked slowly, making sure he did not scratch the tiles or the ceramic pedestal by his chin.

Standing again, he took hold of the basin. He could feel it give slightly; he tugged at it, praying it would not crash to the floor. The sink slowly came away from the wall. The pedestal beneath remained in place. It held the weight of the sink and trembled a little as he heaved the basin towards him.

He leaned across and peered into the dark space behind. Two flexible pipes ran from the hot and cold taps, before disappearing into the wall behind. Another pipe, this one from the waste hole in the basin, was connected to a valve assembly beneath the sink and a brass union on the wall. He pushed the basin gently. It rattled, but did not collapse.

He squatted once more. Quickly, he withdrew the rifle assembly from the suitcase and placed it inside the space between sink and wall. The cavity was just big enough to squeeze it through. Holding the cartridge in one hand, terrified that he would drop it and lose it in the hollow of the pedestal, he expertly taped it to the underside of the sink. He tugged at it. The tape held firm. Next came the muzzle, again wrapped in plastic. He leaned across the basin and lowered the muzzle into the hollow gap. He repeated the tricky manoeuvre for the rest of the rifle parts and the small bag of subsonic ammunition before he heaved the sink back against the wall. Sliding once more to the floor, he screwed the back nuts on.

Standing quickly, he took a cotton cloth from his pocket and wiped the surfaces clean. He checked the tiling behind the sink basin and pedestal. There were no marks. He closed the suitcase, locked it and wiped the floor clean. He placed the dirty tissues in his pocket and left the bathroom.

Two minutes later he was back in the lobby and out on to the street. As he crossed Louisiana, he smiled to himself for the first time all day.

The delivery had been made.

Someone else would be back to retrieve it in a few hours.

Elizabeth left the conference room. Across the open-plan space of the war room, her staff had lined up to see her off. She stopped at a few of the desks, chatting with her young volunteers. They applauded her as she made her way to the front of the office. Greenhalgh and Marjorie followed, three Secret Service agents around them.

Elizabeth waited just inside the door that led out on to the sidewalk. The agents had yet to give the all-clear for her to appear. She turned and smiled at Marjorie. They both knew what was beyond the closed doors: a phalanx of media, supporters, critics, nuts. The usual chorus of approval, or otherwise, that followed candidates wherever they went, like seagulls behind a ship. She smiled to herself: Tyler had called them vultures.

'Mrs Forrester?'

She turned to her left; the voice was that of a stranger.

A young man, good-looking, light-haired, dressed in a dark business suit, stood with hand outstretched. On his lapel he wore a Secret Service buttonhole. 'I'm your new Head of Detail, ma'am.'

Elizabeth smiled and shook his hand. 'Oh, I'm sorry, Agent—'

'Shaw, ma'am.'

'Agent Shaw . . . yes, that's right. I thought you were joining us at the airport.'

He shook his head. 'Change of plan, ma'am. I wanted to familiarise myself with the operation as soon as possible. I'm sorry I couldn't get here earlier but there was something I needed to check at Sixteenth Street.'

Elizabeth shrugged off his apology. The agent's face was flushed; he was sweating slightly, his breath short. Elizabeth could understand his nervousness. She also knew she had to be civil. She missed Morrow, longed for him to be with her, but the new agent was just doing his job. She accepted she had better get used to him. He would more than likely stay with her for most of the campaign.

'Agent Shaw, it's good to have you on board,' she said, turning and introducing him to Marjorie and Greenhalgh. Elizabeth couldn't resist a smirk as Marjorie gave the new agent her most seductive smile. The two women locked eyes; Marjorie's glowed and danced with merriment. Elizabeth winked back.

Two seconds later Shaw received the signal from outside. They were ready to move. Elizabeth breathed in, held the breath, counted to five. The doors opened ten feet in front of her, the tumult from outside crashing and whipping through the enclosed space. Out on the sidewalk, she could see the media, the onlookers, the circus held back by the PD's barriers.

She smiled and glanced at Shaw.

'Whenever you're ready, Mrs Forrester.'

Elizabeth could feel the adrenaline rush through her. Now was the moment. The die had been cast. Whether she survived or failed, prospered or withered, led her supporters up the side of the cliff only to find the horizon obscured, none of it mattered to her at that moment. Not really. All that mattered was that she was in with a chance. The ultimate prize was within her reach. She *knew* it. That motivated her enough. After the deaths, the grief, the shattering of what had been dear – *so dear!* – to her, she had paid the price, counted the cost. Now she had nothing more to lose: her dignity, her reputation, her honesty, her husband, her *friends*, the secrets she had hoarded among the dust and corners of her emotional attic . . . they had all been pulled from out of the gloom, unwrapped and exposed to the ruthless, unforgiving glare of the world. It had happened. It was gone.

At that moment, standing just inside the doorway of the war room, with the crowd in front of her captured in freeze-frame, Elizabeth felt as if she could touch the excitement, could *massage* it, like silk through her fingers. Alone amid the chaos that whirled in front of her, behind her, to the sides, over the helmeted heads of the PD officers standing shoulder to shoulder, the networks' videocams – tight little clusters of them – stretching out to her like open-mouthed goslings waiting to be fed, the immense, seething crowd straining for a glimpse of her, aching for a part of her as much as the media that needed its hunger satisfied . . . and beyond even them, past the snake of black limousines by the kerb, the hooting horns, the shimmer of the plate-glass windows from the buildings opposite, the surge and push and shove that pirouetted and swept around her, Elizabeth herself felt oddly calm.

She breathed in, feeling as if she had emerged from a darkened cellar. Feeling free at last.

She held her smile, and headed out into the sunlight.

Riordan folded up the memo.

'Whitey, you're going to have to go public with this.' He wiped his forehead with the back of his hand. 'I mean, fuck it, this is *enough*. You've got it all here. The guy who tried to kill you told you he was working for McQuogue! He was the same bastard who blasted Friedman away! With this memo—'

'I know, I know!' White paced the living room. 'NordFund was channelling the funds to Kelly and McQuogue. But the man signing the cheques is a new one on me.' He spoke quickly, gesticulating, still pacing. 'OK, here's what I'm going to do. I've got to get hold of Belch. I'll ring the stupid fucker and tell him I'm coming in to see him. He can send a car here. Then, we need to find out where Elizabeth Forrester is and, more importantly, McQuogue: where the hell is that slimy sonofabitch?'

White stopped and sat down. He looked at Riordan. 'If Kelly was trying to get hold of Elizabeth, he must have been hoping Tyler had told her something about the memo. Kelly would have trusted her.'

Riordan nodded. 'Sure. So what?'

'Friedman told me that Elizabeth was trying to find out about Kelly. She'd found the covering note to this memo, but nothing else. Plus, her husband's diary worried her enough to send a Secret Service agent to Shenandoah ahead of me.'

'You think she was just trying to cover up, protecting her dead hubby?'

White shook his head. 'No, it's not her style.'

'How do you know?'

I know.

'Everything she's done points against her just trying to bury this. Mick, look, I have enough to run with. There's no doubt that even someone as dense as Bletchman is going to publish this. But what I *don't* know is whether Elizabeth Forrester has anything she's holding back. I might be wrong, but Friedman couldn't believe I was already on to Kelly. He died before he could tell me any more . . . but I need to get to Elizabeth Forrester. Maybe she's been trying to get this memo too!'

Riordan heaved himself up off the sofa. 'Oh, yeah, fine . . . you have dynamite in your pocket and all you want to do is hand it over to Liz Forrester. Great idea, Whitey! Let her take the credit. People will think it's just propaganda for her campaign . . . but for all you know, she still might try and bury it for good! She's not going to want Tyler looking like a prick, is she? And anyway, how you gonna get to her? Just pitch up at her campaign HQ and drink coffee while you wait for her to see you?'

White waved his objection away. 'She sent Lee Morrow to Shenandoah. If she trusted him, then maybe I can too.'

'Sure, let's get the book and just ring the fucker up! He's only her Head of Detail!'

'OK, Mick, OK! I'll ring Belch, tell him what I have. We'll try and get to Elizabeth later. Make some coffee.'

White sat down and picked up the phone. Riordan wandered over to the breakfast bar, turning the television on. White dialled the *Herald*'s number and waited. He idly watched TV as the switchboard connected him with Bletchman's office.

'News editor's office.'

'It's Mark White. Is he there?'

'Mark! Where have you . . . hang on, I'll try and get him. He's somewhere on the floor.'

White heard a clank as the secretary put the phone down.

Riordan stood by the bar, flicking channels. He stopped at CNN. He grunted to White, who looked over his shoulder. The network was broadcasting Elizabeth's departure from Washington. White could see her exiting from the National terminal, the media pack around her.

Riordan laughed and leaned over for the remote control. 'You should've booked yourself a seat on her flight, Whitey,' he said, picking up the remote.

White ignored him. From the other end of the phone there was only silence.

The CNN camera panned back, Elizabeth giving one last wave to the crowd in the airport. White watched as her staff moved with her towards an open door, the tarmac visible through the plate-glass window. The Secret Service agents surrounded Elizabeth, holding back the frenzied group of journalists, soundmen, curious tourists. White casually counted the agents: one, two, three . . . a sandy-haired agent ushering her along . . .

He glanced away from the screen. He could hear the rustling of papers from the other end of the phone. The secretary was back. 'Mark, I'm putting you through to Mr Bletchman.'

'Thanks—'

White froze.

He spun back to the television. '*Jesus Christ, Mick, turn it back!*'

Riordan looked up in surprise.

'*Turn it back!*'

White slung the phone to the floor, throwing himself across the small room. He pushed Riordan aside, snatching the remote control out of his hand. White looked down at the buttons.

'Which one? . . . Fuck!'

He pushed the channel selector, eyes riveted to the screen. The image returned to the scene at the National. Elizabeth's entourage was disappearing down a corridor. The CNN reporter had positioned herself in front of the camera. She was beginning her live report. Beyond her shoulder, White could see Elizabeth's Secret Service agents closing the doors to the tarmac.

'It's him! *It's him!*' White shook with horror, the remote crashing out of his hand. 'Jesus fucking Christ, it's him!'

'Whitey—'

He spun round, eyes blazing. 'Mick, it's him . . . the guy who was the passenger . . .' White stumbled over the words, his voice hoarse and garbled, chest heaving. 'The passenger in the car! In Shenandoah! The guy in the *car*! It's him!'

Riordan took hold of his shoulder. 'Look, you've been—'

White pulled back. 'Mick, I'm not making it up! I saw them! They were trying to find the bastard who surprised me in the cabin! I told you: I recognised the driver . . . and I had a full view of *the passenger*, Mick! He looked me *right in the face*. He was fucking armed! He knew who I was! It's him!'

'OK, Whitey, I believe you, but what are you . . . Jesus, *what* guy?' Riordan turned back to the TV screen. 'Did you see him in the crowd, Whitey?'

'Mick, he's with Elizabeth!' White's finger shook as he pointed frantically at the screen. 'He's one of her *detail*!'

White leaped towards the phone.

'Where the fuck is Lee Morrow?' he screamed, picking up the receiver.

Riordan tried to stop him. 'Whitey, put that down! You can't just ring up the Service, accusing someone you don't even know of being part of a conspiracy against Elizabeth Forrester! You've got nothing—'

White snapped round. His rage and fear were all-consuming. Elizabeth was in danger. And whether he was doing it more for himself than for the woman he had abandoned two decades before White did not know. All he felt was an intoxicating fury, a desperate urge to do something to help her. 'Mick, I've got to alert her! Fuck, McQuogue's people are alongside her!'

'Whitey, listen to me!' Riordan held him by the shoulders. 'You can't start asking to be put through to Lee Morrow. It don't happen like that.'

'Mick, let me go!'

'For fuck's sake, the only way you're going to get near her is to get to Houston. Try and get to Morrow *down there*. If you say she trusts him, then maybe you can. It's the only way, Whitey.'

He nodded. 'Mick, have you got a credit card?'

'Sure.'

'Then book me a flight to Houston.'

Chapter Thirty-eight

Elizabeth stepped forward to the podium. The TelePrompTer was scrolling, although she didn't need it. She knew what she was going to say.

'Good morning, ladies and gentlemen. I doubt this place has been this full in a while, and if it's like my own school, then I think this may be the first time any of you have been in a lecture hall!'

The laughter rose as expected. It calmed Elizabeth, cheered her audience.

She glanced to her right. Marjorie and Greenhalgh were standing in the guest viewing area. The bank of network cameras was behind them. Instinctively, she looked for Ben Shaw: the new Head of Detail was to her left. Morrow had always stood to her right.

Elizabeth ignored the change in routine; every agent was different.

She returned to her speech.

'In a few hours' time, I am due to make an address at the Hyatt Hotel. My audience, an important one, will be made up of the people in Texas who have already declared for my candidacy. Some are friends of mine, and helped my late husband during his own campaign. Others I have never met, but they are people who have of their own volition made a stand for a new kind of America.'

She glanced round the room.

'But you are the real reason I have come to Houston. Every one of you here. You are why I am in Texas, why I shall go to other cities, and towns, and districts, and homes across our great nation. For it is the young people of this nation who deserve better, who are our future . . .'

Elizabeth settled into her address. She had written most of it herself on the plane down from DC. Greenhalgh had tried to censor a few of her jokes; Elizabeth had written them back in. Finally, they had agreed on the text. It had been photocopied on the plane, and handed out to the media during the drive from the airport.

She saw the red light flicker on the TelePrompTer in front of her. She had only a minute of her address left. Effortlessly, enjoying the moment, the rapt attention and goodwill of the young people in front of her, she made her closing remarks.

'I thank you for your time. I wish you well, all of you, in what you decide to do with your lives. And I hope you will leave this great institution with the determination to make the best of your lives, and to do the best for your country. Thank you very much, and God bless all of you.'

She accepted their applause. It rose and thundered around her, waves of noise crashing down and then sweeping up again round the enclosed space. She glanced down at the notes on the podium. The Q&A session would last fifteen minutes.

'Right,' she said as the applause quietened. 'You've listened to me. So now I'm going to do something most politicians don't . . . I'm going to listen to you. Who wants to start?'

A blond-haired girl, her T-shirt a vivid pink, rose from the third row. Elizabeth smiled at her, prompting her to ask a question.

'Mrs Forrester.' The young woman's voice shook, reedy and nervous. 'Ma'am, why do you think a woman would be a better President than a man?'

Elizabeth could sense, rather than see, the media home in on her. 'Well,' she said, raising her hands slightly, 'I don't think that *is* what I am saying. I don't believe a candidate's sex should be a deciding factor. I hope we have moved on from that. What I do I know is that men and women have different skills. Equality of opportunity has shown us that women can contribute the same as men, in any environment. But, equally, I think we have to respect the differences there are between the sexes. As a woman, I think I can bring strength of will and focus to the job. I've had experiences in my life, things I have done, both right and wrong, that make me a more rounded and informed individual. It doesn't matter what sex you are, as long as you can be trusted, as long as you are committed and as long as you ensure that your voice is the one people respect and trust.'

The young woman nodded her head vigorously.

Elizabeth leaned farther into the podium, the microphone right up against her lips. 'And also,' she whispered theatrically, 'because women have more balls.'

There was stunned silence, then an explosion of laughter and applause. Elizabeth glanced at Greenhalgh. 'I was told not to make that joke,' she said loudly, trying to be heard above the noise. 'My campaign professionals were dead against it. But people have to trust me, and to do that, they have to know me. Even if they don't like my jokes!'

More applause.

'Now,' she said, 'who else has a question?'

All the students in the room put their hands up.

White struggled through Arrivals at Houston Intercontinental airport. He crossed the terminal and joined the queue for the airport express to downtown. Fifteen minutes later, he was seated at the back of the shuttle, a sports hold-all on his knee as the bus swept along the Eastex freeway.

The shuttle reached its destination, the terminal at the Hyatt Regency Hotel on Louisiana. White remained seated while the others passengers disembarked. He fell in with the group of schoolchildren standing at the junction of Louisiana and Polk, waiting for the traffic to clear. As he did so, he glanced behind him at the towering edifice of the Hyatt. Limousines and airport minibuses swept up the concrete drive and under the brightly lit canopy that covered the main entrance to the hotel.

Crossing Louisiana, he walked three blocks before he found an appropriate place. The diner was full of lunch-time office workers, a huge plate-glass window overlooking the sidewalk. White was shown to a table to the left of the bar. He ordered a burger and retrieved a guidebook from his bag. He wrote down the number of the hotel he had found and called from the phone by the washrooms. He reserved a double room, paid for his burger and left the diner. A Liberty cab was coming towards him. He strode across the sidewalk, struggling with his bag, as he began waving at the driver.

He gave the address of a hotel near Rice. He would check in and plan his next move.

The Lancaster in Houston is a small hotel, redolent of an English country house, a venue for established Houston families and new money that likes to think it is old. The lobby and bar are quiet, reserved places. It is only seven blocks from the Hyatt, but a world away in style. The suites are small but filled with antiques. Where the Hyatt screams wealth, the Lancaster murmurs in snobbish disdain.

Morrow let the curtain slip back into place. He had not spoken to Willard as Air Force One had delivered the White House team to Houston and then on to the Lancaster. His objection to being taken off Elizabeth's detail still rankled with his bosses. For the duration of the stay in Houston, he had been told to remain within the hotel complex as part of the permanent on-site detail. He would not be required to travel with the

Commander-in-Chief. He smarted at the insult as he paced his small bedroom on the fourth floor of the hotel.

The knock on the door surprised him. He flung it open angrily, startling the man on the other side.

'Hey, Morrow, calm down.'

Bob Russell stood in the doorway. The older man looked at him and strode past into the room. 'Look, Lee, I'm sorry about this,' he said, adjusting the lapels of his jacket and folding a single sheet of fax paper in his hands. 'But it's not my call. I'll try and get you seconded on to another detail when we get back to Washington. I know you were close to Mrs Forrester, but there's nothing I can do about it.'

Morrow ignored him and sat on the end of the bed.

'Lee, she's in good hands.' Russell carried on talking, trying to break the tension. 'Anyway, you need to see this. It's an alert faxed through from DC. This hasn't leaked to the media yet but it probably will. The hotel where John Friedman was shot: a case was found in the trashcans at the back. It belonged to a journalist called Mark White.'

Morrow did not recognise the name. Russell handed him the fax report.

'The guy at the hotel reception in DC has apparently ID'd White as the one who was meeting with Friedman. White himself has gone missing from his office. He's some writer at the *Herald*. His friends have been questioned and there's a feeling he might be in Houston. Keep an eye out. The guy's supposed to have flipped.'

Morrow sat on the bed. He nodded automatically as Russell finished the briefing. Once the senior agent left, Morrow lay down and closed his eyes.

He would do his duty. Like the rest of the detail, he would ensure that Mark White was apprehended, if he was truly in Houston. Friedman's death was still a sore point with Morrow; it still irked him that a man close to Elizabeth Forrester could have been gunned down so brutally. As for White, Morrow knew the Service or the FBI would get to him. Like most of his colleagues, Morrow despised journalists. And if White had had a hand in Friedman's death, Morrow would do anything he could to stop him.

The suite on the twenty-fourth floor of the Hyatt was in darkness. Faint shadows fell through the drawn curtains. The gunman stood alone and tugged one curtain back. The suite was not overlooked, the only view being the shimmer of cars out on the freeway and the broad, hazy sweep of downtown.

He crossed the suite and entered the bathroom. He worked by torchlight. The room was cluttered with a guest's belongings. The gunman carefully stepped over the wet clothes stuck to the marble floor. He smiled to himself. The delegate booked into the suite had been delighted to receive a call summoning him to a private meeting with Elizabeth Forrester after her arrival at the hotel. He had rushed from the suite immediately. They'd told him not to be late.

The gunman crouched under the sink unit. He retrieved the muzzle first; then the magazine and the box of sub-sonic ammo. In the darkness, as he had been trained, he rebuilt the Vaime silenced rifle. The stock slipped in easily, the magazine cold in his hand. He unzipped the ammo bag. The 7.62mm rounds were light. They had been specially formulated for a maximum silenced fire. The barrel was integrally suppressed, again to limit the noise.

He knew there would be a 'crack'. They couldn't avoid that. But the escape plan had been carefully thought through. Through the next-door suite, a service door led down one flight. In Room 2313 was a hidden suitcase in a false panel at the back of the wardrobe. It contained a change of clothes, new ID and false credit cards. In the commotion, he was to join the crowds on the balcony and make his way with them out of the hotel. The meet was arranged one block from the Four Seasons.

He ran through the plan as he double-checked the rifle. It was a single-shot, the magazine containing five rounds.

He stood, left the bathroom in disarray. By the time the guest or the police checked the suite, he would be long gone, heading for New Orleans.

Chapter Thirty-nine

White paid the cab and followed the wide sidewalk that circled one of the immense carports in the Galleria shopping complex. He made his way to the far side, away from the sprawling entrance to the mall. It was quieter here: the air was toxic and heavy, the concrete beneath his feet rumbling and shivering from the highway that thundered fifty yards in front of him. But there were only a few cars. The evening shoppers were way beyond the crash barriers, congregating at the neon entrance a hundred yards from where he stood.

White pressed himself into a call-box. He got the number of the Lancaster from Information then dialled, his story prepared.

'Lancaster Hotel, good evening.'

'Agent Morrow, please.'

The operator hesitated. 'Sir, we have no record of a guest with that name.'

White had expected that reply. 'Ma'am, I know you are not authorised to reveal details of the presidential party. But I need to speak with Agent Lee Morrow urgently.'

'Sir, all enquiries from unauthorised personnel must be directed to the White House. Shall I connect you directly, or do you want to call them your—'

'Ma'am, I know you can do this.'

Riordan had told him to try it this way.

'Please notify Mr Morrow that my name is Benmont Greenhalgh. I am Elizabeth Forrester's Campaign Director and I need to speak with him immediately.'

'One moment, Mr Greenhalgh.'

White waited as he was put on hold. It seemed an eternity. He tried to guess the time he had been holding: one, two minutes.

Was this being traced?

A voice interrupted him.

'Benmont? What are you doing in a pay-phone?'

White tensed at Morrow's startled tone. He leaned farther into the call-box. 'Agent Morrow, it's Mark White. Look—'

'White! Where are you?'

'Agent Morrow, please just listen to me—'

'Mr White, I'm finishing this conversation now! You are under investigation by DC police. It is my duty as a member of the United States Secret Service to warn you that you are wanted as an accomplice in John Friedman's murder! You are to remain where you are—'

'Morrow, what are you talking about? I'm wanted for *what*?' White was stunned. He knew he hadn't dropped anything in the hotel room. He'd checked.

Morrow interrupted his thoughts. 'They found your briefcase, Mr White, in a trashcan. I am now terminating this call and will report—'

'Morrow, I didn't leave *anything* there! I was only carrying a tape recorder, nothing else! That briefcase was stolen from my apartment days before when I was attacked. It's been placed there to incriminate me.'

'Mr White, I have to warn you that—'

'Morrow, *please*! Listen to me, Lee. Just let me talk. Please! This was the only way I could get hold of you! I'm in Houston. I *have* to meet with you and Elizabeth. You can't leave her, Morrow!'

White knew he wasn't making sense but he carried on regardless, desperation and fear fuelling his monologue. 'Morrow, don't you understand? It's what they *want*. Please, she's got to trust me! There's someone who's part of her detail, he tried to—'

White flinched at the venom of Morrow's reply. 'Mr White, you are wanted in connection with the *murder* of John Friedman. I do not know why you have called me. I am not interested in what you have to say. There is no way I am going to put you in contact with Mrs Forrester! Are—'

'Agent Morrow, I know you went to Shenandoah! *Just listen to me!* I know you were looking for Kelly.'

'Mr—'

'Morrow, I have the memo! *Kelly's memo*. I went to the Blue Ridge. OK, I was in contact with Friedman. But Elizabeth Forrester got *him* to contact *me*! Check with her yourself. Go on! Fucking call her on the other line!'

White waited.

Finally, the agent spoke. 'How do I know I can trust you, White?'

'Since I've been on this story I've been attacked repeatedly, nearly killed! Yes, I was with Friedman. But are you seriously telling me you believe that I met with him, left him in the hotel room, then went to a carport across the street and blew his brains out from fifty yards? It doesn't make sense, Morrow! Just let me meet you and I'll give you what I've got. Please! I'm being framed. Can't you see that it's all a little bit *too* convenient? They try to gag me and now I'm being set up for Friedman's *murder*! Morrow, I'm not a killer. Come *on*!'

He waited for Morrow to speak. Eventually, the silence was broken. 'OK, Mr White, stay calm. I'll meet with you. But I'm doing this for Elizabeth Forrester, not for you. I warn you: any fun and games, and you'll be in custody before you know it.'

'Fine. Just make it quick. There's someone—'

'OK, White . . . where are you?'

*

Morrow replaced the phone. He grabbed his Service revolver and ID then hurried from his hotel room. He took a flight of stairs down one storey and dashed along the corridor. The presidential Command Centre was at the end, one floor above Willard's own suite.

The door to the office was open. Morrow rushed in. Five agents were crowded around a conference table, its top covered with maps of Houston and a detailed plan of the Lancaster. They were examining it, checking points of entry and security from a list.

Bob Russell looked up in surprise as Morrow thundered through the door.

'Lee—'

'Sir, I need a word. *Now*.'

Russell blinked in surprise at his vehemence. 'OK,' he replied, ushering Morrow to a corner of the room, out of earshot of the rest of the detail.

'Sir, the fax you gave me earlier . . . the journalist . . .'

Russell nodded.

'I don't know why, sir, but Mark White's just called me. Here! He pretended to be Mrs Forrester's—'

Russell spoke quickly, trying to step round him. 'Lee, come with me. Did you get a trace?'

Morrow pulled Russell back towards him. 'Sir, I think the guy really has flipped! He's screaming about a conspiracy against Mrs Forrester, about John Friedman. He's all over the place. The call was traced to a call-box at the Galleria—'

'Morrow, we have to get there, *fast*—'

'There's no point, sir. White has agreed to meet with me.'

Russell tried to interrupt but Morrow kept talking. 'Sir, you have to let me handle this. Please! I was with Mrs Forrester, I've been there all along. If White is trying to harm or cause trouble for her then it's my call, sir. That's why I kept him talking. I *know* where he'll be in one hour.'

Russell stood in silence. Morrow waited, his breath catching.

Finally, Russell spoke. 'OK, Lee, I'll allow you to get involved . . . but consider it a favour, son. From now on we're quits as far as the Forrester thing is concerned. But you have to inform Mrs Forrester's detail about this. Get on the phone to Agent Shaw. Tell him what you know. The Forrester detail can provide you with back-up, we're too stretched here. *But let me know what happens.* I want a full report within' – Russell checked his watch – 'two hours. If there is a nut out there, then you better damn well bring him in.'

'Mrs FORRESTER! Over here! OVER HERE!'

Elizabeth turned and waved at the crowd. The lights of the press pack competed with the harsh glare of the hotel entrance. She stood alone for a second, her Secret Service detail and entourage off to her left. The press surged forward, desperate to capture the picture: Elizabeth, resplendent in a neat blue two-piece, both arms raised in a victory salute, before she turned and was escorted through the doors of the Hyatt.

The lobby was crowded and hot. As if propelled by an invisible force, Elizabeth crossed the open space, still smiling and saluting the crowd. She clutched at the hands outstretched towards her, stopping now and again to exchange a few words with some of the campaign workers. Marjorie followed, exchanging jokes with Greenhalgh, who beamed at his candidate.

The conference room was off to the right. Elizabeth made her way down the narrow corridor, the crowds pushed back by the security personnel. It should only have taken her a minute or two to cross the lobby. In the end, she was running fifteen minutes late by the time she emerged into the vast room, and the band erupted. More applause. More cameras. More crowds.

She skipped forward to the podium. The audience could see her fully now, surrounded by her campaign team on the small stage at the back of the hall. The roars were deafening. Elizabeth held her smile and tried to silence her supporters.

'Ladies and gentlemen, at last! I'm back in Texas!'

The applause lasted for a full minute.

She raised her hands again and called for silence.

'You know, in front of me here is that thing my campaign professionals call a TelePrompTer. It shows me the speech I'm supposed to make. You can't see it from where you're all standing, but I can. It's telling me what I should be saying.' She stopped and surveyed the men and women in the audience. 'But I'm not going to read it. I don't need a prepared speech. I'm back home in Texas, among friends, and I'm going to say what I want to!'

She stepped back slightly from the podium and waved again. Behind her, Greenhalgh and Marjorie erupted into laughter. Greenhalgh theatrically tore up the cards in his hand and threw them over his head. Elizabeth caught sight of the gesture and pointed towards her Campaign Director. 'See!' she roared into the microphone. 'That man helps to run my campaign. And even he doesn't know what I'm going to say!'

Her performance electrified the crowd.

'My friends, it has been a long road to Houston. There were times when we thought we wouldn't make it. When those who would wish to deprive us of our moment thought they had stopped us. But here we are, beginning our fight to win this nomination. I stand before you today not just as a candidate. Not just as the wife of a brilliant and inspiring President. No, I am here because I want to be! Because I know we can make this happen, and I know you are with me all the way!'

Another minute of applause.

'I have made apologies for some things that I have done in my life. And I have never made any apologies for being a woman. It is not what or who I am that should decide this race. It is what I know I can do for this party and for my country. *That* is why I intend to be the next President of the United States!'

Her voice was clear and compelling. It cut through the cheers and whistles, the murmur of the crowd. She could feel it again:

the momentum was with her, pushing her forward, as unrelenting and as powerful as a tidal wave.

Elizabeth accepted just a few more minutes of applause. Then, her remarks over, she left the podium and was shown to a side room off the conference suite. This quick address had been hurriedly pencilled into the schedule. In one hour, she would make her proper speech of the evening.

As they made their way along, Greenhalgh rushed to her side. 'I never thought I'd say this, Liz, but I think we're going to do it!'

Elizabeth slumped on to a chair and began reapplying her make-up. Marjorie stood to one side, holding her attaché case and her papers.

'How long have I got in the suite upstairs before tonight's speech?' she asked.

Benmont checked the schedule in front of him. 'We stay here for fifteen minutes. You have the TV interview in here and then half an hour upstairs.'

'OK,' she replied. 'Let's bring the crew in.'

White chose the shopfront with care. Across the darkened lot, a Western clothing store remained open, the neon store sign bathing the lot in pink-and-green light. He watched as a pick-up truck rolled towards the store; two men dressed in denim walked through the entrance, laughing.

White was well into the shadows. He saw Morrow approach from the east, off the freeway and down through the underpass. Morrow was in the driving seat of the car. He was alone. The car rolled to a halt at the edge of the lot, just as White had instructed. Morrow turned the ignition off. He got out of the car and stood to one side, again as White had requested. Morrow glanced around the gloomy space, eyes searching the shopfronts directly in front of him.

White emerged from the shadows. His hands lay by his sides, his fingers splayed out. As requested. 'Agent Morrow.'

Morrow turned sharply on hearing his name and peered into the darkness.

'Walk towards me, Lee. I'm not armed. But I'm not coming out into the lights.'

Morrow made his way towards White. 'Mr White, I'm sorry. Please, I have to ask you to do this. Lay on the floor with your arms stretched out in front of you. I shall then—'

'Lee, for fuck's sake! I'm not carrying. Can't you at least—'

'On the floor, Mark. *Now!*'

White dropped to his knees, cursing as the concrete scraped his skin through the thin fabric of his trousers. As he lay there, he could see Morrow jogging towards him.

A bullet richocheted off the concrete two feet from White's left hand.

White spun wildly. He could hear Morrow gasp in front of him. White spun again and rolled into the fierce light of a set of headlights. He was blinded briefly but struggled to his feet, the bullets pecking viciously at the concrete around him. He knew Morrow had a clear shot at him.

White threw himself back towards the storefront. The window to the hardware store disintegrated in front of him. He kept running, dodging from side to side. He was only twenty feet from the darkness now. He lunged forward. A streetlight exploded above his head, the plastic coating raining down. He scrambled over the debris, hurtling towards the relative safety of the shadows.

Morrow, you bastard!

White heard the rattle of more gunfire. He spun around, eyes searching for a hiding place. As he did so, he caught sight of Morrow, crouched behind his car. In the murky light, White could just see the outline of Morrow's pistol jerking in his hand. He was firing.

But not at White.

A blue pick-up truck swerved violently to the left. The windscreen shattered as Morrow's bullets struck home, screams and the roar of its tyres filling the parking lot. Morrow continued firing, spinning now from under the car. The back tyre of the pick-up truck exploded. The truck mounted the sidewalk, swaying and buckling as it smashed against a safety barrier. It carried on, its brake lights extinguished, and roared into the incoming traffic.

White stared wildly around him.

What the fuck . . .

'White!'

He could see Morrow scrambling inside his car. Almost immediately, it began rolling towards White, its headlights still off. Morrow flung open the door, desperately beckoning White towards him.

'Get in!'

He scrambled into the saloon. Morrow pressed his foot on the accelerator. The car screamed forward, White's foot dragging along the concrete. Morrow pulled him fully in with one hand as they thundered after the pick-up.

'Morrow, what the fuck—'

White was thrown back into his seat. The car hurtled under the freeway and swung left down the wrong exit lane. Other drivers swerved to avoid a collision. White flung himself as far into the seat as he could, his hands gripping the dashboard. 'Where the fuck we goin'?' he choked.

'I don't know!' Morrow screamed, slamming across a T-junction and heading towards a suburban street straight ahead.

'What the fuck happened there, Morrow?' White shouted as they raced west. 'Why did your people start shooting?'

The agent stared straight ahead. 'I don't know,' he whispered, undoing his tie and massaging his chest.

'What the fuck do you mean, you don't know? What . . . you telling me they weren't your guys?'

Morrow shook his head. 'I don't know, Mark . . . they started shooting at both of us. They were supposed to be the Forrester detail! I'd told Shaw . . . I don't *know* what happened!'

*

Morrow pulled the car over near the Heritage Plaza. Downtown was unusually crowded. Across the sidewalk, a Western bar had thrown its doors open. White could hear the music and the laughter.

Morrow opened the driver's door. 'Christ, White,' he muttered, 'I promise you, I wasn't expecting what happened back there. I don't know who the fuck they were.'

White joined him on the sidewalk. The two men raced forward, checking left and right. They hadn't been followed. They fell in with the crowds, crossing Main and turning left down San Jacinto. Two blocks down, a plaza opened in front of a skyscraper. White and Morrow hurried across the deserted space. A small bench had been placed to the left of the building's entrance. It was dark here, the street fifty yards in front of them. They slumped down.

'We'd better make this quick, Mark,' Morrow said.

White exhaled and looked at the Secret Service agent. 'Lee, I've just spent the last week trying to stay alive.'

Morrow nodded for him to continue.

'You need to read this.'

White took the memorandum out of his pocket. He watched as the agent unfolded it hesitantly. Morrow began reading, turning to face the streetlights so he could see more clearly. When he had finished, he handed it back to White. 'Where did you get it?'

White told him about Kelly's cabin. 'Lee, McQuogue is the link with Vale Investments and NordFund.'

Morrow slumped forward. 'How do you know?'

White handed over the bank statements. 'It's all there.' Morrow said nothing as he glanced through the NordFund accounts. 'Christ,' he said eventually, 'he used his wife! After the attack in the private quarters—'

'*What?*'

Morrow looked at White. 'John Friedman was attacked in the White House the day Tyler Forrester died. An usher was set up for it. Two days later the usher was dead.' Morrow held Kelly's memo in his hand. 'They were looking for this.'

White cursed and looked back at the memo. 'Lee, McQuogue was behind all of it! He's got to have been. He had the run of the White House. But before they could stop him, Kelly disappeared with the paperwork.'

Morrow looked again at the torn bank statement, then pulled out of his pocket the photocopy of the list of figures Elizabeth had found. He laid the two pieces of paper on top of each other. He turned and looked at White. 'McQuogue and his wife have received nearly two million dollars! Elizabeth found one half of the bank statement in the President's pocket watch. I tried to find out who held the account but without a court order, we couldn't do *anything*. Jesus, Mrs Forrester thought it was her husband taking the bribes!'

White spoke quickly. 'Lee, whoever's behind this has covered their tracks brilliantly. They bought Kelly off; they owned his fucking house, they owned him! Maybe Kelly got greedy, and decided to blackmail them by sending this memo to Tyler Forrester—'

Morrow interrupted. 'That's why—'

'They killed him,' White said. He looked at Morrow. 'Friedman was being blackmailed too.'

Morrow remained silent. 'How do you know?' he asked finally.

'He told me. On the day he was killed. Whoever was behind this needed information on Elizabeth,' White went on. 'They had to be close to her. When she announced her candidacy, she threatened to blow this whole thing wide apart. Lee, look at these.' He leaned over and hurriedly leafed through the documents. He spoke as he did so. 'Kelly had got hold of a whole list of accounts at NordFund. He was smarter than they thought, and he was protecting himself. He sent one copy to the White House, and kept another for himself. The accounts show where the money for Kelly and McQuogue was coming from. They mean nothing to me but there were fucking millions of dollars changing hands!' He shoved the papers back at Morrow.

The agent took them again and flicked through. Suddenly, he stopped. '*Jesus Christ!*' He stared at the page. 'There's got to be some mistake here. The money paid to McQuogue came out of five of these accounts—'

'OK, but—'

Morrow spun round to face White. 'But look who paid the money in! Look!'

White hunched over Morrow. 'I know, Lee, but who the fuck is he? The name means nothing to me. I haven't had a chance to—'

Morrow was already standing. 'He's with Elizabeth, White! He's been with her all along—'

'*What?*'

'Clifford Granby!'

White didn't answer.

'Mark, Granby's the name on these accounts! He was the one paying the money all along.' Morrow turned back towards White. 'Mrs Forrester had her husband's diary . . . but a break-in at her cottage relieved her of it.'

'*A break-in?*'

'Granby was there that night! Mrs Forrester had told him about the diary but never showed it to him. He had to get it . . . Jesus, it was the ultimate cover! Granby pretends he's her confidante, and all the time his people are shadowing her. Granby *knew* Elizabeth had found the NordFund account . . . He had to bury it!

'*Jesus!* By standing, Elizabeth has left him with no choice!' He sprang up from the seat and leaped forward.

White grabbed hold off the papers and struggled to follow him across the plaza. 'But, Lee, where the fuck is Granby?'

'Mr President?'

McQuogue moved to Willard's side in the suite at the

Lancaster. Around them, the leading Democratic players were enjoying the party. 'Mr President, just a few moments, sir.'

McQuogue took hold of Willard's arm. 'If I may, I'd just like to drag you away from these good people.'

Willard followed him across the suite. At the door, the Chief of Staff paused. 'Sir, I'm sorry to have interrupted you but there is someone I'd like to introduce to you. He's a very old friend of mine and will be a key contributor to your campaign. He's vital to our success. He worked closely with Tyler, sir, although I don't think you ever met him. He would appreciate a few words.'

'Sure, Wayne, where is he?'

McQuogue pointed to the door in front of him. 'I think it might be best if we were to speak with him alone. He doesn't like these things,' he explained, glancing into the crowded room behind Willard's shoulder.

'OK,' the President said, turning towards his Secret Service detail. 'Guys, leave me with Mr McQuogue.'

Willard followed him through the open door. The room was brightly lit, papers spread out on a large coffee table. A tall man stood by the window, admiring the view of Houston. McQuogue shut the door and directed Willard across the room.

The man turned to greet him.

'Mr President,' McQuogue said, 'it's my pleasure to introduce to you a great patriot and a good friend.'

Clifford Granby smiled as he took Willard's outstretched hand.

White hurried along the sidewalk with Morrow. 'Lee, for fuck's sake, listen to me!' He nearly spat the words. 'I don't know who the fuck Granby is—'

Morrow shouted back at him as he ran. 'Elizabeth trusted him! He's been behind her—'

'Lee, listen to me! When I was in Shenandoah, two guys tried to run my car off the road. I recognised the driver. He was the bastard who broke into my apartment. The other guy was younger, armed—'

'Mark, if Granby—'

White tugged at Morrow's jacket sleeve, the two men colliding to a halt in the middle of the sidewalk. 'Lee, listen to me! This is why I came to Houston. I was trying to get to Elizabeth through *you.* After I'd found Kelly's papers two guys tried to run me off the road! And the younger one . . . I just saw him on TV. *With Elizabeth.*'

Morrow turned round, stunned. 'What, in the crowd?'

'No! He was part of the detail!

'Mark, that's bullshit! Everyone is checked, double-checked! There's no way—'

'Lee, *it was him.* I'm certain of it. I'm a journalist. You get to remember faces, specially if someone's trying to kill you!'

White flinched as Morrow quickly reached into his jacket.

'Mark, I'm not reaching for my revolver.' Instead, he pulled a small leather wallet out of his pocket.

White could see the faint reflection of the streetlight off the shiny leather. 'What the fuck's that?' he said, checking round them.

Morrow explained. 'When I was transferred off the Forrester detail, I was automatically given the photo IDs of any new detail people around her. That way, if we need to be suddenly sent over to the Forrester camp, we have a photographic breakdown of all Service personnel.'

'Don't you know them anyway?'

Morrow shook his head. 'Unlike in the movies, the Secret Service is not made up of only five people. I hardly know half the people designated to protection duties in DC. We all have our lapel badges but this is a back-up. It's what the book's for.'

Morrow opened it. White could see photocopied pictures of the agents assigned to Elizabeth.

Morrow turned the pages over.

'That's him, that's him!' White screamed, pointing at a photograph.

'*This one*? Impossible, White. No way! This guy might be new but—'

'Lee, it's fucking him! What's his name?'

Morrow held the small wallet in his hand. 'Agent Ben Shaw. I'd briefed him back in DC. And he was the agent I told about meeting you . . .'

The two men looked at each other.

'So what's his job?' White barked. 'I mean, can we get him away from Elizabeth?'

Morrow shook his head. 'No way, White. Shaw is *my* replacement. He's the one member of the detail whose job it is never to leave Mrs Forrester's side.'

White tried to speak again but Morrow had set off.

'Where *is* Shaw?' White screamed after him

Morrow was running fast. Ahead White could see the lights of the Hyatt blinking back at him from two blocks away.

Chapter Forty

'Well, are we done?'

Elizabeth waited for Greenhalgh's signal.

'Yes, ma'am. We're through. Shall we go to the suite?'

She nodded and collected her things. 'Marjorie, do you have my bag?'

'It's here, Liz,' she said, stepping over the cables the television crew had laid across the floor. 'Shall I carry it for you?'

Elizabeth nodded and stood. 'Yeah . . . yeah, that's fine. I'll be able to wave with both hands.'

The small group made their way out of the room through a side entrance. Greenhalgh led, Marjorie followed. Elizabeth was a few paces behind, her Secret Service detail watching the people around her.

She looked radiant. The onlookers could tell she was enjoying her moment. Whatever the result of the convention in a few months' time, Elizabeth Forrester had made her mark in Houston.

She smiled and stopped to speak to a few of the delegates as the Secret Service circled around her in the Hyatt's lobby. Elizabeth missed Morrow, but Shaw seemed reliable. She made a mental note to talk with him later. If he was to shadow her through the rest of the campaign, she'd have to make more of an effort with him.

The group made its way slowly across the lobby. As they neared the main entrance to the hotel, Elizabeth could see the Secret Service making a path towards the back of the hotel.

'Where are we going?' she asked quickly, keeping her smile in place.

'To the main lifts, ma'am,' Shaw replied. 'They're already prepared.'

Elizabeth stopped and surveyed the lobby. 'But I thought we were going up in the service lifts. Wouldn't that be quicker?'

She could feel Shaw's hand in the small of her back. 'Mr Greenhalgh thought you'd prefer to let the crowd see you as you left, Mrs Forrester. The lifts have been checked, ma'am.'

Elizabeth turned and tried to catch sight of Greenhalgh, but he was buried deep within the crowd behind her. She shrugged and gave Shaw the go-ahead.

She strode on as the crowd opened up in front of her. She turned to her right, revelling in the crush, both arms raised in a victory salute. Within seconds they were at the elevators. As Shaw held the doors open, Elizabeth and Marjorie pushed through. Elizabeth made her way to the back of the confined space, facing the crowds through the glass of the elevator. She saw Greenhalgh arguing frantically with one of the agents in the lobby beneath her. She couldn't catch his eye.

Elizabeth squinted as the flashguns erupted in front of her. She continued waving as the elevator began its slow ascent to the twenty-seventh floor.

The sniper nestled the butt of the Vaime rifle against his left shoulder. The door to the suite was propped open. Fifty yards ahead, he could see the Secret Service scanning the balconies. But the angles of the hotel ensured they could not see him. He opened the door just a fraction more, gently pushing the dark muzzle through the open space. The rifle had almost no recoil but he steadied himself anyway against the door jamb.

He squinted through the sight. The open elevator shaft was ahead of him, slightly to the right.

He saw the lights of the elevator first, eight startling white bulbs surrounding the top of the egg-shaped 'bubble'. Then, slowly, the top pane of glass came into sight.

He had not expected the light to be so fierce. The glare of television cameras and flashguns from the lobby twenty-four floors below ricocheted off the glass.

The top of Elizabeth's head came into his sight. Her arms were still outstretched. She was waving at the delegates, the crowds craning for a view from the terraces.

He counted the seconds.

One, two . . .

'Marjorie, isn't this incredible!'

Elizabeth looked behind her and caught her friend's amazed stare. Then she turned back, smiling, and carried on saluting the crowd. Across the vast open space people were standing around the terraces, waving, applauding, as the elevator carried her even higher.

She felt enlivened, purposeful. Houston had given her an extraordinary welcome. Later, she planned to watch Willard's speech at the Lancaster on television. She knew he wouldn't have matched this.

'I feel as if I'm in a glorified cage! I hope no one out there can lip-read.'

One more wave at the crowd.

She looked at her feet. 'Marjorie, do you have my bag? I want to check—'

'No, it's beside you.'

Elizabeth turned to her right and bent down.

He pulled delicately on the trigger.

The 7.62mm bullet exploded from the silenced muzzle. It took half a second to cross the hundred-yard space. There was, as expected, no recoil, but the crack of the discharge surprised him. Through his sight, he saw the glass of the elevator shatter and explode. He could not be certain but he thought his target had moved. He was unable to tell whether it was in the millisecond before or after he had fired. The exploding glass from the elevator obscured his view.

He fired twice more.

Chapter Forty-one

Morrow and White reached the security cordon around the Hyatt. Morrow signalled to a Houston cop and flashed his ID. The cop nodded him through but lunged to prevent White. Morrow screamed his objections, dragging White along with him. They dashed under the concrete canopy. The security personnel stood motionless as Morrow raced up to them, his Secret Service ID held out in front of him.

'United States Secret Service! Get out of the way!'

They heard the screams as they lunged through the hotel doors.

The crowd in the lobby surged back against them. Morrow pushed and shoved his way through, snarling at the men and women trying to escape.

'Fuck! Fuck, Lee, what's happened?' White yelled, pummelling people aside.

Morrow was just ahead of him now. White followed his gaze. Above them, splinters of glass rained down on to the lobby. It was almost beautiful: the small fragments of glass twirling and twinkling in the glare of the chandeliers that swung one hundred feet up in the air.

White groaned. He could see the elevator, still moving slowly. What had once been a marvel of engineering and design was twisted and buckled now. Not one pane of glass remained intact.

White could see the agents on the terraces above frantically pointing downward, their guns drawn.

The white bulbs at the base of the elevator were still working, apart from one. It blinked playfully at White as the screams echoed around the vast space.

Morrow struggled to stay standing as the crowd slammed against him. His eyes were glued to the balcony high above him. The panic among the onlookers swept over him again. He nearly toppled over.

Frantically, he looked around him. He had lost White in the crowd. Morrow lunged forward, pushing people aside. He held his Secret Service badge in one hand. In the other, he had his gun.

He made it to the left side of the lobby. By a pillar, he stopped and looked up.

Twenty-seven floors above, he could see commotion. Two, maybe three floors below, the elevator was still moving.

He turned, hurrying between the gargantuan plant-pots. By one, a group of hotel staff stood transfixed, gazing at the scene above. Morrow grabbed one of them, a small Latino man. 'Is there another elevator here? Tell me!'

The man trembled, trying to wrestle free from Morrow's grasp. 'A service elevator! Over there!'

Morrow spun on his heel and began running to the far side of the hotel. He jumped over a row of potted plants, careering into a small group of women who had taken refuge behind them. He ignored their screams and made it to the service elevator. The doors were open, a bemused hotel guard standing inside. Morrow flashed his ID and flung the man out. He had to get to the detail, find Shaw. He pushed the button for the twenty-seventh floor. The doors slid closed.

The elevator began its grinding journey upward. Morrow focused his mind on one thing.

Elizabeth.

The elevator doors slid back.

Elizabeth opened her eyes. She could feel a weight on her, heavy and suffocating. She tried to move but was unable to. She struggled to lift her head but flinched as shards of glass cut viciously into her cheekbone. The cold tiles of the elevator floor were harsh against her face.

She managed to cry out. 'Agent Shaw! *Anyone!* Jesus, is someone there?'

Suddenly, the weight was lifted off her. She sat up and screamed in surprise. The elevator's glass sides had disintegrated. She was peering into a two-hundred-foot drop to the lobby below, with nothing to protect her.

Elizabeth felt a pull from behind.

'Mrs Forrester! We're getting out of here! *Now!*'

It was Shaw.

She clambered to her feet. 'My God! *Marjorie!*' She yelled her friend's name, oblivious to Shaw's pleas. 'Marjorie! Oh, no, please, *no!*'

Elizabeth squatted down again, sobbing and shaking in horror. Marjorie lay slumped on the elevator floor. She was covered in blood, limbs splayed unnaturally, hair matted and congealed. She was not moving.

'Marj—'

Shaw took hold of Elizabeth's arms, heaving her backward. She began screaming, yelling for the medics to come and help her friend.

Within a second, she was dragged from the elevator. Shaw grabbed her wrist and propelled her forward.

'Mrs Forrester! This way!'

'But I must get back to Marjorie! Where are we—'

'No, ma'am. Please, this way!'

Elizabeth was pushed forward again and spun to the right, Shaw's immovable arm around her. She tried to focus on what was happening. 'But we're on the . . . Christ, the twenty-fifth floor! There's no one here to get at Marj—'

Shaw kept his hold on her. 'Mrs Forrester, I have to get you out of here! *Now!* You must be safe!'

The agent pushed her forward along the balcony. Across the open terraces, Elizabeth could see her full detail two floors above, pointing at her and screeching instructions to each other. She almost stumbled and tripped, Shaw half dragging her up.

'Agent Shaw, I think I'm bleeding! I want to go back!'

'This way! Hurry!'

Elizabeth allowed herself to be propelled forward again.

They reached the far side of the terrace. She could hear the screams and shouts emanating from the lobby below. She longed to peer over the ledge, to raise her arms and tell the people beneath that Marjorie needed assistance.

Shaw manhandled her along, Elizabeth pleading with him to radio the rest of the detail.

'I will, ma'am, I will. But you must be made *secure!*'

Elizabeth struggled against his weight, trying to break free. 'But the rest of the detail are up there—'

Shaw tightened his grip. 'It's OK, ma'am. Through here now!'

Elizabeth struggled to breathe, to focus. She was hurled through an open door. Shaw pushed through behind her. They were into a service corridor. The door slammed shut behind them. With it, the noise evaporated. It was quiet now, eerily so. The corridor was brightly lit, the walls brilliant white, the floor concrete and scarred. Elizabeth ran ahead, the sound of her heels ricocheting off the solid floor. She willed herself forward, suppressing the need to scream.

'Shaw, get the goddam detail over to Marjorie!'

Ahead was a fire escape. The blue sign above it was bright; there was a metal handle across it. Elizabeth reached for the handle.

'We'll wait here for the rest of the detail, ma'am.'

She stopped and let herself collapse against the cold wall. Her legs were beginning to shake. Her heels scraped along the concrete, her knees buckling. She managed to stay standing and laid her hands against the hard wall. Her head slumped between her outstretched arms, the noise of her breathing harsh in the confined space.

'Agent Shaw?'

She turned, half reaching towards him.

'Yes, ma'am?'

The agent was ten feet away from her. Elizabeth glanced around. They were still alone. 'Agent, what about *Marjorie*? My friend! Christ, *Marjorie!*' She began sobbing again, her body shaking. 'Where *are* the rest of my detail? You should be getting all of us out of here!'

Morrow saw the flash of colour below him, away to his right. It was only a glimpse. He did not recognise the woman's outfit. But he didn't need to. He knew it was Elizabeth. He shouted her name but his voice was lost in the commotion.

He saw a man – *Shaw!* – push Elizabeth through a doorway. They were two floors below.

White had been right.

Morrow flicked the safety catch on his gun and began running.

'Agent Shaw?'

Elizabeth's voice echoed down the long corridor. Shaw remained where he was. It was just the two of them. She saw the agent look behind him. Elizabeth followed his stare. The door at the end of the corridor remained closed. She watched as Shaw holstered his gun.

'Agent Shaw, what are you doing?'

Adrenaline and fear made her shiver. She tried to make sense of what was happening. She knew the procedure: she should not be in this corridor. Not with just one agent. She should be in a secure place, with her detail, well away from the hotel.

She lunged forward, trying to make a break for the door that led back towards the twenty-fifth floor. 'Where's Marjorie! For God's sake, I *have* to get to her!'

Shaw raised his hand to stop her. 'Mrs Forrester, please stay calm.'

Shaw was smiling. He was smiling at her. Elizabeth relaxed a little, just wanting someone to take her away, grateful she had survived, was protected, albeit only by one man. She wished that he would come nearer. She wanted that animal sense of protection, the smell, the feel, of another living human being near to her. She didn't want to be alone. But she longed to know about Marjorie.

Shaw opened his jacket. Elizabeth watched. She felt as if she were witnessing the scene from far away. The agent reached under his jacket, bending slightly down and to the left.

Elizabeth saw him remove a gun. It wasn't the one he had just put back in his holster. This one was thinner, longer. The silencer gleamed under the lights.

She stood still. Shaw lifted the revolver. She saw that he was wearing gloves. She focused on them, the starched, white material. Clean and soft. The long fingers. The solid, metallic object in his hand. Pointing at her.

He seemed to move with a slow, almost balletic grace. No hurried movements. Elizabeth felt as if her body were floating upward. She could see what was happening in front of her, but almost a second too late. She was here, but not here. She felt herself sway.

The agent had stopped smiling. She looked into his eyes. They held hers for a second. She thought she was peering into darkness.

The noise of the shot consumed her.

Her head was flung back, the pain in her neck vicious. She could see the ceiling above her as she spun, the long strip lighting coming towards her. The whiteness was absolute. She was lifted off her feet, whiteness all around her now, the explosion deafening. Her legs gave way and she began to fall.

It was almost reassuring. She could feel herself tumbling gently, half floating, her limbs light and still.

The wave of blood splashed hard against her.

It carried on up and over her head. The walls in front of her suddenly turned red, a great sweep of colour, brutal and shocking against the clinical white of the corridor.

There was no pain. As she trembled again, and spun around for the last time, all she saw was red and white. Lights, concrete and dirt. Hard corners. The grooves of the skirting board. The brilliant column of whiteness. More red. Instinctively, she reached for her chest.

McQuogue placed the papers back on the desk. He grimaced and knotted his hands together. He lowered his head and began picking at a nail. Behind him, a small desk lamp highlighted his balding pate. Granby sat facing him.

'I see,' McQuogue said gently. 'The President will be grateful for this contribution, Clifford. Obviously, we can ensure the arms licences are processed as quickly as possible. However, I have to tell you—'

'Wayne, be quiet!'

McQuogue flinched at the insult. Instinctively, he checked behind him. There was no one else in Granby's Lancaster suite. The two men had retired to it after the meeting with Willard.

'Clifford, look—'

'Wayne, I *have* to bag this deal. You know that. Kelly was useful but only up to a point.' Granby slid the papers back towards him. 'Wayne, the survival of the Granby Foundation depends on you granting these licences. When you do – sorry,

Willard does – the shares in five of these arms companies will double in value overnight. It will be the biggest order placed with domestic arms manufacturers for over thirty years: half for the US military, half for overseas. At the moment, those shares are almost worthless. Tyler saw to that. It's a shame he had to stick to his principles but rather useful that you didn't.'

'Well, yes—'

'Wayne, Tyler Forrester made two mistakes. The first was refusing to expand his own defence budget. Bad move. Not just for him but also for me, as you well know.' He looked hard at McQuogue. 'I didn't invest what is left of my fortune in the domestic arms industry to see Tyler try and crucify it with his liberal guilt. It wasn't just jobs he was destroying; it was *me*.'

'I lobbied against his cuts, Clifford,' McQuogue muttered. 'I ensured that Congress and the Defence Trade Advisory Group moved against them also.'

'Yes, you did, Wayne, which is why you were rewarded. Forrester made one other mistake: he died. Bad for him, good for us. But not quite good enough. *I need this deal*.'

McQuogue felt his face redden. 'Clifford, the licences that were already pushed through at your insistence were extremely profitable. You—'

'Wayne, I need *this* profit. Kelly was just dealing with the small fry.' Granby stared hard at McQuogue. 'You can make a much greater contribution.'

'Clifford, I understand your predicament—'

'No, I don't think you do, Wayne.' Granby rose from the chair and stared out over the lights of Houston. 'I have spent the last four years trying to prevent the collapse of the Granby Foundation.' He turned back to McQuogue. 'Oh, I've no doubt that like most people you considered my funds to be endless. Clifford Granby, the quiet philanthropist! Well, you were wrong. I'm afraid my bastard of a father would be turning in his grave if he knew. You see, Wayne, you become accustomed to money and power . . . but these days, power demands rather more money than it used to. Although I hate to admit it, I'm afraid my life is something of a sham.' He sat down heavily. 'My restructured debt is such that, within a matter of days, I will be unable to facilitate my creditors. I will not be able to maintain my repayments. The first is fifty million dollars, Wayne. And that's the *smallest.* When that fails, all the wolves will come to the door.'

McQuogue flinched as Granby clapped his hands together. 'But you own NordFund, Clifford. Surely—'

'*All* of the wolves, Wayne. Oh, I've manipulated the figures. That's why I had enough to fund the payments through NordFund. Owning the bank was useful in terms of propping up my debt, which is why I moved Calthorp in as CEO. But I'm afraid that cannot go on for much longer. And with it will go what little money I have left . . . money that, of course, I had earmarked for Willard's re-election. You do understand me, don't you?'

McQuogue nodded. He watched as Granby drew heavily on a cigar. 'Of course, Clifford. We're most understanding—'

'*Understanding?*' McQuogue felt Granby's cold, penetrating stare wither him. 'You'd better understand! If I fall, so will *you.*'

'Cliff—'

'Please listen, Wayne. You *understand* that I had Friedman blackmailed? Without that we wouldn't have learned about Elizabeth's less than savoury past. At least it gave us something to throw at her, even if she's managed to survive.' He stopped and glared at McQuogue. 'The fact that Elizabeth will launch an investigation into NordFund if she's elected is something of an inconvenience, Wayne. Perhaps if it had been dealt with a little more expertly she wouldn't currently be such a threat to our candidate and to my future. Oh, and *yours,* of course.'

He smiled. It was a playful, teasing smile. 'Wayne, let me tell you a few facts of life. It is, I believe, the right moment to do so. I also think it might help you agree to this deal.' He waved nonchalantly at the papers spread out in front of McQuogue. 'You see, Wayne, Friedman's death was no accident.'

McQuogue felt the room sway in front of him. He had heard what Granby had said but his mind was trying to reject it, to rewrite the words.

'Wayne, John Friedman did not die in a drugs war. You actually thought that was *true*?'

'Well, *yes!*' McQuogue half laughed. 'Clifford, I saw the police reports! The hotel was a notorious meeting place. The PD received information from their informants that a drugs deal had gone wrong! Fried—'

'Wayne, I didn't kill John Friedman. No one individual dealt with the Friedman problem. We *all* did.'

McQuogue felt his throat contract. He tried to swallow, but failed.

'You did, Wayne! You were more than helpful. It was unfortunate that Friedman was snooping around the White House while my man was in there, but we only had to go looking because *you* couldn't find Kelly's diary!'

'Well, yes, I was prepared to frame Danello for that—'

Granby snorted. 'Wayne, you are extraordinary! For such a ruthless man, you're amazingly stupid! Are you going to pretend to me that Danello's death was *another* accident?'

McQuogue glanced away. 'I prefer not to dwell on it.'

Granby laughed loudly. 'I bet you don't!' He glared at McQuogue. 'After all, you and your lovely wife are more than comfortable now, aren't you?'

McQuogue didn't answer.

'Wayne, I'm sorry to be so forceful but, you see, either you agree to this or I'm afraid the game is up!'

McQuogue held his stare. 'What are you saying, Clifford?'

Granby shrugged impatiently. 'Wayne, cut the crap. You knew what Kelly had discovered. And *you* should have been more careful over ensuring Elizabeth Forrester didn't stumble across Kelly's betrayal!'

McQuogue leaped from the chair. 'Fuck you, Granby! I'm not having any part—'

Granby remained seated. He smiled again. 'Keep your voice down!' he commanded, then motioned to the chair opposite. 'And sit down.'

McQuogue wanted to storm out of the room, to blank out the appalling realisation of what was happening. What had happened.

He felt light-headed. The fear was all-consuming. He sank into the soft cushions, his legs trembling. He knew he would have to listen to Granby. He was drawn towards him like a sacrificial lamb seeking shelter in the temple.

'Wayne, I'm telling you this because you are an accomplice.'

'I am not! I never discussed *killing* Friedman or Kelly. I'm Chief of Staff to the President! Yes, I accepted your money, but I didn't go around having people—'

'Wayne.' Granby's voice was hard. 'Whether you intended to or not, whether you knew or not, you're implicated now, aren't you? Do you think people will split hairs if this comes out? You were kept fully informed that I was blackmailing Friedman, and you were a willing recipient of that information. I am sure your friends in the media will confirm it was from the West Wing that rumours first started to emerge about Elizabeth's abortion. The finger points at you, Wayne.'

McQuogue felt the heat in his chest. It rose up, more painful and intense than heartburn, and almost caused him to gag. The room went in and out of focus. His head slumped forward. He fought against the rising panic, trying to think.

He could only manage a defiant whisper. 'You bastard, Granby!'

'Thank you, Wayne. I wondered how long it would take for you to see sense. Look,' Granby said, his voice softer now, 'there was no other way. And besides, Friedman was a nuisance who had to be dealt with. He had given us what we needed, even more than we'd expected, but he could *not* be allowed to talk to White. I would actually have preferred to have kept him alive for a while but his duplicity was unacceptable. Friedman thought he could get away with it. He hoped that one day this would all just go away. Well, it did. At least for him.'

McQuogue flinched at Granby's harsh laughter. He spoke over it. 'And so,' he said as calmly as he could, 'you now have me precisely where you want me too? You need the deal and I need you to get it.'

Granby shrugged. 'If you care to put it that way, I suppose that's right.'

McQuogue refused to look at the man opposite. He could not bring himself to do so. Still, he could not resist one last vicious taunt. 'Well, Clifford, we haven't exactly *stopped* Elizabeth, have we?' he sneered, his mouth twisted in controlled rage. 'She's still set to beat us at the convention in a few months' time! She's wooing everyone here. I mean, for all of your cleverness, Willard is hardly secure in the nomination, is he?'

McQuogue was surprised to see Granby smile, then shrug lazily. 'I think you will find, Wayne, that Willard Morgan will be—' he checked his watch – 'yes, almost certainly, the President is now the *only* candidate currently in this race. And should you consider telling *that* to anyone, Wayne, make sure you've got a good lawyer.'

Before McQuogue could speak, Granby leaned to his right. He picked up the remote control, checked his watch again, smiled and turned on the television set. McQuogue's eyes moved towards the screen.

He sat riveted. He heard police sirens, thought the noise was coming from the screen. Then he realised the long, harsh wails were also from the street outside.

Granby grimaced. 'I do believe we're within earshot of the Hyatt!' He laughed quietly to himself.

McQuogue felt the bile rise in his throat.

'Ma'am, get down!'

Elizabeth almost smiled at the command. It was all too

surreal. She just longed for the brightness to end. She felt her head slump to the floor, bouncing harshly against the concrete. An arm took hold of her hand. She closed her eyes, felt warm. She wondered if she had wet herself.

She tried to focus her eyes. Still the brightness. Then she saw the body.

'Shaw . . .'

She found she couldn't speak properly. She was aware of people around her, confused commands. Someone shouted an order, the male voice ricocheting off the walls like a tennis ball.

She lifted her head, tried to focus. Shaw's limp body lay slumped at her feet. His head oozed blood on to the floor. Elizabeth panicked. 'What—'

'Relax, ma'am. You're fine.'

A male voice. Familiar.

She heard more voices. More shouting. The warmth was still there. She struggled against it, trying to test its strength. Only then did she realise it was soft, human. She moved her head to the left, eyes focused now. She strained to catch sight of whoever was holding her. Someone was. That was the warmth. She almost wept with relief.

'Who—'

'Can you stand, Mrs Forrester? Ma'am?'

She wondered where she had been shot.

'It's Lee, ma'am. You haven't been hit. *Mrs Forrester*? Can you stand up for me?'

Chapter Forty-two

Elizabeth sat slumped in the hospital's VIP suite. Her left arm was bandaged where shards of glass from the shattered panes had torn her flesh. The suite was quiet. In a corner of the room an agent kept careful watch; armed guards stood on the other side of the teak door. Morrow had yet to see her at the hospital, yet to talk to her. She knew that he had gone to telephone his report through to Command at the Lancaster.

She did not remember being rushed out of the Hyatt. She could not recall Morrow's comforting words as her limousine raced towards the hospital. She had not really reclaimed her senses until she was in ER, a bank of doctors checking that she had not been wounded.

She looked across the room. Greenhalgh sat opposite her, resting his head in his hands and talking quietly on a mobile phone.

Elizabeth placed her feet on the coffee table in front of her. She was still wearing the dark blue skirt and white blouse, the latter torn around the collar, its double cuffs marked by blood. Her jacket rested on her shoulders. She shivered, pulling it around her.

She knew they had been after *her*. She had not had time to ponder on why, or how. That would come later. All she thought about was Marjorie. About the doctors fighting to save her life.

She let her head slump back against the chair. It felt removed from her body, as if someone were playing pinball in her cranium. Her make-up was smudged and dried; she hadn't even seen a mirror, would not have cared anyway.

The suite smelt vaguely of disinfectant and stale coffee. The carpet was stained in places. A vase of flowers rested by her feet on the table, withered by the warm central heating that purred from ceiling ducts. She could hear the fragile rattle of trolleys and medical equipment from the other side of the door.

Greenhalgh finished his call and placed the mobile phone on the armrest of his chair. He caught Elizabeth's eye.

'How're ya doin', Mrs Candidate?' he drawled, trying hard to summon a smile.

Elizabeth sat staring ahead. 'Benmont . . . why is there so much death in this business? So much . . . I don't know . . . *hatred*?' She rubbed her eyes and sat forward. 'You never expect this, you know, never think this will ever happen. And then, like Tyler's death, just as you are getting somewhere, they reach out and grab you.'

She could see her reflection in the glass top of the table. She held her own stare for a second before turning towards Greenhalgh. 'I just can't help thinking perhaps it wasn't worth it . . . Marjorie is down there dying, and it's me up here. *Me!* I'm the one they wanted to kill.'

Her fingers scraped hard against her cheek.

She heard a faint knock on the door. The Secret Service agent opened it a fraction and peered outside. Then he stood back. Morrow entered the room, taking in Greenhalgh as his eyes searched for Elizabeth.

'Lee!'

She rushed towards him, knowing she shouldn't do it, knowing that even in the midst of this tragedy she should retain her composure. But she hugged Morrow tightly, the tears returning. After a moment she pulled back, drying her eyes.

'Can I see Marjorie now?'

Morrow escorted her out into the corridor. The medical staff and doctors stood back to let her pass. She felt Morrow's hand on her shoulder. 'Three doors down, ma'am.'

She entered the small ward. It contained two beds, but one had been pushed to the far side, its green mattress covered in torn packages, bandages, a doctor's apron.

Marjorie was in the other bed, plugged into a bank of drip-feeds and saline bags. Her hair was pushed back, eyes closed, a swathe of bandages wrapped tightly round her chest. The first bullet had entered and exited through her shoulder bone; a second had pummelled through her right hip-bone. Her normally healthy complexion was shadowed, wan, and although her eyes were closed, she seemed to be wincing as if an unspoken, terrible pain had replaced the smile that usually laid claim to her features.

Elizabeth composed herself and turned back to Morrow. 'Lee, leave me for a few minutes.'

He closed the door and she stood a few feet from the bed before pulling a chair towards her. Lightly, as if putting her hand into a fire, Elizabeth stroked her friend's shoulder. Marjorie's eyelids opened a fraction.

'Liz?'

She leaned forward and kissed her on the forehead. 'Marj, stay still,' she whispered. 'You're OK now. Keep your eyes closed. Try to go back to sleep.'

Marjorie didn't obey. 'What happened, Liz? Are you OK?'

'Marj, I'm fine. Don't worry about me. Just stay still. The team here are superb. They've done a great job, Marj. You're going to be absolutely fine.' Elizabeth brushed her hand against her friend's forehead, trying to ease her back to sleep.

Marjorie spoke again. 'You've been reading too many books on Reagan, Liz.'

'Shhh, Marjorie.'

'You learned to duck.'

Elizabeth smiled and kissed her friend's hand. Marjorie's eyes closed again. Instantaneously, her face seemed to sink in on itself, her strength momentarily gone. She fell asleep with the suddenness of a handclap.

Elizabeth stayed with her for five more minutes. Then she walked back across the room and opened the door. Morrow was outside.

'Lee, I wish to go now, please.'

She was escorted back to the VIP suite. Greenhalgh was waiting inside with a Secret Service agent. As she gathered her jacket and possessions, it was Morrow who broke the silence in the room.

'Mrs Forrester, there is something I need to tell you.' He turned and looked at Greenhalgh. 'Sir, would you mind giving me a few moments with Mrs Forrester?'

As Greenhalgh made for the door, Morrow spoke quietly to the agent standing beside him. 'Please, I need you to leave as well.'

The agent looked confused, glancing at Elizabeth.

'It's fine,' she said, trying to catch Morrow's eye.

He waited for the door to close again. 'Mrs Forrester, there is an awful lot that you need to listen to.'

He rose from his chair and walked to the door. 'But before that,' he said, opening the door, 'there's someone else you need to hear from first. It will explain an awful lot.'

Morrow looked out into the corridor. Then he stepped back.

Mark White stood in the doorway.

'Elizabeth.'

She rose from the chair, her face flushed red.

'Mark?'

They both tried to speak at the same time, stopped at the same time. Neither noticed Morrow leave the room. They watched each other, silent.

Ten feet separated them, over two decades reduced to a few

small steps between them. Two lives that had been so different, so vastly different, only to come back on themselves, the distance between them now reduced to an arm's length. Ten quick paces that were still an eternity, a chasm of misunderstanding, pain, absolution, fear.

It was Elizabeth who spoke first. She heaved the words out, slung them across the room like a spear. 'What are you doing here, Mark?'

'Liz . . . er, can we just sit and . . .'

Elizabeth sat down on a sofa as White pulled up a chair. A coffee table sat between them. They both looked at it. They both knew what the other was thinking: best to keep a barrier, a fence between us. Other fences, other high and solid barriers, had been erected between them, hammered in, only to be torn down, new ones built in their place.

'Are you . . . are you OK?' White asked timidly, watching her. He spoke like a man stepping through a minefield, just waiting for the final, tentative placing of his foot in the wrong place.

Elizabeth arched her back and nodded silently.

'Liz . . . sorry, Mrs Forrester . . .'

'Liz will do fine, Mark.'

White nodded in acceptance, caught her eye. They both looked away.

'You haven't answered my question, Mark. What are you doing in Houston? Why are you here?'

'Liz, this may not . . . I don't know . . . this may not be the best time, but there are things you need to know. I don't know whether John Friedman told you' – he looked up at her, looked away again – 'but I have been investigating Ronald Kelly's death and its links to the White House.'

'Go on.'

'Liz, both Kelly and McQuogue were being paid by Clifford Granby.'

Elizabeth stared at him wide-eyed. '*Clifford?*'

White nodded. 'Granby needed Kelly to process the arms

deals. McQuogue ensured that there was no trouble from the White House.' He looked at Elizabeth. 'It wasn't your husband receiving the funds, Liz. It was McQuogue and Kelly. And Granby was doing the paying.'

'But, my God, *why*? Clifford was never involved with the military.'

White shook his head. 'Not publicly. But Granby needed the deals badly, Liz. According to the accounts Kelly had got hold off, Granby used a company named Vale Investments as a front for his Foundation. The trouble was, there wasn't any money left, Liz. Granby was nearly bankrupt. If Kelly or McQuogue hadn't delivered on the arms deals, Granby would be penniless.'

She looked at White. 'But Hiscock House . . . I mean, he inherited a fortune! He was—'

'Almost broke.'

She stared at him. 'So *this* is what's it's all about? *Money?* Just that?'

White shrugged. 'Money and pride. Granby had to maintain his position. He could not face the prospect of going to his grave a pauper, maybe even to prison. He had been juggling the books, Liz. Money was his god and the thought of losing it was too much.'

'So when I began investigating what Kelly had discovered, Granby was terrified I'd uncover the entire scam?'

White nodded. 'Granby couldn't allow that to happen . . . he was playing you and Friedman and Morrow along all the time. He hoped that if he sent you the wrong way, you'd give up. But you didn't.' White smiled at her. 'You never were one to give up. So—'

'Clifford had to stop me? He had to win my confidence, but at the same time, he had to stop me. My God, *Clifford!*'

White nodded, then spoke more gently. 'Liz,' he said, 'John Friedman was being blackmailed.'

Her head snapped back, a look of deep, terrible pain etched

on her face. '*Oh, no!*' she whispered, her eyes closed. She let out a deep, ragged sigh; her head slumped forward.

'Granby's people had got to him,' White said. 'I don't know what they had over him. But before he died he spoke about having made a mistake.'

'He was gay.'

White looked up.

She nodded, her composure returning. 'I always knew . . . well, I didn't *know*, but I suspected.' She stopped and breathed in deeply. 'So they picked *him*.'

White nodded. 'It would appear so, yes.'

'*Bastards!*' She hissed the expletive, staring at White. 'So it wasn't you who leaked the abortion story?'

She had said it. She'd wanted to slap him with his betrayal, twist him and pummel him verbally. But it hadn't been him. He had still been loyal: quiet, reserved, weak, but ever-so-loyal Mark.

'No, Liz,' he muttered finally. 'I didn't leak the abortion story. I never had, and never would. It was Friedman. Granby had the information, and through McQuogue it was leaked in order to finish off your campaign. When I met Friedman at the hotel, Granby's people had followed him. They couldn't risk Friedman helping me.'

She sat back and covered her face with her hands. Another betrayal, another loss. She had grieved for Friedman. And all along . . .

'Liz . . .'

She looked up.

'You need to read this,' he said. 'It's all there . . . well, most of it. Until Granby and McQuogue are questioned.'

She took Kelly's papers from White's hand and read them in silence. When she had finished, she nodded to herself and placed the package on the table between them. 'Can I keep this, please?' She looked up at him.

'Yes.'

'I'll pass it immediately to the FBI. There will have to be an independent counsel appointed.' She held her head in her hands. 'Christ, this is not going to be pleasant.' She looked up and watched him closely. 'So I suppose I owe you my life, Mark.'

'Liz—'

'In fact, I owe you much more. When I first discovered the NordFund bank account in Tyler's watch, I thought it was my husband who was taking the money.' She looked at him. 'That nearly killed me, Mark. The thought that Tyler was corrupt. I couldn't face it, couldn't accept what I was seeing and hearing. And all along, Granby *knew*! He could see how much I was suffering, thinking Tyler had betrayed all of us, but Granby was the one pulling the strings.'

She shook her head slowly.

'I bet neither of us . . . Well,' she went on slowly, 'I don't think we ever expected to find ourselves in this situation, did we, Mark?'

He held her stare.

Elizabeth felt a surge of emotion: the man she had tried to write out of her life, the man whom she had loved and lusted after, then expunged from her memory, only to find his ghost threatening to destroy her . . . he had finally come through for her. It hadn't been Tyler. It hadn't even been Friedman. Fate had thrown herself and White together as adolescents; now it had finished its bizarre, inexplicable circle, had joined the lines, here in this hospital room, surrounded by death and betrayal, where once they'd been cushioned by the glow of a student summer.

White sat in silence. He knew what she was thinking, dared not show it.

Elizabeth broke the silence. '*Granby!*' She spat his name out. 'He gave McQuogue the greatest prize of all . . . he gave him John Friedman.'

'Yeah, I'm afraid so.'

'But when that didn't work, when I was still on the scene and getting stronger, Granby had no choice. He knew that if I was successful in this campaign, I'd launch an investigation. I was the one in the way. And he couldn't allow that to happen.'

'Yes. Granby had thought he was clear once he'd learned about . . . about your abortion. But without realising it, you outmanoeuvred them. Your television broadcast—' White had to look away again. 'It was, well, in Granby's eyes the broadcast put him back at the beginning. You looked unstoppable. He couldn't take the chance that you might go public. He had to act fast and his reach was such that someone like Shaw was waiting to be put in the right place.'

'What about you, Mark? Why did you never reveal what you knew about me?'

He avoided her stare. 'I'd left you when you needed me most,' he said quietly. 'I was cruel because I was frightened. I'd never expected that to happen to me. Never thought that—'

'You'd be snared that quickly?'

He started to speak then shrugged. 'Maybe, Liz, maybe. I'm not proud of what I did. Whenever I thought about it, what I'd lost, how selfish I'd been, I'd just try and bury the emotion, try and forget it. I was naïve, of course. It was always going to be with me. Always.'

'Did you marry?'

'Yes. Badly.'

'Who was she?'

He shrugged. 'A secretary with a heart of grit. She left me two years ago. She's somewhere in Detroit now, living off what she got of my immoral earnings.'

Elizabeth smiled and sat back in the sofa. 'I knew you were in DC,' she said. 'Throughout Tyler's primary campaign, I was waiting, just waiting, for the roof to fall in. I suppose I underestimated you. I thought that you'd probably do it when Tyler had the nomination, but when you didn't, I hoped I was in the clear. Did you ever think of contacting me?'

He nodded. 'Often. But the First Lady isn't someone you invite over to your house for old time's sake.'

'Thank you, Mark.' She said it quietly, let it float between them, then repeated it. 'Thank you.'

'I've changed, Liz. I let you down once, I wasn't going to do it a second time.'

She got up from the sofa and walked round the coffee table.

She sat beside him, her head resting on his shoulder, the tears flowing once more.

'What will you do now?'

He asked the question gently.

She turned and looked at him. 'What I've always done, Mark. I'll pick myself up and carry on.'

'And the Kelly memo?'

She breathed in heavily, exhaled, staring ahead. 'We'll expose them, don't worry.'

'It could harm you . . . whatever went on in the Tyler White House, even if you and your husband didn't know about it . . . it will haunt your campaign.'

She nodded. 'I know that. But Tyler went to his grave with that fear in his mind.' She glanced at him. 'I can't allow that to happen to me. I can't live with that, not the way Tyler did.'

There was a knock on the door off to their left. She stood, walked quickly across the room and opened it. Morrow entered the suite and glanced at White. 'Mrs Forrester, the Houston PD . . . the media . . . we need to get moving, ma'am.'

She nodded, putting her jacket on. She turned to White and held out her hand.

They stared at each other.

'Thank you, Mr White, for all that you've done. I am most grateful.'

Elizabeth let go of his hand and began walking towards the door. Then she stopped and turned back towards him. 'Mr White, perhaps you'll find time to call me when all this is over.'

White smiled. 'Of course, Mrs Forrester. Is it true what they say about the White House?'

She frowned. 'What do you mean?'

He took a step towards her, lifting his own jacket off the sofa. 'Well, that the telephone operators can find anyone, anywhere?'

'Yes.'

'Well, when you're back in the Mansion, make sure they find me, ma'am.'

She smiled and then was gone through the door.

Epilogue

Eighteen months later.

'Goddammit, Whitey, what the hell have you got in here?'

White watched as Riordan struggled down the apartment building steps. The Irishman was carrying a large box, its sides and lid taped shut.

'My books,' he shouted back.

'Jesus, I never knew *Zipper* magazines could be so heavy.'

Riordan squatted down, the box tumbling on to the sidewalk. 'Is that it?' he asked, mopping his head with a handkerchief.

'Think so.' White checked the contents of the van. It was piled high with furniture and boxes, suitcases, his precious stereo and guitar. He lifted the final package into the van and slammed the door shut.

He looked back at the apartment. 'Did you lock up?'

The Irishman handed over the keys. 'All done,' he said, sweating and short of breath.

'Well, I'd better get going, Mick. It's a long drive.'

Riordan snorted. 'Yeah, it's best you get out of my sight before I start charging you for my time.'

White held out his hand. Riordan looked at it as if it were a dead fish. 'Get outta here!' he roared, throwing his arms around White and pulling him towards him. The two men embraced awkwardly. 'You take care of yourself, Whitey,' the Irishman said, pulling back eventually.

White could see Riordan trying to avoid his eye. It wasn't the easiest of goodbyes.

'Thanks, Mick,' he said quickly, slapping him on the shoulder.

He winced inwardly at the pathetic, macho gesture. These two knew each other better than that.

'Send Roxie my love,' he said, walking towards the front of the van. 'I'll see you at the wedding.'

'You'd better, Whitey. Someone's got to lead her down the frigging aisle.'

'Oh, and settle my check at Mort's, will you!'

White gave a final wave and slipped into the driver's seat. He started the engine, checked the mirrors and rolled out into the DC traffic. He honked the horn, and looked in the rear-view mirror. Riordan stood on the sidewalk, his hand raised in a final wave. White watched as he turned, pulled a packet out of his pocket and lit a cigarette, strolling down the street.

White concentrated on the heavy afternoon traffic. He was heading for the I-95, the bullet-straight highway to the East Coast, the thin missile of an interstate that begins down in Florida, hurtles up past Richmond, Baltimore and DC, before thundering through the eastern states and on beyond Boston.

He was looking forward to New York. A new apartment. A new job, this one with the *Times*. Finally, he had been headhunted: his exposé of the Granby affair had brought most of America's editors to his door. Eventually he had accepted the *New York Times*' offer. It was where he'd always wanted to be. Riordan had been horrified; but then Riordan didn't like to lose a friend, though White knew they would always be there for each other, even if McReedy's was no longer their umbilical cord.

He settled into the drive, skirting through Adams-Morgan. He waited for the lights to change at the junction of 16th and Euclid. To his right, way down beyond Scott Circle, was the

White House. He couldn't see it but he knew it was there, in all its miniature glory and global importance.

He eased his way into the uptown traffic. He opened the window, breathing in the cool air. Instinctively, he reached for a cigarette, then remembered he had given up. He laughed loudly and turned on the radio. Jefferson Airplane: 'Somebody To Love'. He felt his heart leap.

No, he thought, he didn't need somebody to love. Not yet, anyway.

Lee Morrow eased the car into West Executive Avenue. Security was tight around the White House. The President was welcoming the British Prime Minister in a few hours' time. It was to be the highlight of the Washington season. Morrow viewed it as yet another professional exercise in which his men and women would have to stand guard.

Still, he thought, life could be worse. The Service had survived the scandal of Shaw's murderous duplicity. A Senate investigation was on-going; Morrow himself had spent nearly a week giving evidence. But there were no more clouds on the horizon. He was back in the White House, promoted to head of the presidential detail.

He strolled towards the West Wing basement entrance, the sun breaking through a light layer of cloud.

He knew he wouldn't get home for at least twelve hours. His one regret in accepting the promotion was that he would see even less of his family.

Morrow shrugged to himself. There weren't many people who could say they loved every minute of their job. And the new boss was someone he knew he could work with.

The light from the windows was stronger than it had been in previous days. It was the kind of Washington morning that the natives of the city welcome whole-heartedly. It was still cold at times; the wind down Pennsylvania and Massachusetts slashed and cut at exposed ears and necks. But the paralysing chill had lessened. The sky was brilliant blue, cloudless. And the smell of the city had changed subtly overnight: gone was the sodden, rank odour of a long, hard winter; of dead trees and rotting rubbish. The fleeting warmth of the sun had brought a sweetness to the air.

The curtains in the private quarters of the White House had been drawn. In one corner of the bedroom suite a television was switched to CNN, the volume turned down. The *Post* lay on the bed.

A maid knocked on the door and waited.

'Come in.'

She walked across the small sitting room, balancing the breakfast tray in her hands. To her right, she could see through the double doors to the bedroom. She placed the tray of coffee on the mahogany table, then turned as the door to the bedroom opened farther. She stood ramrod straight, adjusting her apron.

'Good morning, Constance,' the President said, gratefully taking a cup and pouring some coffee.

The President looked at that morning's *Post*. The main headline was no surprise: the Granby scandal still dominated Washington. Clifford Granby himself was in a penitentiary ten miles outside DC. He had been diagnosed with prostate cancer. So far, he had refused to co-operate with the federal authorities. His companies' records had been seized: the Granby Foundation had been on the point of bankruptcy. Granby himself was charged with multiple counts of fraud, blackmail and extortion; bribing government officers at the Pentagon, State and the Secret Service; falsifying Type 73 licences and myriad tax returns; and, most damagingly, with conspiracy to murder and pervert the course of justice. Kelly, Danello and Friedman would receive posthumous justice.

Granby's cancer treatment had rendered him frail and disoriented. He was a dying man. His lawyers did not expect him to make it to the trial. They thought he would die before he told what he knew.

According to the *Post,* his lawyers had failed yet again to convince him to accept a plea bargain.

The President flipped the paper over. Wayne McQuogue's familiar shy smile filled half the page. This item the President did not know about.

According to the report, McQuogue had agreed to turn government witness in the Granby affair. He had joined Jim Appleton on the prosecution side.

The President smiled.

The former Chief of Staff had finally failed in avoiding the fifteen counts of conspiracy and fraud the DA had thrown at him. McQuogue had tried every trick in the book, funding his flailing legal manoeuvres by selling his Georgetown house. Now he had caved in. According to the *Post,* the best he could expect was a ten-year jail term.

The President left the newspaper on the table by the window. A schedule for the state visit lay next to it. It could wait.

The bathroom lights had been turned on. The President washed, and dressed in the small anteroom off to the left. The quiet of the private quarters was welcome. The White House rattled and creaked with the constant sounds of conversation, telephones, doors opening and closing.

But in here, deep in the silent sanctuary of the presidential bathroom, there was the chance to think, to cherish the precious few moments of being alone.

The grave was to the left of the cemetery entrance. Very few visitors recognised John Friedman's name. His mother came every day to tend his grave. The pain of her loss never left her, never would. But she took solace from the fact that her son was near to her. Just up on the hill, perhaps watching from an even higher place.

She still did not know the identity of the person who, once a week, sent a bunch of lilies in remembrance.

The President exited the bathroom. The telephone console was on a lowboy by the door, the red CRASH button the only clue that this phone was out of the ordinary.

The President walked back towards the bed. It had been made, the staff appearing silently, as if by magic, before swiftly finishing their task and vanishing again.

The telephone rang.

The President strolled back towards it, momentarily annoyed at being disturbed.

'Yes?'

'It's Lee Morrow. Marjorie Wallace is here and—'

'Lee, I'm sorry. Am I running late?'

'Well, we need to—'

'Give me five minutes. I have the schedule here. Has Benmont arrived?'

'Yes, he has.'

'Very good. I'll be out shortly.'

'Thank you, Mrs President.'

Elizabeth turned back to the bed. She glanced at the photograph of Tyler and smiled. She had yet to grow used to being called 'Mrs President'.

But then again, perhaps she never would.